PERFORMING THE INTERCULTURAL CITY

THEATER: THEORY/TEXT/PERFORMANCE

Series Editors: David Krasner, Rebecca Schneider, and Harvey Young

Founding Editor: Enoch Brater

Recent Titles:

Performing the Intercultural City by Ric Knowles

Microdramas: Crucibles for a Theater and Time by John H. Muse

Haunted City: Three Centuries of Racial Impersonation in Impersonation in Philadelphia by Christian DuComb

Long Suffering: American Endurance Art as Prophetic Witness by Karen Gonzalez Rice

Alienation Effects: Performance and Self-Management in Yugoslavia, 1945–91 by Branislav Jakovljević

After Live: Possibility, Potentiality, and the Future of Performance by Daniel Sack

Coloring Whiteness: Acts of Critique in Black Performance by Faedra Chatard Carpenter

The Captive Stage: Performance and the Proslavery Imagination of the Antebellum North by Douglas A. Jones, Jr.

Acts: Theater, Philosophy, and the Performing Self by Tzachi Zamir

Simming: Participatory Performance and the Making of Meaning by Scott Magelssen

Dark Matter: Invisibility in Drama, Theater, and Performance by Andrew Sofer

Passionate Amateurs: Theatre, Communism, and Love by Nicholas Ridout

Paul Robeson and the Cold War Performance Complex: Race, Madness, Activism by Tony Perucci

The Sarah Siddons Audio Files: Romanticism and the Lost Voice by Judith Pascoe

The Problem of the Color[blind]: Racial Transgression and the Politics of Black Performance by Brandi Wilkins Catanese

Artaud and His Doubles by Kimberly Jannarone

No Safe Spaces: Re-casting Race, Ethnicity, and Nationality in American Theater by Angela C. Pao

Embodying Black Experience: Stillness, Critical Memory, and the Black Body by Harvey Young

Performing the Intercultural City

Ric Knowles

UNIVERSITY OF MICHIGAN PRESS

Ann Arbor

Published in the United States of America by the
University of Michigan Press
Manufactured in the United States of America
♾ Printed on acid-free paper

2020 2019 2018 2017 4 3 2 1

A CIP catalog record for this book is available from the British Library.

Library of Congress Cataloging-in-Publication data has been applied for.

ISBN: 978–0-472–07360–3 (hardcover: alk. paper)
ISBN: 978–0-472–05360–5 (paper: alk. paper)
ISBN: 978–0-472–12306–3 (e-book)

For Christine, as ever

Preface

By the time this book appears in print it will have been over ten years since I started work on it. Why has this taken so long?

I began work on *Performing the Intercultural City* by applying for and getting a three-year grant with which I started carrying out interviews and working as a dramaturge, initially on two intercultural productions, both of them of Filipino Canadian plays. I knew right away I was in trouble. Working with just one culturally specific community, I was already daunted by the complexities, the pre- and postcolonial histories, the cultural geographies, the myriad of cultural forms with which I had to become acquainted, the food, and the experiences of different generations and seasons of immigration to the West. As I write this preface I am a research fellow at the International Research Center "Interweaving Performance Cultures" at the Freie Universität in Berlin, surrounded by scholars from all over the world working from different perspectives on similar problematics, and I still feel more than a little out of my depth.

For one thing, I realized shortly after I began work that this was not like other research projects I had undertaken. Work across significant cultural difference involves a different kind and level of engagement than I have had with archives and repertoires, processes and productions, however new and experimental, that sit well within my cultural comfort zone and closely reflect my training and experience. I had to find different ways of approaching the people and material that I was writing about and working with than had served me in the past. I had to adopt an approach that was humble before the myriad of cultural forms and individual experiences that I was encountering. And although I had worked in various kinds of collaboration prior to undertaking this project, I had to take a great deal more time doing my homework, building relationships, negotiating, and engaging in research that was necessarily more collaborative, and collaborative in different ways, than had previously been my scholarly habit.

I also had to reconcile two parts of my life—as a theater artist and a scholar—that I had never really been comfortable keeping separate anyway. I had throughout my career engaged in both scholarship and theatrical practice, but if I were to do justice to the work I was writing about this time, I found I needed more systematically to participate in it, not simply by bringing my already-formed knowledge and expertise to the table but by offering what resources I had in support of projects that were out of my control and about which I knew, at the outset, very little. I never did or could have become expert. In the past ten years I have had the huge and challenging pleasure of working with many of the theater companies and artists whose work I discuss in these pages. I expect that, as a white male with scholarly pretensions, I was, initially at least, greeted with suspicion by many, but they never let this show, and whatever doubts they may have had about my intrusions into their space, most treated me with unfailing generosity. Many have even hired me to work on their shows as a dramaturge in the hopes that we could learn from one another to work productively together across our differences.

But working together, building trust, and learning from one another take time, especially when you're in rehearsals for each production for up to six weeks (not including development workshops), when each new production involves a different community and a vast cultural learning curve, and when each culture with which you're working turns out to be *internally* intercultural in complex, heady, and multiplicitous ways. And I had a three-year grant.

I also realized early on that I had to learn more about theatrical interculturalism more generally, and that I had to learn more about different kinds and modes of meaning production across cultures. I couldn't assume, as many Euro-American interculturalists had before me, that audiences—so-called target audiences—were either "Western" or monocultural, nor could I assume that meaning production—semiotics—worked in the same ways in all cultures. This meant that I had to do research beyond the bounds of my initial project, supported by another three-year grant, which led in several directions and issued in two small books on meaning production and theatrical interculturalism, as well as two coedited collections and four edited or coedited special issues of journals on performance across cultures. I was trying to learn the ropes, and to contextualize my original project.

Finally, I realized that to work on intercultural performance in the Americas was to face the basic fact of the "firstness" of the First Nations and Indigenous peoples of Turtle Island, and to try to address what contemporary performance native to this continent might look like. I had developed a working relationship with a few Indigenous artists, and in particular had worked with senior Guna and Rappahannock performer and playwright Monique Mojica, who since 1991 had been a prodigious collaborative researcher (with Indigenous artists Floyd Favel, Pura Fé, Muriel Miguel, and others) on the use of Indigenous cultural texts and artifacts in the creation of contemporary Native performances.

This important Indigenous work, I felt, was central to my concerns, and at the same time was seriously underfunded and under-recognized in Canada and the United States. This realization led to another grant, "Indigenous Knowledge, Contemporary Performance," initially involving seven artist-researchers, five of them from various Indigenous Nations in what are now Canada and the United States, in yet another three-year project. Chapter 4 of this book deals with this project directly, but the book is informed by it methodologically throughout.

My initial plan for *Performing the Intercultural City* was to provide a slice of the contemporary present in the newly intercultural environment of "the global city" (Sassen). But the decade since I began it has been full of changes, not only for me, but for my "object of study." This book is still intended to deal with the ecology of contemporary intercultural performance in Toronto, but performance ecologies continue to shift, theater companies come and go, artistic direction and management change, and every change in one corner of the ecosystem effects change in all the rest. Nothing, that is to say, will sit still for analysis, and even the gap between the preparation of a manuscript and its appearance produces change. The "contemporary" scene that I am studying, then, is a shifting target that covers the past decade and a little more, and while it is as up-to-date as I can make it, I can vouch for its identifications of roles, responsibilities, leaderships, and mandates being accurate only at the various times of writing.

Acknowledgments

This book, which appears under my authorship, has been the product of many hands, and I must begin by acknowledging some people who have served as actual or virtual coauthors. The first of my debts goes to Jessica Riley, who coauthored chapter 7 and who also contributed to the larger project as one of several research assistants who worked on it along the way. Other research assistants and research partners to whom I am deeply indebted are Brittany Brassard, Sabrina Hope, David Lee, Ingrid Mündel, Nicholas Murphy, and Marta Zeamanuel.

I owe an equal debt to several artists who have allowed me to work in close collaboration with them. Chief among these are my friend and longtime collaborator Monique Mojica, who has been an inspiration for this work at a fundamental level. Also central to much of this work is the friendship and collaboration of Nina Lee Aquino, who has provided me with opportunities that have had a significant and direct impact on almost every chapter. And constant conversation over the years with Yvette Nolan, and friendship with her and with Philip Adams, has changed the ways I think. And then there are Soheil Parsa and Majdi Bou-Matar, who have allowed me to work with them and who have been consistently stimulating interlocutors. There are many others: Kawa Ada, Chadwick Allen, Leon Aureus, Sue Balint, Jill Carter, Marjorie Chan, Marion de Vries, Peter Farbridge, Brenda Farnell, Floyd Favel, Michael Greyeyes, Catherine Hernandez, LeAnne Howe, Erika Iserhoff, Thomas Morgan Jones, Oswaldo De León Kantule, Camellia Koo, DD Kugler, Sandra Laronde, Jani Lauzon, Richard Lee, Keira Loughren, Anita Majumdar, ahdri zhina mandiela, Gloria Miguel, Gia Nahmens, Marilo Nuñez, Martha Ocampo, Pam Patel, Béatriz Pizano, Brian Quirt, Renna Reddie, Anusree Roy, Michelle St. John, Trevor Schwellnus, Djanet Sears, Jovanni Sy, Diana Tso, Kate Ann Vandermeer, Guillermo Verdecchia, Nadine Villasin, Donald Woo, David Yee, and d'bi.young anitafrika. I must also thank the theater companies with whom I have worked, who have been unfailingly generous with me. These include Cahoots Theatre Company, Carlos Bulosan Theatre, the Chocolate Woman Collective,

Factory Theatre, fu-GEN Theatre, Modern Times Stage Company, MT Space, the Red Snow Collective, Theatre Passe Muraille, and Turtle Gals Performance Ensemble, where I served on the board of directors.

Many scholars, consciously or not, have had a hand in this work that exceeds the contributions made by their publications. These include Natalie Alvarez, Karen Bamford, Roberta Barker, Rustom Bharucha, Leo Cabranes-Grant, Jill Carter, Dong-Shin Chang, Tracy Davis, Heather Davis-Fisch, Penny Farfan, Brenda Farnell, Barry Freeman, Helen Gilbert, Jen Harvie, Ajay Heble, Smaro Kamboureli, Harry Lane, Esther Kim Lee, Daphne Lei, Laura Levin, Diana Manole, Marc Maufort, Charlotte McIvor, Michael McKinnie, Yana Meerzon, Roberta Mock, Ingrid Mündel, David O'Donnell, Patrice Pavis, Ramón Rivera-Servera, Eugenia Sojka, Kim Solga, Jenn Stephenson, Joanne Tompkins, Caroline de Wagter, Jerry Wasserman, Robin Whittaker, Patricia Ybarra, and Harvey Young. While working on this book I was a member of the "Belonging Differently" interdisciplinary Humanities Task Force of the Canadian Institute for Advanced Research (CIFAR), chaired by Jonathan Arac and Robert Gibbs, where I learned a great deal and benefited in particular from conversations with John Borrows and Lauren Berlant. I also spent a blessed year in Berlin in 2013–14 working on the later stages of this book at the International Research Center "Interweaving Performance Cultures" at the Freie Universität, and for that I have to thank especially Erika Fischer-Lichte and Christel Weiler, Holger Hartung, Claudia Daseking, and everyone else at the center, especially Torsten Jost, for inviting me, looking after me, and creating such a stimulating intellectual and theatrical environment. I'm grateful, too, to all of the fellows who provided feedback and intellectual stimulation throughout the year, including Khalid Amin, Stephen Barber, Ananda Breed, Paul Carter, Catherine Diamond, Richard Gough, Lydia Haustein, Lynette Hunter, Biodun Jeyifo, Navtej Singh Johar, Jean Graham-Jones, Peter Lichtenfels, Kuan Wu-Lin, Susan Manning, Rabih Mroué, Kate O'Reilly, Bill Worthen, Hana Worthen, Philip Zarrilli, and especially Hypatia Vourloumis. Finally, the book has benefited greatly from the comments and suggestions of two anonymous readers for the University of Michigan Press and from the advice and help of LeAnn Fields as press editor; I would also like to thank David Krasner, Rebecca Schneider, and Harvey Young as general editors of the press's Theater: Theory/Text/Performance series, to which I'm honored to contribute.

Many chapters in this book had their first life as papers presented at the Association for Canadian Theatre Research (three times); the American Society for Theatre Research (twice); the Australasian Drama Studies Association; the Drama Department at Queen Mary University of London Quorum lecture series (twice); the PhD program in Performance Studies, the Theatre Program, and the Dance the Performance Studies Graduate Group at the University of California at Davis; the Canadian Studies Program at the University of Silesia, Poland; the Alternative Dramaturgies of the New Millennium conference in Tangier and Tétouan, Morocco; the Shipping of Souls conference at Theatre Passe Muraille, Toronto; the Interculturalism & Performance Now conference, National University of Ireland, Galway; the Canadian Studies, English, and Drama Programs, Mount Allison University (twice); the TransCanada Institute at the University of Guelph; the FOOT Festival, "Dissolving Borders" at the (then) Graduate Centre for the Study of Drama, University of Toronto; TaPRA, in Plymouth, UK; the Improvisation, Community, and Social Practice research project at the University of Guelph; and the Signatures of the Past: Cultural Memory in Contemporary North American Drama conference, Centre for Canadian Studies and the Languages and Literatures Department, University of Brussels. In every case, I benefited from the opportunity to try out my ideas and from the helpful feedback and discussion that took place, and I am grateful to the many and various organizers of these events, whose names are included above.

Some of these chapters have appeared, mostly in earlier versions or in different arrangements, in previous publications. They are published here with permission and with gratitude to the editors, who helped shape and hone my thinking:

An earlier version of chapter 1 first appeared as "Multicultural Text, Intercultural Performance: The Performance Ecology of Contemporary Toronto." *Performance and the City*. Ed. D. J. Hopkins, Shelly Orr, and Kim Solga. Basingstoke: Palgrave Macmillan, 2009. 73–93.

Chapter 2 had its first life as "Performing Intercultural Memory in the Diasporic Present." *Signatures of the Past: Cultural Memory in Contemporary Anglophone North American Drama*. Ed. Marc Maufort and Caroline de Wagter. Brussels: Lang, 2008. 49–71.

Chapter 3 first appeared as "The CBT Collective: Towards a Filipino Canadian Dramaturgy." *Asian Canadian Theatre*. Ed. Nina Lee Aquino and Ric Knowles. Toronto: Playwrights Canada, 2011. 130–47.

Parts of chapter 4 have appeared in various places in various versions and configurations. These include: "Calling Off the Border Patrol: Intercultural Dramaturgy in Toronto." *Performance in the Borderlands*. Ed. Ramón H. Rivera-Servera and Harvey Young. Basingstoke: Palgrave-Macmillan, 2011. 161–81; "Native Performance Culture, Monique Mojica, and the *Chocolate Woman* Workshops." *Crosstalk: Canadian and Global Imaginaries in Dialogue*. Ed. Diana Brydon and Marta Dvořák. Waterloo: Wilfrid Laurier UP, 2012. 73–92; parts of the final two chapters of my *How Theatre Means*. Basingstoke: Palgrave-Macmillan, 2014; and "Mounds, Earthworks, *Sideshow Freaks and Circus Injuns*." *Enacting Nature: Ecocritical Perspectives on Indigenous Performance*. Ed. Birgit Däwes and Marc Maufort. Brussels: PIE Peter Lang, 2014. 47–58.

Chapter 5 was first published as "to be dub, female, and black (queering the revolushion): towards a womban-centred afro-caribbean diasporic performance aesthetic in toronto." *Theatre Research in Canada* 33.1 (2012) 78–105.

A short, very early abstract of chapter 6 first appeared as "The Modern in Modern Times." *Canadian Theatre Review* 139 (2009): 63–68.

Chapter 7, coauthored with Jessica Riley, first appeared as "Aluna Theatre's *Nohayquiensepa*: The Intermedial Intercultural and the Limits of Empathy." *Latina/o Canadian Theatre and Performance*. Ed. Natalie Alvarez. Toronto: Playwrights Canada, 2013. 36–63.

The research for this book has been generously supported by funding from the Social Sciences and Humanities Research Council of Canada, to whom I am very grateful.

I am also grateful to Lewis Bold Wark (in Canada) and Florian Thamer (in Berlin) for keeping my computers functioning.

My greatest debts, both personal and scholarly, are to Christine Bold, who has had a hand at every stage in shaping my thinking and making it clearer, in pushing and encouraging me to do the work, in refusing to let me get away with glib overstatements, in reading and commenting on individual sections and on the whole, and in serving as both conscience and inspiration for the work. It is to her that this book is dedicated.

Contents

Introduction

The playwright and solo performer was Chinoy (Chinese Filipino) Canadian, the director was Argentinian Canadian, the venue was an upscale demonstration kitchen at downtown Toronto's teemingly diverse St. Lawrence Market, and the producing company was Toronto's intercultural Cahoots Theatre Company ("theatre in full colour"). The audience seemed to be from everywhere. The show, *A Taste of Empire*, involved the real-time preparation and consumption of a Filipino national dish, *rellenong bangus* (stuffed milkfish), while the harried sous-chef, left to his own devices, told the global stories of conquest, colonialism, exploitation, and consumption that account for the dish's varied ingredients, their sources, and their means of production. Meanwhile, in the heat of summer at the end of June, as the show was moving from dress rehearsals into previews, Toronto's downtown was staging before the world the brutal containment by municipal, provincial, and federal police of protesters against the 2010 G20 summit of global economic leaders. In its personnel, its context, its staging of cross-cultural and international encounter, its politics, and its reception the show was exemplary as one of many nodes in a relational network that constitutes the intercultural performance ecology of a characteristically multiethnic global city. This book sets out to explore how such an ecology functions in one such city, and what cultural work it performs.[1]

Two significant developments in scholarship drive this project. The first, the constellation of critical multiculturalism, new cosmopolitanism, critical race theory, and postcolonial, diasporic, and whiteness studies, concerns itself with intercultural negotiations and the local proliferation of cultural diversity globally. The second, performance studies, concerns itself in part with the performative constitution of social identities (or subjectivities). One aspect of performance studies, deriving from 1980s and 1990s intercultural performance, links these developments and is particularly pertinent here, though it is in urgent need of revisionist thinking in its application to the twenty-first-century city, where the constitution of performances and, crucially, audiences, is increasingly heterogeneous. Performance has always been a technology of intercultural exchange, but in the modernist period intercultural performance solidified and was appropriated in both practice and discourse by Western universalists (such as Antonin Artaud) and materialists (such as Bertolt Brecht) alike, and it devolved in the twentieth century into an East-West binary in the work of Peter Brook, Ariane Mnouchkine, and Eugenio Barba and the scholarship of Patrice Pavis and others. Late in the twentieth century, however, the postcolonial beginnings of a discursive practice of "decolonizing the stage" (Balme) emerged in scholarship by Rustom Bharucha, Christopher Balme, Julie Holledge and Joanne Tompkins, and Jacqueline Lo and Helen Gilbert and proposed new ways of thinking about a more productive and complex "interculturalism from below" that *Performing the Intercultural City* develops. This book explodes the binaries of source-to-target culture on which traditional intercultural theories are based and rethinks interculturalism as a complex set of negotiations across multiple sites of difference, on stage, between the stage and the audience, and within audiences.[2]

Cities around the world, particularly major theater centers, have become increasingly heterogeneous in their cultural makeup. Amsterdam, Delhi, Dublin, London, New York, Rio, Stuttgart, Sydney, Toronto, Yokahama, and many other cities have become sites of both contestation and exchange, as well as key locations for the intercultural performance-into-being of new, diasporic—or hyphenated (see Chaudhuri)—subjectivities. *Performing the Intercultural City* concerns itself with the performance ecology of one unique but also representative global city in which cultural and national identities no longer coincide, and in which the performative constitution of such identities is increasingly recognized as formative.

In the promotional discourses of the city of Toronto there have typically been two key claims: to be the world's most multicultural city (the sheer number of cultures and languages represented on its streets and streetcars lends the claim weight), and to be the third most active theatre center in the English-speaking world (after London and New York). It is also the largest city in the first country in the world to legislate, however problematically, a policy of official multiculturalism. On all of these fronts it is a resonant case study with significant implications for other global cultural crucibles. Toronto is also a place where the traditional hegemony of whiteness on the city's stages is actively being challenged "from below" by an informal coalition of artists of color working in solidarity across difference to create a theater scene that increasingly reflects and challenges the cultural makeup of the city. Finally, Toronto is distinctive in that, in addition to serving as home to a greater range of immigrant cultures than perhaps any other city in the world, it is also home to a significant and mixed urban Indigenous population, and to one of the world's largest and longest-standing Native theater companies, Native Earth Performing Arts.

Indeed, the work of Indigenous artists and theater companies is as central to this book as it is to the city's intercultural performance ecology, and it is essential when researching and writing about things Indigenous to be guided by the important work that has been done by Indigenous scholars, mostly in the social sciences, on Indigenous research methodologies (Archibald; Denzin, Lincoln, and Smith; Kovach; L. Smith; Weber-Pillwax; Wilson). This work is applicable, in its general principles and local variations, to all ethical work on Othered or minoritized cultures. I will outline the application and implications of these methods for my work below and will try throughout to follow their fundamental principles of respect, reciprocity, responsibility, and relational accountability. Within the overarching context of those principles, *Performing the Intercultural City* models an approach to intercultural performance analysis that involves the intersection of theoretical, critical, and thick archival research, employing a materialist approach, collaborative practice, case study method, and what anthropologist George E. Marcus calls "multi-sited ethnography" (79). Its materialist approach considers the work of culturally specific and intercultural theater companies less as cultural texts than as cultural production. Its collaborative practice works *within* interculturalism across difference, drawing upon my own engaged professional work as a dramaturge with Aboriginal; East, Central, and South Asian Canadian; African Canadian; Latinx Canadian; Iranian and Lebanese Canadian; and explicitly inter- and cross-cultural theater companies and festivals. The decision to use case study method derives from the materialist view that theory must always be practiced, and practice theorized; that is, any move toward a general theory must emerge from engagement with local practice, which is my focus here. I adapt multisited ethnography, theorized by Marcus as a way of insisting on the need for a processual "mobile ethnography [that] takes unexpected trajectories in tracing a cultural formation across and within multiple sites of activity" (80), in application to my work in rehearsal across the city as an urban intercultural microcosm of what Marcus calls a "world system." I have had variable access, engaged in what Dwight Conquergood would call "co-performative witnessing" (149), to the multiple sites and rehearsal processes of the different companies that I write about here, who nevertheless constitute a single, complex theatrical ecosystem. For some I have served as co-creator, some as dramaturge, some as witness, and some only as observer. As such, what Indigenous scholarship would call my "relations" to the work, my perspective, and to some extent my authorial voice necessarily vary, as appropriate, from chapter to chapter, and even within chapters, depending on the degree of my participation in any given process.[3] This is, in the end, what multisited ethnography requires: "Multi-sited fieldwork is . . . always conducted with a keen awareness of being within the landscape, and as the landscape changes across sites, the identity of the ethnographer requires renegotiation" (Marcus 97).[4] And in each case I am writing not simply about a completed and consumable work of art but about a process—including a rehearsal process—and a complex and shifting set of relationships.

Performing the Intercultural City uses contemporary Toronto's theater scene and the unique work performed within it as case studies of the larger issues surrounding intercultural theater, multiculturalism, the performative constitution of social identities and intercultural memories, the development of diasporic cultural forms, performative cultural mediation, and the emergent circulation of performance networks. It explores Toronto's complex intercultural theatrical ecosystem by tracing the work of dozens of artists, companies, and individuals who are working performatively across various cultures. The purpose of this exercise is to come to some understanding of how individual gendered, raced, and classed subjectivities and community identities within the contemporary multicultural city are not just reflected or given voice but are *constituted* through performance *as*, for example, Filipino Canadian, Asian Canadian, Caribbean Canadian, African Canadian, or First Nations or Native Canadian. How does this processual, performative (re)construction of subjectivities through practices of surrogation (Roach) relate to what Himani Bannerji sees as the oppressive *state*-constructed and static ethnic communities of official multiculturalism (10)? How do these performatively constituted subjectivities interact with one another in shifting networks, coalitions, and solidarities? How do they relate to societally dominant understandings of the city's social space, understandings that constitute the dominant culture as unified and monolithic and minoritized or immigrant non-European cultures as variously "authentic" ethnic enclaves?

PERFORMANCE ECOLOGY, ACTOR-NETWORK THEORY, RHIZOMES, RADICANTS, AND HETEROTOPIAS

To try to answer these questions, I draw throughout the book, within the larger methodological context of Indigenous research protocols with which they are in many ways congruent, on four related metaphorical/theoretical frames toward which I've already gestured: the ecology of performance, as articulated by Baz Kershaw; actor-network theory (ANT), as introduced by Bruno Latour and John Law; rhizomatics, as articulated by Gilles Deleuze and Félix Guattari and supplemented by Nicholas Bourriaud's concepts of relational aesthetics and radicants; and heterotopics, as introduced by Michel Foucault and developed and explicated by Kevin Hetherington. To lump these four frameworks together in a blunt and summary way—I hope their details and differences will emerge as I tease them out below and as they apply locally throughout the book—I argue that the city of Toronto functions as *heterotopic* space, with heterotopias understood as *ecologies* in which *reassembling the social* can happen *relationally* and *rhizomatically*.

I treat contemporary Toronto as a complex intercultural performance *ecology*, drawing on Kershaw's articulation of performance as a kind of ecosystem. Kershaw describes within such a system "the complicated and unavoidable inter-dependency between any element of a performance event and its environment," where "the smallest change of one element in some way, however minutely, effects change in all the rest" ("Oh" 136). He also suggests that, as in all ecologies (and contra the totalizing tendencies of early versions of theater semiotics), the health of the ecosystem is best judged by the diversity of its species rather than by the competitive success of individual elements ("The Theatrical Biosphere"). It is for this reason that *Performing the Intercultural City* focuses not on individual "stars" such as Tomson Highway and Djanet Sears who are expected to represent their communities internationally but on the network of companies and actants that constitute the ecosystem. Both of these features—interdependence and healthy diversity—are singularly applicable to the performance ecology of a successful intercultural city.

I am not using the phrase *performance ecology*, however, in quite the same way that Kershaw does. He uses it, in contradistinction to "performance ecologies" ("how particular performances operate ecologically as ecosystems") and "ecologies of performance" ("how humans might arrive at better appreciation of performance process in the Earth's ecosystem through ecology"), to mean "how performance is an integral part of global ecology and ecosystem" (*Theatre Ecology* 14)—though as he admits, he adheres to these definitions somewhat inconsistently. I use the same phrase, *performance ecology*, to talk about the complex ecosystem that is constituted by a city's shifting network of "actors"—performers, performances, institutions, artists, administrators, and audiences—organized variously into companies, caucuses, committees, and communities. I use it, that is, as a metaphor. "Ecology," as Kershaw notes, "references the inter-relationships of all the organic and non-organic factors of ecosystems, ranging from the smallest and/or simplest to the greatest or/and most complex. It is also defined as the interrelationships between organisms and their environments, especially when that is understood to imply [their] interdependence" (*Theatre Ecology* 15). The performance ecology of a city such as Toronto, then, can be understood to consist of a shifting and unstable constellation of human and nonhuman actors and factors operating interdependently to constitute an ecosystem. And like networks and heterotopias, as I will argue throughout, ecosystems are always in process and in the contemporary world are always threatened, most often by the operations of unfettered global capitalism (see Guattari). Like heterotopias and networks, too, they operate as what Kershaw calls "edge" phenomena, at the intersection, in this case, of local and global environments.

I have already used the words *network* and *constellation* to refer to the groupings and regroupings that occur in the intercultural performance ecology of a global city, and it may be useful to consider for a moment how to think about and analyze the relationships within and among such groupings. Actor-network theory (ANT) is useful here. John Law defines ANT as follows, though he refers to it as a practice rather than a theory and immediately disclaims the validity of any *firm* definition of a practice that exists only in its application:

> Actor-network theory is a disparate family of material-semiotic tools, sensibilities and methods of analysis that treat everything in the social and natural worlds as a continuously generated effect of the relations within which they are located. It assumes that nothing has reality or form outside the enactment of those relations. Its studies explore and characterize the webs and practices that carry them. Like other material-semiotic approaches, the actor-network approach thus describes the enactment of materially and discursively heterogeneous relations that produce and reshuffle all kinds of actors, including objects, subjects, human beings, machines, animals, "nature", ideas, organizations, inequalities, scales and sizes, and geographical arrangements. (2)

What is most useful about actor-network theory, for my purposes, is its insistence that the social—in which I include theatrical practice—consists of "webs of heterogeneous material and social practices that are *performative*, that generate realities" (Law 12, emphasis added)—webs, that is, through which realities are explicitly *enacted into being*. This is extremely suggestive for the analysis of Toronto's (or any city's) intercultural performance ecology, as are Bruno Latour's arguments that this enactment has to do, not with dispersion and deconstruction, but with "*reassembling* the social" (11, emphasis added) and that identity consists of difference. "To exist is to differ," he says; "identity is a minimum and, hence, a type of difference" (15–16). For within that ecology new identities (or subjectivities) can be understood to be continuously (re)enacted, (re)performed into being through difference and differentiation, as various human and nonhuman "actors" (or in semiotic terms that Latour also uses, "actants," or forces) function as the centers of relational networks.

The metaphor of the network does capture something of the shifting, decentered, nonhierarchical and horizontal quality of the relationships within Toronto's intercultural performance ecology. In applying it, however, particularly in terms of the structure of my book and my selection of specific case studies, I want also to invoke anthropologist Tim Ingold's modification of actor-network theory, in which he replaces *network* with *meshwork* to invoke a network with "uneven and fluctuating distribution of agency" (Ingold 92; Donald 121), in which some actants temporarily and provisionally acquire different degrees and kinds of agency. This has certainly been the case within Toronto, where the meshwork of culturally specific, cross-cultural, and intercultural companies tosses up hubs and nodal points from time to time. Some of these nodal points have been small companies with explicitly intercultural mandates whose influence and importance have often been disproportionately large and who form the subjects of the chapters that follow.

Both Latour and Law have acknowledged the relationship between actor-network theory and Gilles Deleuze and Félix Guattari's key image from the introduction to *A Thousand Plateaus* for certain emergent types of books, languages, psyches, worlds, and ways of thinking: the rhizome, as opposed to the "root-tree" (7). Indeed, Latour has observed that "we might talk of 'actant-rhizomes' rather than 'actor-networks'" (qtd. in Law 6). Rhizomes are subterranean stem systems, assemblages rather than vertical structures. They consist of bulbs and tubors rather than roots and branches. For Deleuze and Guattari, "the fabric of the rhizome is the conjunction" (25), which grammatically links elements of equal value arranged horizontally rather than hierarchically. They outline six "certain approximate characteristics of the rhizome" (7): principles of "connection and heterogeneity" ("any point of a rhizome can be connected to any other and must be" [7]); of multiplicity ("a multiplicity has neither subject nor object, only determinations, magnitudes, and dimensions that cannot increase in number without the multiplicity changing in nature" [8]); of asignifying rupture ("a rhizome may be broken, shattered at a given spot, but it will start up again on one of its old lines, or on new lines" [9]); and of cartography and decalcomania—the decal-like transference between surfaces (" a rhizome is not amenable to any structural or generative model," it is "a *map and not a tracing*," "it always has multiple entryways," and, crucially, it "has to do with performance" [12]).

But perhaps most importantly, in terms of the intercultural performance ecology of the city of Toronto, rhizomatic systems are decentered, "finite networks . . . in which communication runs from any neighbour to any other, the stems or channels do not pre-exist" (17). "The rhizome," they conclude, "is alliance, uniquely alliance" (25). I have suggested elsewhere that "what is needed [in intercultural performance studies] is a model of scholarship that understands the multiple performances of difference, local and global, as *processes*, circulations of energy, in which previously marginalised cultures are seen to work *together* rather than *against*, constructing genuine, rhizomatic, and multiple intercultures that respect difference while building solidarities" (Knowles, *Theatre and Interculturalism* 59). This is what I aspire to provide in the pages that follow.

Deleuze and (especially) Guattari are among the thinkers most frequently cited in Nicolas Bourriaud's *Relational Aesthetics*, which sets out to consider whether it is still possible "to generate *relationships* with the world" in a context traditionally dominated by its *representation* (9, emphasis added). Most scholarship about intercultural performance derives from a semiotic approach that is centrally concerned with representation, and in particular the representation of difference *by* one culture *to* another (usually dominant) culture. What would it mean to consider what Bourriaud calls "the possibility of a *relational* art (an art taking as its theoretical horizon the realm of human interactions and its social context, rather than the assertion of an independent and *private* symbolic space)" (*Relational Aesthetics*14)? What would it mean to apply what he calls "relational aesthetics"—"aesthetic theory consisting in judging artworks on the basis of the inter-human relations which they represent, produce, or prompt" (112)—to the performance ecology of a city such as Toronto? For according to Bourriaud, relational art is an urban phenomenon, it "stems essentially from the birth of a world-wide urban culture, and from the extension of this city model to more or less all cultural phenomena" (14). It might mean considering specific performances, personnel and other actants, theater companies, arts organizations and funding bodies, the city's inter- and micro-cultures, and its audiences as "'formations' rather than 'forms,'" where "form only exists in the encounter and in the dynamic relationship with other formations, artistic and otherwise" (21).

In a subsequent book Bourriaud has explicitly extended Deleuze and Guattari's nomadism and its biological metaphor from "rhizomatic" to "radicant," which he uses at once to describe and promote a contemporary form of global art production that involves journeys, transfers, migrancy, and above all translation but that unlike the "rhizome" (a root system) is *superficial* (above ground) and takes into account questions of identity and subjectivity (Bourriaud, *The Radicant* 55). Bourriaud uses *radicant* as "a term designating an organism that grows its roots and adds new ones as it advances. To be radicant," he argues, does not mean being rootless but "means setting one's roots in motion, staging them in heterogeneous contexts and formats, denying them the power to completely define one's identity" (22). Although I find some of Bourriaud's conceptualizations of identity and difference problematic for my purposes (as I will discuss below), his proposing of "a system of thought capable of making connections between disparate cultures without denying each one its singularity" (40) has considerable appeal, as does the project of "unsticking identities and signs" (44) in what he describes as a "laboratory of identities" (51).

What kind of radically intercultural place, what kind of ecology, hosts rhizomatic or radicant art? What kind of space is constituted by the networks, relationships, and "horizontal negotiations without an arbiter" that Latour and Law set out to describe (Bourriaud, *The Radicant*, 188, citing Latour)? What kind of geopolitical space might serve as Bourriaud's global "laboratory of identities"? A possible answer is provided by heterotopics. "Heterotopia," in Latin, means "place of otherness." Foucault explores the concept briefly in his essay, "Of Other Spaces," where he contrasts heterotopias with utopias. The latter, he says, are "fundamentally unreal places"; the former are "places that do exist and that are formed in the very founding of society—which are something like counter-sites, a kind of effectively enacted utopia in which the real sites, all the other real sites that can be found within the culture, are simultaneously represented, contested, and inverted" (24). A heterotopic space, then, can be understood to be "a sort of simultaneously mythic and real contestation of the space in which we live" (24), and as Foucault's brief discussion of them in the preface to *The Order of Things* reveals, they can be textual as well as geographical sites, in which form they "secretly undermine language . . . desiccate speech, stop words in their tracks, contest the very possibility of grammar at its source; they dissolve our myths and sterilize the lyricism of our sentences" (xviii).[5] This, in terms of the grammar of performance rather than text, is what many of the productions examined in this book undertake to do, providing heterotopic possibilities for the performance into being of new grammars, new lyricisms, and new performatives across radically disruptive differences within and between communities.

What does it mean to suggest that the performance ecology of a "global" city such as Toronto constitutes heterotopic space? Kevin Hetherington is helpful here.[6] In *The Badlands of Modernity: Heterotopia and Social Ordering* Hetherington describes historical heterotopias as "spaces which acted as obligatory points of passage" (12). "Almost like laboratories," he argues, anticipating Bourriaud, "they can be taken as sites in which new ways of experimenting with ordering society are tried out" (13). Importantly, Hetherington sees heterotopias as heterogeneous mixtures of old and new, dominant and marginalized, to the point that what is central or dominant and what is marginal is "not always clearcut" (6):[7] "The image of a counter-hegemonic margin that acts as a site of resistance, offers us an image that oversimplifies, through a process of polarization, the issues of marginality, difference, and Otherness" (7). "I do not define heterotopias as sites of resistance, sites of transgression, or as marginal spaces," he concludes, "but precisely as *spaces of alternate ordering*" (9)—"spaces of deferral, spaces where ideas and practices that represent the good life can come into being, from nowhere, even if they never actually achieve what they set out to achieve" (ix). Fundamentally, in heterotopias as in ecologies, networks, and rhizomatic or radicant structures, "hierarchy gives way to a series of exclusively lateral relations," which is, for Hetherington, "the main principle of a heterotopia for Foucault" (43, quoting Harkness 10).

I suggest that the intercultural performance ecology of Toronto, consisting of complex and shifting relationships among many individual actants, broadly defined, can usefully be understood to constitute heterotopic space, where new "ideas and practices" can come into being. To repeat, merging my selected metaphors: the city of Toronto functions as a *heterotopic ecosystem* in which *reassembling the social* can happen *relationally* and *rhizomatically*. When the artists and companies in part 1 of this book perform official texts differently, or constitute new intracultural memories; when those in part 2 draw upon and refigure cultural texts in startling and productive new assemblages; when those in part 3 find innovative ways of (re)mediating across cultural difference, they are reassembling the social in ways that are at once relational, nonhierarchical, and heterotopic. They are constituting the intercultural city as, in Hetherington's terms, "a space of alternate ordering."

INDIGENOUS RESEARCH METHODOLOGIES

I am conscious that all of the theories, methods, and metaphors I have outlined in the previous section derive from the writings of European men, mainly French, as I'm conscious that the works and practices that I am examining in *Performing the Intercultural City* are by non-Europeans, mostly women. I am also conscious of the role played by the application of enlightenment and post-enlightenment western theory in the project of European colonialism.

This is, of course, a problem, and it returns me to the intersecting methodologies I outlined earlier, to a kind of research that is fundamentally collaborative and a kind of writing that privileges the voices of those it writes about. This means that I use quotations a lot, as ethnographers do, but it means more than that. It also means that I attempt to engage the reader with the practices I am describing and analyzing in ways that are less critical than relational—not in the sense of Bourriaud's relational aesthetics, which are primarily about aesthetic *judgment*, but as in the relational bases of Indigenous research methodologies. These methodologies, as I have indicated, constitute the overarching theoretical and political frame for this investigation, and they might usefully serve as a kind of umbrella under which the theories and metaphors I've introduced above can function *insofar as they fit within and are compatible with* what Opaskwayak Cree scholar Shawn Wilson calls an "Indigenous Research Paradigm" (6). There are variations on how this is understood, but its general principles are those outlined by Māori scholar Linda Tuhiwai Smith, who is held by many to be the progenitor of the field:

1. Aroha ki te tangata (a respect for people).
2. Kanoha kitea (the seen face, that is, present yourself to people face to face).
3. Titiro, whatkarongo . . . korero (look, listen . . . speak).
4. Manaaki ki te tangata (share and host people, be generous).
5. Kia tupato (be curious).
6. Kaua e takahia te mana o te tangata (do not trample over the *mana* [authority, status, dignity[8]] of people).
7. Kaua e mahaki (don't flaunt your knowledge). (120)

I draw primarily upon Wilson here, however, because he systematically develops an Indigenous research paradigm in some detail and is writing for both Indigenous and non-Indigenous researchers. I do so as a non-

Indigenous scholar trained in the western academy in order to articulate the practices I have learned from him and from my Indigenous colleagues and have tried to adhere to in researching and writing this book—though I am also conscious that there are key Indigenous stories and aspects of Indigenous knowledge that are not mine to recount and that, as a settler scholar, I cannot access. The principle with which to begin, however, and which can be applied to othered cultures beyond the Indigenous community, is that of "doing research *with* Indigenous people and communities rather than *on* them" (Wilson 108).

In the opening "Foreword and Conclusion" to his book *Research Is Ceremony: Indigenous Research Methods*, Wilson posits that

> The shared aspect of an Indigenous ontology and epistemology is *relationality* (relationships do not merely shape reality, they are reality). The shared aspect of an Indigenous axiology and methodology is *accountability to relationships*. (7, emphasis added)

An Indigenous ontology, with which most aspects of ecological thinking are congruent, is relational because "we could not *be* without *being in relationship* with everything that surrounds us and is within us. Our reality, our ontology, is the relationships" (76). Relationality, moreover, involves "the epistemological inevitability of inclusiveness and egalitarianism" (134). Finally, relationships extend not only to family, friends, immediate community, and ultimately all peoples, but also to animals, plants, minerals, the natural world, and the cosmos. When an Indigenous speaker ends an address with the phrase "all my relations," it is these to which she or he refers. An Indigenous *epistemology*, then, with which central aspects of actor-network theory are entirely congruent, involves "thinking of the world around us as a web of connections and relationships" (77).

An Indigenous axiology (ethics) "is built upon the concept of relational *accountability*. What is . . . important and meaningful is fulfilling a role and obligations in the research relationships—that is, being accountable to your relations" (77, emphasis added). It follows, then, that Indigenous *methodology* "must be a process that adheres to relational accountability" (77). "The methodology needs to be based in a community context (be *relational*) and has to demonstrate *respect, reciprocity* and *responsibility* (to be accountable as it is put into action)" (99, emphasis added; see Weber-Pillwax): "It has to benefit the community" (102).

Wilson places ontology, epistemology, axiology, and methodology, moreover, on a medicine wheel, where, as in an ecosystem, "a change in one affects the others" (70). From this he builds an ethical research paradigm that involves attention to the relational context within which, and only within which, an idea exists and attention to the position from which it is realized and articulated ("reality is in the relationship that one has with the truth" [73]). Within this paradigm a research project is both cumulative and collaborative, and it pays ethical attention to how knowledge is acquired and disseminated. As in actor-network theory, moreover, Indigenous knowledge is holistic: it rejects the atomization of the western scientific method *as well as* poststructuralist processes of deconstruction, both of which can be understood to *destroy* relationships, in favor of syntheses, which *build* them (119, 121). Wilson claims, in a statement that is entirely congruent with an actor-network approach even in some of its language, that "any analysis must examine all of the relationships or strings between particular events or knots of data as a whole before it will make any sense" (120). Unlike the proponents of actor-network theory, however, Wilson doesn't claim for this analysis any form of scholarly objectivity: his analysis is explicitly positional and purposeful. The analyses that follow in this book are intended to be similarly positional and purposeful and explicitly to support the work of the individual artists and intersectional communities that are its subject. And they are analyses of performance, of work *in formation*, of processes of subjectivity- and knowledge-production rather than of ownable, consumable, or appropriatable products.

In Wilson's Indigenous research paradigm, finally, research is ceremony, "a ceremony for improving your relationship with an idea" (110), and *as* ceremony it is "a means of raising our consciousness" (69) or achieving heightened consciousness that might "bridge the distance between our cosmos and us" (137). It involves preparation and dedication, but finally, at its climax, research, as ceremony, involves a coming together of ideas, when all the connections are made (see 89).

This, then, is the larger context within which the metaphors drawn from western theorists that I have outlined will be employed and by which their usefulness and appropriateness will consistently, if not always explicitly, be measured. For performance ecologies, actor networks and meshworks, rhizomes, radicants, and heterotopias all work best not as theories but as explanatory metaphors, ways of thinking that, like all metaphors and analogies, are rhetorically useful but analytically suspect: metaphors always displace and are always in danger of consuming their objects. In Indigenous praxis, however, the relationality that the western theorists I've cited employ metaphorically is real.

It is perhaps important to demonstrate more concretely how and why, in drawing upon western theorists, I nevertheless do so with some circumspection and test them against their compatibility with Indigenous protocols and practices. Bourriaud, as read against the work of Nishnaabeg scholar Leanne Simpson, provides a useful example. Bourriaud's metaphor of the radicant is compelling, and its image of a series of rerootings (or serial installations), which "implies a subject, but one that is not reducible to a stable, closed, and self-contained identity" (*The Radicant* 55), is a valuable one for this book insofar as it imagines new and flexible ways of dealing with diasporic identity construction. But Bourriaud's radicant is proposed within the context of a critique of (unlocated)[9] multiculturalism as the reification of identities that he feels are inappropriately and oppressively tied to place and culture, and within a promotion and celebration of contemporary nomadism that he feels is liberatory. He spins out the metaphor of the radicant in dazzling but (ironically) ungrounded ways that are, however, incompatible with Indigenous worldviews, and that I find problematic in the specificity of their application. In his celebration of the migratory contemporary artist, for example, Bourriaud cites the English novelist and travel writer Bruce Chatwin rather than any Aboriginal source when he offers Aboriginal Australian "walkabouts" as "a wonderful metaphor for the contemporary art exhibition as the prototype of the journey form" (121). In doing so, he ignores the facts that walkabouts are tied to very specific landscapes, that Aboriginal peoples have very specific relationships to those landscapes, that Aboriginal peoples *are* contemporary, and that Indigenous people and their cultural productions have for centuries been appropriated (a concept Bourriaud resists) and used as metaphors for western art practices.[10]

Leanne Simpson, in her exemplary book *Dancing on Our Turtle's Back: Stories of Nishnaabeg Re-creation, Resurgence and a New Emergence*, discusses a very specific radicant—the strawberry plant—in very different ways, and the methodological comparison is salutary. Simpson works with the worldviews that are embedded within Indigenous language, specifically the language of her own Michi Saagig (what many non-Indigenous people refer to as Mississauga) Nishnaabeg (Anishinaabe, Ojibwe) people, and her discussion begins with an exploration of the name of the river—the Odenabe (Otonabee)—that runs through her home city, Peterborough, Ontario, northeast of Toronto in the southern expanse of her people's traditional territories. *Ode*, she establishes in discussion with an Elder, means "heart," and the river's name, Odenabe, refers to its rapids, which "bubble like the beating of a heart." *Odeena* means city, "the place where the hearts gather." *(O)debwewin* (truth) literally means "the sound of the heart." And *odeminan* (heart berries) means strawberries, "their runners connecting the plants in a web of inter-relationships, much like cities" (Simpson 94). For Simpson, unlike for Bourriaud, the runners of the radicant strawberry plant are not simply metaphors but models from which to learn about and practice a very particular kind of interconnectedness and mobility that is grounded in both language and territory. She draws on Anishinaabe scholar Gerald Vizenor's concept of "transmotion" (Vizenor 15, qtd. in Simpson 88) and Anishinaabe understandings of their territory as defined not by borders but by language, philosophy, way of life, and political structure. Unlike Bourriaud's migrants, the traditional Anishinaabe were not simply wandering, or moving on, or moving from place to place but were moving outward from a territorial center to a place of encounter, "where one needs to practice good relations with neighboring nations" (Simpson 89).

Not surprisingly, Simpson comes to a very different understanding from Bourriaud's of both movement and multiculturalism. She quotes Anishinaabe Dakota scholar Scott Richard Lyons:

> The Ojibwe[11] were a people on the move. The Ojibwe envisioned life as a path and death as a journey; even *Ojibwemowin*, the Ojibwe language, is constituted by verbs on the move. What does migration produce? As we can see in the story of the Great Migration [from the mouth of the St Lawrence to the more dispersed inland territories the Anishinaabe now inhabit, in response to a vision predicting the coming of the white men] it produces difference; new communities, new peoples, new ways of living; new sacred foods, new stories, and new ceremonies. The old never dies; it gets supplemented by the new, and the result is diversity. (Lyons 4, qtd. in Simpson 92)

"The [radicant] heart berries," Simpson concludes, "serve as a reminder of the importance of working together in a good way, the importance of working through conflict in a manner that doesn't hurt one another, and the importance of letting go. . . . They remind us that the heart is the compass of life" (95). Her interweaving of language, place, mobility, relationships, personal integrity (truth), negotiation, and difference is itself a model of Indigenous scholarship, one from which we can learn in thinking about the intercultural performance ecology of a city, Toronto, whose name is traditionally understood to derive from the Huron-Wendat word *toronton*, or "meeting place."[12]

I write as a third-generation settler/invader of Anglo Scottish ancestry, but the protocols that Wilson outlines and Simpson models are not entirely foreign to me. I too want to position my research and writing in relation to my immediate context, the larger environment, and the people—Indigenous, immigrant, and dominant culture—with whom I live and work. I try to work, to paraphrase Wilson, *with* the individuals, companies, and communities that I am writing about, rather than *on* them. This, for me, as both dramaturge and scholar, means adopting the three Rs of respect, reciprocity, and responsibility, as well as the principle of relational accountability, and it means adapting my own goals—the exploration of my own research questions—to the goals and purposes of the intercultural theater community of Toronto with whom I work in solidarity. This means, in part, that the "outcomes" of my research take the form of contributions to the ongoing production and (re)constitution of an intercultural performance ecology in Toronto through working *with* other actors in that ecology both as a collaborator on their productions and as a scholar on the written work that is published under my name. In both instances, a core requirement is the one articulated by Wilson: it has to benefit the community.

SCOPE AND FOCUS

It is customary in writing the introduction to a book to talk the reader through its contents and concerns. In this instance part of that task is to articulate the book's exclusions. A broader perspective than I take here would consider the myriad ways that the city of Toronto performs itself, and it would constitute a massive and truly interdisciplinary performance studies project that would take into account urban planning, cultural and physical geography, political studies, economics, architecture and landscape architecture, media and communications studies, marketing theory, and other disciplines too numerous to mention much less engage.

My focus is much more narrow. Indeed, I am not even considering some of the more theatrical or formal performances of the city that include such things as music, dance, sketch or stand-up comedy, walks, tours, installations, parades (Toronto hosts Pride and Caribbean parades and celebrations that are among the largest anywhere), the city's many and various cultural festivals, or the annual Nuit Blanche, Luminato, and other events explicitly designed to perform the city before the world. And although my focus is on theater, I am not much concerned here with the occasional tokenistic forays into multiculturalism undertaken by the city's larger theaters, which sometimes fill what Filipina Canadian director Nina Lee Aquino calls "the dim sum slot" or "the curry slot" in their seasons in order to gain coveted multicultural funding (qtd. in Knowles, "Between" 80). I am even less interested in the city's commercial theaters, its mainstream "Regional" theater, Canadian Stage, or its classical theater, Soulpepper. Finally, although the many "one-off" amateur, semiprofessional, or professional productions by theater artists of varying cultural backgrounds, including, for example, productions that emerge from European communities; Jewish, Roma, or other diasporic communities; or indeed even disability communities and communities of gender and sexual difference do not exceed my interest, they do, for the most part, exceed my scope (except insofar as these communities are constituted as cultures by the companies on which I am focusing). My attention here is squarely on the networks of professional, culturally specific, racialized, and explicitly intercultural theater companies that populate the city's small-to-medium-sized stages and occasional or one-off performance spaces and focus primarily on the work of people of color.

Toronto is home to a dizzying and always changing number of such companies and collectives, some of which exist only on paper (or on websites). This is so in part because of various idiosyncratic funding requirements that force theaters to function on a project-by-project basis and because some funding programs will not accept applications from individuals. Applicants, then, are forced to form companies and collectives on an ad hoc basis, some of which survive and thrive for a time, some of which exist only for a single production, leaving online traces and "paper" trails. These companies constitute a significant part of the city's performance ecology, they are populated by artists who also work elsewhere, and they will figure periodically in the pages that follow. My main focus, however, is on a number of core companies that have established a record and reputation and have contributed significantly to the emergence, over the past few decades, of a vibrant, interdependent ecology of intercultural performance that crosses cultures and performance disciplines, challenges the hegemony of whiteness on the city's stages, and begins to reflect the cultural differences that are visible and audible on the city's streets and streetcars.

Some of these companies are dedicated to supporting and reflecting specific cultural communities—though even these communities are far from homogeneous. Others have primarily performed work from more broadly defined cultural "homelands," representing largely expatriate "communities" that exist as such only in diaspora. Others still *constitute* internally diverse and sometimes conflicted cultural communities *as* "African Canadian," "Asian Canadian" "Latino/a Canadian," "Indigenous," or "Native Canadian," developing and performing new work that speaks across such differences. Finally, companies such as Cahoots Theatre Company and Modern Times Stage Company are yet more broadly and explicitly *inter*cultural, bringing together and addressing the broad spectrum of the city's hyphenated cultures.

Few of these companies have their own performance spaces, and most rely on quickly disappearing rental space downtown or on coproduction with resident companies—usually Factory Theatre, Theatre Passe Muraille, Buddies in Bad Times, Native Earth at Aki Studio Theatre since 2012, or the Theatre Centre. Each mounts a limited season of one or two major productions per year, but many of them are also and crucially involved in developing, "workshopping," and presenting new work at fringe and play development festivals such the Toronto Fringe, Summerworks, b-current's rock. paper.sistahs Festival, fu-GEN's Potluck Festival, Alameda's De Colores Festival (until fall 2014), Nightwood Theatre's Groundswell Festival, Buddies in Bad Times' Rhubarb! Festival, and, until 2006 and 2008 respectively, the AfriCanadian Playwrights Festival and Factory Theatre's intercultural CrossCurrents Festival, the latter replaced by Performance Spring before being absorbed into the company's larger cross-cultural and play development mandates. Finally, some of this work is appearing more and more often in the regular subscription seasons of resident companies such as Tarragon Theatre, Theatre Passe Muraille, Buddies in Bad Times, even the "mainstream" Soulpepper and Canadian Stage, and, particularly since 2013, Factory Theatre.

Appendix 1 provides, for reference purposes, an account and categorization of the companies that this book takes as its primary focus. While this mapping might suggest a certain atomization that would validate critiques of multiculturalism by Bourriaud, Neil Bissoondath, and others that I survey in chapter 1, in practice traffic in plays, productions, and personnel among and across these companies and communities is fluid, as I argue in the conclusion. Recent productions on which I have worked as dramaturge, for example, in addition to *A Taste of Empire* (2010), with which I opened this introduction, include Chinese Canadian Diana Tso's *Red Snow* (2012), developed through fu-GEN Asian Canadian Theatre and produced by the Red Snow Collective and the Latinx Canadian Aluna Theatre at Theatre Passe Muraille before touring to a theater festival in Shanghai; Filipino Canadian Flerida Peña's *Sister Mary's a Dyke?!* (2013), developed first at Buddies in Bad Times (queer) Theatre, then at Carlos Bulosan (Filipino) Theatre Company, and finally produced by Cahoots (intercultural) Theatre Company at Native Earth's Aki Studio; Afghan Canadian Kawa Ada's *The Wanderers* (2014), developed by Cahoots Theatre Company and coproduced with Buddies in Bad Times; and Algonquin playwright Yvette Nolan's *The Unplugging* (2015), produced at Factory Theatre and directed by Filipina Nina Lee Aquino.

Part 1 deals with this type of fluidity and attempts to place it in context, first, in chapter 1, as a conscious tactic of performing what I call "the multicultural script"—Canada's official multicultural policy documents—in ways that work to circumvent its structural limitations and containments. Chapter 2 contextualizes the work differently, attempting to theorize beyond the atomization of traditional understandings of cultural memory to develop a view of "intercultural memory" as a site where negotiations happen across difference in the performative constitution of newly intercultural subjectivities and community identities in diasporic space.

Part 2 deals with examples of the ways in which those subjectivities and identities are shaped and structured through the conscious development of culturally specific dramaturgies: Filipino Canadian, Indigenous, and Afro-Caribbean Canadian. Chapters 3 and 4 concern themselves with ways of returning to Indigenous performance forms in the Philippines and in the Western Hemisphere for dramaturgical models that predate colonization and thereby circumvent the reifications implicit in "resistance," while also engaging with contemporary realities. Chapter 5 engages with attempts by the Afro-Caribbean community in Toronto to revision and regender a more recently developed performance form, dub poetry, as a dramaturgical model that queers performative identity formation.

Part 3 focuses on some of the many ways in which negotiations across cultures in performance are mediated in contemporary Toronto. Chapter 6 examines the work of Modern Times Stage Company and its deployment of modernist form as a surprisingly flexible mediator across difference, insisting on the specificity of different global modernisms while taking advantage of the adaptability of modernist performance to local application. Chapter 7 looks at the ways in which intermediality, in the work of Aluna Theatre, can mediate intercultural negotiations, problematizing universalizing understandings of empathy while simultaneously working effectively across difference. And chapter 8 considers the work of Cahoots Theatre Company (formerly Cahoots Theatre Projects) as a discursive nodal point, a mediator across cultural differences within the city's "brown caucus," and a site where many of the main "actors" in the city's intercultural performance ecology converge and the culturally specific becomes definitively intercultural.

Performing the Intercultural City concludes with cautious optimism around an increasing transnationalism within Toronto's intercultural performance ecology, an increasingly focused intraculturalism across difference within and among its community, and the beginnings—at Factory Theatre and especially at Aki Studio, now administered by the Indigenous Native Earth Performing Arts—of the material realization of the growth in influence and presence of the hitherto "other" on the city's stages: a room, or rooms, of their own.

PART ONE | Contexts

Intercultural performance, in Toronto as elsewhere, does not happen in a vacuum. While detailed consideration of all the material and theoretical contexts that shape intercultural performances, their production, and their reception in Canada is beyond the scope of this book,[1] the policies and practices that have shaped immigration and "official multiculturalism" in the country deserve examination in some detail. These policies have had an overwhelming impact, first on the funding and economics of cultural production, including theater, and second on the discourses of heritage and cultural memory—and therefore the formation of intercultural subjectivities—in an officially multicultural society. This section concerns itself with an analysis of these policies, their critiques, and the ways in which they have been officially and unofficially performed, as well as a consideration of the extensive body of literature on cultural memory that proliferated in cultural, visual, and literary studies in the 1980s and 1990s and merits reconsideration today within the context of what I call "intercultural memory."

Both the practices of official multiculturalism and theories of cultural memory have been sites of struggle for interculturalism in performance. Both have been enabling in many ways, the former for creating, at least theoretically, conditions in which full participation in Canadian society is possible for people from all cultural and ethnic backgrounds, the latter for providing an understanding of the ways in which embodiment, and hence performance, work to constitute specific community identities. Both also, however, have had a tendency to atomize culturally based identities as self-identical, and both have struggled to accommodate a definition of culture that is fluid, dynamic, and responsive to heterogeneous, culturally diverse, and always-emerging ecologies. Both are understood here to constitute "scripts" for performances that may not always follow their terms.

Chapter 1 addresses the official "multicultural script" as one that has real, material, and to some degree determining consequences, particularly on the funding, housing, and support of theater, but has nevertheless consistently been performed differently in Toronto by "actors" who take advantage of the opportunities it hierarchically presents while simultaneously re-creating its terms, crossing its boundaries, and troubling its categorizations. One of the potentially most restrictive aspects of the multicultural script is its tendency to constitute cultural memory as "heritage"—the static and nostalgic preservation of a cultural past in a faraway land—rather than as something that happens in and contributes to a present-tense constitution of subjectivity. Chapter 2, therefore, considers some of the ways in which the traditional scripts of cultural memory in diaspora are reimagined and rewritten across difference. It considers emerging versus inherited memories, interculturality as at once a continuum and rupture between "home there and home here" (Nina Lee Aquino, qtd. in Knowles, "Between" 77), embodied memory (in dance and movement) versus inscribed historical memory, and casting and rehearsal as deliberate sites of contingency and improvisation. It looks at the ways in which theater can employ the temporally bridging powers of memory synchronically to work across different communities of memory and to forge alliances and identities based on newly minted memories that are inter- rather than monocultural.

Part 1 provides a range of small-scale examples of some of the ways in which minoritized communities in Toronto have performed the multicultural script differently, carving out their own communities of memory in the diasporic city. Later chapters will explore specific theater companies and performances in more detail.

ONE | Multicultural Text, Intercultural Performance

> Multiculturalism is not a buzzword. It is not a trend. It is the new reality. As the premier theatre company in this country, we are best positioned to capitalize on these shifting demographics. While some of you may see fear, I see opportunity.
>
> —Bobby Del Rio, *Professionally Ethnic*

Bobby Del Rio's play *Professionally Ethnic* is a satiric fantasia about a large Canadian theater company hiring a token "ethnic" actor to symbolize its newly "diverse" corporate brand: "COLOUR YOUR WORLD" (77). But the play directly addresses the fact that one of the key contexts within which theatrical activity takes place in Toronto, and one of the key actors putting pressure on its performance ecology, is Canada's official multiculturalism policy, which functions hierarchically to dictate what I call Canada's "multicultural script."[1] This script is intended to function in the way that many traditional understandings of scripts would suggest: as a template and container for performances that are understood to "realize" it. But the actual intercultural performance practices taking place within that ecology, I suggest, function more rhizomatically. This chapter positions theatrical activity within the city of Toronto in relation to that multicultural script. It articulates multicultural *texts*—the policies, documents, and official discourses of Canadian multiculturalism (the archive)—against intercultural *performance* (the repertoire)—the complex ecology of grassroots interculturalism that refuses to be contained by the official script and plays itself out among and across the many culturally specific and intercultural theater artists and companies that attempt to construct culturally alternative communities and solidarities across difference.[2]

I don't wish to discount the importance or impact of the official policy, but neither do I want to reify a text/performance binary that gives primacy to that policy's text or denies performance practices independent authority.

I read the city's performance of the official multicultural script through the work of W. B. Worthen and Robert Weimann, understanding the relationship between text and performance as mutually constitutive. For multiculturalism, as for a dramatic text, "performance is not determined by the text . . . : it strikes a much more interactive, performative relation between writing and the spaces, places, and behaviors that give it meaning" (Worthen 12). Intercultural performance in Toronto operates in relation to multicultural text as "a formative force, as an institutionalized power in itself, as a cultural practice in its own right" (Weimann 4–5), and one that performs official multiculturalism in ways that are independently generative, at once instantiating, qualifying, and complicating that text in ways that constitute its social effect. At the same time, these performance practices are continually (re)constituting the city as heterotopic space, in which the order imposed by official multicultural policy is being processually *re*-ordered, as the essentially idealist utopia of official multiculturalism meets the messy materialities of heterotopic practice.

My purpose in this chapter is to come to an initial understanding of how individual gendered, raced, and classed subjectivities and community identities within the multicultural city are not just reflected in, or given voice by, but are *constituted through* performance. How does this processual, performative (re)construction of subjectivities relate to the "ethnic" communities of official multiculturalism? How do these performatively constituted subjectivities interact with one another in shifting coalitions? How do they relate to dominant understandings of the city's social space, which constitute the dominant culture as unified and monolithic and minoritized non-European cultures as "ethnic" enclaves?

MULTICULTURAL TEXT

Canada's multicultural policy has been widely celebrated for its utopian vision and its potential use by marginalized groups and individuals to gain access to full participatory democracy. And there is no doubt that considerable Pierre Trudeau–era idealism clings to what was the world's first state-sanctioned multiculturalism policy. Indeed, in 2005 Caribbean Canadian sociologist Cecil Foster envisioned a realizable nation "*Where Race Does Not Matter*" emerging from Trudeau's "idealist dream" (ix). But it is important while acknowledging the aspirational value of utopias to recall the historical dystopias that have emerged when such ideals have been imposed monologically, to historicize the emergence and development of the Canadian multicultural script since the 1960s , and to take into account the ways in which that script continues to play a key role in shaping the material conditions within which intercultural performance in Toronto happens.

The federal policy "Multiculturalism within a Bilingual Framework" was introduced by Prime Minister Pierre Elliott Trudeau in 1971 as a response to concerns expressed by "ethnic minorities" about the establishment of the Royal Commission on Bilingualism and Biculturalism.[3] The commission was appointed in 1963 to determine how to develop Canadian nationhood based on equality between French and English "charter groups," with "other ethnic groups" taken into account only as a secondary issue. In this narrative, "official multiculturalism" emerges as an afterthought in the effort to contain the independence movement in Quebec. Within Toronto's arts, education, and theater communities, this meant the availability of targeted arts funding for francophone or bilingual (English-French) work, but not for work from "othered" cultures.

A second determining context from which the 1971 policy emerged was the 1960s liberalization of Canada's immigration policies. The 1962 policy, formalized in the Immigration Act of 1967, initiated an idealist system that eschewed discrimination on the basis of race, national origin, or culture. The unspoken purpose of the policy change, however, was to bolster a dwindling labor force with cheap, easily policed bodies at a time of exuberant economic expansion. It had the effect, nevertheless, of opening Canada's borders for the first time to significant numbers of non-European immigrants, who came to be known as "visible minorities" and who settled disproportionately in the city of Toronto, where street life was transformed and the possibilities for intercultural exchange increased dramatically.[4] It is possible, then, to see those policies as having produced the felt need to both exploit and "manage" diversity, particularly racial diversity, through means other than immigration. Enter multiculturalism.

A third context that leaves traces in Canada's multicultural practice is more symbolic than material. This was the felt need, following Canada's 1967 centenary, to establish a distinctive national identity, if only to differentiate Canadians from Americans. Canadian multiculturalism became a widely broadcast symbol, and Toronto became the poster city for Canadian identity as one "tolerant" of diversity—one of the policy's stated goals, but one that problematically positions "diversity" as non-Canadian, something "other," that "real" Canadians "generously" tolerate.

In its 1971 "White Paper" articulation, its 1982 entrenchment in the Charter of Rights and Freedoms, and its passage into law in 1988 as Bill C-9, the focus of the multicultural script was on "preserv[ing]" the "cultural heritage" of people of diverse ethnicities and "advanc[ing] multiculturalism throughout Canada in harmony with the national commitment to the official languages of Canada" (Multiculturalism and Citizenship Canada 13, 15).[5] This combined focus on the culturalist preservation of the heritage of the "other" and on containment within a French-English charter-group dominant has been the basis for the most salient critiques of the multicultural script. Neil Bissoondath attacks it for ghettoizing cultural communities through the rhetoric of preservation, resisting assimilation while controlling access to material and cultural capital, and limiting cultural production to folkloric exhibitions and multicultural festivals. Himani Bannerji (125–50) critiques the liberal discourse of "tolerance" embedded in the script as articulated by philosopher Charles Taylor, where a (white) liberal "we" is seen to "tolerate" "others" rather than to dissolve into a more inclusive multicultural entity. As Bourriaud argues, Taylor's "courtesy . . . leads us to view non-Western artists as guests to be treated with politeness, and not as full-fledged actors on the cultural scene in their own right" (*The Radicant* 27).[6] Sneja Gunew points to "state multiculturalism" in Australia and Canada as a bureaucratic tool for "managing" diversity. State multiculturalism, she argues, has been "framed by a liberal pluralism where cultural differences are paraded as apolitical [ahistorical and static] ethnic accessories" (17) and where women are positioned without agency as the stolid bearers of the "ethnic" tradition.[7] Bannerji has scrutinized what she calls "capitalist state inspired multiculturalisms" (1) for their capacity to obscure "a hidden class struggle being conducted behind cultural-historical masks of 'authentic' identities." She also critiques the Canadian multicultural script's capacity to function "as an epistemology of occlusion which displaces the actual living subjects, their histories, cultures, and social relations, with ideological constructs of ethnicity" (11) while attributing various social and economic inequalities, together with racialized and gendered violences, not to systemic racism and sexism but to untouchable "cultural differences." Smaro Kamboureli provides a nuanced reading of the Act itself, exposing its internal contradictions and its tendency, fueled by veiled racist and assimilationist principles, toward the legitimation and commodification of ethnicity (*Scandalous* 96–106)—commodification that often manifests itself within Toronto theater as the display of exotic difference on the city's mainstream stages for dominant-culture subscription audiences.

For these and other critics, the central reference points for the multicultural script, against which a conflation of "visible minorities" can be defined, are the inscribed charter languages of French and (for Toronto) English,[8] and "a consolidated and hegemonic 'whiteness' as the encompassing sign for all forms of socio-economic and political privilege" (Gunew 19). Finally, and scandalously, "the 1971 policy does not mention First Nations peoples, and the 1988 Act specifically excludes them" (Kamboureli, Introduction 11). As it turns out, this, in application if not intention, may not be a bad thing. Dakota scholar Philip Deloria argues that in the United States, "with its focus on difference and rigid categorizations . . . a multiculturalism based on pluralism proved troublesome to those who lived identities along more complicated racial-ethnic, gender, sexual, occupational, and geographic lines" (173). What Deloria calls "incorporative multiculturalism" (176), on the other hand, involving a "cosmopolitan focus on culture-crossings and simultaneities . . . suggested that one's identity was a matter not so much of descent as of consent and choice" (173). Both remain problematic propositions for Indigenous peoples subjected over the centuries simultaneously to stereotyping and to a kind of cultural identity theft. Nevertheless, the exclusion of Native peoples from the multicultural script has left the relationship between multiculturalism and Indigeneity a vexed issue to this day, particularly in urban centers such as Toronto, with its significant off-reserve "urban Indian" population. Indeed, the only peoples with genuine claims to "founding" status in relation to the places now called Canada are, in the multicultural script, "relegated," as Bannerji says, "to the status of footnotes" (101).

The multicultural script has had its most determining impact on cultural festivals, folk arts, and amateur community theater, where it has, as its critics suggest, tended to create ethnic enclaves and to play a fundamentally preservationist role in relation to immigrant cultures. But as the next section demonstrates, it has also laid the foundation for arts and culture funding policies and structures within which professional theater by minoritized artists has had to work, and against which it has had to struggle.

PERFORMING THE MULTICULTURAL SCRIPT: FUNDING

Official performances of the multicultural script, as realizations of the text inscribed in official discourse, have borne out the concerns of its critics. One of the most determinative official performances, the funding of arts practice, provides a salient example, one that intercultural performance practitioners in Toronto have been forced to negotiate for decades. As sociologist Peter Li demonstrated in 1994, in the first two decades following the implementation of multiculturalism, arts funding under the policy produced separate and unequal support structures for "occidental" (365) and so-called minority arts. Throughout the 1970s and 1980s, artists from "the high-status art world of mainly white Canadians" (366) enjoyed a formal system of arms-length, peer-reviewed funding through the Canada Council for the Arts. Meanwhile, "the more nascent multicultural circle [was] sustained by Canada's official policy of multiculturalism through the Government's direct funding and control of activities under . . . multicultural programs" designed to promote heritage activities among minoritized cultures (366).

Not surprisingly, funding allocated throughout the 1970s and 1980s through the federal Multiculturalism Directorate, available to individuals only if they were "supported by recognized community [i.e., multicultural] organizations/groups or institutions" (qtd. in Li 387), went almost exclusively to nonprofessional "national and regional multicultural festivals, which involved folkloric dancing, ethnic theatre performances, and craft exhibitions" (Li 378). In short, multiculturalism as performed through arts funding practices kept othered cultures in their static, nostalgic, and dehistoricized ethnic place, allowing dominant cultural expression to flourish within an established European tradition. Arts funding practices created "the institutional framework for reproducing minority art, culture, and heritage in forms and manners that are consistent with maintaining the hegemony of the dominant group" (Li 369).[9]

The effects of this for theatrical practice are clear, as Mayte Gómez demonstrated in 1993. Locating her study within an analysis of official policies that anticipated Li, Gomez examined Toronto's Cahoots Theatre Projects' 1993 Lift Off! Festival. She found that the universalist discourse encouraged by the multicultural script resisted interaction across genuine, shifting, materially and historically located cultural or formal difference within the city. Theater that set out to simply realize the script, that is, reinforced rather than disrupted the dominant/other binary on which colonialism rests, inscribing *diversity* rather than, and without, real *difference*. This has remained true, as large "mainstream" companies in Toronto, complying with the multicultural script, fill the "diversity slots" in their seasons with "ethnic" exotica (the curry slot, the dim sum slot, the chitlins slot, rarely the bannock slot) without significantly shifting their audience base or comfort level.

Arts funding practices shifted in the 1990s, as the Multiculturalism Directorate was replaced in 1991 by the Department of Multiculturalism and Citizenship. This was in turn split in 1993 between the new Department of Canadian Heritage and the Department of Citizenship and Immigration, when a Secretary of State (Multiculturalism) was appointed at a junior level not represented in Cabinet. The Department of Canadian Heritage, moreover, was given responsibility not simply for multiculturalism but for an array of other areas, including fitness and amateur sports, the parks component of Environment Canada, and cultural broadcasting. In 1997–98, in response to criticisms by the new right-wing Reform Party, the Liberal government eliminated funding for "ethnocultural" groups altogether on the grounds that multicultural funding, which in any case had been steadily shrinking, should be available to all, not just "ethnic" Canadians. One consequence of this, as Paolo Prosperi notes, was that "for ethnocultural organizations who were in the past the beneficiaries of core funding, those wanting to secure funding from [that] point forward [had] to do so on a project-by-project basis" (qtd. in Abu-Laban and Gabriel 114–15).

The binary system of providing arts funding to individuals and companies from the dominant cultures while funding "ethnic" groups through multicultural grants had nevertheless been broken, and artists from various cultural backgrounds, including Indigenous, began to gain (limited) access to arts funding.[10] The shift improved the optics but did not mark a substantive change. Canadian Heritage has continued to provide direct funding to projects from "othered" cultures, often privileging them in their folkloric guise and managing cultural and artistic expression directly. But the pot was diminished, with a higher percentage of direct (vs. arms-length) funding from government increasingly diverted to dominant-culture "heritage" projects—with "heritage," particularly under the Conservative government of Stephen Harper from 2006 to 2015, increasingly defined as Canada's "whitestream" settler-culture history.[11] Funding from the arts councils, meanwhile, perpetuated the inequity that the realignment seemed designed to mend, because along with the restructuring came not only the discontinuation of core funding for "ethnocultural" groups but also a redefinition that in practice constituted a virtual freeze on ongoing operating funding. Because of budget cuts and increased demand, operating funding, in effect if not explicit policy, was only available to already established companies, and when extended to new applicants often had the unanticipated result of *diminishing* the total funding that had been available through project grants. (Companies on operating funding are not eligible to also apply on a project-by-project basis.) In Toronto this means that a handful of companies, most of whom have secure production venues and most of whom are "white,"[12] remain on operating funding and control the theater seasons and performance spaces on which "other" companies rely for co-productions or rental space. The "other" companies, meanwhile, must apply for one-off project grants from funding agencies that can and do claim to privilege "multicultural" ventures. The companies identified as "multicultural" are thereby placed in dependency relationships to the "charter" anglo companies, which are de facto given the power to police what productions from the "ethnic" communities are staged and which tend to favor work that is nonthreatening to their largely middle-class anglo audiences. Meanwhile, "ethnic" companies are forced to compete with one another for small pools of one-time funding, a situation that threatens to fracture potential solidarities among them.

The Canada Council for the Arts and (especially) the Ontario and Toronto Arts Councils, responding to pressure since the 1990s by activist artists of color, have made serious efforts, within the shrinking confines of their respective mandates and budgets, to address the changed face of Canada's arts communities. The Canada Council now has an Aboriginal Arts Office and designated Aboriginal programs as well as an Equity Office mandated to support "Canadian Artists of African, Asian, Middle Eastern, Latin American or mixed racial heritage and their artistic practices," and the mandate of its Theatre Office also includes a statement that it "respects diversity of practices, cultures and company mandates" (Canada Council). The Ontario Arts Council similarly has an Aboriginal Arts program and is proactive in promoting diversity in the arts, as is the Toronto Arts Council.

But the federal government's performance of the multicultural script in the past two decades has invoked an increasingly corporate version of the utopian vision, as politicians and bankers, using the slogan "multiculturalism means business," have argued for the "competitive advantage" of "internal globalization" in the new world economy.[13] The concerns this raises for those interested in the social justice potential of multiculturalism have to do with how an economic emphasis on "productive diversity" turns attention away from antiracism, how it impacts on minoritized groups whose home countries do not offer opportunities for trade, how it impacts on Aboriginal groups, and how it inflects issues of class and gender (Abu-Laban and Gabriel 117). In the delicate performance ecology of Toronto, meanwhile, the ongoing loss to condo developers of crucial venues for the city's intercultural companies has increased those companies' dependency on established theaters for inclusion.[14]

INTERCULTURAL PRACTICE

Intercultural practitioners in Toronto are forced to work with the official multicultural script because it directly shapes their material realities. Fortunately, however hierarchical or monologic in intent, that script is not monolithically pre-scriptive: the constitutive relationship between policy and practice, text and performance, archive and repertoire is not unidirectional, and performance has its own horizontally and independently generative regimes. This is true in part *because* of the otherwise problematic material reality that few of the city's culturally specific and intercultural companies can offer significant full-time employment, most theater artists for purely financial reasons work in a range of ways with a variety of companies, and the ghettoes of multiculturalism have porous walls. For both positive and negative reasons, then, within Toronto's performance ecology interculturalism is able in many cases to work dialogically and rhizomatically to reconstitute the official script's social effects across many communities of difference. As Toronto activist, cultural critic, and sometime playwright Afro-Caribbean Canadian Marlene NourbeSe Philip argues,

> Multiculturalism may have been a cynical ploy by Liberal politicians to address the balance of power in Canada, but the creativity and inventiveness of the people in being able to turn to their own advantage policies that may not have their interests at heart can never be underestimated. (8)

Some of these people are theater workers who perform the official script in ways that ignore the folkloric enclaves into which they have been slotted, forming horizontal networks, performing into being new diasporic subjectivities, and establishing relationships and solidarities across acknowledged difference. Coalitions are being constructed around what Ella Shohat and Robert Stam call "*mutual and reciprocal relativization*" (359, emphasis in original) in order to counter both exclusionary practices from the outside and compensatory nostalgias from within specific communities. These coalitions are also reinserting Indigenous peoples as central to Canadian multiculturalism in performance, without surrendering their Nations' status as "First"—and this has been particularly true since 2012, when Native Earth Performing Arts took over the administration of Aki Studio in the Daniel's Spectrum building in Regent Park, coordinating seasons that include those of resident companies Cahoots Theatre Projects, fu-GEN Asian Canadian Theatre, and Kaha:Wi (Indigenous) Dance Theatre (see this book's conclusion). Finally, these companies, individually and collectively, have evinced a continuing capacity to get their work onto the city's stages more broadly, forming shifting collaborations, coproducing with one another, and fundraising in inventive ways that allow them to remain at once professional arts and "multicultural" organizations. They have consistently found ways, that is, to speak *as professional artists* out of *specific cultural positions*, in defiance of the exclusionary binaries of the official script and the routine dismissal of "community theater" as nonprofessional. While alliances among these companies are proceeding *intra*nationally, theater workers from various communities are attempting to establish broadly diasporic networks beyond the nation-state. There are (at least) three overlapping practices undertaken within and across Toronto's multicultural theater companies as performative rewritings of the multicultural script: strategic reappropriation, diasporic transnationalism, and urban intraculturalism. I provide some examples below as a kind of baseline in order to demonstrate how each complicates and performs the multicultural script differently. But variations on these strategies, in isolation or in combination, permeate this volume.

Strategic Reappropriation

The most familiar of these strategies involves reappropriation by the colonized of the symbolic capital of the dominant culture, as canonical texts and forms are rewritten and reconfigured through difference. Thus a play such as Djanet Sears's *Harlem Duet*, a "prequel" to Shakespeare's *Othello* featuring Othello's first, Black wife, Billie, first produced in 1997 by the feminist Nightwood Theatre under its mandate to privilege "creative alliances among women artists of diverse backgrounds" (Nightwood Theatre) and subsequently produced by theaters large and small across the continent, not only engages in postcolonial "talking back" to empire but also reverses Shakespeare's representation of Othello as an isolated character in an overwhelmingly white world (and naturalized European culture). *Harlem Duet* relocates the action to Harlem, sometimes seen as the center of African North American diasporic culture, where it is Shakespeare who is isolated and decentered, surrounded on the bookshelves by *African Mythology* and *Black Psychology* and in the play by central moments from Black history. Among the venues at which the play has been performed is the Stratford Festival, heavily supported by government arts funding and dedicated to the work of Shakespeare. The production was directed by Sears herself, the first Black person to direct at North America's largest classical repertory theater.

Or consider Joseph Jomo Pierre's 2013 play *Shakespeare's Nigga*, coproduced by Obsidian Theatre, Theatre Passe Muraille, and 3D Atomic Entertainment. Here Shakespeare becomes a plantation owner who has fathered a child, now his foreman Othello, with a "Dark Lady" who died in childbirth. He is facing a slave rebellion led by Aaron (of *Titus Andronicus*), who himself has had a child by Shakespeare's daughter Judith. The play opens with Othello whipping Aaron under Shakespeare's supervision; it closes with Shakespeare reading a book to Aaron's child: "There's music from the most crude of instruments" (Pierre 63). The play, as its dramaturge says in his notes to the published script, is "Aaron's chance to rewrite his own story.[15] It is Shakespeare's chance to listen" (Hague).

Native Earth Performing Arts has also reappropriated Shakespeare, but to quite different effect, in *The Death of a Chief,* their adaptation of *Julius Caesar,* which had three public workshops in 2005–6 before premiering in 2008 at the symbolically central National Arts Centre in Ottawa, hitherto virtually unavailable to Indigenous theater artists. In *Harlem Duet* Sears both claims and rejects Shakespeare—"the Shakespeare's mine, but you can have it," says Billie, dividing the bookshelves at the dissolution of her marriage (52). The anticipated postcolonial critique in *The Death of a Chief,* however, is replaced by an acceptance of the cultural authority and "universality" of Shakespeare, but one that *lays claim* to that authority, and with it the right, in the words of artistic director, playwright, and director Yvette Nolan, "*to say those words if they feel like it,*" in full consciousness that "language is power" (Nolan, "Death" 2, emphasis added). *The Death of a Chief* uses Shakespeare for its own ends, analyzing through Shakespeare the postcontact poison that has infected Native communities since the beginnings of the colonial project. One of the goals of the creation of *The Death of a Chief* as a process was to provide classical training that is often denied to Aboriginal actors; another was to deflect the pain of internal betrayals within the community, and of the public exposing of those betrayals, onto Shakespeare's exposition of the dysfunctions at the root of European history. But chief among the goals of *The Death of a Chief* was to negotiate and perform into existence a Native community in Toronto out of the many displaced Indigenous nations that find themselves there. Each workshop began with a negotiation within the company about the ceremonial elements of ritual performance in their various cultural traditions. As Nolan says,

> When you put people in a room together, you end up with a discussion of what those traditions are, and who they've learned them from . . . . When we work on a project like *The Death of a Chief,* which has, at any given time, between eight and fifteen Aboriginal artists in the room . . . all of those people bring their traditions to the room . . . and it works just like it says in the stories that it works, in that we sit and discuss it until we figure out what everyone can live with. (Interview)

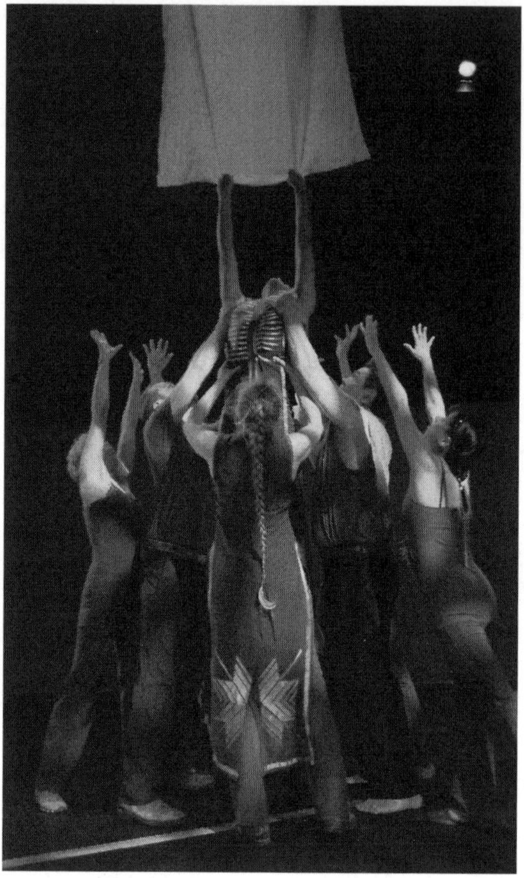

Fig. 1. Waawaate Fobister as the shaman/soothsayer surrounded by performers from a wide range of Indigenous Nations in the Native Earth Performing Arts production of *The Death of a Chief*, adapted from Shakespeare's *Julius Caesar* by Yvette Nolan and Kennedy Cathy Mackinnon. Photo by Nir Bareket.

Ultimately, "we created our own ritual," Nolan says (Interview). It is important to notice here the ways in which Native Earth drew upon and respected traditional performance forms without engaging in the preservationist rhetoric of the multicultural script. These are respectful but created and negotiated rituals, used to forge diasporic urban identities across First Nations. The *Death of a Chief* creation process, then, was heterotopic in intent. Here as elsewhere, the hope, according to Nolan, is that "*if we can work it out in this play then maybe we can work it out in our lives too*" ("Death" 4, emphasis added).[16]

Other Indigenous artists have performed intercultural appropriations of non-Shakespearean canonical work, chief among them Ntlaka'pamux (Thompson Salish) playwright Tara Beagan, who seems to be making something of a specialty of Indigenous adaptations of realist classics, or as she says, of "reclaiming the canon . . . , making it clear that our stories are relevant to one another." "Indigenizing the canon," she argues, "is the most obvious way of demonstrating to both First Nations and non–First Nations folks that we are irrevocably connected" (Beagan, qtd. in Solga 242). In *Miss Julie: Sheh'mah* (*sheh'mah* is a derogatory Ntlaka'pamux term for "white person," or "whitey") she relocates Strindberg's 1888 Swedish play to the interior of British Columbia in 1929 (traditional Salish or Sushwap territory), casts Miss Julie as the Canadian-born daughter of an immigrant British rancher, and transforms Strindberg's Jean and Kirsten into the Secwepemc Sushwap Jonny and Ntlaka'pamux Christie Ann. She also shifts the action from midsummer's eve to a winter night on which, slumming it as a class *and* cultural tourist, Miss Julie has given consent for the Indigenous servants on the farm to dance—a practice made illegal by the colonial government of the day. The play says a lot about the racism of white society, and it says more about the complex humanity of its Indigenous characters, but perhaps most importantly it serves as a work of intercultural appropriation: "To place figures like Jonny and Christie Ann into a realist European text . . . is to argue that the lives lived by these utterly marginalized persons *are real*" (Solga 242), unlike the merely symbolic "ethnics" of the multicultural script or the static, ahistoric subjects of the Indian Act.

In *Free as Injuns* Beagan performs similar reconstructive surgery on Eugene O'Neill's *Desire under the Elms* (1924), her title picking up on the irony of the vision the brothers Simeon and Peter have in O'Neill's play of going to California to be "free as Injuns" (O'Neill, I.4)—California being among the regions where Native Americans in the period were least "free" and most decimated by violence and disease. In Beagan's version, the entire cast, with the exception of Ephraim, is mixed race. Ephraim's son Even (Eben in the original), Even's mother, and Ephraim's new wife, Be (Abbie in the original), are all Indigenous, and like Be, Even's mother is from the territory on which the play is set: Ephraim's farm, we hear, is on "her land. Her people were here long before his line got hold of it" (Beagan, "Free" 16). The racial backgrounds of Ephraim's other two sons by other mothers (Ephraim, with a fetish for racial "Others," seems nevertheless to have worked all his wives to death), are determined by casting. But this show, permeated by the thick dirt covering the floor of Mushkegowuk Cree designer Andy Moro's set in the original 2012 Native Earth production at Buddies in Bad Times, was all about lineage, land, territory, and the earth from which Evan emerges at the outset and to which his and Be's son is returned—"planted"—at the end. It is all, that is, about sovereignty, though the word is never spoken in the play. *Desire under the Elms* has frequently been called "the first important American tragedy" (Bogard); *Free as Injuns* rewrites it as a tragedy of the First Americans.

These are only a few examples of what in its simplest form can be read as postcolonialist reappropriation, "talking back to empire," but the subtlety, complexity, and variety of the adaptations of canonical drama that have been undertaken by marginalized communities in Toronto is unusual. This perhaps points to the fact that many of these communities, working in English in western performance spaces within the material conditions framed by the multicultural script, are always engaged in a kind of reappropriative adaptation of, or to, dominant-culture forms, institutions, languages, and horizons of expectations.

Diasporic Transnationalism and Trans-Indigeneity

In recent years, as Abu-Laban and Gabriel have argued, the multicultural script has moved increasingly toward "selling diversity," appropriating multiculturalism in the service of globalization. But they have also noted the capacity for strategic transnationalisms to perform globalization differently, rehearsing heterotopic modes of alternate ordering, pointing to "groups and individuals who contest policy changes and new directions," "actors" who "may themselves be part of new transnational networks and organizations that supercede national boundaries" (22).

The simplest theatrical expressions of this type of transnationalism have to do with maintaining connections with cultural "homelands." Companies such as the AfriCan Theatre Ensemble, the now-defunct Rasik Arts, and to a lesser extent Theatre Archipelago have been dedicated to producing plays from their respective countries or continents of origin. In spite of some residual tendency to promote compensatory nostalgias for lost homelands, these companies have nevertheless introduced to Toronto major works from the international repertoire, contributing to the productive internationalization of Canadian multiculturalism and introducing new performance forms to the city. They have also excited new diasporic awarenesses, in that the communities they performatively constitute cut across the boundaries of nation-states within their respective homelands. As Theatre Archipelago's artistic director Rhoma Spencer has said of her complex 2006 setting of the Jamaican two-hander *Fallen Angel and the Devil Concubine* in Toronto's mixed Parkdale district, close to the Theatre Centre where it was performed, "'the Caribbean' only *exists* in the diaspora" and can only be addressed there (Spencer). The original play was first produced in Jamaica in 1987 as a national allegory, and as one of its writer-performers says, it "explore[d] how women who are positioned on opposite sides of the colonizer/colonized divide, continually perform memories of this colonial relationship and in doing so recreate, reiterate and transform it" (Ford-Smith 233). The relocation of *Fallen Angel* to Toronto in the Theatre Archipelago/b current coproduction, the cross-casting of a white Jamaican Canadian male, John Blackwood, in the role of Katie, and the decision to cast Lettie as Trinidadian and Katie as Jamaican, all expanded the original play's concerns to address diasporic issues specific to the shifting intercultural landscape of Toronto's "pan-Caribbean culture." There, as Spencer says, the characters, suffering from mental illnesses, "have a double whammy of dispossession. . . . Not only are they distanced from everyday reality, but they're also uprooted from their homelands" (qtd. in Kaplan, "Parkdale").

Companies such as Modern Times and Aluna Theatre, discussed at more length in chapters 6 and 7, practice a different and somewhat more politicized transnationalism. Modern Times, in its international "Dialogues Project," has used its production of Iranian playwright Bahram Beyza'ie's *Aurash* to make connections in various parts of the world that have been riven by conflict. Aluna has worked with Bogotá's Corporación Colombiana de Teatro in Colombia, developing its creation process in part by way of cross-national collaboration, and has also cultivated a rhizomatic transnational network through its Panamerican Routes/RUTAS Panamericanas Festival, which in its 2014 and 2016 manifestations also involved collaboration with Native Earth Performing Arts and New York's Hemispheric Institute. Panamerican Routes consists of workshops, classes, "conservatorios," and conversations, exhibitions and installations, papers, panels, and performances that are represented in the festival's programs by way of the routes—Mexico City and San Francisco, Valdivia and Vancouver, Medellín, Montevideo, Caracas, Bogotá, Edmonton, and Ottawa—by which each one arrived in Toronto, each stop along the way contributing differently to the creation process. The 2014 edition featured keynotes by the Hemispheric Institute's Diana Taylor and Inga (Indigenous Colombian) artist Waira Nina, together with panels on such topics as "maiz in the americas," "femicide in the americas," "the migration of youth," "urban displacement + renewal," and "re-staging treaty (no 9)."

First Nations companies in Toronto such as Red Sky Performance, Native Earth, and Turtle Gals Performance Ensemble, in spite of Aboriginal peoples having been excluded by official multiculturalism, in spite of their having little purchase in the realm of global capital, and in spite of working within very different diasporic contexts,[18] have proven themselves to be expert at forging transnational connections with other Indigenous peoples. Since its founding in 2000 by Anishinaabe artistic director Sandra Laronde, Red Sky has worked out of Toronto with Indigenous artists from Canada, the United States, Mexico, Australia, and Mongolia to bring the traditional performance forms of a worldwide Aboriginal community into the realm of the modernist avant-garde. Red Sky is producing neither "issue plays," "authentic" Aboriginal performance (with all the colonialist preoccupations with purity that implies), nor tourist shows but contemporary dance/theater productions that draw upon, develop, and juxtapose traditional Aboriginal performance forms from various Indigenous cultures. Their productions remain in repertory and tour within Canada and internationally, creating work for Aboriginal performers, replacing racist stereotypes with representations of astonishing beauty and skill, and exploiting tactically (de Certeau, *Practice* xix–xx, 34–39) the pieties of Canada's official multiculturalism in order to advance the cause globally of Aboriginal people in the arts. *Tono*, first performed in 2010, brought together theater, live music, and dance from communities in Canada, the United States, Mongolia, and China to celebrate strength, beauty, and grace among trans-Indigenous plains horse cultures.

Under the artistic direction of Yvette Nolan Native Earth also negotiated the discourses of globalization through collaborations with Indigenous peoples rather than national governments, but theirs has been a transnationalism that, unlike that of Red Sky, circumvents the industrial, "foreign relations" model of production and diplomatic exchange or of free trade in commodified cultures. Rather than collaborations within a single production, Native Earth's Honouring Theatre project involved a repertory system of mounting and touring shows by Aboriginal companies from Canada, Australia, and Aotearoa New Zealand to all three countries in 2006–8. It involved forging strategic alliances, "establishing," as the tour's program puts it, "indigenous trade routes through the arts" that echo pre-contact trade routes among Indigenous nations (Native Earth, Program) and anticipated their collaboration with Aluna on Panamerican Routes/RUTAS Panamericanas in February–March 2014. This ambitious project staged Nolan's own play, *Annie Mae's Movement*, Injibarndi Palku playwright David Milroy's memory play, *Windmill Baby*, and Samoan playwright Makerita Urale's text and movement piece, *Frangipani Perfume*. The companies include actors and directors from a wide range of Indigenous Nations from North America and the Pacifica coming together over three countries and three years, and these collaborations have continued: in the fall of 2014 Native Earth's new play development festival, Weesageechak Begins to Dance, showcased a new and ongoing collaboration between Indigenous artists in Toronto and Māori artists from Tawata Productions in Aotearoa New Zealand, and the companies have continued an active program of visits and exchanges since.

Like Red Sky and Native Earth, Turtle Gals Performance Ensemble, founded in Toronto in 2000 by Jani Lauzon, Monique Mojica, and Michelle St. John, was concerned with exploring "a continuum of past, present, and future" and developing "non-linear multi-disciplinary theatre forms" out of Indigenous performance traditions (Turtle Gals, Information). And like Red Sky and Native Earth, their interest exceeded and exploded national boundaries to take in hemispherically, in their case, the Indigenous peoples of the Americas. The form of Turtle Gals' work was hybrid, growing out of the performers' own mixed race, which also served as the hemispheric and autobiographical content of their work. This, however, was autobiography in the broadest sense of the term: autobiography that included the performers' blood memories of their hemispheric ancestors, disregarding the latter-day borders of nation-states. Turtle Gals discontinued operations in 2008, but its three founding members continue their work in the hemispheric city along developing but similar lines, one strand of which, the ongoing work of founder Monique Mojica, is explored in chapter 4. But all of this—the autobiographical, the hybrid, the hemispheric, the traditional, and the contemporary, together with a deeply rooted sense of First Nations cultural memory—played itself out in Turtle Gals' complex interdisciplinary productions and is an important part of their ongoing legacy. *The Scrubbing Project* was the company's signature piece and its most directly autobiographical show, dealing with the writer-performers' own hybridized identities, their internalized racism, and their experiences "living with genocide" (Turtle Gals, *Scrubbing Project* 363). But it also dealt, as Anishinaabe scholar Jill Carter points out, with "recovery, remembrance, revitalization and reintegration of *all* Aboriginal peoples," regardless of their current national location ("Writing" 14, emphasis in original).

What these variations on transnationalism perform within Toronto is a constitution of the city's *intra*cultural performance ecology, discussed below, as effectively heterotopic space, countering the multicultural script's drive toward globalization through the exploitation of its diversity in the global marketplace. These projects are not about the cross-border flow of capital and goods but about the reconstitution of borders themselves as expansive border*lands* that encompass the city, are neither guarded nor traversed, but are productively embraced and inhabited differently.

Urban Intraculturalism

If Red Sky, Native Earth, and Turtle Gals have used strategic transnationalisms to complicate the dominance of globalization from First Nations perspectives, theater companies across Toronto have developed a kind of cooperative intraculturalism from below in order to perform differently the corporate drive within the multicultural script toward what Royal Bank president John Cleghorn in 1995 called "internal globalization" (qtd. in Abu-Laban and Gabriel 105)—multiculturalism deployed as market advantage for Canada within the "home" nations of immigrant communities. By constructing a heterotopic space within the city, these companies might be thought of as adapting Rustom Bharucha's call for a grassroots theatrical *intra*culturalism in the face of prevailing utopian discourses of theatrical interculturalism that leave power within the hands of charismatic and well-funded westerners such as Peter Brook, Ariane Mnouchkine, and Eugenio Barba (Bharucha, *Theatre*). I am here following Mayte Gómez in applying Bharucha's concept of intraculturalism to Canada, and specifically Toronto, as a "second world" settler/invader society (Slemon), thinking through interculturalism "from below," practiced "tactically" in relation to the monological "strategies" of the dominant (de Certeau, *Practice* xix–xx, 34–39; see also McClintock, Mufti, and Shohat; Moss).

The intercultural performance ecology of Toronto features a complex web of interconnections among individuals and companies working in solidarity across their acknowledged differences. Yvette Nolan, former artistic director of Native Earth, calls this network "the brown caucus"[18] and gives a sense of how it functions:

> The Native Earth office [in 2006] consists of two Aboriginal women, one Black woman, and one Asian woman, and we bring all our communities to the work. We always choose *other* in the work. When we choose directors, designers, dramaturges, we always choose *other*. Even though Weesageechak [Begins to Dance] is an Aboriginal festival developing work by Aboriginal writers, we first choose *other* dramaturges, dramaturges who are Aboriginal or Asian or queer. *Other* as in not white, not from the dominant culture, those who have a sense of self outside of the dominant culture. (Interview)

The geography of contemporary downtown Toronto facilitates working across difference. As urban planners Mohammed Qadeer and Sandeep Kumar found in 2006, the city's downtown is free of what they call "ethnic enclaves." Downtown neighborhoods are mixed. They flow into one another, allowing for the performance of intercultural exchange and intercultural identities not pre-scripted by official multiculturalism. The offices of Toronto's intercultural theater companies coexist and share resources in locations like the Distillery District and 400 Richmond Street West (both former industrial complexes now devoted to galleries and arts offices), Wynchwood Barns (a former streetcar repair facility near St. Clair and Christie and just northeast of Aluna Theatre's offices and studios in a warehouse complex north of Dupont), and similar buildings in the former garment district on Spadina Avenue. These companies also share workshop and performance spaces at such places as the Great Hall, the Theatre Centre, Factory Theatre, and Theatre Passe Muraille, all on or near Queen Street West and close to the cluster of offices on Spadina and Richmond Streets, and increasingly in clusters in the city's east end, where fu-GEN, Cahoots, and Native Earth have offices in or near the Aki Studio on Dundas Street, which they share, and where the offices of Obsidian Theatre are a little farther east on Dundas beyond the Don River.[19]

When Nina Lee Aquino, then artistic director of fu-GEN Asian Canadian Theatre Company, was approached in late 2006 about taking up residency at the Richmond Hill Centre for the Performing Arts in the largely Asian Canadian north Toronto suburb of Richmond Hill, she turned down the otherwise attractive offer in fear of ghettoization: she was aware that the company's real constituency was located within the performance ecology of the city's downtown (Aquino, Interview). Similarly, South Asian Canadian writer-performer Anita Majumdar's popular one-person show, *Fish Eyes*, grounded in various forms of Indian classical dance, was designed for the downtown core. Majumdar believes, moreover, that it reached its diasporic South Asian Canadian community in part because it did *not* have its premiere in the heavily South Asian suburb of Brampton[20] or any of the other ghettoized suburban community centers of official multiculturalism (Majumdar, Interview). It has reached its South Asian Canadian as well as its more general audience precisely because she resisted folkloric imagery and targeted established professional theaters. *Fish Eyes* proved itself downtown, where its success validated the show within its home community and where it began to play its role in reconstituting that community as South Asian Canadian.

Theater workers within the intercultural theater ecology of Toronto move fluidly across cultures and companies, working in different capacities with many over the course of their careers, often simultaneously, and engaging in a kind of productive cross-fertilization that defies "ethnic" ghettoization. One example is Filipino Canadian Nina Lee Aquino, who launched her career in the early 2000s apprenticing at Factory Theatre, where she gradually assumed responsibility for four years for that company's Crosscurrents Festival of intercultural theater and then ascended to the role of apprentice artistic director and later associate artist. Meanwhile, she founded fu-GEN Asian Canadian Theatre in 2002 with David Yee and Leon Aureus and was the company's first artistic director, worked on staff at Native Earth Performing Arts until 2006, and directed productions at Carlos Bulosan (Filipino) Theatre and Young People's Theatre. She resigned from fu-GEN in 2010 to take over the artistic directorship of Cahoots Theatre Company, which she ran until 2013. In 2012 she was appointed co–artistic director with African Canadian Nigel Shawn Williams at Factory, and since fall 2014 she has been sole artistic director of the company. Over that time she wrote two plays that premiered at Carlos Bulosan and Factory and taught at the National Theatre School in Montreal and the theatre program at Humber College in Toronto's west end. Aquino's career has been exceptional in some ways—not everyone founds a theater company and serves as artistic director of three over the course of little more than a decade—but in terms of its cultural range it is representative of dozens of theater workers within the city's intercultural performance ecology.

These theater workers are cumulatively answering Bannerji's call for the creation of solidarities, for the opening up, in the face of racism, eurocentrism, ethnocentrism, and official multiculturalism, "a space for a broader community among us" (158). They are creating a heterotopic space for alternate ordering that is neither static, folkloric, nor merely symbolic, in which new social identities and social formations are performatively forged out of the crucible of traditional performance forms, the technologies of contemporary theatrical practice, and the daily work of negotiating across real and acknowledged social and cultural difference.

CONCLUSION

I have been able here to cite only a few examples of the ways in which the official multicultural script is being performed in contemporary Toronto and how those performances change the nature of the city's complex performance ecology. What is key is that the companies I have been discussing and others discussed throughout this book do not set out merely to realize that script as prescriptive, as governmental bodies and "mainstream" theater companies have done in an "add-on" fashion ("what we've always done plus diversity"), nor do they simply resist its prescriptions and thereby reify its dominant position in a counterproductive binary logic. Rather, they work to reconstitute that script and its social effects by performing it strategically through the technologies of the traditional and contemporary performance practices to which they have access. Through strategic solidarities across acknowledged difference and a kind of intercultural performative excess, they continually rewrite, reconfigure, and restage multiculturalism in ways that are cumulatively heterotopic, moving "the world's most multicultural city" from below toward an ever-evolving mode of alternate ordering.

TWO | Performing Intercultural Memory in the Diasporic Present

Historical memory . . . is not what it used to be.
—Andreas Huyssen, *Present Pasts: Urban Palimpsests and the Politics of Memory*

One of the most insidiously restrictive aspects of the multicultural script has to do with the ways in which it relegates cultural memory to ethnic heritage and mandates the protection and preservation rather than the growth and development of minoritized cultural practices. One of the most productive ways of performing that script differently in Toronto has been through the often collaborative but always performative constitution of memories that work to bridge difference in the present-tense moment of memory making.

All memory bridges difference. It takes place in the present but recalls, incorporates, or appropriates the past. All *cultural* memory is performative. It involves the transmission of culture through bodily practices such as ritual, repetition, and habit. I consider here some of the ways in which communities in diaspora interact and constitute themselves as communities through the performative enactment of *inter*cultural memory. In chapter 1 I considered Toronto's intercultural performance ecology within the context of official Canadian multiculturalism. In terms of cultural memory, the multicultural script problematically constructs memory in essentialist, static, and nostalgic terms in relation to dehistoricized ethnic "homelands," atomizing communities of memory into separate "ethnic" enclaves and relegating memory to history. But as Huyssen notes in the epigraph to this chapter, historical memory isn't what it used to be—at least not what it used to be for nineteenth-century nation-states, when "the discourse of history was there to guarantee the relative stability of the past in its pastness" (1). But the form in which we think of the past, Huyssen argues, "is increasingly memory without borders, rather than national history within borders" (4). This does not mean, however, that cultural memories have become dissociated from identity formation. Within Toronto and other global intercultural cities, the increasing detachment of memory from national histories is contributing to the performative formation of newly complex intercultural and intr*a*cultural subjectivities. Over generations of border crossing within the city, as once-segregated communities of memory increasingly meld, there develop urban memory banks that migrate across cultures and begin to forge new interdiasporic subjectivities. It makes sense, then, that much of the grassroots *intra*cultural performance practice of a city such as Toronto works against the essentializing pressure of the official script performatively to forge intersecting and fluid diasporic identities in the city.

In focusing on intercultural memory, I am attempting to take into account scholarship on cultural memory as both social (Halbwachs) and a function of social ritual and habit, embodied, performed, and transmitted across generations (Connerton). Taking into account the performative nature of social identities—gendered, classed, and raced—as constituted through ritual repetition (Butler), I use Joseph Roach's concept of "performance genealogies," which he sees as drawing upon "the idea of expressive movements as *mnemonic reserves*, including patterned movements made and remembered by bodies, residual movements retained implicitly in images or words . . . and imaginary movements dreamed in minds not prior to language but constitutive of it" (Roach 26, emphasis added). I also find useful Roach's concept of "surrogation" (2) as a mode of cultural transmission by replacement ("the king is dead, long live the king"), together with Diana Taylor's elaboration that sometimes, particularly in postcolonial cultures, the doubling repressed by surrogation *preserves*, rather than erases, its antecedents (174–75). In introducing the concept of intercultural memory I am attempting to understand the transmission *and transformation* of cultural memory in diaspora across various kinds of difference.

If it is true that all memory bridges difference, it is equally true that all cultural memory involves transference, in which the individual subject remembers events that she or he did not, in fact, experience, practices that she or he did not perform. Ross Chambers has examined the phenomenon of "orphaned memory" to explain the ways in which the memories of a dead generation of Holocaust children survive in bodies to whom they do not, in any experiential sense, "belong." They are "fostered"—technically "false" as individual memory, but as cultural memory embodying profound and otherwise inaccessible truth: the memories of the dead. Similarly, Marita Sturken suggests that so-called false memory syndrome, in which individual subjects recall the experience of sexual abuse that did not happen to them, can be considered to *be* cultural memory. She argues that events that may not have happened to the person who "remembers" them are nevertheless culturally "true" insofar as they rightly characterize a lived, embodied culture of systemic sexual violence.

How are these transferences affected? Marianne Hirsch puts considerable faith in the power of art to produce empathy among audiences who do not simply witness representations but undergo "emotional and bodily experience" that is incorporated and felt as embodied memory ("Marked" 72). Alison Landsberg, considering the transcultural power of mass culture to "suture" to spectators memories of events through which they have not lived, labels this process "prosthetic memory" (14).[1] Empathy, as will be discussed in chapter 7, can be a complex, double-edged sword, its effects ranging from the easy catharsis of the "good cry" to the appropriation, without cost or context, of others' experiences. But in specific performance contexts certain forms of nonappropriative empathy can also provoke the genuine transference of embodied, practiced memory across difference. When, in Roach's terms, "patterned movements made and remembered by bodies, residual movements retained implicitly in images or words . . . and imaginary [or imagined] movements" come to inhabit the muscles and socialization of the body, the possibility exists of the transference, across difference, of embodied "mnemonic reserves" (26). For this reason movement and dance, as conduits of both cultural memory and its performative transformation, play a significant role in this chapter, as they do throughout this book.

Addressing the question of transference, Paul Connerton claims that "if there is such a thing as social memory" it is performative, operating through commemorative ceremonies, bodily practices, and habit (4–5). It is, consciously or not, *taught*, as when young girls learn by unspoken example to cross their legs when sitting, young boys to take up space in ways denied their sisters. If this is so, then cultural memories can be transferred, not only generationally within a family or community, as in Hirsch's concept of "postmemory" (*Family Frames*), but also across other kinds of difference.

In diaspora this transference crosses both generations and geographies, and it involves the intercultural transformation of the very performance practices it employs. There are various kinds of theatrical practice in Toronto that use the performance forms of "home" communities, invoking embodied cultural memories to (re-)constitute different kinds of diasporic community. Some companies, such as Carlos Bulosan (Filipino) Theatre Company, are dedicated to supporting and reflecting fairly specific (though far from homogeneous) communities of memory. Others, such as the Afri-

Can Theatre Ensemble, Theatre Archipelago, and the former Rasik Arts, primarily perform work from cultural "homelands"—Africa, the Caribbean, and South Asia—evoking, sometimes nostalgically, cultural memory in diaspora. Others, such as Obsidian Theatre, b current, fu-GEN Asian Canadian Theatre, Red Sky Performance, and Native Earth Performing Arts, constitute internally diverse or even historically conflicted communities as "African Canadian," "Asian Canadian," and "Indigenous," developing new work that speaks across such differences and producing intercultural memory among potentially affiliated communities of interest. Finally, companies such as Cahoots Theatre Company (formerly Cahoots Theatre Projects) and Modern Times Stage Company are more broadly intercultural, creating performance forms that bridge explicit and acknowledged differences.

Chapter 1 has considered what this activity means for the constitution of Toronto as a multicultural city and the (re-)constitution of its broadly diasporic subjectivities. Here I want to look at five recent performances that employ the performance forms of minoritized cultures, not to retrieve memories from a static memory bank but actively to "build memory" (Turtle Gals, *Scrubbing Project* 37). At the level of representation, the memories the shows considered here address, suture, and transform are increasingly traumatic in terms of the levels of displacement they portray. They move from voluntary immigration (and voluntary memory), through harrowing refugee experience, to involuntary trauma memories of enforced migration, colonization, and genocide. My examples also move from the individual effort to suture a divided cultural identity, through the communal building of shared cultural memory, to the actual *constitution* of new forms of community through a kind of "prosthetic" memory making that works to reconstitute diasporic subjectivities through embodied practice. In no case are the memories built in these shows the nostalgic or recuperative ones prescribed and pre-scripted in official multicultural policy; these memories are not evoked, but enacted.

FISH EYES

Fish Eyes, a solo show written and performed by South Asian Canadian Anita Majumdar, began when Majumdar was a theater student at the University of British Columbia (UBC). Having grown up an only child in the Vancouver suburb of Port Moody, where she was "one of maybe three South Asians in my school, from elementary school to graduating in grade twelve," Majumdar says that when she went to UBC "it was important to me to own my culture and investigate what this other side of me was" (Interview)—to re-member it. Although she had taken and quit classes in ballet, piano, and figure skating as a child, her father wouldn't allow her to take Indian dance, so she set out at UBC deliberately to construct a set of embodied memories—"patterned movements [as] mnemonic reserves"—of her South Asian self. These were not specific to her own Bengali heritage in East India but were both diasporic and pan-Indian. As a theater student at UBC she enrolled, outside the program, in classes in Kathak, a narrative dance form from northern India that fuses Hindu and Muslim cultures. She also took language classes in Hindi—ironically, from a white American—where she was exposed for the first time to "a sea of brown faces." Majumdar performed with a dance troupe in Vancouver but kept her dancing separate from her theater training, which at UBC was overwhelmingly western. Only later, in her final years at the National Theatre School, was she encouraged by faculty and fellow students to integrate her dance life into her acting—which meant merging her cultural identities. *Fish Eyes* developed over several years from a fifteen-minute in-school exercise to a full-length professional production opening at Factory Studio Theatre in 2004 as part of Toronto's Summerworks Festival and touring nationally and internationally since; in 2015–16 it toured as part of *The Fish Eyes Trilogy*.[2] But it retained its interdisciplinarity as dance and theater, as well as its interculturalism as both Canadian and "pan-Indian." Majumdar describes being in India when *Fish Eyes* was first conceived:

> We were on a . . . 12-hour trip back from the Taj Mahal to where I was staying in Lucknow [both in Uttar Pradesh, northern India]. We were stuck on the national highway . . . and I was looking through these fields, this vast land, and I suddenly felt this great need to be able to fuse the two countries that I come from. . . . And when I got back to Calcutta [in West Bengal][3] I had a blue costume stitched for what my idea of what the play was going to be. (Interview)

At first, *Fish Eyes* seems to be a simple sketch about Meena—short for Meenakshi, meaning "Fish Eyes"—a teenage Canadian born to South Asian immigrant parents, caught between the pressures and pleasures of her last year in a very white high school and her parents' requirement that she take classes in Indian classical dance. Meanwhile, her friends "are going to parties . . . and making out in closets with hot, popular boys like Buddy Cain, and drinking lots of beer and making best friends with popular girls like

Candace Paskas because she holds your head back while you throw up" (Majumdar, "Fish Eyes" 2–3).[4]

The play is autobiographical in form, not content. While Majumdar chose at the age of eighteen to take dance and language classes as performative entrées into the South Asian side of her culture, Meena grows up under the wing of Kalyani Aunty ("happy cow" ["Fish Eyes" 1]), an exuberant if lovelorn woman who "lactate[s] butter chicken" (2), readies Meena for the Lord Ganesh Festival and the All-India Dance Competition (where she will perform "Extreme Nimbooda"), and accompanies her in her pink Volvo to Toronto's "Little India" (3), where they purchase Indian foods, Thumbs Up, henna, and other trappings of the homeland.

Kalyani Aunty provides the play's most trenchant, if comic, postcolonial critiques: "You know how many places British colonize? 77! 77 in whole of the world, Meena! They have so much land, SO MUCH LAND, then be giving us generous gift: two blocks of East Gerrard Street?! Oh thank you, *thank you* British Raj!" (9). And she speaks in the play for the immigrant community's compensatory nostalgia for all things Indian, while at the same time aspiring to take her students' work back to the old country to demonstrate its quality. But her most significant role is as one dance teacher in an intergenerational chain, making regular calls to her own teacher in India to report her students' progress. As such, she serves as the agent for the transmission of embodied, if transformed, cultural memory through dance.

For of course the play is not reverent about India, nor is it purist in its treatment of the rigid traditions of Indian classical dance. "I don't like purist work," Majumdar says. "I get bored with it. . . . What I really like is seeing the invention of new forms" (Interview). In fact, the play includes elements of the south Indian Bharatanatyam, the northern Kathak, and the northeastern Odissi dances, sometimes combined within a single movement sequence. It also includes one parodic, cross-dressed Punjabi dance and a comic toothbrush dance, conceived early on as a way of imagining how a Canadian might find her Indian mudras—symbolic gestures—informing her work as a dental hygienist. These various positions and mudras function in the play in clear and uncomplicated ways as Roach's "mnemonic reserves . . . made and remembered by bodies" in which they can be combined, complicated, and clustered. But, as Majumdar says, "We never said, 'Meena studies Kathak, or Meena studies Odissi.' It's a mix of all those" (Interview). And of course the play is not Indian classical dance but South Asian Canadian dance theater—itself a newly minted form and an embodiment of a new diasporic identity.

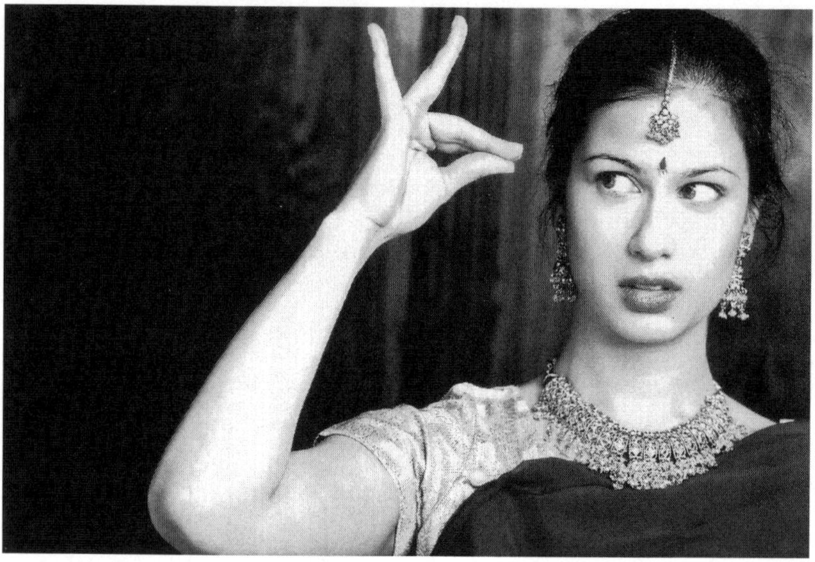

Fig. 2. Anita Majumdar in *Fish Eyes*, making the Katakamukha mudra that is used in both Bharatanatyam and Odissi dance. Photo by Rob Daly.

Nevertheless, the play *is* structured around Indian classical dance. Meena's narrative and Majumdar's character transitions are signaled by specific mudras—Kartarimukha (scissors), from the Bharatanatyam dance tradition; Katakamukha, the gesture usually used across the chest and indicating the lotus of purity; and so on. And the play incorporates a mixture of forms that bring together within Toronto a "South Asian" community, a kind of "pan-Indian" experience that can only happen in diaspora. As such it helps to constitute a performative reinvention of embodied, intercultural memory mediated through humor, and along with it community identities and individual subjectivities that have not previously existed.

Fish Eyes was first intended for a broad, non–South Asian Canadian theater audience. It was first directed by Gregory Prest, a white male classmate of Majumdar's from National Theatre School. And together with other work by Majumdar and others, it is contributing to the performative reconstitution of the intercultural performance ecology of Toronto. But the play has also reached a more specific South Asian Canadian community, partly because it has *not* been folkloric, targeted to the ghettoized community centers of official multiculturalism. It has reached its South Asian Canadian audience partly because Majumdar developed and has performed it at established theaters, refusing to play multicultural or South Asian community venues in suburban Mississauga, Scarborough, or Brampton. In spite of some early criticism in the South Asian press of the show's perceived critique of India (Syerah), *Fish Eyes* proved itself downtown, where its success validated the show within its home community and began to play its role in reconstituting that community within a globally pan-Indian diaspora. Majumdar talks about how the show serves South Asian audiences as a site of memory making, where they come together to compare traditions, across classes, castes, and South Asian cultures and to negotiate, without ever taking itself too seriously, new, crossover identities in diaspora. The show's success also led to a well-received production in late 2006 at the prestigious diasporic Other Festival in Chennai, Tamil Nadu, in eastern India (since replaced by the New Festival), where—who knows?—it may have contributed to the reconfiguration of inter- and intranational subjectivities *within* the subcontinent through the transformative injection of embodied, performative and diasporic, intercultural memories.

SINGKIL

Singkil, written by Filipina Canadian Catherine Hernandez and produced in 2007 by fu-GEN Asian Canadian Theatre Company, directed by Nina Lee Aquino, also centers on dance, in this case Filipino folk dance, the Singkil of the play's title. And like *Fish Eyes*, the play is concerned crucially with the intergenerational teaching, learning, and transformation of cultures in diaspora through embodied performance. But both as process and product *Singkil* moves from the individual reinvention of self through more complex performative memory making and more directly into the knitting together of a larger community. Moreover, the displacement the play represents at its heart—a mother-daughter rift—is more traumatic. Indeed, as Eleanor Ty has argued, "The play is an important piece because it explores a number of topics that are not usually talked about in Asian North American families: depression, infidelity, and matrophobia"—together with "the entangled web of connections between home, history, memory, fantasy, nostalgia, and belonging in the diasporic subject" (214).

Singkil began with an event that is represented in the finished play, and one that bespeaks the intergenerational transmission of embodied mnemonic reserves: Filipina playwright Catherine Hernandez, rifling through family photos on her eighteenth birthday in an effort of conscious memory making, discovered an image of her mother, Cecille Hernandez, dancing the Singkil. Looking at the date on the back, Hernandez discovered herself in the picture: her mother had been pregnant with her when the photo was taken. An accomplished dancer herself, Hernandez had not realized she had been "dancing this dance my entire life" (Interview).[5]

As both process and product, deliberately and inadvertently, *Singkil* is very much about mothers (to whom the published script is dedicated), daughters, and the transmission of cultural memory through performance. The play deals with the struggles of the partly autobiographical Mimi, played by Nadine Villasin, to come to terms with the memory, and loss, of her mother, Maria. She does so in part by learning the Singkil, the dance that her mother had abandoned—and along with it her sense of self—when she came to Canada. Two weeks into rehearsal for the show, the company learned that Nadine's own mother, Fely Villasin, who founded Carlos Bulosan, the Filipino theater company Nadine had inherited as artistic director, had died suddenly from cancer. Nadine, playing a woman coming to terms with her mother's death by learning her performance traditions, missed only one rehearsal, and the company, for whom her mother was an icon, rallied around her. Less than two weeks later, a week before opening night, director Nina Lee Aquino's water broke while she was setting cues. She finished the cue she was working on, made notes for the next day's scheduling, and went into labor with her own daughter, Eponine. Hernandez, a prenatal educator, was present at the birth. But it had been all about mothers and daughters from the beginning. In the workshop presentation at Factory Theatre in 2005, the mother-daughter team of Cecille and Catherine Hernandez attended rehearsals to teach the cast the Singkil, the latter carrying her own one-and-a-half-year-old daughter Arden on her hip. "[It was] three generations of us doing this dance," says Hernandez (Interview).

In a very real sense, teaching and learning the dance across generational and cultural differences internal to the Filipino community, teaching one another Tagalog (one of the major cross-cultural languages of the Philippines and its diaspora, used in the play), teaching the use of the traditional *kulintang* gongs, and exploring informally, in breaks, the respective foods, traditions, and behaviors—the embodied memories—of the largely Filipino company constituted not simply the rehearsal of a play but the rehearsal of a community in diaspora.

Not everyone spoke Tagalog, and the one best versed in the language was the youngest cast member and most recent immigrant, Rose Cortez. Not everyone knew the Singkil, in spite of the dance's being a major archetype of Filipino identity, a traditional Muslim dance that nevertheless cuts across the different religious and geographical communities in the country's dispersed northern and southern islands. Hernandez talks about the central importance of teaching the dance to Karen Ancheta (Maria), a Filipina Canadian raised in Hamilton, Ontario, "totally, you know, a steel-town girl, who doesn't speak Tagalog" (Hernandez, Interview).

Rehearsals began with the actors creating, with movement designer Clare Preuss, movement vocabularies associated with motifs in the play and aspects of their characters that were then invested with the gestural vocabulary and physical embodiment—the mnemonic reserves—of the Singkil. Hernandez taught the cast the rhythms, the walk, the way the body is carried, explaining all of this in culturally specific ways, invoking cultural memory: "you're regal, with the half smile of a Buddha"; "it's a patriarchal society, so the men move differently"; "the hands (and fans) go in opposite directions, because this is the east, and we move in opposite ways"; "older Filipino men have a rhythm when they walk, or even stand: you could put a song to it"; and so on.[6] The music, too, was adapted from Filipino Muslim chants, folk songs, and the Singkil rhythms deployed by the also Filipino composer, Romeo Candido, using, among other things, the traditional *kulintang* gongs live amid an electronic soundscape. In a very real sense the rehearsal process involved the company learning embodied memory from one another, embodied ways of being Filipino in diaspora.

This learning process was also represented in the action of the play, as Mimi's "Tita" (loosely "Auntie") Norma, who had danced the Singkil with Mimi's mother in the Philippines, arrives in Toronto and after considerable struggle begins to teach Mimi the movements, rhythms, modes of embodiment, and cultural significance of the Singkil—a dance form based on the story of a Muslim princess who dances gracefully through the crashing forest of an earthquake and emerges unscathed. This was not simply folkloric, nor was it the nostalgic reproduction in diaspora of a slice of the homeland. Even as rehearsals negotiated and the show represented invented rituals of birthing and bereavement, so the dance that Mimi learns and finally performs in reconciling with her mother's ghost (who we see perform the traditional Singkil early in the play, and who haunts Mimi throughout) is one of continuity, homage, and transformation. Mimi entered at the end carrying the Singkil fans she had inherited from her mother, assuming a traditional pose, but early on she threw down her fans, and performed a dance that combined elements of the dances of the Asik girl (the traditional supporting role that had been danced by her Tita Norma) and the princess (that had been performed by her mother). But, without the fans or the traditional *sarimanok* headgear, she constituted her own independent mode of expression on a stage without even the bamboo poles (and symbolic dangers) of the traditional dance.[7]

The production finally offered its own model of contemporary, transformative, and interdisciplinary interculturalism both within and beyond the Filipino community and built its own performative memory. Because of course, like *Fish Eyes,* this was not dance but movement-based theater, transforming a traditional performance form while using its modes of embodiment to inform an innovative theatrical practice within Canada. The production was intercultural, moreover, in the constitution of the company and in its audience address. The playwright, director, composer, and four of the five actors were from various Filipino geographical and cultural backgrounds and generations of immigration, and much of the rehearsal process explored those relationships and identities, cultivating a shared intracultural memory. But it was important to the playwright that the show was staged *not* by the specifically Filipino Carlos Bulosan Theatre Company but by fu-GEN Asian Canadian Theatre—"it's a work for fu-GEN," Hernandez says (Interview)—and no small part of the cultural work it performed had to do with fu-GEN's ongoing project of constituting diasporic pan-Asian subjectivities in Toronto through shared intercultural memory. The set and costume designers—Camellia Koo and Jacqueline Chau—were both Chinese Canadian; the fifth cast member, David Yee, Chinese Scottish Canadian; the stage manager, Dale Yim, Korean Canadian; and the lighting designer, Arun Srinivasan, South Asian Canadian. The production's intended audience constituted a series of concentric circles: the Filipino community, expanding outward to the Asian Canadian community, beyond that to a burgeoning arts and culture audience from nondominant cultures collaborating in various kinds of solidarity, and finally, least importantly to the creators, to a dominant-culture audience—all united in a kind of embodied but "prosthetic" memory functioning to shift and complicate dominant understandings of the city as imagined community.

THE SHEEP AND THE WHALE

> In Africa, when a young man begins to think and ask questions, they give him a potion. When he takes it, he loses his memory, he doesn't know where he's from or what his name is anymore, and his body only knows how to do one thing: walk North, always North without ever looking back. . . . Then, they take out the young man's heart, bury it

> in the sand and say, "Now, leave your heart in the South, and go find your memory in the North." I can't stay in the South, because I won't have a memory, and I can't stay in the North because I won't have a heart. . . . Here, halfway between North and South, I'm more fragile than a spider web, because I don't have either a heart or a memory.
> —Ahmed Ghazali, *The Sheep and the Whale*

These lines are spoken by the African Stowaway, who is ultimately thrown overboard "here, halfway between North and South," by the crew of the ship that constitutes the setting of *The Sheep and the Whale*. The play was written in French by Moroccan Canadian Ahmed Ghazali, translated into English by Quebecker Bobby Theodore, and directed at Theatre Passe Muraille by Iranian Canadian Soheil Parsa in a coproduction by Parsa's Modern Times Stage Company and Cahoots Theatre Company in February 2007. *The Sheep and the Whale* presents a very different relationship between intercultural memory and ritual performance than those I've been looking at, a differently gendered setting from the women-centered spaces of *Fish Eyes* and *Singkil*, and a very different vision of diaspora. The immigrants here are illegal, desperate refugees and the stakes are literally life and death. Cultural memory as represented here is certainly performative but is also traumatic and involuntary.

The Sheep and the Whale is set in the Strait of Gibraltar onboard a dilapidated, once Russian, now multinational "Oceans International" freighter.[8] The ship has just come upon a storm-ravaged boat that has sunk while smuggling Moroccan refugees into Europe. As the play opens, the crew is fishing ten dead bodies, plus the surviving smuggler, out of the sea, and the subsequent action occurs as the Russian captain requests permission to take the bodies into port—somewhere. Gibraltar won't take them because it's not their problem, Algeciras won't take them because "it happens all the time" (Ghazali 9), and Tangiers isn't responding because they are celebrating Aïd El-Kebir, the festival of sacrifice at which each family slaughters a sheep or ram in memory of the prophet Ibrahim.

Ghazali's stage directions articulate the setting allegorically as the ship of the world: its containers, corridors, and dark places represent "the South, Africa, the jungle, the north of Paris, the ghetto, housing projects, shantytowns of Bombay, Harlem, the cemetary, a mess, the 3rd World, the tribe, the medina of Fez"; its cabins represent "Europe, the Western World, the modern city, the rich North, the skyscrapers, the bourgeois neighborhoods"; and its deck "the gulf between North and South, between Europe and Africa, between the West and the East, between Blacks and Whites, rich and poor, modern and primitive" (2–3). The characters also function in part allegorically: the stowaways, the survivor, and the dead represent the dark places of the ship and the world, the crew the liminal space between that is also the Strait of Gibraltar, and the passengers Europe.

But those passengers consist of an interracial couple, the French Hélène, metonymic of Europe, and her partner, Hassan, who, we discover at the same time she does, arrived in France illegally, "snuck across the Strait . . . like them"—the dead refugees (46–47). It is Hassan's crisis of involuntary memory on which the action hinges. The couple is returning to Paris from a holiday on the Canary Islands, which Hassan has unconsciously chosen because of its proximity to his native Morocco. He has spent his time in Europe, like the Stowaway, acquiring a new memory, suppressing his heart and his memories of Africa. But confronted with the fate of his compatriots, his European identity begins to crumble. He begins, involuntarily, to speak with an accent, and later in Arabic, as he becomes increasingly disoriented. He dredges up memories of his failures as a child to perform the sacrifice required at Aïd El-Kebir, failure that he associates with his repression of memory: his refusal to allow Hélène to learn Arabic, his refusal to entertain the idea of a holiday in Morocco, his refusal of a Moroccan identity in diaspora. But as the action proceeds he comes increasingly to identify with the drowned Moroccans, his "brothers" (49), as his embodied, repressed cultural memories surge to the surface with a vengeance. He catches himself "humming Moroccan songs. Then words started slipping off my tongue like pieces of wood coming off a wreck" (44). He chooses, finally, to join the corpses on the deck as a "museum of humanity" (48), and ultimately the play stages his nightmarish reenactment of Aïd El-Kebir—this play's performative equivalent of the dances in *Fish Eyes* and *Singkil*—in which he is stripped to the waist and forced to perform the ritual of sacrifice. He emerges from the dream letting out "great screams of rage, like someone undergoing an exorcism" (42).

What issues from this is Hassan's brutal offstage sex with—rape of?—Hélène-as-Europe[9] and his equally nightmarish, prophetic vision of Europe overcome by its "others" literally walking across the accumulation of corpses filling the strait (47–48). He and Hélène finally separate, each returning to her or his native culture, their embodiment of any kind of utopian intercultural vision a dismal failure. It is this pessimistic vision that Korean Canadian actor, playwright, and activist Jean Yoon lamented in her keynote address to the Shipping of Souls conference held at Theatre Passe Muraille in association with the run of the play (Yoon, Keynote). It would seem that both Hassan's and Hélène's cultural memories are intransigent, determinate, and militate against any final form of intercultural exchange.

In terms of what is *represented* in the play, in the Strait of Gibraltar, Yoon's reading is convincing. But the rehearsal process in Toronto, the production's embodiment of that process, and its reception represent something different. Parsa cast the show, as he does most Modern Times' productions (see chapter 6), broadly interculturally, and with the exception of roles that require specific racial identification—the Black Stowaway, the white European woman, the Russian captain—across racial lines. Parsa trained in Western acting methods in Tehran, ironically, and after fleeing Iran in the wake of the Islamic revolution educated himself in Persian/Iranian performance forms—acquiring "mnemonic reserves" as Majumdar had done at the University of British Columbia—while studying theater at Toronto's York University. As I describe in more detail in chapter 6, his company is dedicated to working interculturally across Eastern and Western performance forms, and he casts actors from different traditions and styles of theater in his shows, which rely heavily on a kind of neomodernist stylization, including stylized movement.

Parsa's staging of Hassan's nightmare vision of the Aïd El-Kebir ritual is a case in point. The production process modeled communal ways of dealing with trauma memory through ethical witnessing, performance, and testimony, the multicultural cast and audience engaging in what Roger Simon (with Mario Di Paolantonio and Mark Clamen) calls "remembrance as praxis," where "public practices of memory can have a transitive function . . . as actions that 'pass over' and take effect on another person or persons" (132–33). Parsa describes early rehearsals of the scene:

> The actors read the piece, and at the end they started dancing. Some people tried to please me and do some Sufi dance, turning around. And I said, "Oh my god, this is so deadly. It's so folkloric. . . ." I stopped everybody and said, "Look, the worst thing in theater, especially in terms of movement—if you don't know the dance, if you don't know the culture—is to start imitating. . . . Let's simplify it. What is the essence of this scene?" (Interview)

What the actors finally performed was less imitation than homage and witnessing, as their bodies assumed the truth of traumatic events that, through performing the play, they and the audience were witnessing (that is, "bearing witness to"). Like the bearers of Ross Chambers's "orphaned memory," the players and the play in *The Sheep and the Whale* became the bearers and transmitters of the memories of the dead—"their bodies strewn across the bottons of the oceans and the seas"—to whom the play was dedicated (Ghazali 2).

If in its *representation* of interculturalism, then, *The Sheep and the Whale* was pessimistic, as process and production the show embodied broad intercultural solidarities in Toronto and enacted a transference of embodied performative forms of cultural memory—in this case, trauma memory—through transformative movement. The cast member who came closest in performance to the Sufi dance tradition was an African Canadian dancer with no cultural links to Morocco or to Islam. There was nothing folkloric and certainly nothing nostaligic in the performance; rather it represented a collaborative, transformative process of witnessing and working through trauma.

BODY 13

The MT Space, located just down the road from Toronto in the culturally diverse city of Kitchener, Ontario, has nevertheless become an important part of Toronto's interculturtal performance ecology, having performed three of their major works at Theatre Passe Muraille since their founding in 2004 by the Lebanese immigrant Majdi Bou-Matar, who is recognized within the city as a key "actor" in the network.[10] The company has also become, through its biennial international IMPACT Festival and accompanying conference, an important site for the negotiation and discussion of what intercultural Indigenous and immigrant theater in Toronto and Canada might consist of and might perform.

MT Space presented the first workshop version of their widely performed and wildly successful devised piece *Body 13* at IMPACT '11 in Kitchener in September 2011. The fully developed version arrived in Toronto at Theatre Passe Muraille in January 2013, and it has since toured within Canada from Halifax, Nova Scotia, to Whitehorse, Yukon Territory. *Body 13* began as an exploration of love and sex across (various kinds of) difference, and as reviewers noted it remained that (see Coulbourn, "Theatre Review"; Kilborn; Slotkin). But it quickly became apparent that it was also and always centrally about memory.[11] *Body 13* is what would widely be considered devised, movement-based theater. The play takes place on a beach somewhere in Canada over the course of a single day, moving from a morning funeral toward an evening wedding. In its movement vocabu-

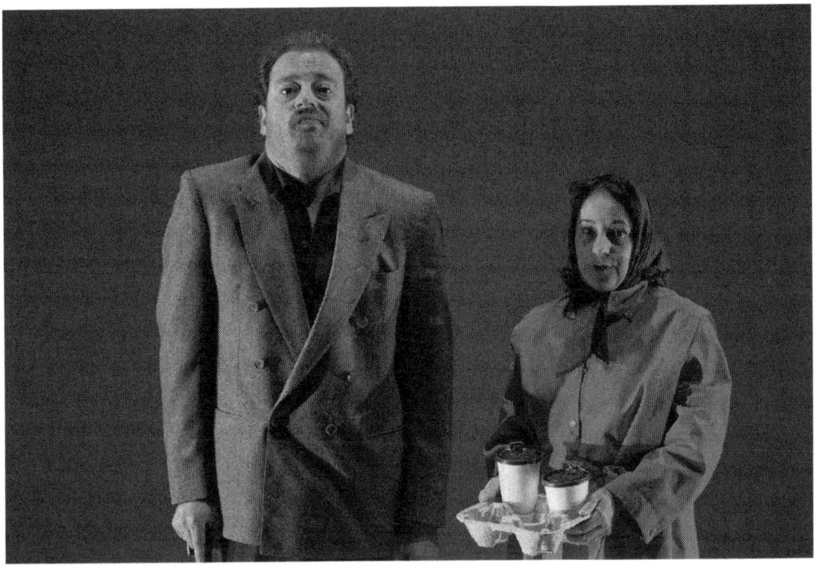

Fig. 3. Badih Abou-Chakra as Asaf and Nada Humsi as Iman in the MT Space production of *Body 13*, directed by Majdi Bou-Matar. Photo by Andy Wright of Andy Wright Studios.

lary and its almost balletic arias it is centrally and sensuously about sexuality across differences in gender and sexuality, race and culture, age and experience. The audience witnesses gloriously orchestrated scenes involving sunbathing, sunscreen, and swimming; the violent BDSM erotics of hockey and the sinuously sexual stimulations of running; the homosocial erotics of male competitiveness; and, in various manifestations, the sensual and sexual pleasures of hair.

But the spoken and embodied languages of the play[12] are often about memory and loss. The older, Syrian refugee applicant, Iman, dancing with the entire cast, each in her or his cultural tradition, tells her younger immigration officer and would-be lover Rhea about the parties they would have "back home" in Syria. Rita, a young woman from Gujarat, India, and her surrogate father, Assaf, a wounded former colonel in the Lebanese civil war ("*that was serious shit!*"), share stories of lost worlds elsewhere. "It's gonna be dark soon," says Assaf, to which Rita responds, "It's barely noon." Ato, the young Ghanaian Canadian, struggles to overcome his ancestral spirits and recover from childhood beatings because of his sexuality. Tristan suffers from anxiety attacks that began when he was eleven and gay at a hockey camp in Newfoundland. And Thomas Christian Kressman, preparing a speech for his best friend's wedding, is unable to come to terms with the passage from adolescence to adulthood. Throughout the play run several refrains, lines that recur in different contexts, all of them having to do with memory and loss: "one moment you are waiting, the next moment you are 89," is one; "that's sad"—that Rita's father is dead, that she feels nothing about it, that she feels he didn't love her, that Assaf, secretly attracted to men, feels nothing for his wife, who is not dead, that Rita doesn't know even so much as what she would *like* to feel—is another; and most prominently, "I'm sorry for your loss"—of a father, of youth and freedom, of a coherent sense of self, of a way life, of community, cat, cufflink, or country.

But the play is also about recovery. As the young Ghanaian Canadian beach runner Ato, prone to giving advice, tells Thomas—the play's white, normative "best man," who is trolling the beach for women and a lost ancestral cufflink—"People lose things in the sand all the time. You'll find something else, but you'll never find what you're looking for." The play ultimately turns to that "something else" for hope and healing, as most of its characters—with the exception of the recalcitrant, homo- and xenophobic Thomas, clinging to his past—come together in surprising pairings and join together in a closing, healing ritual that literally strips away inhibitions and differences. As reviewer John Coulbourn says, "While they are all eager to embrace a new day, none of them are quite so eager to completely abandon the memories of the past. Yet, slowly, as the day wears on, six of them find companionship and, through compromise and compassion, romances blossom. That leaves the seventh in their midst trapped completely unaware in a world and a Canada as outdated as the heirloom cufflink for which he's been searching" ("Theatre Review"). Ultimately, then, we witness the characters in *Body 13* as they adapt deep-seated cultural memories and begin to forge new ones across their own sutured identities in alliance with those of others. As Rhea says to Iman, whose refugee application has been refused because of the official story of her past in Syria,

> RHEA: I'm going to change your story.
> IMAN: But it's true.
> RHEA: It's not enough.

THE SCRUBBING PROJECT

> I will carry you. I will care for you, I will feed you, and I will sing you songs of comfort.

I will wash away the dirt, and the ragged flecks of flesh and skin
And you will be warm
And you will be loved
And I will build memory.
—Turtle Gals, *The Scrubbing Project*

These lines are spoken by Esperanza, "the massacre collector" (339) played by Monique Mojica in Turtle Gals Performance Ensemble's 2005–6 production of *The Scrubbing Project*. She says this as she gathers up the bones of her ancestors that she carries with her always, along with, as Mojica says, "the history of Native women on this continent" (Mojica, "Chocolate" 164). *The Scrubbing Project*, collectively written and performed by Turtle Gals Performance Ensemble (consisting at that time of its founders, Jani Lauzon, Monique Mojica, and Michelle St. John),[13] is entirely about, as the flyer for the 2002 production said, "Identity, Tradition, and Memory" (Turtle Gals, Promotional flyer). It extends still further the role of the audience as participant-witnesses of involuntary trauma memory, while also consciously attempting to reconnect with, rebuild, and reinvent precontact cultural memories and communities as a "project" in healing. The play moves between the celestial, Broadway-inflected "Star World" realm of three "angels," Winged Victory, Dove, and Valkyrie, and the abject human world of "three raggedy-assed half-breeds at the turn of the 21st Century" (Turtle Gals, *The Scrubbing Project* 331), Esperanza, Blessed Ophelia, and Branda X, to whom the "Star World" characters are sent by an ethereal, voice-over "Lydia" to help. Branda's daughter has been taken away and is lost to her; Esperanza can't get beyond the victim position, bury the bones of her dead, and move to recovery; and Ophelia is trapped at age thirteen in her self-image as a Catholic saint. All, in the words of the play's darkly comic support group, are "living with genocide": "My name is Blessed Ophelia, and I am living with genocide. / Hello, Blessed Ophelia" (339).

This is not a play about diaspora in the same sense as the others I've been dealing with, nor is it about immigration, though immigration plays a role. These Indigenous women, *as* Indigenous, are displaced, spiritually and materially, *within* the land of their ancestors and, as mixed-race women, within their own bodies. The scale of the rupture effected in cultural memory by colonization, moreover, is monumental, defeating any of the pieties or potential nostalgias of the official mulitcultural policies from which Native peoples were excluded. But *The Scrubbing Project* is nevertheless deeply, personally intercultural, dealing as it does with the mixed races of its creators, and indeed, through the sexual technologies of colonization, of most

Indigenous peoples throughout Turtle Island. Lauzon, Mojica, and St. John are from diverse heritages: the Métis Lauzon, as she says, is "Finndian" (Turtle Gals, *Scrubbing Project* 347); Mojica is Guna, Rappahannock, and Ashkenazi, her father being a European Holocaust survivor; and St. John is Wampanoag and Ashkenazi, her immediate Jewish roots being in Brooklyn. But their cultural memory is no less real or material for being mixed:

> We will build memory . . .
> A *wailing wall* that will stretch across this *grandmother turtle*.
> (364, emphasis added)

The mandate of Turtle Gals was to explore "a continuum of past, present, and future expressed as stories using our bodies and voices. We draw on traditional forms of story telling, oratory, song and dance integrating them with current technology and popular culture to develop non-linear multi-disciplinary theatre forms" (Turtle Gals, Information), including, in the case of *The Scrubbing Project*, Broadway musicals, vaudeville, Marx Brothers' and other slapstick routines, medicine shows, and a ritual of remembrance invented before our eyes, in which the performers' different backgrounds, memories, and traditions come to the fore—as when Ophelia brings gefilte fish and Branda Kentucky Fried Chicken to the Native ceremony (335–36), or when Esperanza finds death camps in her "bundle" and genocide on both sides of the family (347, 363).[14]

The hybrid form of *The Scrubbing Project* grows out of the writer-performers' own hybridized identities and their own internalized racism as a manifestation of trauma. But the play also centrally deals, as Anishinaabe scholar Jill Carter points out, with "recovery, remembrance, revitalization and reintegration of *all* Aboriginal peoples":

> With *The Scrubbing Project* Turtle Gals has invented a container—and imagined a ceremony in which to frame it—that unabashedly celebrates our dualities, that suggests a methodology for their integration and balance, and that locates (and locates us around) an essential centre. ("Writing" 13, 14)

The Scrubbing Project, then, draws upon traditional performance forms, remixed and reconstituted, as it re-members the dismemberment that was colonization and *assumes* and *heals* the trauma memories of that history. It attempts to perform into being new intercultural memories and new ways of living in the world through new rituals that are nevertheless rooted in the blood memories of the Indigenous and mixed-race first peoples of Turtle Island.

CONCLUSION

The Scrubbing Project ends with the unfurling into the audience of three very long scrolls listing the names of the intercultural dead, which spectators pass back through the house, linking those onstage and off as participants in a powerful ritual of testimony, witnessing, and remembrance. As Jill Carter argues, "This *Project* does not simply evoke mood, invite identification, or solicit sympathy. The performers demand my participation in the conversation: They remember that *we might remember together*—'I add my breath to your breath'" ("Writing" 14, quoting *The Scrubbing Project* 355, emphasis in original):

> It is a *project* that demands our utter engagement and active participation. . . . *The Scrubbing Project,* as a contemporary rite of re-membering and healing, does not merely *show* us the way: It moves our feet along the path, and transforms us from passive receptors into active agents in the ongoing *project* of creation and re-creation. ("Writing" 17, emphasis in original)

Carter is writing as a Native woman, albeit from a different Nation than any of Lauzon's, Mojica's, or St. John's. But she is describing an experience and a project that reaches across greater differences than this, to which each of the shows I have been discussing contributes. Each of these shows at its best creates, and contributes to the constution of Toronto as a genuinely heterotopic space "of alternate ordering" (Hetherington viii)—"the place Indians talk about" (Ortiz 45)—in which the troublesome doubling of Roach's surrogation becomes a prosthetic suturing together of new, re-membered forms with the traditional performance forms that haunt them. Rejecting the atomizing nostalgias of official multiculturalism, each of these shows, at its best, represents, enacts, and transmits to diverse Toronto participant-audiences a genuinely transformative, border-crossing, intercultural memory, the visceral stitching together from below of a larger intercultural community in the city through performative acts of re-membering across real, acknowledged, and respected difference.

•

Part 1 of this book has concerned itself with some of the policy contexts in which, and through which, the intercultural performance ecology of the city of Toronto has developed, as examined in the remainder of the book. Canada's multicultural script as written through its immigration, bilingualism and biculturalism, and official multiculturalism laws, acts, and policies has at once enabled and contained this development. The influx of mainly economic migrants to Canada from beyond Europe in the wake of 1960s changes to immigration policy has meant that the children of these first-generation immigrants have been able to take tactical advantage of the multiculturalism policies of the 1980s that were not necessarily designed for their benefit. This, together with their activist work in realizing the rhetoric of a beneficient (if paternatlistic) multiculturalist policy, has allowed them to use the theater—in rehearsal and performance—as a laboratory of identities for the bridging of inherited and emerging embodied memory and the rehearsal of new intercultural subjectivities. In the pages that follow the strategies that I have isolated and identified in part 1—strategic reappropriation, diasporic transnationalism and trans-Indigeneity, urban intraculturalism, and the performative activation and transformation of embodied mnemonic reserves and cultural texts—will be seen to play themselves out across Indignous and diasporic communities in various blends, combinations, and juxtapositions that taken together have come to constitute the city as potentially transformative heterotopic space.

PART TWO | Dramaturgies

Dramaturgical forms and structures, including those that claim transcultural universalism, are inevitably culturally and ideologically coded. For decades so-called alternative theater in Toronto has attempted to infuse classical, neo-Aristotelian, and naturalist forms with politically resistant content in ways that have most often defeated the creators' best social justice intentions.[1] In Toronto a dominant tradition of poetic naturalism is one of the representational technologies with which culturally specific and intercultural companies have had to contend. The development of culturally specific dramaturgical forms emerging from the histories and historicized bodies of the performers is often an essential step in the performative constitution of intracultural community identities in diaspora. Part 2 of *Performing the Intercultural City* deals with the efforts of three different communities in Toronto to forge dramaturgical structures and theatrical forms that are derived from cultural texts that resist, complicate, or precede the ruptures of colonization or immigration, ground and bridge new diasporic subjectivities, and perform individual and community identities into being.

The Carlos Bulosan Theatre Company may appear to outsiders to be the most culturally specific, least genuinely intercultural company under consideration in this book, focusing as it does on the specifically Filipino community in Toronto. It quickly becomes apparent in the company's rehearsals, however, that the Filipino Canadian community is constituted through and across very significant internal cultural differences. The Philippines itself, of course, is plural. In addition to remarkable natural biodiversity, the archipelago of over seventy-one hundred islands is divided into culturally distinctive island groups, Luzon, Visayas, and Mindanao, in which there are seventeen regions and eighty provinces. Its population derives from hundreds of distinct Indigenous peoples—many of them loosely grouped as the Igorot in the north, Lumad on the southern island of Mindanao, and Mangyan in the central islands (see "Indigenous"). It derives, too, from three periods of colonization (by the Spanish, the Japanese, and the Americans) and from various communities tracing back, for example, to Chinese settlement as early as the ninth century, accounting for the prominent Chinoy (Chinese Filipino) community, and to Islamic settlement dating from the fourteenth, accounting for dominant Muslim cultural influences in the southern region of Mindanao.

In Toronto this complexity is further compounded by the various generations of immigration to the city, which receives ninety-five hundred new Filipino immigrants each year, adding to a population that that began to grow in the 1980s in response to Canada's "Live-in-Caregiver Program," expanded further in the 1990s with a different economic class of independent immigration, and grew exponentially in the early 2000s. At the time of the 2006 census 5.5 percent of Torontonians claimed the Philippines as their "ethnic origin" and since then the Philippines have bypassed both China and India as the number-one source of new immigrants (see K. Smith). Taken together, all of this means that any rehearsal process involving a Filipino company also involves negotiations across differences of cultural and religious background, generations of immigration, class and economic positioning, and language (not all Filipino Canadians speak Tagalog, or do so with equal fluency). Filipino identities, then, are always already plural and intercultural, the search for new dramaturgies based on Filipino cultural texts is a search for new definitions of and grounds for community identities, and the performance of works based on these cultural texts functions as the ongoing performative constitution of new diasporic subjectivities rather than the recovery of old ones. This is the subject of chapter 3, which traces the Carlos Bulosan Theatre Company's efforts at working within the context of Toronto's institutional structures "Towards a Filipino Canadian Dramaturgy."

Toronto's Indigenous community is very different, most fundamentally in its being not an immigrant community but an urban, off-reserve assemblage of Indigenous peoples from different First Nations still living as colonized people on their own land. Indigenous peoples, particularly those living off-reserve, are engaged in a continuing process of negotiation between the rock of pan-Indianism and the hard place of fragmentation, and if there is little danger of succumbing to the tranquillizing lure of compensatory nostalgia for a faraway lost homeland, neither is there the rallying potential of anything resembling Rastafarian repatriation, Ethiopianism, Negritude, or back-to-Africa movements.

The search for dramaturgical structures that might serve the larger project of performing contemporary Indigenous subjectivities has been a fraught one. A key technology of the genocidal project of colonization has been the rupturing, through prohibitions, removals, reserves, and residential schools, of the relationship between Native peoples and their land, languages, cultural forms, and traditional practices. As a consequence many of those forms and practices have been lost, and even when they haven't, rehearsal processes that attempt to observe them inevitably involve negotiations across cultural differences within the room, resulting in hybrid and even newly minted ceremonial practices.

Algonquin playwright and director Yvette Nolan describes the creation process for the opening sequence of the Native Earth Performing Arts production of *The Death of a Chief* (an adaptation of Shakespeare's *Julius Caesar* performed at the National Arts Centre and Buddies in Bad Times Theatre in 2008) as having emerged from negotiations in rehearsal among the diverse Aboriginal cast, each member attempting to find connections between the play and her or his own traditional culture. "Naturally," according to Nolan, "people began to sing and drum, because that's what always happens, and so the piece became scored by the company. The seven-minute opening . . . brings all of those elements into it—those traditional elements. We created our own ritual" (Interview). Like many Native productions in Toronto, this workshop was in part about building, and negotiating, a diasporic Indigenous community in the city. Nolan is acutely conscious that Toronto's Native community is engaged in the ongoing act of performatively (re)inventing itself: "We're the Indian diaspora—we're Cree from Manitoba, and Haida from way out west, and Salish, and Mi'kmaq, and we're from everywhere" (Interview).[2] Asked if she is consciously bringing the very different communities that constitute Toronto's "Indian diaspora" together, performatively constituting it *as* a single community, Nolan responds,

> I'm always conscious of it, because whenever we do anything, we have to start with some kind of ceremony. So we're always inventing ceremonies. . . . When we have an Elder, it's generally not an Elder from this neck of the woods; it's whoever's Elder is around. And certainly, as we, as Native people, try to rebuild a bridge between ourselves and our histories, pasts, cultures, we're reclaiming stuff that is not ours. Nations that have never done sweat lodges and sundances are doing sweat lodges and sundances, and we see tipis in places where there are no tipis and have never been tipis, there have been lodges. (Interview)

Nolan is concerned about the loss of cultural specificity and the disconnect from specific traditions that this involves, particularly when the mix of

Nations and cultures within the theater community necessitates casting shows from across, and sometimes even outside of, First Nations and Aboriginal communities. But she is also concerned with the question of by whom and in whose interest tradition is controlled:

> I'm very wary of who gets to say what tradition is. But when you put people in a *room* together, you end up with a *discussion* of what those traditions are, and who they've learned them from, and that's what they bring *into* the room. It's interesting when we work on a project like *The Death of a Chief*, which has, at any given time, between eight and fifteen Aboriginal artists in the room. . . . All of those people bring all of their traditions to the room and then we have a negotiation, and we agree on the things that we can agree on, and it works just like it says in the stories that it works, in that we sit and discuss it until we figure out what everyone can live with. (Interview)

In the case of the opening sequence of *The Death of a Chief*, the result was simple: what began as a circular procession evolved into something closer to a figure eight, as performers from different cultures negotiated their different needs for ceremony to move in a clockwise or counterclockwise direction. Something similar happened in the first development workshop in 2007 for Monique Mojica's play *Chocolate Woman Dreams the Milky Way*, with a similar result: Plains Cree workshop director Floyd Favel was uncomfortable when Mojica stepped over a circle of cacao beans to move to a different part of the stage. In his tradition, it is unthinkable to step over people or objects. Guna artist and designer Oswaldo De Léon Kantule, however, noting that the cacao beans were dormant (they had not been smudged), was uncomfortable opening a portal in the circle because doing so would disrupt the symmetry that is so sacred for the Guna. The negotiated solution, after some time, was to open four portals, one for each direction, offending neither Favel's nor De León Kantule's traditions (see Carter, "*Chocolate*" 169).

The most systematic work on the building of contemporary dramaturgies out of culturally specific Indigenous cultural texts has in fact been done by Mojica, working with her intercultural team of primarily Indigenous collaborators from many different nations to build "Dramaturgies of Decolonization" that are nevertheless based on culturally specific forms and practices deriving directly and consciously from her own Indigenous traditions. This is the subject of chapter 4.

Like the Philippines, the Caribbean archipelago consists of a dizzying plurality of islands, communities, peoples, and in this case postcolonial nation-states, prominently including but by no means limited to Barbados, Cuba, the Dominican Republic, Haiti, Guyana, Jamaica, St. Lucia, and Trinidad and Tobago.[3] The Afro-Caribbean community is manifestly an intercultural one, and unlike the Filipino or Native communities, as Rhoma Spencer points out in chapter 5, it exists *as* "Caribbean" only in diaspora, and in many ways its epicenters are Toronto and London, England (a point that is significant given the assumption by many that the United States, and in particular Harlem, is the heart of the African diaspora). Toronto plays a unique role in the Afro-Caribbean diaspora, and as chapter 5 argues this has in part to do in the theater world with the creation of new dramaturgical forms of play- and identity-formation that explicitly wom(b)anise and queer the largely masculinist genealogy of both theater and dub poetry in the Caribbean archipelago itself. (It is perhaps not accidental that the Philippines and the Caribbean literalize the now-popular trope among cultural theorists in which the multiple shores and overlapping jurisdictions of the archipelago replace the unifying metaphors of the body politic or ship of state as organizing principles [see Kukathas]). What is striking about the Afro-Caribbean Canadian companies and artists that are the subjects of chapter 5 is that they are not only developing new theatrical forms and performing-into-being new diasporic subjectivities largely independent of "home there," but they are also (re)constituting Toronto itself as heterotopic interculture, an expansively queer Black woman's ecosystem capable of incubating and generating performance forms that are at once broadly and interculturally Caribbean *and* unique to Toronto as "village."

The work that part 2 addresses, in different ways, involves the search for culturally specific forms upon which to build new dramaturgies in diaspora. In no instance discussed here does this consist of an essentialist search for or recovery of stable or fossilized cultural identities or the mere replication of dramaturgical forms or cultural texts from the homeland; rather, it consists of a search for flexible, adaptable formal models in the here and now that are nevertheless grounded in the cultural histories and historicized bodies of specific communities.

THREE | Toward a Filipino Canadian Dramaturgy

The Carlos Bulosan Collective

Perhaps the simplest versions of Canadian interculturalism in performance are theater companies founded to represent a single national immigrant community in diaspora, in spite of the fact that those national communities, as I have argued, are often internally diverse. These companies also offer some of the clearest examples of intercultural efforts to meld specific cultural texts with western forms to create new, hybrid dramaturgies in diasporic space.

The story of Carlos Bulosan Theatre is in some ways representative of such companies and such efforts. The company was founded in 1982 by activists Martha Ocampo, the late Fely Villasin, Voltaire de Leon, Ging Hernandez, and Bernie Consul as the Carlos Bulosan Cultural Workshop (CBCW), the cultural wing of the North American organization CAMD (Coalition against the Marcos Dictatorship). In its early years it functioned as a nonprofessional community theater concerned with the struggles of the Filipino people at home and in diaspora. It mounted new plays, often collectively created, with and for its community base on urgent social and political issues.[1] It was funded not by arts councils but by sources such as the Ontario Women's Directorate and what was then the Federal Multiculturalism Directorate. In 2001, when its artistic direction passed from Fely Villasin to her daughter Nadine, it changed its name to the Carlos Bulosan Theatre (CBT) and assumed its present fully professional status as a key "actor" in Toronto's intercultural performance ecology, funded by the municipal, provincial, and federal arts councils, including Canada Council "equity funding."[2] Along with that shift came the shift away from the concerns of a first-generation immigrant community to those of the so-called 1.5 and second generation and the carving out of new, hyphenated subjectivities, together with the development of new dramaturgical strategies and structures for performing those subjectivities into being. It is the evolving strategies and processes used by the Carlos Bulosan Theatre company in forging new Filipino Canadian dramaturgies—by which I mean play structures as cultural forms—on which I will focus here.

Under the direction of Nadine Villasin, a graduate in political studies from Queen's University who had previously worked as a performer and facilitator with the workshop, the company formed a partnership with the Kapisanan Philippine Centre (*kapisanan* is Tagalog for "community") and the Digital Sweatshop (a Filipino film and television production cooperative) and in 2005 opened the Kapisanan Philippine Centre for Arts and Culture in Toronto's trendy, multicultural Kensington Market (see Keung). The Kapisanan Centre has been central to the development of the Filipino community in Toronto, of the Carlos Bulosan Theatre, and, through CBT's annual play creation unit and Tales from the Flipside showcase, of distinctly Filipino Canadian dramaturgies. It was founded as a place of mentorship, to fill a void in the community, and to help fulfill the company's goals of, according to Nadine Villasin, "education, activism, growing a community of artists, and providing positive cultural identification" for Filipino youth (Villasin). In quite short order the play-creation unit and Tales from the Flipside showcase produced a thriving community of Filipino theater artists, many of them working in innovative and culturally specific ways with interdisciplinary dramaturgies that involve culturally specific music, dance, and spoken word. "Theater in our community can't just be about plays," Villasin argues.

Much of this work is continuous with that of the CBCW, dramaturgically and otherwise, but the turn to professional status and to the work of new generations of Filipino artists and audiences involved some difficult transitions and produced some significant shifts in focus. In the early years, according to Filipina playwright and director Nina Lee Aquino, the Carolos Bulosan Cultural Workshop "was for the Filipino community that immigrated, the overseas workers, and the plays were centred on immigrant issues," and while she feels that "Carlos Bulosan will always be politically based; they will always tackle political issues . . . the new generation is taking over . . . , working to develop new voices, new Filipino *Canadian* voices, playwrights and actors" (Knowles, "Between" 77). Indeed, the new generation since 2010 has been represented by work at Tales from the Flipside and in the development of shows such as Flerida Peña's *Sister Mary's a Dyke?!* (produced by Cahoots Theatre Company in 2013) that began to deal in inventive ways with such things as mixed-race and LGBTQ subjectivities among second-generation Filipino Canadians.

As a professional, contemporary Filipino Canadian theater company

CBT's mandate is "to reflect on social issues affecting the Filipino and broader community"; its commitment is "to creating work that is new, innovative, and reflective of a vibrant, new generation of Filipino-Canadian artists" (Carlos Bulosan Theatre). Although the shift to professional status meant significant changes in the company's practices—hiring and paying professional actors for full, daytime rehearsal schedules has a considerably different feel from feeding volunteer actors lavish Filipino meals in return for devoting their evenings to staging plays—in many ways the continuities with CBCW were more apparent than the differences. Under Nadine Villasin CBT maintained the feeling of shared community engendered by such hospitality and food continued to feature at every opportunity, from festivals to opening nights and parties. Its dramaturgical practices of new play development, particularly collectively devised work, evolved out of rather than turned their backs on those of CBCW, and became one of the company's most characteristic features as it continued to develop distinctly Filipino Canadian dramaturgical forms.

MISS ORIENT(ED)

CBT's first professional, explicitly Filipino Canadian production, *Miss Orient(ed)*, was written by Nina Lee Aquino and Nadine Villasin, and under the direction of Argentinean Canadian Guillermo Verdecchia had a very successful run at the Factory Studio Theatre in 2003 and, in 2005, under the direction of anglo Canadian Sarah Stanley, at Montreal's Teesri Duniya Theatre. The play was created out of a desire to address identity topics that were "hot" with Filipino youth. After a workshop with young Filipinos the playwrights decided that they wanted to deal with questions of identity and to represent three synchronic elements of the Filipina Canadian community: "the Filipina born in Canada, who doesn't know a lick of language but looks Filipino; the Filipina immigrant who wants to completely erase the past, pretends she does *not* speak the language and dyes her hair blonde . . . ; and the fresh-off-the-boat, newly arrived, wide-eyed, naïve Filipina" (Aquino, qtd. in Knowles, "Between" 81). But they needed a logical setting in which these three might meet, and they needed a dramaturgical frame. The breakthrough on both fronts was the idea to locate the play at, and structure it around, "one of the most sacred things in Filipino culture": a beauty pageant. There, offstage, the three contestants support or deceive one another, quarrel, and expose insecurities. Onstage they compete in:

- the opening ceremony (dancing to *West Side Story*'s "America" [Aquino and Villasin 86]);
- the talent competition (karaoke ""I Will Always Love You" versus a "box-ercise version of "Survivor" and the Tinikling Filipino bamboo dance [91]);
- the evening gown competition; and
- the question-and-answer segment ("How can we bring about world peace?" "What is your definition of beauty?" "What does being a Filipina mean?" "When was the first time you realized you weren't white?" "What's your favourite food?" [87–88], and "What, in your own words, makes the ideal modern Filipina?" [97].

The winning answer to this last question is "a woman who is modest, submissive and obedient, venturing no ideas and owing no opinions in polite society or . . . to her mother" [98]).

As the reviewer for the *McGill Tribune* wrote, "Cultures collide, blend, and sometimes make friends throughout the show. . . . The play offers a lesson in Filipino-Canadian identity, playing with stereotypes and breaking them completely. Wrongs are not 'right' by the end [the westernized blonde and breast-enhanced 'Carrie' (aka 'Caridad Makapante') inevitably wins], but each contestant learns some form of lesson about her background—and her attitude towards it" (Treutler). Ultimately, as another reviewer notes, the play asks, "Which sector of society allows you to fully claim Canadian culture? Why can't you also say you're fully Filipino? Who owns culture? Who's to say what's Filipino and what's Canadian?" (Dlodo). Most importantly for my purposes here, as a contribution to the evolution of a distinctly Filipino Canadian dramaturgy, *Miss Orient(ed)* made the bold move of structuring itself around a contemporary, widely popular, and distinctly Filipino Canadian pop-culture form and committed itself to its formal principles. It focused, not on an individual hero or heroine, and not on a single Aristotelian action, but on the messy identity issues of a conflicted, intergenerational community in diaspora.

THE ROMANCE OF MAGNO RUBIO

The five-woman *Miss Orient(ed),* the cast featuring in its premiere both playwrights together with CBCW founder Fely Villasin, was followed in 2005 by a five-man show, the Canadian premiere of *The Romance of Magno Rubio,* a play by Steppenwolf Theatre's Lonnie Carter with Loy Arcenas and Ralph Peña, first produced by New York's Ma-Yi [Asian American] Theatre Company in New York. The play is based on a short story by Carlos Bulosan and was directed imaginatively in Toronto by actor, musician, sound designer, and filmmaker Romeo Candido. The play deals with the duping of a Filipino American itinerant laborer by the lovelorn-column object of his affection. Insofar as *Romance* was not a new script and emerged from the Filipino *American* community, *Magno Rubio* didn't contribute directly to the evolution of a distinctive dramaturgy for Filipino Canadians. Insofar as it was written largely in traditional rhyming couplets and was modeled on various traditional Filipino performance forms, including the *eskrima* (a martial arts practice involving stick, staff, or knife play), it nevertheless did provide an example of engaged political playwriting on historical themes that are in danger of being forgotten by second-generation Filipinos and beyond. It also, and perhaps more importantly, provided the company with a tentative contemporary Filipino diasporic dramaturgical model for further exploration.

PEOPLE POWER

From 2006 to 2013 CBT's mainstage productions focused on the collective rewriting of Filipino history by five core members who called themselves the CBT Collective: Leon Aureus, Rose Cortez, Nicco Lorenzo Garcia, Christine Mangosing, and Nadine Villasin. The group was internally inter- or intracultural: each member had her or his own first-, 1.5-, or second-generation immigrant history; each had her or his own family heritage of class, cultural, and geographical positioning within the Philippines; and each had her or his own degree of familiarity with Filipino languages and cultural forms. These productions served a conscious community-building function within Toronto, as well as an educational role for Canadian-born Filipinos who may have lost touch with the (particularly) colonial history of the island and its languages. And they followed a deliberate agenda of developing uniquely Filipino Canadian dramaturgies. What follows are accounts of the collective's work on two shows from my own (intercultural) position as a non-Filipino Canadian working as associate dramaturge on the first production of *People Power* at Theatre Passe Muraille in 2008 and as dramaturge on its remount in 2010, as well as on the long development process of *In the Shadow of Elephants* from April 2009 to the show's premiere in June 2013, a difficult and lengthy period of transition for the company.[3]

People Power, the collective's first project, revisited the company's origins in the Carlos Bulosan Cultural Workshop and the anti-Marcos movement. It drew upon research about and interviews with members of North American CAMD to tell the story of the "People Power" (EDSA) revolution in the Philippines in 1986, a nonviolent, spontaneous uprising that toppled the brutal Marcos dictatorship and inspired subsequent nonviolent resistance movements around the world, including those that brought down the Berlin Wall three years later. Many in the collective had family histories of participation in the resistance and revolution. Nadine Villasin's father, Ruben Cusipag, a journalist in the Philippines, was imprisoned by Marcos in the 1970s, and the family moved to Canada upon his release in 1974. Her mother, Fely, in addition to founding the theater company, was a Torontonian and later North American leader in CAMD (see Kaplan, "Vocal"). Leon Aureus's father ran a newspaper and magazine that were shut down by the Marcos regime (see Ouzounian). Rose Cortez was a child of six at the time of the uprising, and she remembers playing with her friends when they were interrupted by the noise of hundreds of helicopters overhead, marking a climactic moment in the revolution and the play. Nicco Lorenzo Garcia, whose great-grand-uncle had served as one of Marcos's top security officers in the early 1970s, remembers the helicopters passing when he was walking to church with his family in Mutinlupa when he was eight years old. "Gera na ba [will it be war]?" he asked his father. Christine Mangosing's family moved to Canada in 1984, a year after the assassination of Ninoy Aquino that precipitated the events depicted in the play. As a child she had a doll of Cory Aquino, the widow of Ninoy, who became president in the wake of the revolution (see Ouzounian). The show's director, Nina Lee Aquino, was charged in *People Power* with the difficult task of staging her *tito* (uncle) Ninoy Aquino's assassination and funeral, a staging that including a graphic photojournalist's image of his corpse.[4]

Only two members of the collective had significant prior experience as playwrights: Leon Aureus (*Banana Boys*, produced by fu-GEN Asian Canadian Theatre in 2004, revived in 2005, 2008, and, by Factory Theatre, in 2015) and Nadine Villasin (*Miss Orient(ed)*, 2003, revived at Teesri Duniya in 2005). Two had formal theater training (Rose Cortez and Nicco Lorenzo Garcia, at Toronto's York University and Humber College, respectively). One, Christine Mangosing, trained in fine arts and works as a graphic designer. The collective had several goals entering the multistaged two-year creation process that resulted in the first production of *People Power* in 2008.[5] Some of these goals were continuous with the company's history but extended to a new generation and were both political and dramaturgical. According to Christine Mangosing,

> I feel deeply connected and enthusiastic about the new narrative traditions emerging from young Filipino-Canadian and Filipino-American artists today. As the offspring of a post-colonial society, and what my sister, Caroline, has labelled the "first postmodern culture," modern Filipinos bear no identity outside of a colonized one.
>
> Hundreds of years of colonization by the Spanish . . . the Japanese and the Americans erased the Philippine Islands' rich history of tribal traditions. . . . These traditions have been embraced and reinterpreted by a new generation of young Filipino artists in North America eager to piece together a history and a culture that they can truly and proudly call their own.[6]
>
> Examples of this at work are local Filipino-Canadian filmmakers' The Digital Sweatshop's film *Ang Pamana: The Inheritance*, which draws from age-old Filipino mythological creatures set within a modern-day Filipino-Canadian context; another local Filipino artist, accessories designer Melissa Clemente, calls her designs an "interpretation of folk dance costume focusing on art forms from the mountain regions of the Philippines." Len Cervantes, a spoken word artist, borrows from ancient Filipino poetic forms such as *balagtasan* (a form of debate in verse) and *tanaga* (a set rhyme and syllabic scheme) in his work.

But the work that Mangosing most admires and wishes to create is neither folkloric nor tinged with the types of compensatory nostalgia that often plague first-generation immigrant communities; rather, it is deeply political:

> I believe art and social commentary go hand in hand. Art, in whatever form, has served as a means to relay social and political events, opinions, and ideas throughout history. It is more important than ever to use art as a means of challenging systems of oppression. . . . Society needs to be reminded on a constant basis that oppression exists—racism STILL exists, misogyny STILL exists, the list goes on and on. Art, whether it be visual, performance or literary, loses its weight if it's not saying anything at all. ("Theatre Is Territory")

In addition to attempting to fulfill their aesthetic and political goals, the collective also structured the creation process as an opportunity to learn, and this entered them into a complex negotiation. Alongside "creation" work on the show the actor-writers held workshops. The first phase, in 2006, involved Aureus and Villasin along with three others who eventually left the collective (Caroline Mangosing, Len Cervantes, and Christine Florencio—though a poem by Cervantes remained prominent in the show). This phase was facilitated by Ethiopian Canadian director Weyni Mengesha (director of the long-running *da kink in my hair*, by Jamaican Canadian trey anthony), who was at that time associate director and resident dramaturge at Theatre Passe Muraille.

For the second and subsequent phases, in 2007, Aureus and Villasin were joined by Rose Cortez, Nicco Lorenzo Garcia, and Christine Mangosing, completing the collective. This group held workshops with Filipina playwright, director, and actor Mary Beath Badian (who served as the show's first dramaturge) on creation process and audience-stage interaction, which they were determined to explore in the show as part of what performance means in the Philippines. They were convinced that a performance form rooted in the culture of the Philippines would necessarily involve the audience as active participants rather than passive observers and were determined to make this a central part of the *People Power* experience. In this phase they also held productive workshops with Swiss Canadian Clare Preuss on movement and the development of movement vocabularies grounded in Filipino sensibilities and the events of 1986. But perhaps most formatively, and perhaps most problematically for this show, they held creation workshops with Paul Thompson. Thompson trained in the mid-1960s with activist and antinaturalist director Roger Planchon in France and on his return to Canada became the father of collective creation in Canada, at Theatre Passe Muraille and across the country. Thompson taught the CBT collective his techniques of collective creation through improvisation and physical and vocal mimicry rather than psychological identification (see Knowles, *The Theatre of Form* 87).

People Power was created, rehearsed, and in April–May 2008 staged within the storied walls of Theatre Passe Muraille. Not surprisingly, the show bore some resemblance to the early and still iconic Passe Muraille collectives, particularly *1837: The Farmers' Revolt*, a 1973 collective creation involving playwright Rick Salutin and directed by Thompson. *1837* was hugely influential in Canada in its day. It modeled a dramaturgy that, as reviewer Brian Boru described it in 1974, involved "a cool, matter-of-fact geometric form, the inevitable choice of a social situation rather than a character as protagonist, a passion for local history and an uncompromised belief in individual rights and public good. . . . What happens to the characters . . . is less important, dramatically speaking, than what the enacted events imply for the community as a whole":

> In choosing to look for drama in circumstances rather than personalities, Theatre Passe Muraille becomes a subscriber to the view that the theatre's prime function is to present publicly and in dramatic terms those conditions which most affect social well-being and stability. Such a premise would make Passe Muraille a political theatre in the most basic sense of the word, that is, the sense which derives from the notion that government is an activity and a responsibility rather than an institution. The intention of this kind of theatre is to awaken the slumbering social conscience through artistic means: art and politics being seen, in this context, to intersect at the point where men [*sic*] are moved to act for social change. The methods which such a theatre needs to employ are deliberately demonstrational and the attention of its drama is fixed on the effects of ethical, political and economic issues rather than on behavioural causes. (157)

People Power works recognizably within this tradition in combination with the political and community-based traditions of the CBTW. Like *1837* it focuses on the social and political rather than the individual and psychological. Both plays take pains to represent the social causes of their respective revolutions in vignettes such as, in *1837*, the "Family Compact's" nepotism and its abuse of land grant distribution[7] and, in *People Power*, the strict control of the press, death threats to CAMD members, and murders of opposition, including student, leaders. Like *1837*, too, *People Power* combines an episodic structure with fragments of evolving narrative. In both, characters that are never fully fleshed out in psychological terms reappear across several interwoven scenes to tell fragments of representative stories. In *1837* the audience (particularly in the second act) follows ordinary people such as Thomas, who quits his store job to join the revolution; Isaac, who locks his tavern to take part, and his locked-out customer Jamey, who joins for the supposed rum ration; and Edward, a farmer and newlywed who sets out, with his new wife Mary's blessing, to join the rebels at the crossroads as momentum gathers for the climactic and lopsided April battle. In *People Power* we similarly see the servant Flor, whose brother is one of a small and threatened group of rebel soldiers; the student leader Anna, in conflict with her Marcos-supporting family; the photojournalist Victor, torn between his family connections to the Marcoses and his sense of social justice; and the beleaguered taxi driver Manny, who at first resents the protesters for blocking the streets but is drawn into the action as all converge upon the EDSA parkway where the peaceful but revolutionary conversion of the pro-Marcos army occurs.

Like its Passe Muraille predecessor, *People Power* used a small group of five actors to portray a vast sweep of characters, and both productions used objects such as (in *1837*) a giant head (the historical figure Sir Francis Bond Head, with the actors playing the eyes, nose, mouth, etc.)[8] and (in *People Power*) tanks and helicopters. In both productions the cast also staged iconic, gestic events, such as (in *1837*) the farmers' makeshift military drill with pitchforks instead of rifles and (in *People Power*) a young girl's passing of a flower to an armed soldier in combat gear. Finally, and crucially, like *1837*, *People Power* consisted of a collective of actors portraying collective action that constituted grassroots revolution—the collective theatrical process mimicking the political and antihierarchical character of the revolution—though unlike the farmer's revolution in *1837*, the People Power Revolution was both nonviolent and successful.

The Passe Muraille heritage was both a blessing and a curse. It provided CBT, through Paul Thompson's instruction, with a way of working together collectively, transforming traditional historical research and material generated through interviews, by means of an improvisatory process, into character, action, and scenes characterized by startling immediacy and the freshness and commitment of work performed by its creators. Without the Passe Muraille model, it's difficult to imagine the invention of such scenes as that in which a threatening fleet of helicopters interrupts a children's game or another representing the contested election between Marcos and Cory Aquino, consisting of a movement piece in which the cast lined up in rotation to vote (or accept bribes), effectively representing through their rotation a large crowd, as Passe Muraille had done in the "The Rope" scene in *1837* (Salutin and Theatre Passe Muraille 62–63).[9] But *People Power* also shared with *1837* a susceptibility to critique on the grounds of a reliance on melodrama "of the most traditional sort," as the reviewer for the *Canadian Historical Review* wrote of *1837* (Westfall 163), or on sentimentality, as the reviewer for the *National Post* wrote of *People Power* (Cushman). This led to *People Power*'s having a somewhat old-fashioned feel in places, and while most reviewers were overwhelmingly enthusiastic, at least one, Robert Cushman, pointed to such things as its cardboard characters and sometimes stilted writing—charges that had also frequently been leveled at the political collectives of the 1970s and have been leveled throughout western history at political plays.[10]

More seriously, however, the Passe Muraille connection tended to work against the collective's ambitions to piece together new, postmodern, and specifically Filipino Canadian cultural and dramaturgical forms grounded in "the Philippine Islands' rich history of tribal traditions," as Mangosing put it. The subject was the Philippines, but the process and form were largely borrowed, the Filipino part of its distinctly Filipino Canadian character subsumed, at least in its dominant-culture reception as evidenced by reviews,[11] within its largely episodic docudrama form. Ultimately the show sits comfortably within Christopher Balme's second category of what he calls syncretic theater, in which "the existing system remains dominant" (17)—the existing system, in this instance, being the now-traditional 1970s Passe Muraille house style.

IN THE SHADOW OF ELEPHANTS

The process shifted for the CBT collective's next work, *In the Shadow of Elephants,* where the creators made a significant move toward a theatrical syncretism in which, in Balme's terms, "a new equilibrium [is] established" (17) and there is a fusion of traditional performance forms from the Philippines with the formal properties of western dramaturgy, retaining the formal integrity of both. The project was initially intended to focus on the Japanese occupation of the Philippines during World War II and was inspired by the opening lines of Filipina American novelist Tess Uriza Holthe's *When the Elephants Dance* (a poetic revision of which occurs early in the final version of the show):

> Papa explains the war like this: "When the elephants dance, the chickens must be careful." The great beasts, as they circle one another, shaking the trees and trumpeting loudly, are the Amerikanos and the Japanese as they fight. And our Philippine Islands? We are the small chickens. (3)

The collective's early research on this period, however, betrayed a significant American bias in the archive, which presented the Americans overwhelmingly as liberators. But less than half a century earlier they had themselves brutally pillaged the country, torturing and murdering its peoples during the Filipino-American War (1899–1902 and beyond)—now popularly known, insofar as it is known at all, as the "First Vietnam" (see Francisco).[12] This led the collective to broaden the scope of its project, and by the time the first development phase began in April 2009, it was with the expressed intention of writing the postcolonization history of the Philippines as "a story of resistance rather than one of colonization or victimization, told through a recuperation of what in the culture was *not* introduced by the colonizers" (Knowles, Dramaturgical notes). This meant a conscious return to the cosmology, belief systems, and cultural forms of the Indigenous peoples of the Philippines—the Bukidnon, the Kalinga, the Ibaloi, the Ifuagao, the various Igorot tribes, and many others. Most prominent among these are the Subanon, whose story of the destruction of their sacred land on Mount Canatuan by a Canadian mining company frames the play in its final form, and the T'boli, from whose textile arts the collective drew a central healing figure in the play, the guiding Dreamweaver, and a central metaphor based on that culture's famous woven *t'nalak* cloth. The *t'nalak*, indeed, is threaded throughout the play as an emblem of the wholeness or, when ripped, the threatened destruction of the culture.

Rather than workshops on western techniques of play creation, then, including collective creation, the process as designed for the show that was first titled *When the Elephants Dance* centred on embodied Filipino cultural forms.[13] The initial creation schedule was set up as a series of five three-week workshops, with the mornings spent training with facilitators in traditional Filipino arts and the afternoons dedicated to creating stories, scenes, and characters out of archival, library, and Internet research and the interviews the collective had undertaken, mostly with survivors of the Japanese occupation. Some of these workshops, with facilitator Catherine Hernandez, were on traditional Filipino dance, including, for example, the harvest Dugso (dance) of the Manobo people; the Bogobo Rice Cycle harvest dance; the Bumayah thanksgiving dance of the Ifuagao (used in the show for a threatening procession of elephants representing the colonizers); the Vinta drum song and dance from Mindanao; the Kalinga peoples' Banga (pot) dance (without the pots); and the Kadal Tahaw, a T'boli bird dance that was eventually performed by the Dreamweaver with the *t'nalak* cloth around her shoulders at the show's opening .

In other workshops, led by Alexander Punzalan (who ultimately designed the show's sound and music), the company learned to play traditional Filipino musical instruments such as the *angklung* (bamboo tubes that produce different pitches attached to a bamboo frame and are shaken by the player to produce its characteristic quavering sound); the *kubing* (the bamboo mouth harp of the Maguindanao and Maranao peoples in the south); the *cajóns* (wooden beat boxes not unique to the Philippines); the *kulintang* (a series of differently pitched gongs); and the *agong* (a large gong worn on a strap over one shoulder). They also learned traditional chants, songs, and rhythms, including the "war-like beat" (the Vinta) that finally ended the show with a gesture of defiance before it resolved into the healing swish of the Dreamweaver's loom.

Next Amihan Bonifacio-Ramolete of Teatrong Mulat in Manila was brought to Toronto to teach the company Asian puppetry (not exclusively Filipino), shadow puppetry, and mask work, including mask and puppet construction—workshops that profoundly influenced the show's visual palate and its ways of representing the "elementals"—representatives of the ancestral and spirit worlds. It was at this point, too, that the title of the show, perhaps influenced by the shadow puppetry, was changed to *In the Shadow of Elephants*.

The company also experimented during this period with emblematic movement and tableaux deriving from work with the *malong*, a traditional southern Philippine tube skirt or tube dress made of handwoven multicolored cotton cloth (though it is now often machine-made), with geometric *okir* designs based on leaf or vine patterns. One hot and humid summer week was even spent in the woods near director Karen Ancheta's home in Ancaster, Ontario, approximating an embodied sense of what guerrilla resistance in the hot and humid jungles of the Philippines might feel like.

These "cultural texts," as Yuri Lotman calls them (6), from which the collective drew its inspiration, were in fact *inter*cultural, cutting across the various primarily Indigenous cultures and communities of the Philippines, and the company did not attempt to derive from them coherent and clearly articulated dramaturgical principles.[14] Nevertheless, entering the creation phase in the afternoons, the group's bodies inevitably retained the sounds, rhythms, patterns, and imagery of the morning's work, and the improvisations and writing were naturally informed by them as they proceeded almost organically toward a distinctly Filipino Canadian dramaturgy.

This was how the first three workshop phases, of three weeks each, were structured. Later phases, facing the pressure to produce a final script (funding and production schedules can be stretched only so far), dropped the morning workshops and focused exclusively on creation, which quickly devolved to collective writing, much of the time table-bound. The participation of the director, Karen Ancheta, and dramaturge, myself, was funded only for the final, rehearsal phase of the project in 2013, though we both attended the earlier workshops frequently and provided input as we could.

It is difficult and time-consuming work, when at every stage naturalized western dramaturgical instinct must be challenged by cultural difference and cultural specificity and when the relationship between the cultural texts on which the work was drawn, its dramaturgy, and the historical record of resistance that was its subject had not been explicitly pinned down. Within the material constraints of time and funding, there were, pre-

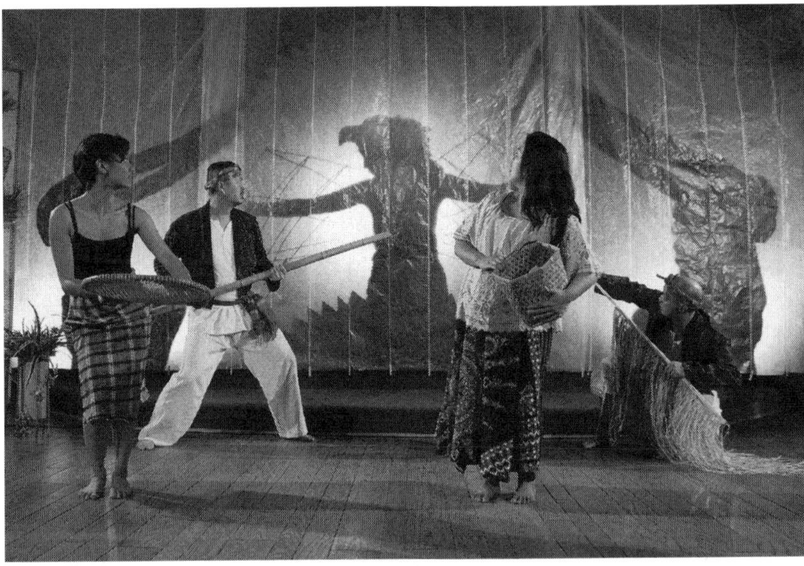

Fig. 4. Belinda Corpuz, Leon Aureus, Jennifer Maramba (in shadow), Aura Carcueva, and Nicco Lorenzo Garcia in the CBT Collective's *In the Shadow of Elephants*. Photo by Alexander Punzalan.

dictably, slippages into comfortable compromises. These included such things as the abandonment of early plans to have the Indigenous ancestors and "elementals" (the Dreamweaver, the *diwata* fairies, the *babaylans*, the Maya bird) speak using *tanaga*—a disciplined, haiku-like Filipino verse form consisting of four lines of seven syllables each, with the same rhyme at the end of each line. A major slippage occurred in October 2009 when, facing an imminent public presentation of the work-in-progress, the collective went into minor meltdown and in short order restructured the play as a kind of naturalistic Filipino family drama—the fallback form for western-influenced theater. I had missed two days of the workshop while this happened; when I returned I told the company that I admired their courage in making so dramatic a shift but, rightly or wrongly, as a cultural outsider, I also reminded them of their original intention (which I had recorded) to work from and with Indigenous Filipino forms to tell Filipino stories in new, Filipino Canadian ways. The moment of panic passed, the group reconsidered, and the restructuring was rejected; nevertheless, operating at a remove from the embodiment of morning workshops meant that in the fourth, fifth, and, several years later,[15] final phases the writing was more cerebral, more table-bound, focused to a greater extent on character and action, and the epic expanse of the show was shoehorned into a tighter and somewhat more familiar dramaturgical frame.

Nevertheless, in its final form at Toronto's Music Gallery in June 2013 *In the Shadow of Elephants* retained the central features of an evolving, syncretic Filipino Canadian dramaturgy that brings together Indigenous Filipino cultural texts and belief systems within the frame of the western theatrical practice to rewrite the history of the Philippines as one of resistance. The show is primarily in English, but like *People Power* it includes significant amounts of Tagalog and is partly imagined through that medium. Passages in the Indigenous languages Cebuano (for the representation of Magellan's arrival and fatal encounter with "the natives") and Subanon (for the Indigenous confrontation with Canadian mine operators in the play's final movement) did not, unfortunately, survive the final revisions. In its current form and pending future revisions, the show covers four periods and many types of resistance: to the Spanish, American, and Japanese colonizers and occupiers, as well as to the current multinational—in this case Canadian-based—corporate colonizers, the mining companies that are razing sacred land, polluting the country's rivers and forests, and destroying its agricultural base. And it explicitly portrays and promotes resistance to each of the sexual, military, political, economic, educational, and cultural forms that colonization has taken throughout the history of the islands.

In the Shadow of Elephants is structured around several intersecting organizing principles, including the guiding and framing mythopoeic Dreamweaver, the recurring trope of the torn *t'nalak* cloth, and the staging of two key scenes that bring the play's time periods together, as when women raped by Spanish and Japanese soldiers during their respective periods of occupation meet and comfort one another across time and when, in the final sequence, characters from each of the show's four time periods unite in resistance. Each actor in the show, moreover, plays multiple linked roles (indicated by the first letters of their names) across the play's different time periods. One actor, for example, plays the healers Sora and Sita in the Spanish and US occupations, respectively, as well as Selma, who orchestrates the escape of a group of "comfort women" from the Japanese occupiers. The actor playing Lando in the sequences of Spanish occupation morphs into Lamug during the American and the guerilla hero Luis during the Japanese sequences, and so on. The actors do not perform psychologically realistic characters, then, but enduring roles in a long-standing resistance.

And of course the play remains grounded in movement, sound, and visual patterns, images, and rhythms indigenous to the Philippines, using dance, music, masks, puppetry, and projections most directly to represent Indigenous belief systems and the (resistant) presence of "the elementals." But these forms are never used in ways that are folkloric or nostalgic, nor do they lay claim to fundamentally colonialist and repressive notions of "authenticity." Indeed, the show's central mythological figure, the Dreamweaver, who provides a unifying and motivating spine to the stories, although inspired by an actual weaver from the T'boli people, is almost entirely invented. The show, finally, uses each of the cultural texts on which it draws in the service of a dramaturgy that is both political and transformational, negotiating new diasporic subjectivities across internal cultural, generational, and other differences and collectively performing them into being.

FOUR | Indigenous Knowledge, Contemporary Performance

Dramaturgies of Decolonization

The most systematic and sophisticated attempt to develop new, culturally specific dramaturgies that I have worked on or know of has been a Toronto-based project funded by a Research/Creation Grant from the Social Sciences and Humanities Research Council of Canada called "Indigenous Knowledge, Contemporary Performance." The project involves seven core coinvestigators and collaborators, five of them from various Indigenous nations in what are now Canada and the United States. This chapter focuses on the dramaturgical portion of the project, for which I am most directly responsible, as it applies to two of its productions on which I have worked as dramaturge: *Chocolate Woman Dreams the Milky Way* and *Side Show Freaks and Circus Injuns*.

"Indigenous Knowledge, Contemporary Performance" is a practice of "decolonizing methodology" as outlined in the introduction to this book, employing Indigenous research methodologies that are fundamentally relational (that is, that locate the researchers in relation to their subjects and to all of creation) and that consider research, as Shawn Wilson says, as ceremony. It involves new, collaborative, and mutually beneficial co-creations that privilege Indigenous over western theoretical frames. Through embodied field- and studio-based research the project develops contemporary creation strategies for Indigenous performance that involve neither the appropriative nor touristic representation of traditional practices, nor the creation, as Plains Cree director Floyd Favel argues, of "artificial trees" (Favel Starr, "Artificial" 71)—"the superficial or clichéd presentation of ritual and social structures" (Favel, "Shadowed," qtd. in Mojica, "Chocolate" 164).

The overall project is grounded in contemporary art practice that investigates and employs culturally specific (as opposed to "pan-Indian") Indigenous formal principles—the deep structures of specific traditional practices—rather than their external qualities (Favel Starr, "Artificial" 70). Its intention is to open a space for contemporary practice that is not nostalgic, that does not function in a simplistic binary relationship of dominance versus resistance, that is not imitative or reproductive of Western forms, that is not stuck in the victim position nor subject to specious demands for static authenticities, and that respects and protects the sacredness of Indigenous ceremonial practices.

First Nations and Aboriginal cultures on Turtle Island are diverse, but all share a central characteristic: they are *performed*, created not out of texts but out of practices and stories. The contribution of the "Indigenous Knowledge, Contemporary Performance" project rests in its capacity, drawing on Indigenous traditions and relationships to the land, performatively to support the revitalization of Aboriginal cultures and communities in the contemporary world and to provide ways of reimagining trans-Indigenous and transcultural relationships. It is the project of a city, and of an urban Aboriginal theater community, that is necessarily intercultural, working across a number of (First) Nations that constitute a diaspora within their own land, attempting to forge new Indigenous subjectivities and identities grounded in traditional forms and practices.

CHOCOLATE WOMAN DREAMS THE MILKY WAY

Chocolate Woman Dreams the Milky Way tells Guna and Rappahannock playwright-performer Monique Mojica's veiled autobiographical story of Dule Wagwa, or Dule Girl, a "lost" woman of Guna ancestry trying to find herself by finding her way home.[1] The show is framed by "Sky Woman Falling," the creation story from Mojica's Rappahannock and adopted Haudenosaunee cultures, in which Sky Woman falls (or is pushed) from the Sky World and is supported by birds as she falls and lands on Turtle's back in the middle of otherwise undifferentiated ocean. Once there, she sends animal after animal—the loon, the beaver, the otter—to try to bring back mud from the ocean floor, with no success until the body of the lowly muskrat floats to the surface with a bit of mud clutched in his paw. From this, Sky Woman—or in some versions the trickster Nanabhozo—creates Turtle Island (North America). "Woven into this creation story" along with the story of Alice's fall down the rabbit hole, a key memory from Mojica's childhood, is "a re-telling of the [G]una story of Olonadili, the youngest of the Nis Bundor (Daughters from the Stars). She who was caught and trapped by human men, taught the people to sing to the babies, to feel emotions, to sing their grief, to mourn in verse, to make poetry from their sorrow" (Mojica, *Chocolate Woman*).[2]

These stories develop throughout the show, and the *stages* of the stories parallel those of Dule Girl's return to Guna Yala, guided by the Mugana (the Guna Grandmothers of Creation): Nan Kapsus (Mother Night), Muu Osiskun (Grandmother Ocean), Ibedon (the Earth), and finally Buna Siagua (Chocolate Woman), who rescues Dule Girl's spirit by catching her in a healing golden net. These elemental female figures tell traditional Guna stories that illuminate and culturally contextualize Dule Girl's/Mojica's own autobiographical stories of, as she says, "clawing and crawling [my] way back to wholeness" (Mojica, "Artist Statement"). Through them she is taught, and healed. For example, the story of the people's successful revolution against the evil *nia boni* and the "fat man" who sits at the top of the *palu wala* tree hoarding all of nature's goodness for himself is interwoven with Dule Girl/Mojica's fictionalized personal story of "once in a time of war" when, as a girl soldier in the 1970s, she fought in an armed people's revolution, the American Indian movement (AIM). In another example, the autobiographical story of Dule Girl's betrayal by her partner, "the light bearing warrior," is intercut with the parallel story of the betrayal of Olonadili, the youngest daughter from the stars, by the four human brothers who entrap her. Though not as mechanically as it may seem in my account, four pairs of cultural and personal stories are interwoven throughout the play as Sky Woman falls to Turtle's back and Dule Girl makes her way back to Guna Yala, the homeland of the Guna people. The dramaturgical significance of the number four will become apparent as this account develops.

Key moments in the show marking Dule Girl's transformation include a powerful wordless moment toward the end when Alice has arrived in Wonderland, Sky Woman has landed, and Dule Girl has arrived "on sacred land . . . where the grandmothers walked." Dule Girl shares a bowl of water with Ibedon, who proceeds to rouge Dule Girl's cheeks with bright red dye made from achiote seeds and to draw a black line down the centerline of her nose.

To the Guna, the face paint has many meanings, some of them practical (it protects from the sun) and some too sacred to divulge. In the context of the show, however, as the culmination of Dule Girl's journey and the beginning of the transformation and healing that conclude the show, the primary meaning has to do with the completion of a search for self: it is not until her face is painted that she is able to encounter Buna Siagua (Chocolate Woman). As Mojica says,

> For me it has always been one of those Guna things that I was missing. I knew I was supposed to have it on when fully dressed in mola,

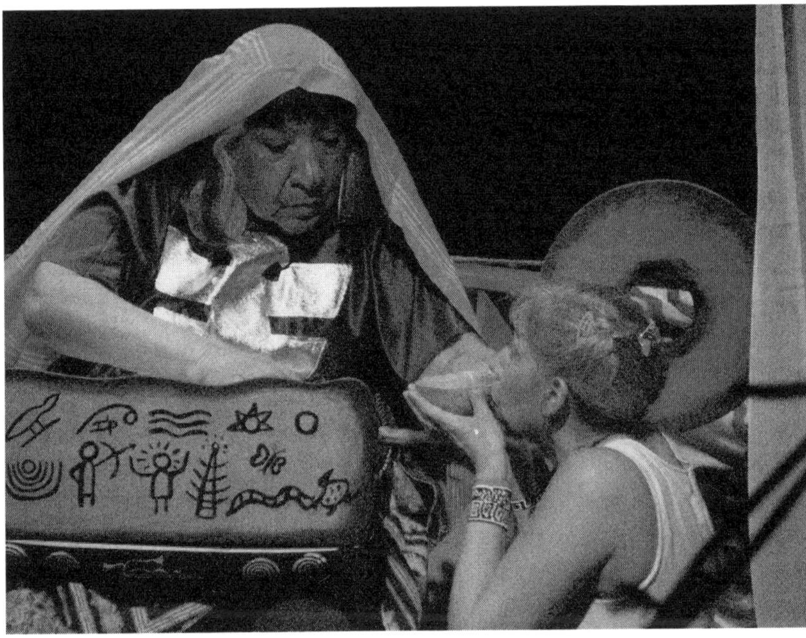

Fig. 5. Gloria Miguel as Ibedon (the earth) and Monique Mojica as Dule Wagwa in *Chocolate Woman Dreams the Milky Way*. Photo by Ric Knowles.

> but using conventional make up to do it always felt hollow. When I went to a chichi ceremony for the first time,[3] the women made it very clear that I had to be painted. For me (and in the play) it's about being endowed with marks that signify identity. (Email)

The world of *Chocolate Woman* is the Guna cosmos, and the play takes place, according to the production script, "in the present, between the eight layers of reality." On stage this was represented in a variety of ways. The star world was painted in a swirling Milky Way on the stage floor. Located centrally was a hammock, "the heart of [G]una culture," according to the show's designer and cultural consultant, Oswaldo De Léon Kantule: "One is born in a hammock; one sleeps in a hammock; leaders sit in hammocks at the Gathering House to tell stories; and after death the [G]una body is wrapped in a hammock to be buried" (Carter, "*Chocolate*" 174). Mojica performed athletically in, around, above, and beneath the hammock, and many of Dule Girl's crises and revelations occurred there. Upstage of the hammock was a brightly coloured *galu*, or spirit house. *Galus* for the Guna are portals. They provide access to different layers of the cosmos, and this construction served as the main set piece for the show, housing all of the characters—the Grandmothers of Creation—played by Gloria Miguel. This set piece grounded the production and served as a site and symbol of connectivity around which the action swirled and circled. Rigged above and in a semicircle upstage were three fifteen-foot-by-three-foot silk panels painted by Guna designer Oswaldo De León Kantule, which Mojica released sequentially. These panels served as actors (or actants) in the show, putting different kinds of pressure on the proceedings. Dule Girl interacted with them and derived specific energies associated with the figures that were painted on each of them.

The three panels represented different elemental female figures in Guna cosmology and different aspects of Mojica herself. The stage right panel represented Muu Bilii, Grandmother Ocean, but also, below her, Mojica/Dule Girl as mermaid (a complex and not entirely positive figure in Guna culture). At the bottom was a representation of Mojica's/Dule Girl's dream, recounted near the end of the production, of arriving at the beach on Guna Yala to be greeted by Kikadiriyai, the prophet Ibeorgun's sister, who introduced mola-making to the Guna people. The central panel was Buna Siagua, Chocolate Woman, rising in the purifying smoke of smudged cacao beans, with her net extended to capture the spirits of illness and rescue the spirit of the sick person. At the top of the panel was the pictographic symbol for cacao, which is a staple in the Guna diet, the only plant in the culture that can heal on its own. Finally, the stage left panel depicted Nis Bundor, the Daughters from the Stars after whom every Guna woman is named, including Mojica, who was given the name of the youngest, Olonadili, when she was a child. This last identification formed a central layer of *Chocolate Woman*'s theatrical weave: the key narratives of the show told the traditional Olonadili stories interwoven with Mojica's "*personal* Olonadili stor[ies]" of her own life (see Carter, "Chocolate" 170, emphasis in original). It is this interweaving of traditional with personal stories that constitutes Guna (and much Indigenous) pedagogy: the passing on of healing wisdom through the repetition and renewal (and reliving) of the ur stories that give events their meaning.

De León Kantule's panels, together with the painted floor, galu, and hammock, constituted the "set" of the production and made manifest its world, but they were not mere set decoration, nor, as Jill Carter argues, were they "emblems or static mnemonic devices, but . . . living texts" with which Mojica, herself a living text, interacted ("Chocolate" 175). They also bodied forth the principles by which the world of the production operates, one overseen by the creator, Baba/Nana (Father/Mother), in which the ancestors are very much alive and active in the (eternal) present, in which under certain conditions traffic is possible between the earth plane and the eight levels of the cosmos, and in which cultural values are communicated intergenerationally through rich, patterned textiles, stories, songs, and chants.

The development of *Chocolate Woman* began at an intersection of urgencies. Mojica initiated the project at a time of deep personal crisis (Carter, "Chocolate" 171) but also at a turning point in her professional life and her sense of purpose around her art (she had left Turtle Gals Performance Ensemble, which she had cofounded consciously as a successor/inheritor to New York's Spiderwoman Theater, founded by her mother and maternal aunts and still the longest running women's or Native theater on Turtle Island). She initiated the process, as she says, to save her life, but also to try to find a way for both herself and for Native theater more generally to move beyond "rehashing a victim narrative" (Mojica, qtd. in Bimm), a trap laid by colonization for Native artists. She began by asking, "In the midst of dislocation and (oft-times) despair, how can the actions of the disaffected and spiritually embattled change the world? Or more to the point, how does the representation of action . . . reassemble the world and restore harmony?" (qtd. in Carter, "Chocolate" 171). "What stories would I tell if I started from a place of connectedness instead of from a place of rupture?" (qtd. in Knowles, "Native" 74).

Like the rest of the "Indigenous Knowledge" project, *Chocolate Woman* builds on two preexisting pursuits: Storyweaving, as developed by Mojica's Guna and Rappahannock mother and maternal aunts at Spiderwoman Theater, and Native Performance Culture research, as developed by Plains Cree director Floyd Favel working with Mojica, her aunt Muriel Miguel, Tuscarora musician Pura Fé, and others in a series of workshops beginning in 1991.

As described by Muriel Miguel, Storyweaving derives from traditional forms of Indigenous storytelling and an Indigenous belief system rooted in relationality and the interconnectedness of all things. It is used by Spiderwoman in very specific ways "to entwine stories and fragments of stories with words, music, song, film, dance and movement, thereby creating a production that is multi-layered and complex; an emotional, cultural and political tapestry" (Miguel qtd. in Mojica, "Chocolate" 165).

Native Performance Culture research is centrally concerned with the relationship between contemporary performance and the traditional forms of Indigenous cultures, including "dances, songs, weaving, myths, and ceremonies" (Favel, "Poetry" 34). Native Performance Culture research had previously focused, in particular, on the Plains Cree Round Dance (Favel Starr, "Artificial" 70) and the Sioux winter count glyphs on which Favel drew for the rehearsal/creation of *The House of Sonja*, his Indigenous adaptation of Chekov's *Uncle Vanya* (see Appleford, "No" 253). The method attempts to "isolate the technical principles" of specific Indigenous cultural texts and use them as starting points for contemporary performance that doesn't simply react *against* colonialist inscriptions but bypasses them (Favel, "Waskawewin" 114). *Chocolate Woman* constituted an extension of this research, neither imitating nor representing but attempting to build upon the deep structure of Guna cultural forms.

A third evolving methodology used in the *Chocolate Woman* workshops, in addition to copious library, Internet, and archival research, is a combination of what Mojica calls "embodied research" and deep improvisation (which she considers to be a process of excavation) ("In Plain Sight" 219, 221). Embodied research is a deeply experiential process of immersion in a culture, its forms, and its artifacts; deep improvisation emerges from embodied memory as activated though this research. "I placed myself on the land, in the ocean, on a river, among [my Guna] relatives, and embodied them by assimilating and integrating myself with their vibrations," Mojica explains. "I listened to what [these experiences] had to tell me, and listened to how my body responded. I put it all in one big vat until I couldn't hold it anymore" (qtd. in Bimm). She then brought all of this information, stored in her body, into the studio, where she typically engages fully and deeply in an improvisatory process from which movement, gesture, and language emerge in a complex weave that constitutes a fully embodied "first draft" that is much more than simply text.

But she doesn't work alone. Like most theatrical devisers, Mojica works with an assemblage of resources, including practices, artifacts, archives, histories, stories, personnel, and land. For *Chocolate Woman* Mojica turned to the Guna part of her heritage—the people, stories, and material culture of Guna Yala, a territory on coastal Panama that has existed autonomously since the Dule Revolution of 1925 and that retains uninterrupted many of its precolonial traditions and practices. These traditions and practices constituted, for her, "a place of connectedness" with that which is "not broken" (Mojica, qtd. in Knowles, "Native" 74, 73). She assembled a powerful constellation of resources, beginning with an almost entirely Indigenous but broadly intercultural creative team. Oswaldo De León Kantule, set designer and cultural consultant, is the grandson of a leader of the 1925 revolution, the son of a *saila* (spiritual leader) on the island of Ustupu, and the brother of exquisite mola-makers there. He's an internationally known visual artist whose work is grounded in the sacred stories of Guna culture. Floyd Favel, who led the early development stages of *Chocolate Woman*, is a Plains Cree director from Poundmaker First Nation in Saskatchewan, one of the last pupils of Polish director Jerzy Grotowski, and one of the prime developers of Native Performance Culture research. Jill Carter, witness and scribe, is an Anishinaabe scholar, the first Indigenous person in Canada to complete a PhD in theater studies. Her expertise is in the Storyweaving work of Spiderwoman Theater. These four constituted the creative team who entered the first *Chocolate Woman* workshop in 2007.

After the initial workshop others were added to the team. Guna and Rappahannock Gloria Miguel, cofounder of Spiderwoman Theater and Mojica's mother, joined as actor and Elder. Omushkego Cree designer Erika Iserhoff, with a specialized knowledge of Indigenous textile arts, joined as costume designer, Mohawk and Anishinaabe designer Michel Charbonneau did the lights, and Mushkegowuk Cree designer Andy Moro served as technical director. After Favel left the project, Guna actor José Colman came from Panama City to take over its direction, assisted by Nicaraguan Canadian theater artist Alberto Guevara. Guna musician Marden Paniza, also from Panama, joined as composer. In addition to these major Indigenous artists, Brenda Farnell brought her expertise in the annotation of Indigenous movement and gesture to the project, while I joined the team as dramaturge. Venezuelan Canadian Gia Nahmens, of Basque heritage, was stage manager.

Beyond the assembled personnel, resources included an extensive gathering of the mola textile arts of Guna women, pictographic annotations of Guna council house chants, and the culturally coded paintings of De León Kantule and his explications of their representations (a selection of these paintings was displayed at the show's premiere). In addition to these visual resources, the team collected cultural stories of female figures in Guna cosmology, Haudenosaunee and Powhatan creation stories, and research on Guna cultural texts and practices, including library, online, and archival work; the embodied research of travel to Panama City and Guna Yala; meetings with contemporary Guna artists, artists who work with traditional forms (including molas), *sailas* (spiritual leaders), and *kantules* (healers); ceremonies; and lived encounters with the land, river, and sea environments. A key resource was Mojica's own personal and cultural (auto) biography, (blood) memory, and lived experience, including childhood memories of *Alice in Wonderland*, Jefferson Airplane, and Perry Como's version of the Paul Vance and Lee Pockriss hit song from the 1950s, "Catch a Falling Star."

Mojica drew on this extraordinarily rich assemblage of personnel and other resources in the deep improvisations that constituted the creation of *Chocolate Woman*. But I will focus here on two elements that were central to the development of the show's dramaturgical principles: molas and pictographs. Molas are appliqué and reverse-appliqué panels hand stitched and embroidered by Guna women in several layers of fabric and sewn together to form the fronts and backs of their blouses. The most traditional patterns, originally painted or tattooed on women's bodies, at once tell layered narratives of Guna culture and conceal/protect those narratives through abstraction. The layers of fabric and detailed stitching give the molas intricacy and depth of a very different kind than the perspectival and characterological depth of most western dramaturgy.

Mojica relates the making of molas to the Storyweaving methodology that she inherited from Spiderwoman Theater. She compares the process of cutting away layers of cloth in the creation of molas to reveal the colors beneath to the creation of her own performance as a process "of cutting away to reveal what is contained within our blood memory, between the cells" (qtd. in Knowles, "Native" 81). Under De León Kantule's guidance and in tandem with a detailed consideration of his paintings, the Chocolate Woman collective pored over dozens and dozens of molas, analyzing them for the stories they tell; their structural principles; their designs, dualities, and abstractions; and the windows they provide into Guna life and belief systems. The team ultimately distilled these into the dramaturgical principles for the production to the extent that Jill Carter calls the show itself "a dense theatrical mola" in four layers, each encoded with its own palette of colors and specific detailing that stitch together a fragmented self ("Chocolate" 171).

Unlike molas, which in their traditional incarnations emphasize geometry over iconicity and patterning over symbolism, Guna pictographs are abstracted iconic records of verb- and action-based healing chants, mnemonic devices that evoke text, movement, and most importantly, cultural memory and recovery. "The pictographs represent the *kwage* [heart]," Mojica explains, "of the vibrational frequency and energetical fields created through the language, chants, rattles, drums, flutes, and dancing during ritual and prayer. Therefore, embodying these . . . create[s] an energetic effect in the body" ("Excerpt" 61–62). The collective analyzed not only the pictographs themselves as they snaked from right to left, then left to right, and so on down the page (originally wooden tablets) but also their use in the council houses by Guna apprentices to learn and eventually embody the chants (Severi 252). As Jill Carter says, "The investigative process for

Chocolate Woman followed Guna protocol in that rehearsals began with tellings and retellings of traditional stories by De León Kantule to the 'apprentice' (Mojica), who began to more deeply explore these and her relationships therewith" ("Chocolate" 174).

Even as the *dramaturgy* of *Chocolate Woman* constituted the show's score as a theatrical mola, the performance text evolved, again through deep improvisations and the pictographic annotation of improvised movement, as an embodied, three-dimensional, and animated pictograph. And astonishingly, when Mojica emerged from the earliest improvisations and began to record them, her notations unconsciously took the form of pictographs, drawn right to left, then left to right down the pages of her notebook (Mojica, "Chocolate" 166). The play's "script" exists in what to date is its most fully realized form as wordless pictographs on nine, nine-foot-by-three-foot scrolls of newsprint, though Mojica and Farnell are exploring the possibilities of three-dimensional digital "publication."

It became apparent in the course of the creation workshops for the production that both molas and pictographs embody four central principles of Guna cosmology that would inform its dramaturgy:

1. *abstraction* (Guna art operates through several levels of abstraction, in part to protect the sacred);
2. *metaphor* (in Guna language and culture everything is protected by being evoked indirectly through figurative imagery);
3. *duality and repetition* (deriving from the Creator Baba/Nana's duality, which means that everything must be repeated. Even Guna households consist of two buildings, one for living, one for sleeping); and
4. *multidimensionality* (everything in Guna cosmology exists simultaneously on four levels above and four below the earth plane; Guna language also operates on four levels, from the quotidian to the sacred).

Through abstraction and metaphor Guna arts participate with other Indigenous semiotic systems that scholar Chadwick Allen, of Chickasaw ancestry, has called "deep patterning" (*Trans-Indigenous* 115),[4] which he finds across the trans-Indigenous world and which he analyzes in the "dynamic symmetry" and "semiotic geometry" of Navajo weaving (117–19).

Structurally it became very clear that Guna art operates very differently from the taken-for-granteds of dominant dramaturgical models, at least in the anglophone world, which tend to rely on tripartite organizational principles—beginning, middle, and end; rising action, climax, and falling action; thesis, antithesis, synthesis—and cherished scene structures in which a third character provides the complication that moves the action forward. These structures embody an understanding of time as linear and progressive and an understanding of narrative as one of conflict, crisis, and resolution. The Guna world, however, is structured around multiples of two, with four and eight being particularly sacred. And of course two-part structures and their multiples embody different understandings of time and story, in which contrast and balance replace conflict, past and future coexist in an eternal present, and stories renew themselves in ongoing re-creations and recitations/re-citations.

This understanding led to a conscious structuring of the show around two actors playing four roles each. Mojica played her fictionalized self (the lost Dule Girl), Olonadili (the youngest of the Daughters from the Stars),Olowaili (the morning star), and Sky Woman. Gloria Miguel played the four Muugana (Grandmothers of Creation), women from Guna cosmology who are encountered by Dule Girl. These elemental Guna women are the fundamental actantial forces in the play world. Their stories guide Dule Girl on her journey, and they were interwoven in rehearsal with "personal," internalized versions (re-creations, re-citations) of them as they played out in Mojica's life. All of this was framed and punctuated by the overarching and conflated journeys of Sky Woman falling to earth, Alice falling down the rabbit hole, and the lost Dule Girl coming home to Guna Yala. *Chocolate Woman*'s is not a familiar structure, but it emerged from our dramaturgical analysis as the way its stories had to be told.

Language is always a fraught issue in Indigenous work. Floyd Favel has written that "when a native language is not spoken, an understanding of the worldview of that nation is purely theoretical" ("Theatre of Orphans" 32). "English," on the other hand, "does not belong on this part of the world [North America]. It does not know the trees and rocks, brooks and gnomes, and all manner of sentient beings" (34). It is "a foreign language which has colonized the soul's expression" (34), or in Australian scholar Sneja Gunew's construction, "a kind of virus inhabiting the body" (61). And yet it is the language of even most Indigenous theater on Turtle Island, and the first language of most Indigenous people there. The *Chocolate Woman* process was, therefore, a particularly complex negotiation. Not only did the production draw on the languages of divergent nondominant cultural forms, resulting in new ways of telling its stories, it also involved the use of two spoken languages in performance—English and Dule Gaya (the language of the Guna people)—and three different spoken languages in the rehearsal hall—English, Spanish, and Dule Gaya, with no one person speaking more than two of them.

English, like most western languages, tends to function representationally in its everyday use and to use as its foundation a grammar of subjects doing things to objects, treating them as value-free raw material for its meanings. English grammar tends, as a structure, both to objectify the world and immediately to relegate it to completeness, to history. The Guna language works very differently. It's driven by verbs and dominated by present participles. Considering this difference, the devising team for *Chocolate Woman* privileged *story* over narrative. The former in Dule Gaya is an embodied oral form taking place largely in the present, peppered with intransitive verbs and centrally concerned with keeping the ancestors alive; the latter, in English, often requires the violence of objectification and the relegation of the past, and the ancestors, to history (see de Certeau, *Writing* 86–102).

Part of the *Chocolate Woman* process was to take text generated in English and put it through a process of double translation into Dule Gaya and back again into a much-altered English, leaving syntactical traces. This means, for example, that the show is replete with present participles—one central monologue begins "I rise rising," and other stories are of "twirl-twirling, whirl-whirling" and the like. It also employs words, phrases, sentences, songs, and sections in Dule Gaya throughout, and this is crucial: as Favel says, "the sound of our native languages on stage is a totally different experience of theatrical sound from English. . . . It is richer, and more musical, and a whole different mood is evoked. Present in the immediate words are the ancestors, who go back generation by generation, right back to the day our language bubbled up from the springs and whispers of the trees and grass" ("Theatre of Orphans" 33–34).

In addition to English, Dule Gaya, and Spanish, *Chocolate Woman*, as we've seen, employs the embodied pictographic language of movement and gesture. The use of Guna pictographic language in performance added another productive complication to the dramaturgical process. Saussurean semiotics is grounded in phonetic western languages and is, in Charles Peirce's terms, overwhelmingly symbolic. Applied to ideographic or pictographic writing, there are significant slippages. Derrida argues that western structuralism, including that of Saussure, is ethnocentric: it privileges phonetic writing as the record of originary speech, the language of civilization, and the basis of metaphysics while disregarding pictographic, ideographic, and other traditions of writing that have nothing to do with phonetics (3). The use of iconic, pictographic languages in *Chocolate Woman* forced the devising team analytically to treat movement, image, and symbol *as* writing, as expressive and performative "literature" imbued with meaning and productive of action.

SIDE SHOW FREAKS AND CIRCUS INJUNS

Although *Chocolate Woman* was intercultural in the sense that it was a devised piece involving collaborators from various First and other Nations, and insofar as its audience was intercultural, it nevertheless involved developing a show in which the cultural texts on which the dramaturgy was based emerged from the same Indigenous culture as that of its primary creator and as the stories that it told. *Side Show Freaks and Circus Injuns*, which remains under development, is more complex. Its stories emerge from a broader range of cultures and none of them are traditional "ur texts," as in *Chocolate Woman*. Its dramaturgical models, moreover, cross several ancient and traditional cultures and have no immediately obvious connections with the manifest content of the show. Indeed, while the molas and pictographs that formed the dramaturgical core of *Chocolate Woman* reinforced and supported the show's action, in *Side Show Freaks* the show's form works to contain, overcome, and outlast (or endure) the sideshow displays that are its content. The dramaturgical models for *Side Show Freaks*, however, *are* more immediately performative than *Chocolate Woman*'s, and more literally foundational. Molas, finally, are well known and have become familiar from gallery exhibitions, tourist sales, and a thriving collectors' market; the dramaturgical models for *Side Show Freaks* are another matter.

In summer 2012 I was part of a panel at the annual conference of the Association for Theatre in Higher Education in which we were asked to discuss "foundational documents" for theater in America. The conference was in Washington, DC, a city famous for its monumental architecture—the neoclassical Capitol, the White House, the Jefferson Memorial, and the US Supreme Court Building—all, in their domes, columns, and domination of the landscape, evoking the European so-called "enlightenment, a moment in history that wasn't kind to the world's Indigenous population.[5] Just down the Potomac but beyond the awareness of most politicos and tourists alike, there are much older kinds of monumental architecture, with a far different relationship to the land. These, and the thousands of other ancient Indigenous mounds and earthworks that populate Turtle Island, were what I chose to discuss as *literally* foundational for American performance. Performances were held on them, they themselves constituted performances, and they remain the dramaturgical basis for *Side Show Freaks and Circus Injuns*.

A lengthy discussion followed our panel; none of it acknowledged the mounds. This isn't surprising. Few in the academy, myself included until recently, know what *kinds* of questions to ask these monumental but also invisible earthworks, which sit on the landscape as they did in the air after my presentation, apparently inscrutable. What follows in the remainder of this chapter chronicles my experience as a non-Native dramaturge working with Indigenous artists trying to listen to and honor the wisdom of the mounds.

My choice of the mounds as foundational documents began with a premise: that foundational to performance on Turtle Island are the foundational performances of the first *peoples* of Turtle Island, performances too often relegated to "prehistory" and cataloged by archaeologists, anthropologists, and other researchers whose relationship to the land is that of the settler/invader. Even much contemporary Indigenous theater fails to take into account formative cultural texts native to this place, this land, this ecosphere. I offered my chosen documents as a corrective to what seems to be a widespread neglect: of the earthworks—platform, conical, pyramid, ridgetop, geometric, burial, and effigy mounds—that date back millennia and reach across much of the continent. The building of these mounds was performative, and they served as the sites of performance for those who built them.

There are mounds from Brazil to northern Manitoba, but the major extant sites stretch north from the Lower Mississippi Valley, across Ohio, and into Ontario, including Toronto. At their peak, tens of thousands of mounds dotted Indigenous North America, beginning as early as 4000 BCE, and they functioned not to dominate the land but as a means of living in harmony with it. As Choctaw artist and scholar LeAnne Howe says, "The very name Turtle Island connotes a vast effigy mound rising out of the oceans" (81). And the mounds have a precise relationship not only to the surface of the natural world but also to dimensions above and below it. As Chadwick Allen observes, "Earthworks parallel natural embankments, follow the waterways of rivers and creeks, mirror the regular seasons of the sun and moon, the patterned coordinates of stars in transit. They occupy symbolic positions, too, aligning within North American systems of representation, within complexes of ceremony and ritual, with economies of power and exchange"

("Serpentine" 815–16). At the time of their construction, many mounds were legible only from a then-impossible height, either in their totality as effigies of birds, animals, or reptiles or in their relations to one another: precise geometric mounds sixty miles apart near Newark, Ohio, were designed to "nest" inside one another and were linked by straight two-hundred-foot-wide "star roads" aligned at certain times of the year with the Milky Way.[6] They were not, it seems, intended for human viewing.

The building of the mounds, formed of interlaced layers of different types, colors, and textures of soil from different locations, required a precise knowledge of physics, mathematics, engineering, astronomy, and architecture. As non-Native archaeo-astronomer Anthony Avilo suggests, these mounds constitute "a marvellous way of connecting . . . the ecological environment, with the heavens. . . . We modern astronomers tend to cut off the heavens from the rest of the world—the mountains, the water, the plants, the animals—to which . . . most ancient cultures would have forged a connection" (qtd. in *Earth Works*). Indeed, as Tewa ethnobotanist Gregory Cajete argues, "The historic efforts of Native cultures to resonate with the heavens *also* represent their attempts to live up to an ideal ecological relationship with the *Earth*" (256).

The mounds performed many different functions, marking territorial boundaries, creating focal points for exchange, and serving as sites for spiritual practice. Some of the platform mounds, such as the massive, 13.8-acre terraced Monks Mound at Cahokia in Illinois, may have been constructed over centuries and served as foundations for structures, games, and ceremonies. Others, such as the Great Serpent Mound in Ohio, the largest serpent effigy in the world at 1,370 feet, include figural representations and multiple astrological alignments and appear to have been built to maintain cosmic balance among the heavens, earth, and underworld (see C. Allen, "Serpentine" 817–19). As Allen argues, the mounds

> represent achievements in science and aesthetics on a monumental scale. They integrate the precise observation of natural phenomena with geometry and other abstract forms of knowledge, as well as with practical skills in mathematics, architectural design, engineering, and construction. Many earthworks were sculptured to mirror perceived patterns in the sky, both in the bodies of individual works and in the arrangements of multiple works into complex sites and cities; moreover, particular works were often aligned with specific celestial events, such as an equinox or solstice sunrise or sunset point on the horizon. (809)

Many of the once thousands of mounds have been looted or destroyed, and many are hiding in plain sight, often unknown to those who live closest to them. But there are mounds that have been largely preserved and subjected to historical, anthropological, astronomical, and archaeological interpretation and analysis by Native and non-Native scholars. Among the most prominent extant mounds are the astonishing and mysterious constructions at Chaco Canyon, New Mexico; Monks Mound at Cahokia; and various serpent mounds, most prominently the Great Serpent Mound at Peebles, Ohio. All are located near water, aligned with significant solar or lunar events, and closely oriented to the natural lay of the land.

Chadwick Allen, who eventually joined the *Side Show Freaks* creative team as associate dramaturge, argues that the mounds constitute "a form of Indigenous writing that employs 'geometric regularity' and 'geometrical harmony' in order to record natural, human, and cosmic relationships within durable structures" ("Serpentine" 812). He uses as an example the Great Serpent Mound:

> The body of the extant Serpent Mound runs roughly a quarter of a mile in length and is mounded to a height of about three feet. It begins at its southern end with its tail in a triple-coiled spiral, undulates along the plateau above the Brush Creek Valley in seven distinct body convolutions, and then straightens out toward its broad, horned head. The Serpent's mouth hinges wide open, poised to swallow a large, oval-shaped disk. (817)

Allen demonstrates that the mound has eight lunar and solar astrological alignments and that it embodies the philosophical and spiritual concept of cosmic balance (818). According to anthropologist William F. Romain, "The Mound Builders celebrated world renewal ceremonies at the site, in order to help strengthen the powers of the upperworld in the continuing struggle against the forces of the underworld. . . . In this way," Romain concludes, "the Serpent Mound builders would have been able to exercise some control over the forces that ruled their universe and affected their lives" (253, qtd. in Allen, "Serpentine" 817–18). Romain's speculation is strengthened by Cajete's characterization of the motivations behind Indigenous astronomy and, more broadly, behind attempts by Indigenous peoples "to align themselves and their societies with what they perceived was the cosmic order" (217). Cajete argues that "'Native astronomers were driven not only by their own awe and curiosity, but were also serving the innermost needs of their societies'—to resonate with the cosmos and to be the power brokers of their worlds" (217–18, qtd. in Allen, "Serpentine" 818).

For Allen the mounds constitute *literature*, "Indigenous writing systems" ("Serpentine" 829n2). In a world in which Native cultures are often considered to be *pre*literate, in spite of winter counts, codices, bark scrolls, petroglyphs, pictographs, wampum, and other forms of writing, this is important. But one of the key co-creators of *Side Show Freaks*, LeAnne Howe, argues that the mounds also constitute *performances*, with a clear relationship to the rhythms of the natural world from which they emerge. She provides the example of the Great Bird Mound (Mound A) at the extensive Poverty Point site in Louisiana, an ancient center for trans-Indigenous trade. At *seven stories high* the Bird Mound is the largest surviving Archaic period earthwork, second only to the Mississippian-era Monks Mound, yet it was created in only three short months. The builders moved 238,000 cubic meters of soil in fifty-pound baskets in just ninety days, Howe argues, as a performance of the creation story of the red-tailed hawk, whose own gestation period from conception to first flight is also ninety days. Both the conception of the hawks and the building of the mound began at the vernal equinox; the completion of the mound coincided, three months later, at summer solstice, with the fledgling hawk's first flight. Both equinox and solstice, moreover, would subsequently have been celebrated at the mound site (Howe 82–83).

But these mounds didn't only constitute ancient performances. Mounds are now being restored and a new one built at the American Indian Cultural Center in Oklahoma City in a project designed explicitly to participate in a centuries-long tradition by "expanding the vocabulary of earthworks as an iconic landscape" (Wasserman 2). Indeed, the mounds *continue* to perform their peoples across time, and this mound performance manifests itself in contemporary Native poetry, as in Alison Hedge Coke's *Blood Run*; in fiction, as in LeAnne Howe's novel *Shell Shaker* and Phillip Carroll Morgan's *Anompolichi: The Wordmaster*; in the visual arts, as in the paintings of America Meredith (Cherokee) and the mixed-media work of Alyssa Hinton (Tuscarora); and in theater, as in *Side Show Freaks and Circus Injuns*. *Side Show Freaks* involves Choctaw LeAnne Howe and Guna and Rappahannock Monique Mojica as writer-performers, six designers from various Indigenous Nations in the United States and Canada, and myself and Chadwick Allen as dramaturges. Directors working on the project have included Plains Cree Michael Greyeyes, Anishinaabe Jill Carter, and exiled Cuban American Jorge Luis Morejon, living in Trinidad. In the rest of this chapter

I will discuss this show's manifest content (the side shows), its form (the mounds), and the process of its creation (mound building).

Side Show Freaks listens to and attempts to embody the mounds and uses their architectures and construction processes as its dramaturgical model in an attempt to reconnect and return Indigenous memories to the present. It addresses in its content a history of the exploitation and display of Indigenous peoples, who, like the mounds, have been at once invisible and hypervisible, overlooked and yet also subjected to the scientific, scopophilic, or pornographic gaze. The show centers on the Saint Louis World's Fair of 1904. Mojica and Howe will play two "freaks" on display there. The first, Invisible Woman, or Izzie, is a Rappahannok potter, rootworker, and midwife who has escaped from the Hiawatha Asylum for Insane Indians in Canton, South Dakota, where between 1902 and 1934 recalcitrant Natives were judged to be insane, incarcerated, and put on weekly display for townsfolk. At once invisible and hypervisible (on display), Izzie embodies the sideshow equivalent of the simultaneous invisibility and hypervisibility of the mounds and of contemporary Indigenous peoples. The second "freak" is Panther Woman (Underwater Panther), a powerful figure common to many Indigenous cultures over thousands of years.

> **Panther Woman** (as a young girl): Panther That Flies, I'm soaring through the underworld, the stars grow brighter and brighter, until I track *issa Fickick*, the Deer Star, through a net of veins, breathing in *okshamali*, the blue-green waters of life, swimming, pawing my way back home. (Howe and Mojica)[7]

In the show, Invisible Woman and Panther Girl are survivors of the famous train wreck on the way to the World's Fair in St. Louis, where they met crawling out of the wreckage. They share the sideshow stage with, among other ethnic and disability "freaks," the mechanical talking head of the great Apache leader Geronimo (reportedly removed from his body, stolen, and put on display at Yale University's Skull and Bones Club by George H. W. Bush's father and George W.'s grandfather, Prescott Bush—also a character in the show).

> **Geronimo's Head**: Coming down the pike . . . Fancy Pants. Every Sunday they send for me . . . Buffalo Bill's Wild West and Congress of Rough Riders. Show bow and arrow, use my rope in the contest—me and an Indian cowboy—Will Rogers.

> Make believe, always fallin' off their horses. One gun shot—10 Indians fall. They get more money they fall. (Howe and Mojica)

This is a sample of some of the show's manifest content. But it employs the environmental and astronomical optics of the mounds to construct, as its foundation, a contemporary Indigenous dramaturgy that both returns the scopophilic gaze and reassesses the peoples' relationship with the universe. Preliminary sketches of the set by Choctaw designer Marcus Amerman nest the sideshow within the frame of a mound, so that the mound is hidden from immediate visibility but the show is nevertheless contained by it. Props and costumes will be in contemporary "steampunk" style (or what the creative team is calling "steam injun punk"), as inspired by misplaced nostalgia for the industrialized, steam-powered nineteenth- and early twentieth-centuries, the heyday of sideshows, medicine shows, and ethnographic displays, when men were men, women were either domesticated or eroticized, and, proverbially, the only good Indian was a dead Indian. But the dramaturgical form of the show derives from a deeper temporality.

Side Show Freaks is under development.[8] From June to October 2011 members of the team researched and visited all the major mound sites and many lesser ones, engaging, as for *Chocolate Woman*, in embodied research, making kinesthetic connections with the mounds and the sacred sites that they inhabit. And again we brought that research to a creation workshop in June 2012 where the performers engaged in "deep improvisation" followed by analysis, rewriting, and refining, crafting the material into a performance score, but to different effect from that of *Chocolate Woman*. As Mojica describes it,

> I practice an Indigenous artistic research methodology that speaks to the embodiment of place. The land *is* our archive and our embodied relationship to the land defines Indigenous identities, history, science, cosmology, literature—and performance. . . . *Side Show Freaks* . . . regenerates my creative source by placing me on the life-giving land in an embodied research process that requires me to walk on, touch, feel, smell, and absorb the stories, forms, and structures of effigy mounds and earthworks to connect to the ancestors who built them and to the peoples who still inhabit the region. Simultaneous to this sacred work, I am challenged to "talk back" to colonial erasure, to peel away that veil, to refocus my lens. Once we were not victims. (Mojica, "Artist Statement")

The first week of the workshop involved distilling our research into basic principles, knowing that we had to invent a process analogous to that of the Mound Builders. While in the *Chocolate Woman* process it took us some time to realize that we were in fact constructing a theatrical mola, this time around we knew from the outset that, in creating this play, we were, in effect, building a theatrical mound. This involved:

1. layering and texturing of materials and "ribboning" ourselves as a creation group;
2. aligning ourselves and our work according to the Mississippian-era cosmological model, "a three-level configuration composed of the Above World or Overworld (i.e. the sky), the Middle World, and the Beneath World or Underworld," with a central axis connecting these levels in the form of "a center pole or sacred tree" (Reilly 127);
3. thinking durationally: considering the relationship between our development time, the duration of the performance, and that of its afterlife;
4. building a *ceremony* of moundings (recalling Shawn Wilson's research *as* ceremony); and
5. maintaining processual openness in order to allow the mounds, in a very real sense, to perform *us*.

Once in studio we began by doing exercises that explored duration ("deep time") and ribboning: ribboning bodies, sound, and imagery even as the Mound Builders ribboned colors, textures, and densities of earth. In the June 2012 creation workshop director Michael Greyeyes introduced an exercise in duration, the actors improvising to his instructions: beginning with familiar actorly practices of breathing and connecting to the floor, he gradually talked Mojica and Howe through the exercise—"Your duration is of generations. Your duration is measured in eons. . . . Even if your movement is sudden, like an earthquake," he intoned, "one million years of shifting produced it. Your breath is the wind that shaped the landscape. You are earth and ground and rocks—but that doesn't mean that you move glacially. You always move gently, and it is formed by breath, the way the wind changes the dunes from night to night. The landscape rolls; you may roll. You are a continent, and you move because your breath moves." This last became a refrain. "You move because your breath moves. As you move, parts of you move internally. Sediment shifts, even if there may be no external movement visible. Your breath is the duration of an epoch. . . . Then you gently shift back into where you entered this. . . . You breathe, you shift. Your breath will bring you home, like a glacier that melts, like a rock that weathers, you find a beginning place. Your movement is the language of duration."

As the actors emerged from the exercise, we discussed its applications and the questions that it raised: how is duration expressed in movement? how does it affect language? what words speak duration? what words take an eon to say? what is the duration of this space, this place? what is the *language* of duration? We talked about the rhythms of the show as intercutting two different durationalities, those of the mounds (the sacred) and those of the sideshows (the profane), and this led us to an awareness of the sideshow chronotope as one that is *not* alive, does *not* breathe, and has no organic relationship to place. It is the chronotope of pornography.

A second time-travel exercise ensued, one designed to make the bodies of the performers experience and endure "mound time," getting to know, too, what we came to call "the stealth nature of mounds"—their capacity, over eons, subtly to commune with contemporary consciousness. Greyeyes asked the performers to lie on the ground next to a chair and to take a full twenty minutes to move continuously and purposefully—"because the mounds are purposeful"—into a seating position on the chair. The exercise was extremely difficult, "making the body endure," as Greyeyes said, "the interminable time function: what happens to the body in mound time as it moves."

When we moved into creation mode we began by reading an excerpt from an account Mojica had published about our research travels:

> *Across the thirteen moons on Turtle's back, across multiples of centuries the Mother Mounds are calling to their children: "Come home. . . ." They call, sing, coo, echo, hum. They infiltrate our sleeping and our waking dreams with whispers of thoughts they make as if our very own: "Come home . . . it's time. Come home to rest your hearts in the layered folds of Mother's skirts." They send out a call.*
>
> *We who think these thoughts as if they were our very own search for the source of the song, the Mother voice, and then gently lay down each boney vertebra of our spines one by one on the ancient, textured soil. Then, vibrating, we align our frequencies to the constellations and join a dialogue begun long ago, mirrored from the Upper World onto nodes and nerve centres on Turtle's back, creating the World Between through earthworks imagined,*

> *crafted, and mounded, basket by fifty-pound basket, by minds, hands, thighs, and muscled backs, through Earth itself.*
>
> *We are in conversation.*
>
> (Mojica, "In Plain Sight" 218, italicized in original)

The improvised monologue that emerged from a process that had begun with Mojica lying on her belly on the mounds—communing with them, embodying them—and proceeded through Greyeyes's exercises in deep time was highly charged. Mojica's improvisation moved from the Great Serpent Mound to the magnificent effigy mounds at Effigy Mounds National Monument in McGregor, Iowa, overlooking the Mississippi River (Little Bear Mound, Great Bear Mound, Fire Point, and Eagle Rock); it moved from outside the mounds, visiting, to inside, embodying the mounds themselves, which seemed to speak *through* her, rather than the other way around. What follows is an edited excerpt from a transcription of this first rough improvisation:

> We weep, belly down. Sobs. Sobs, heart on the serpent, belly on the snake, we feel it, undulate, beneath our bellies, bringing us its song. Thank you. Thank you, for leaving this for us to see, when all is almost gone, your bones pulverized to dust. . . . We reconstitute our broken bodies from your bones. . . . Buzzard watches. Shadow bird. Song begins. Serpent writhes . . . : three coils of its tail, seven undulations and release. Then circle. The Great Serpent reaching towards water. Buzzard watches. We weep, we weep belly down on serpent's body, riding, undulating beneath our bodies. Heart to serpent. Reaching toward water we weep. Reconstitute our bodies from the pulverized bones of our ancestors who left this for us to see when all was almost gone. . . . Thank you for leaving this place for us. . . . The song begins, and we who think these thoughts as if they were our very own, answer the call.
>
> It's time. It's time, come home and rest yourself in the folds of mother's skirts. There's something I must tell you, there's something you need to know. Once there was conversation, come closer, come closer, I almost have you. Here. Here, my most prized possession, needles made from bird bone tucked under my arm, come, come, come . . . *Pause.*
>
> Mounds of light and shadow. Breathing, breathing, breathing. Built basket by 50 pound basket. Breathing. (Mojica, "Outside/Inside").

If the creation *process* for *Side Show Freaks* is based on mound *building*, it stands to reason that the dramaturgical *structure* of the show that results will be that of a mound. The four structural principles that our collective field research has identified as being characteristic of ancient mounds and earthworks are: *duration, alignment, convergence,* and *integration*. These principles will constitute the bones of the show-as-mound that we're building. Like *Chocolate Woman*'s, they are very different from dominant dramaturgical models that have privileged three-part structures supporting dramatic action based on conflict and a myth of linear, progressive time. But duration, alignment, convergence, and integration constitute a culturally specific deep structure that is also different from that of *Chocolate Woman* and supports a very different dramatic action than one based on the Guna principles of abstraction, metaphor, duality/repetition, and multidimensionality. These new principles model a dramaturgy that embodies the patience of the mounds, which outlasts the frenetic, empty, and exhibitionist thrills of the sideshow, of which audiences will tire quickly, and reflects a profound effort to operate at a deep level in a negotiated harmony with the ecosphere, with the universe. The mounds, as Mojica argues, "were built with deliberate creative intent. . . . They have been lovingly mounded to carve out ceremonial spaces conscious of their theatrical impact in order to prepare the human body to be aligned in body, mind, spirit, and heart with the *cosmos*" ("In Plain Sight" 221). We build with the same intent.

FIVE | to be dub, female, and black

toward a womban-centred Afro-Caribbean diasporic performance aesthetic

African Canadian theater is distinct from Black theatre as it has developed in the United States, the U.K., and elsewhere in the African diaspora, in part because of a "nativist" or nationalist strain that locates itself largely in Nova Scotia and in part because of the influence of a broadly diasporic sensibility introduced by a more recent urban immigrant community.[1] In Toronto, a large part of the distinctiveness of African Canadian theater has to do with the contributions of immigrant women from the Caribbean, many of them queer-identified, including centrally the early work of Vera Cudjoe and the subsequent contributions of Rhoma Spencer and the dub-based work of ahdri zhina mandiela and d'bi.young anitafrika that I wish to explore here. Building on Cudjoe's foundations, each of Spencer, mandiela, and young anitafrika has consciously challenged received Canadian and Caribbean theatrical and performance forms, as well as heterosexist and masculinist cultural nationalisms and colonial modernities, by developing woman-centered Afro-Caribbean diasporic performance aesthetics rooted in island traditions but grounded in Canadian realities. What these women have done is to constitute Toronto, already one of the most culturally diverse cities in the world, as heterotopic, transformative space within which they can work at the intersection of nations, sexualities, and performance forms. They have constituted the city, that is, as a space that enables them at once to womanize and queer "the revolushun," building on Caribbean performance practices such as carnival, 'mas (masquerade), calypso, pantomime, satirical musical reviews, agitprop, and crucially, dub to create expansive new performance forms and theatrical hybridities in a diasporic space that is reimagined as not merely (and negatively) in-between but as productively self-standing and independently generative.

Although Black theater in Canada has a history dating back to at least 1849 (see Breon, "Black"; Breon, "Growth"; Saddlemyer 14; Sears, Introduction iv), the first professional theaters were an outgrowth of a wave of immigration from the West Indies that began in the 1960s. In Toronto, the first of these companies, Black Theatre Canada (BTC), was founded by a Trinidadian immigrant woman, Vera Cudjoe, in 1973.[2] BTC was unapologetically Caribbean from the outset, and although it staged such work as Lorraine Hansberry's iconic African American play *A Raisin in the Sun* in 1978, under Cudjoe it was also dedicated to the early development of an Afro-Caribbean Canadian performance aesthetic. This commitment manifested itself in the production of plays by Caribbean writers such as Trevor Rhone, Roderick Walcott, Daniel Caudieron, and Mustapha Matura and in the bringing to Toronto of major Caribbean performers such as Paul Keens Douglas and, crucially, Louise ("Miss Lou") Bennett. In these ways BTC introduced and exposed the community to Afro-Caribbean performance forms and languages that were to have a powerful influence on new work developed by the company itself and by many others in subsequent years, including Spencer, mandiela, and young anitafrika. "Miss Lou," in particular, was crucial, in that her published and performed poetry legitimized the popular "nation language" of Jamaica on which dub poetry came to be based—the rich African-influenced creolized language spoken by the descendants of slaves, laborers, and servants of the colonizer that had hitherto been denigrated as substandard English. Bennett lived for a number of years in Toronto, and her work was crucial to the development of the city's Caribbean community and its art forms. BTC also made direct contributions to the cultivation of an Afro-Caribbean diasporic dramaturgy by developing such things as playwright Amah Harris's school-touring *Anansi Tales* beginning in 1977, structured by the stories and rhythms of African folk tales (Gingell, "jumping" 11n12), and by producing the award-winning "Caribbean" *Midsummer Night's Dream*, directed by Azra Francis in 1983 and structured by the rhythms of carnival, 'mas, and calypso.[3]

BTC folded in 1988, but over its fifteen years it had helped to develop a generation of Black theater artists, predominantly of Caribbean origin, who would lead the way in subsequent years. BTC alumni included Amah Harris, whose Theatre in the Rough focused much of its efforts on training Black youth through its hugely influential Fresh Arts program, alumni of which in turn include d'bi.young anitafrika. Neither BTC nor Theatre in the Rough were revolutionary in their politics, or even in their aesthetic experimentation, but both paved the way, though exposure to African and Caribbean storytelling and performance forms, through mentorships and training, and through the validation of Caribbean cultural texts for the more radical experimentation that was undertaken by their alumni and successors over subsequent decades.

B CURRENT, THEATRE ARCHIPELAGO, AHDRI ZHINA MANDIELA, AND RHOMA SPENCER

Toronto is now home to four major continuing Black theater companies,[4] the earliest of which to emerge, b current, being the most direct descendent of BTC. b current was founded in 1991 by Jamaican-born BTC alumna ahdri zhina mandiela to nurture exploration, engage community, and develop talent that reflects the aesthetics, language, and speech of the Black diaspora. mandiela says that BTC was "how I got hooked on the scene here" (Knowles, "Having"), and in many ways she inherited the mantle of Vera Cudjoe both in terms of her mentoring role, particularly for women, and her (more radical) exploration of Caribbean performance forms. In 1998 her company mounted its first raiZ'n the sun ensemble training program of workshops and classes for young career-oriented artists, and in 2001–2 it launched its annual rock.paper.sistahs festival because, according to mandiela in an interview with Toronto's gay and lesbian weekly, *xtra*, "I needed a forum within the company where we could do some unconventional presentation of work, particularly by sisters. . . . Shorts, experimentations, out-on-a-wire stylistic wrangling, where it wasn't just productions as usual" (qtd. in Alland). Broadly diasporic in mandate, the company nevertheless began with a Caribbean, Jamaican-based form, dub poetry, and with a landmark production of mandiela's own *dark diaspora . . . in* dub!, of which more below. It also launched the Canadian careers of many key Afro-Caribbean artists, most notably d'bi.young anitafrika—then debbie young—Rhoma Spencer, and mandiela's daughter Jajube Mandiela, who together with Ngozi Paul assumed the artistic directorship of b current in 2013.

The most recently formed African Canadian company now operating in Toronto, Theatre Archipelago, grew directly out of the 2004 edition of rock.paper.sistahs. In 2005 Trinidad-born Rhoma Spencer turned two one-woman one-acts mounted there into the first production of her own company, Theatre Archipelago: Jamaican Canadian Honor Ford-Smith's *Just Jazz* (an adaptation of Dominican writer Jean Rhys's *Let Them Call It Jazz*) and Spencer's own *Mad Miss* (an adaptation of Jamaican-born Canadian Olive Senior's *You Think I'm Mad, Miss?*). Theatre Archipelago, named of course for the Caribbean archipelago, is dedicated to serving "as a catalyst for propagating Caribbean theatre in the diaspora" and staging plays "by Canadian and Caribbean playwrights at home and abroad" (Theatre Archipelago).[5] Its productions, frequently coproduced with b current, have been dominated by plays by and/or about women.

Like mandiela, Spencer is interested in the discovery and development of a uniquely Afro-Caribbean diasporic aesthetic. For Spencer—and I believe this is crucial for each of the women I am discussing—Caribbean (as opposed to island-specific) culture exists only in diaspora (see Knowles, "Having") and a Caribbean aesthetic is at once fundamentally African and globally hybrid—what Trinidadian playwright Tony Hall calls "creolization, hybridity, betweenity and assimilation" (qtd. in Citron, "When"). But this diasporic space is enabling for Spencer in part because it is more possible for her, as a woman, to direct in Toronto—" back in the Caribbean, theatre seemed to be a man's space" (qtd. in Knowles, "Having")[6]—and because Toronto is also broadly constituted, as one key component of its ecology, as queer. In an interview in *Xtra* in March 2011, Spencer explains that part of the draw of Toronto for her was that "I was aware of the black lesbian movement taking place in the city, and I felt like I wanted to be part of it. . . . When you come from a space where you have to hide who you are, coming to Toronto is an awakening" (Dupuis). Spencer, then, deeply critical of Canadian multiculturalism,[7] is nevertheless consciously using Toronto as a heterotopic, enablingly queer and female space for the development "from below" of transformative pan-Caribbean diasporic performance forms, and her work extends that of BTC in its explorations of carnival, 'mas, and calypso. Indeed, the company has participated prominently in the Scotiabank Caribbean carnival (formerly Caribana) since 2011, presenting original "Jouvay" (*jour ouvert*, or opening, of the first day of carnival) 'mas characters and costumes in the carnival parade for the first time in its forty-four year history (see Merringer) and reintroducing the political critique inherent in carnival but suppressed in the early years of the festival.

Archipelago's mainstage productions have been equally political and have equally drawn upon and developed Caribbean forms in a Canadian setting. On some occasions this has meant producing Caribbean plays such as Trinidadian Tony Hall's *Twilight Café* in 2007 or the Groundwork Collective production of Jamaica's *Fallen Angel and the Devil Concubine* in 2006,[8] the latter brilliantly transported by its director, mandiela, to Toronto's diverse Parkdale neighborhood and making provocative use of cross-casting. But Archipelago has also developed new work by Caribbean Canadians, such as Haitian Canadian Edwige Jean-Pierre's *Our Lady of Spills* in 2009, the story of an elderly white woman and her Black caregiver. All of the company's work is characterized by a "poor-theatre" aesthetic, a presentational sensibility, exuberant performances, and a richness of language that are typical of Caribbean theater, and all speak in complex ways about the politics of class, gender, and race, with a clear emphasis on women.

The company's evolving aesthetic may be seen to have crystalized in the 2011 North American premiere production of Monserrat-born Edgar Nkosi White's *I Marcus Garvey*, directed by Spencer and coproduced with b current, and in the 2012 world premiere of Nicole Brooks's *Obeah Opera*, again coproduced with b current and directed by mandiela.[9] In telling the politically charged biography of the great Jamaican Black nationalist and pan-Africanist leader in *I Marcus Garvey*, Spencer used a mélange of mostly presentational styles, using extensive doubling, choral speech and movement, direct address, comic exaggeration, a stripped-down set that thrust the action forward to the audience, and a generally carnivalesque atmosphere that was greatly assisted by the presence of an on-stage five-piece band that occasionally joined in the action, feeding the call-and-response, and swelling the crowd scenes.

In *Obeah Opera* mandiela orchestrated the fifteen-woman cast singing Brooks's a cappella mélange of Black musical styles to tell the story of the Salem witch trials from the point of view of the Barbadian-born slave woman Tituba. mandiela used designer Julia Tribe's simple ramped set and modified traverse stage to coordinate rhythmic movement with solo and choric song in a powerfully affecting affirmation of Afro-Caribbean life and spiritual practice that, as blogger Lilia Patias says, "gives a hint of possibilities of female solidarity and freedom to come. . . . It zooms in on the moment when fear stops and turns to anger—when victimhood transforms itself into something that makes political action possible." In an interview first done for *Macomère* (a journal devoted to scholarly studies and creative works by and about Caribbean women in the region and the diaspora), mandiela identifies "having a whole lot of show going on" as "part of our Caribbean aesthetic" (Knowles, "Having"), and the Theatre Archipelago/b current productions of *I Marcus Garvey* and *Obeah Opera* exemplified the style and adapted it for Canadian sensibilities.

AHDRI ZHINA MANDIELA AND DUB THEATRE

It is Spencer's mentor at b current, ahdri zhina mandiela herself, who has been responsible for the invention and naming of the first unique and identifiable Afro-Caribbean diasporic performance form in Canadian theater. With her 1991 show *dark diaspora . . . in* dub!, subtitled "a dub theatre piece," mandiela not only launched b current but forged a new form, not out of carnival, 'mas, or calypso but out of her own political and poetic practice as a dub poet.[10] Dub poetry emerged in the 1970s and 1980s in Jamaica out of the practice of MCs, or "toasters," talking over the "dub," or instrumental side of reggae recordings, where the songs were stripped to their bare, rhythmic essentials and used as dance tracks. The rhythm-driven, embodied, and performance-based poetic form that emerged from this was deeply influenced by the revolutionary and celebratory Black politics, practice, and popularity of Bob Marley and Louise ("Miss Lou") Bennett,[11] their bringing into respectability of Jamaican, or "nation language," and Marley's Rastafarianism.[12] As dub developed and spread globally in the 1980s, the three international centers where it most flourished were Kingston, Jamaica; London, England; and notably, Toronto (see L. Allen 16), where, partly because of the developing feminist scene in the city, many of the form's leading practitioners have been women. And many of these women—including Lillian Allen, Afua Cooper, Motion (Wendy Braithwaite), Dee (Deanne Smith), amuna baraka-clarke, and d'bi.young anitafrika (see Knopf)—have either womanized or queered the dub form itself, in reaction to its mainly masculinist roots. Included prominently among these artists is ahdri zhina mandiela, whose early, 1985 volume *Speshul Rekwes* includes distinctly womanist poems such as "young girls on the street" (12–16), "ooman gittup" (38), and especially "black ooman" (41–41). Although many since the 1980s have rejected the term *dub poetry*, preferring the more expansive terms *performance poetry* or *spoken word*,[13] others feel that these later rubrics for an already expansive form strip dub of its politics; its roots in class, race, resistance, and empowerment;[14] its distinctly Caribbean lineage; and its ties to the nation languages of the archipelago. As Carolyn Cooper argues, "When 'dub' poetry is dubbed 'performance' poetry it goes genteelly up market" (81).

And it is interesting that from the beginning, partly because of the overwhelming influence of Louise Bennett, and evident in the work of early practitioners such as Faybienne Miranda, Lillian Allen (whose 1993 collection of poems was called *Women Do This Every Day*), and Jean Binta Breeze, dub has been amenable to women who brought to it "new agendas and new voices, different sounds and riddims" (A. Cooper, "Utterances" 2). Dub, then, has succeeded in avoiding or derailing some of the masculinist—indeed misogynist—aura of much rap and hip-hop. mandiela herself, noting the expansion of meaning of *dub poet* beyond its original reggae "base" and its increasing use of standard or Black American English, prefers to call herself a "dub aatist": "for me, anything that works against the concept of nation language is a negative" (qtd. in Gingell, "jumping" 10, 7). A large part of the importance of dub poetry for mandiela is that it "bridges traditional and contemporary experience," it "exists as both old and new" and therefore has the potential to become part of what she calls "classical black orality" (qtd. in A. Lee 7), while also advancing the politics and poetics of dub into a more broadly diverse and inclusive future.

In adapting dub for the stage, mandiela was influenced by the distinctly womanist African American playwright and poet ntozake shange's legendary "choreopoem" *for coloured girls who have considered suicide / when the rainbow is enuf* and by African traditions of call-and-response (already incorporated into much dub poetry).[15] *dark diaspora* consists, as script, of a series of dub poems that explore "the present day psyche of the black diaspora," spanning "some 30 years of (social/political/economic) events and emotion influencing the psychological make-up of the black psyche as evidenced in a black woman's journey in 1990's Canada" (mandiela, "about" vii). "In creating 'dark diaspora . . . in *dub*,'" mandiela writes, "the aim was to expand the literary tradition of dub poetry—by producing an integrated stage script composed entirely from dub poems—as well as to present a totally new stage experience: *dub theatre*" (mandiela, "evolution" x). "By working with a dub aesthetic," as Loretta Collins argues, mandiela

> devises a poetic language and form fluid enough to allow her to sift through and mix the cultural fragments, slogans, world-events, icons, public figures, and musical expressions that unify African people. . . . Fusing, weaving, and fragmenting pieces of language taken from distinct struggles and artistic movements from different regions in the African continent, England, the Caribbean, the United States, and Canada, mandiela composes a dramatic sequence of poems that easily code switches between discourses, nation languages, and musical rhythms. The dubbing techniques of the theatrical work provide the ideal means of cutting and mixing in a compressed and dynamic form the diverse "cultural remnants" and varied psychological stages that the work brings to the surface. (45).

The resulting show, located in a generative diasporic space, Collins argues, "generate[s] a vertical velocity with the fluidity of a deejay's wizardry at the sound system controls" (46).[16] And as Rinaldo Walcott asserts, that velocity, fluidity, and movement are evocative of forced and other migrations undergone by Black people globally since the middle passage. As such, they are fundamental "characteristics of Black diasporic consciousness" and form "the bases of a diasporic aesthetics" ("Dramatic" 100). Walcott's insight is important and has implications beyond *dark diaspora* itself. What the play exemplifies are the ways in which traveling between mixed and multiple forms, styles, and sign systems captures and asserts resistant creative control over the often involuntary migration experiences that have characterized Black diasporic life—including the life of mandiela herself and the lives of Vera Cudjoe, Rhoma Spencer, and d'bi.young anitafrika.

But in bringing dub to the stage through women's bodies, the play also womanized a Caribbean form that, grounded in competition and virtuosic display, had been overwhelmingly masculinist. The play is also and crucially, as mandiela says (evoking lesbian womanist Audre Lorde's term "biomythography"[17]), "*auto*mythobiographical" (mandiela, "evolution" x, emphasis added). Biomythography, together with its variants, is a fundamentally womanist form, and in the workshops and productions of *dark diaspora* mandiela herself played the central autobiographical role as "poet maestra" (A. Cooper, "Redemption Dub" 444).[18] The staging involved no less than seven women in its first production, directed by mandiela and Djanet Sears, six of them serving as dancers and "chanters," and the published script in one suggested staging calls for as many as fifteen to fifty women as "*voice/shape/sound*." In each option, however, in addition to the dub poetry at its core, "mandiela used sound, riddims, movement, dance, the spoken word, and [women's] textile art" in what Afua Cooper has called "truly an integrated script" ("Redemption Dub" 444).

dark diaspora—

    one
of many/million
dark tales (mandiela, *dark* 3)

—treats materials that range from personal longings as a lover, as a "sistah," as a Black woman in Canada, through laments about the real and metaphorical coldness of Canada (including, punningly, Canadian "just/ice" [34]), to sequences addressing diasporic issues such as immigration and exploitation, returning home, the neocolonialism of bauxite mining in Jamaica, whiteness, racism, Black politics, resistance, and solidarity. And it evokes love between women throughout, most explicitly in the poem about bisexuality, "who is my lover, now?"

i hear a sister's voice
moan in the recess of my desires
peaking obsessions
in the basal drops of dark sticky tones
this sister sounds/
slide past my throat

unto the lifesongs I peal
she is your lover? now (8)

The show creates, then, an expansive and creatively queer space within the diaspora and ends with the assertion "black/woman.i.be" (8). As Afua Cooper says,

> *dark diaspora . . . in* dub is not simply interested in narrating our grief and loss. mandiela *as woman* and poet, does not suppress her rage. She lets it out, confronts it, wrestles with it, dances with it, engages it, and finally transforms it into positive action. Though *dark diaspora* is a story of sorrow, it is ultimately a story of love. ("Redemption Dub" 442–43, emphasis added)

The show ends with seven strong Black women onstage

chanting arms
chanting arms
chanting arms
chanting

The central contributions of *dark diaspora . . . in* dub! to a developing Afro-Caribbean diasporic aesthetic, then, are to build upon on the heterogeneity and carnivalesque hybridity of existing Caribbean and Caribbean Canadian theatrical forms by introducing into the mix the language and politics of dub poetry "womanized" through the admixture of automythobiography and embodiment in the choreographed movement of powerful Black women's bodies.

In the 1990s, as she ran b current and mentored a generation of Black women in Toronto, mandiela found herself and her collaborators[19] at the center of what she calls "an africanadian theatre aesthetic trek" that continues to this day, in spite of her retirement from b current in 2013 ("africanadian" 69). The trek has taken her backward, to reexplore her own roots in Jamaican pantomime, which she calls "my biggest influence" (Knowles, "Having"); miss lou and mas' ran (Louise Bennett and Rannie Williams); Lorraine Hansberry; ntozake shange; Vinette Carroll; and the early dub poets (mandiela, "africanadian" 69–70; Knowles, "Having"; Gingell, "jumping"; Collins). But the trek has also taken her forward into "the grunt work of carving out a fresh aesthetic . . . a fresh concoction of styles and form, as well as uniquely Canadian content" (mandiela, "africanadian" 70).

And that fresh aesthetic, she acknowledges elsewhere, is "woman-centric" (Knowles, "Having"), if also expansive and inclusive in the ways that the term *queer* itself is expansive.

> by 1995 i was seriously asking the question: how do we as black Canadian folks recognize a homegrown, africanadian aesthetics in our theatre work. . . . i was convinced that elements in the styles and forms we had been generating in our stage work over the previous 10 to 15 years were very closely related to a caribbean, as well as an african american and broadly pan-african strain of aesthetics which we had all been exposed to and with which we had become purposely intimate.
>
> yes, the discussion is about your homegrown africanadian aesthetics. ("africanadian" 70)

"for black people/peoples of african descent," she argues, "our experiences & the way we deal with them are rooted in our blackness/our afrikanness—the ways we talk/celebrate/fight/desecrate/consecrate/rejuvenate—these are elements which determine what our art looks & feels like." mandiela's "africanadian aesthetic trek" "meant searching & developing beyond form & content; toting styles which may be unfamiliar in theatre, but are familiar in other forms of black art" (mandiela, qtd. in A. Lee 4). Much of mandiela's work as a director in the decades since *dark diaspora* has involved "toting" such styles and introducing such "other forms of black art" to the stage, including, in addition to poetic text: music, dance, textile arts, visual arts, games, oratory, and elements of "ring shout" and call-and-response forms of expression,[20] and she has carried this through to her own writing for the stage.

dark diaspora was the starting point in her trek as a playwright—and she admits to not having written for five years after it was first produced while focusing on lobbying for and running her company and its programs (Process Panel) and to at one point having contemplated leaving theater for the film world, where she is also active ("africanadian" 69). The next major nodal point in her own writing for the stage came almost twenty years later, in March 2010, when she directed the premiere production by the African Canadian Obsidian Theatre of her new work, *who knew grannie*.[21] The play is subtitled "*a dub aria in several movements signifying on*[22] *family ties vested in a generation of cousins each attempting to hold onto themselves all the while celebrating/mourning/transporting/grasping/saying so long grannie/forever/in their hearts*." On the title page of the prepublication working draft (though not in the published script) mandiela defines a dub aria as "an emotional flight usually done in a single melodic voice" (mandiela, "who knew"). But the single melodic voice is not that of a solo autobiographical subject, or even a single "character." There are continuities with the automythobiography of *dark diaspora,* but one major step in the development of her particular dub theater aesthetic taken by *who knew grannie* is to move it out of the consciousness of a single character. Here not only are five voices heard but those voices are spoken out of the bodies of five distinct characters played by five actors, though a woman, the titular, recently deceased grannie, remains central; indeed, mandiela maintains that the play "bring[s] several characters in one voice through a single journey" (mandiela, notes). grannie lives and dies in Jamaica, but after her death her four grandchildren are called together from the four major centers of the transnational dub diaspora: kris, now thirty-two, is a queer male celebrity chef in the United States married to a white man; likklebit, now twenty-nine, is a teacher in, and recent immigrant to, Canada who has lost her eyesight and is receiving therapy; tyetye, now thirty-seven, is a musician stuck in prison in the UK on a smuggling conviction; and vilma, now thirty-nine, is an up-and-coming respected politician "at home" in Kingston (*who knew* v–vi).

Like mandiela in her aesthetic trek, and like the sankofa bird that is the play's central symbol and cultural text, *who knew grannie* looks both backward and forward. After a brief "overture" that introduces the cousins, *grannie* is organized into fourteen musical "movements" (rather than scenes) and structured around seven Jamaican children's games: "children children," "bull in a pen," "chick chick chick," "redlite," "rockstone/manuel rd," "show me yr motion," and "what's the time, mr wolf" (mandiela, *who knew* iv), all of which position the children *as* children, answering call-and-response style—or in one instance, *"no call, just random response"* (55)—to grannie's reiterated invocation, "children children." Indeed it is grannie's calling—her vocation and her invocation—*"to bring them back in tune with themselves"* (5). She does this explicitly by taking them back to their childhood and reminding them through her teachings to "walk good" (74), and by invoking, indeed imitating and embodying, sankofa. Sankofa is a crow-like bird of West African myth that flies forward while looking back and taking an egg (the future) off its back; it teaches that we must go back to our roots in order to advance. The bird is pictured on the show's poster and program, where the egg consists of a circle of Black children's joined hands.

In performance *who knew grannie* was deeply moving, mellower than *dark diaspora* in its politics but equally rich in resonance and reference and incorporating an increasingly rich blend of styles and performance genres. It was located on what one reviewer called a "cat's cradle of a set" (Bradshaw) with a scattered diasporic foreground linked together by brightly colored strands and backed upstage by grannie's warm and bright Jamaican hearth, from which the show's live Jamaican music emanated and to which the cousins returned. The show ends with the return complete—"sankofa now" (84)—as grannie signifies on "Swing Low, Sweet Chariot,"[23] and the children urge her to

> bring it home, grannie
> **kris**: with sweet cocoa tea
> **tyetye**: and bush mint
> **vilma**: with a river bursting of rain (84),

and to "walk good." Grannie utters "caaaaawww . . . caaaaaaww", *"in dark sankofa crow and nyabinghi drums continues"* (86).[24]

who knew grannie's use of multiple voices, live music, stylized movement, evocative call-and-response exchanges; its resonant use of signifying on tropes central to pan-African cultures; its formal, "dub aria" structure; and its embodiment of sankofa all significantly enrich mandiela's developing dub theater aesthetic. The play's expansiveness, generosity of spirit, and connection to community are exemplary and are representative of the way the form has developed in the work of her widely successful protégée, the Jamaican-born d'bi.young anitafrika ("young" after her father; "anita" after her mother, anita stewart, a pioneering dub poet in Jamaica; and "afrika" after, well, Africa).

D'BI.YOUNG ANITAFRIKA: BIOMYTH MONODRAMA AND THE SORPLUSI METHOD

d'bi.young anitafrika identifies as "a black, queer, African Jamaican, Canadian, Caribbean mother" (Luhning 11), and she argues significantly that her queerness and "feminist analysis" are both part of her "Canadian reality" within diasporic space:

> The fact that I am openly queer, openly loving women and men within a Jamaican context, within the context of being an artist, within the context of being a woman . . . is challenging so many things. (Flynn and Marrast 38)

young anitafrika's work grows directly out of mandiela's, making still more explicit the woman- (or, for young anitafrika, "womban-") centeredness of mandiela's work from *dark diaspora* through the rock.paper.sistahs festivals to *who knew grannie*.[25] It adopts, adapts, extends, and explicitly queers her dub aesthetic. Some have read the "'bi" in "d'bi" as an assertion of her bisexuality, and young anitafrika welcomes the interpretation, appearing on the cover of the gay and lesbian *Xtra* as a way of explicitly challenging homophobia in the Caribbean community and layering dub, as she says, with her "heavy feminist rhetoric" (Flynn and Marrast 42, 46). Finally, young anitafrika readapts mandiela's "automythobiographical" to "biomyth monodrama," a subtitle that has replaced "dub theatre" for her more recent plays.

But it is clear that young anitafrika's roots are in dub: her practice grows directly out of that of her mother, and she is herself a practicing, published, and recorded dub poet. All of her early work as a playwright was billed as dub theater, including two early two-person plays, *yagayah: two.womyn. black.griots* (2001, coauthored and performed as "debbie young" with naila belvett—now Naila Keleta Mae); and *androgyne* (2004–7), that are the most explicitly queer of her work. Both plays bring to the dub theater aesthetic a new, positive exploration of transgressive Black female sexuality. Indeed, both plays, as Andrea Davis argues of *yagayah* (which was directed by mandiela), directly treat Black female sexuality as a bridge between Canada and the Caribbean (Davis 116–19; see also mandiela and Van Fossen), and this element is characteristic, if not always explicitly so, of all her work. young anitafrika's stage work has also continued to be deeply steeped in a dub tradition, and it is striking how much of it builds upon and directly echoes that of mandiela: the use of sankofa, of children's games, of *grannie*'s "children children" summons, and so on. As her work has evolved, however, young anitafrika has increasingly come to think of what she does less as dub theater than, overarchingly, as "storytelling," but more specifically for her theater work, as "biomyth monodrama," evoking Audre Lorde and, again, mandiela's "automythobiography." young anitafrika defines *biomyth* as

> an abbreviation of the words biography and mythology. biography pertains to the accounting of one's own lived experience; mythology pertains to 1. the poetic reinterpretation of the lived experience and 2. the use of folklore, myth, and magic in the process of reinterpretation. *biomyth* therefore, is the poetic grey space between what we interpret as real and what we deem make-believe. (Email)

"biomyth monodrama," then, is "a mythologized auto-biographical play told by the story's creator/performer" (Email).

As she has worked, particularly on her major trilogy, *the three faces of mudgu sankofa* (now *the sankofa trilogy*), she has been at once focusing on single-actor, multiple-character work and working out what she calls "the sorplusi method." She began theorizing her practice through the four principles of dub poetry taught to her by her mother: "rhythm, political content, language, and orality" (Luhning 12).[26] To these she first added sacredness, integrity, and urgency ("because my own spirit wants to move towards a place of negotiating what it means to be a revolutionary" [Luhning 12]) and eventually one more, inventing the acronym "**sorplusi**" (standing for ***s**elf-knowledge*, ***o**rality*, ***r**hythm*, ***p**olitical content and context*, ***la**nguage*, ***u**rgency*, ***s**acredness*, and ***i**ntegrity*). She argues that

> these ideas form a comprehensive eco-system of accountability and responsibility between the artist/storyteller and the art/stories they choose to create/tell, how they choose to create/tell them and to whom they choose to create/tell them; as well as observing the socio-political and socio-economic effects of the art/stories on everyday life.
>
> the methodology challenges the artist to not only be invested in themselves but to (re)position to the centre of their micro and macro communities, being both accountable and responsible (able to account for and respond to) these communities who gather to witness their art. the artist mirrors society, encourages its self-critique, and inspires its self-growth. (Email)

At her anitAFRIKA studio in Toronto, at the pan afrikan performing arts institute training program that she subsequently ran in South Africa, and at the watah theatre institute that she now runs in Toronto,[27]

> the artist[s] meticulously excavates each *sorplusi* principle, interpreting their findings from a personal, critical-analytical, self-reflective, oppression-aware, point-of-view.
>
> the artist[s] become conscious of their symbiotic relationship with the rest of society and the responsibilities that accompany that relationship; resulting in the simultaneous growth of the artist and their art as they uncover/recover themselves within the magic of personal development, creativity, community and social transformation. (Email)

biomyth monodrama and the sorplusi method are further articulated in her "wombanifesto" on "art for social transformation" posted on her website, and they manifest themselves in *the sankofa trilogy*, consisting of *blood.claat*, *benu*, and *word!sound!powah!* The plays present a complex, nonlinear mapping of versions/myths of young anitafrika's own life: her growing up in the "hard core," "ghetto" area of Whitfield town in Kingston, Jamaica; her schooling from a young age at the legendary Jamaica School of Drama (now Edna Manley College) and at the exclusive Campion (aka "Champion") College; her early engagement with the community of artists, activists, and dub poets; her mother's departure to Canada for three years, leaving her in the care of her grannie; her sexual abuse at the hands of her uncle; and finally her own coming to Canada. She maps these onto three generations of the fictional, mythologized sankofa family women in Jamaica and Canada, descendants of the Maroons, and in particular of "queen nanny," the powerful "obeah woman" who led the slave rebellion in 1730s Jamaica and whose story is most fully told in *blood.claat* but recurs throughout the trilogy. The trilogy does not constitute a linear story. Indeed, like its titular sankofa bird, it looks both backward and forward; in fact, in the original versions of the individual parts of the trilogy the sankofa women moved backward in chronological time as they moved forward through the generations. In the first play, *blood.claat* (2003–5), set mainly in Jamaica "in the present day," mudgu was a young girl who had her first period at the beginning of the play and was pregnant at fifteen years of age at the end (as young anitafrika's own mother had been); in the second play, *benu* (2010), mudgu's daughter, sekesu, was a twenty-eight-year-old new mother in Toronto; and in the third play, *word!sound!powah!* (2010), mudgu's twenty-year-old granddaughter, sekesu's daughter benu, was involved in the "poets in solidarity" movement surrounding the 1980 election in Jamaica, the bloodiest since independence in 1962, in which socialist leader Michael Manley lost to the US-backed Edward Seaga. As revised for production at Tarragon Theatre in fall 2011 and for 2016 publication by Playwrights Canada Press as simply *Sankofa*, *blood.claat*'s "present day" is 1972; *benu*'s title character is only twenty years old and the play takes place in 1992; and *word!sound!powah!*, retaining its 1980 story line, is simultaneously projected forward to be also taking place at a future date.[28]

Each play of the trilogy is framed within different elements of ancient "folklore, myth, and magic," much of it Yoruban, almost all of it womanist, and each play is grounded in a different element (earth, air, fire, and water). Thus *blood.claat* (water, blood) opens stunningly when young ani-

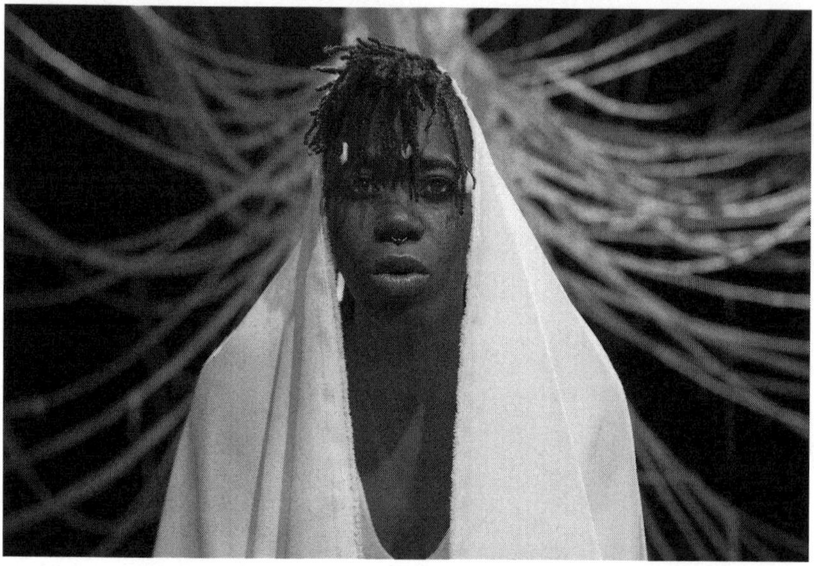

Fig. 6. d'bi young anitafrika in *benu,* part 2 of *the sankofa trilogy* at Tarragon Theatre. Photo by Cylla von Tiedemann, courtesy Tarragon Theatre, Toronto.

tafrika as the storyteller enters naked from the waist up and trailing a blood-red train—a "*river of blood*"—and offers a "*libashun*" to elogua to clear the path and to her ancestors for "*gratitude, guidance, and protection.*" She makes an offering to "*yemosha* [blood], *mawa mother of all,*" and, removing her headdress, asks the goddess ochun for "*permission and her blessing for life birth*" (19) and the goddess oya for "*safe passage*" (20). Elsewhere the play's negative blood energy is wielded by the Yoruba warrior orisha ogun, who "governs metal works [and] misdirects blood fire energy" (18) and whose story is told by queen nanny, who then proceeds to tell her own story of the Maroon resistance.[29] In *benu* (air), the mythical and magical are represented through the benu bird, a predecessor of the phoenix and the bird of life and death in ancient Egypt, who is threaded throughout the play as "bird-womban," with "the beak of a cock, the face of a swallow, the neck of a snake, the hindquarters of a stag, the tail of a fish, the breast of a goose . . . and wings covered in white eagle feathers" (21).

This bird-womban "*sits atop her tree / nesting an egg of myrrh that contains her mother's ashes*" (8) at the play's outset, and her flight to the sun creates the world—her "children, children" (45)—by the end:

> *i am the future of me. i am my past. i am the deep swelling of potential coming. i am water. i am breath. i am the crone. older than blood bleeding wounds which never dry for i am water.* (45)

Part of the magic of *word!sound!powah!* (earth), the most overtly social, political, and historical of the plays in the trilogy, is the poetry itself, as performed by the characters, including the wordless performance of the "physical," or "action poet," "stamma." But the play also incorporates opening and closing invocations of spirits and ancestors as a way of "opening up dem eyes. dem third eye. de one that lead to your soul" (36) and includes a witty and compelling creation myth about the beginnings of race. The play is very much about beginnings. young anitafrika has said of *blood.claat*, but it applies to the whole trilogy, that "a lot of the mythology that comes up in the play is about envisioning new possibilities, new endings—which are also new beginnings" (qtd. in Varty). And the final stage direction in *word!sound!powah!*, the final play in the trilogy, is not "The End," but "Beginning."

The differences in form and content among the trilogy's three parts demonstrate the flexibility of a form that is nevertheless deeply steeped in Afro-Jamaican cultural politics and practices. Formally, *blood.claat* is in part a coming-of-age dub play reclaiming the curse word that is its title[30] and celebrating women's power to give life; *benu* is a social drama exposing the injustices perpetrated on single mothers by the Canadian medical, social, and judicial systems; and *word!sound!powah!* has its dub roots in Jamaican agitprop as it mythologizes the story of young anitafrika's own mother and her activist friends in the Jamaica of the 1980s. The effectiveness of all three shows is their embodiment in a charismatic and chameleon-like dub writer-performer deeply steeped in the histories and specificities of a diasporic culture, including that of contemporary Toronto.[31]

CONCLUSION

young anitafrika's work is at once more transgressive, more political, more personal, more explicitly spiritual, and more expansively queer than that of either Spencer or mandiela, but like mandiela's it is deeply invested in poetic language, specifically the poetry of nation language, and it is deeply "womban-centered." It also, and clearly, emerges from the same developing tradition. "dub theatre" and "biomyth monodrama," as created by mandiela and young anitafrika out of an evolving, womanist Afro-Caribbean tradition in Toronto, go beyond postcolonial resistance with its tendency to reify the dominant *as* dominant (and therefore to be resisted). They expand and extend the revolutionary (and celebratory) politics and principles of dub poetry as it emerged from reggae and rasta into expansive feminist and queer realms not imagined by its inventors. These women, their predecessors, their collaborators, and their contemporaries have constituted a performance ecosystem within the city of Toronto that functions for them as a transformative space operating at the intersection of nations, sexualities, and performance forms to queer traditional theatrical hierarchies, together with the largely masculinist ethos of much Caribbean performance and the narrow chronopolitics of modernist colonial "development." They have created and continue to develop entirely new, empowering, "womban-centered," and "revolushunary" Afro-Caribbean forms that are (re)grounded in traditions of the grannies, the griots, the nation languages of the people, and movement and languages that emerge from and celebrate Black women's bodies in a transnational Canadian-Caribbean diaspora that is dynamic, independent, and forward looking.

PART THREE | Mediations

In theater, as in the rest of the world, intercultural encounters require mediation. Patrice Pavis's model of theatrical interculturalism—which presumes a one-way flow between source cultures, usually "Eastern" or othered and target (western) cultures—positions cultural mediation at the narrow point of a process shaped like an hourglass. This narrow point is where cultural texts are distilled to their presumed essences and subsequently expanded using the decoding semioses of the target culture. In this particular mediating process the cultural and artistic "modeling" of the source culture is adapted through the technologies of theatrical production to the artistic and cultural modeling of the target culture in order to achieve "readability" at the point of reception in the west (Pavis 185), requiring no adjustment of positioning by members of the target culture. The result is a watered-down, decontextualized, and distorted version of the original, one that only benefits the (western) producers and often does violence to the (non-western) source cultures. Pavis's hourglass assumes, moreover, a kind of cultural (and therefore semiotic) homogeneity in each of the (two) participating cultures, including the targeted, presumed-to-be-monocultural audience. This section of *Performing Intercultural Toronto* samples instances in which culture-crossing theater companies explore more nuanced and balanced ways of mediating between cultural formations and at the same time resist constituting their audiences as culturally coherent units.

The most familiar and perhaps fraught form of intercultural mediation is not considered here, though it could be. Many artists from minoritized positions, from stand-up to sitcom, soften the blows of their critique and of the often dire circumstances that they represent through humor, and theater practitioners in Toronto have been no exception. This has been particularly true of Indigenous playwrights such as Tomson Highway (*The Rez Sisters, Dry Lips Oughta Move to Kapuskasing*), Kevin Loring (*Where the Blood Mixes*), and especially Drew Hayden Taylor (*Someday, The Bootlegger Blues, Only Drunks and Children Tell the Truth, Dead White Writer on the Floor*, and others), who have disarmed dominant-culture skepticism through often outrageous comic interventions. Indeed, Taylor has published on numerous occasions about the purposes and efficacy of the technique for Indigenous writers (see *Me Funny*; "Comedic"). And of course it is not only Indigenous writers who have used humor to mediate across cultural difference. Playwrights such as Jamaican Canadian trey anthony in *da kink in my hair*, Chinese Scottish Canadian David Yee in *paper SERIES* and *carried away on the crest of a wave*, Korean Canadian Ins Choy in *Kim's Convenience*, and South Asian Canadian Anita Majumdar in *The Fish Eyes Trilogy* have all won major awards and/or had remounts, tours, and significant commercial success.

Less familiar, and arguably more complex, is the use of modernist formal models, intermediality, and the discourses of cultural critique as mediating devices across difference, and these are what this section will focus on.

It may seem odd to consider modernism—a movement that has not been friendly to the world's "othered" peoples—as a mediating element, especially an equalizing one, but perhaps that is one of its unfinished projects. And as new modernist studies have begun to demonstrate, modernism has not been the same the whole world over or for all of its peoples. In chapter 6 I suggest that the work of Soheil Parsa at Modern Times Stage Company constitutes a reconsideration of modernist formalisms and an exploration of a more elastic modernist model as a mediating element that can facilitate the negotiation between theatrical cultures in a newly global modernity, or across multiple modernities. Through his intercultural productions of high modernist classics, his Persian-inflected productions of Western classics, his adaptations of Persian/Iranian modernist plays, and his productions of new work, Parsa has for over twenty-five years been remediating the problem of modernism itself and working toward fulfilling the broken promises of modernization and of a transnational modernity.

One of the persistent difficulties in staging work that involves the representation of "others" to audiences, including heterogeneous ones, is the too-easy assumption that theater's great traditional tool for bridging difference is empathy. Chapter 7 sets out with Aluna Theatre to at once probe the limits of empathy and explore the possibility of another form of cross-cultural mediation: intermediality. Work on their signature production, *Nohayquiensepa (No One Knows)*, began with a question: how do we deal with the death of a stranger? It proceeded through research that was in large part mediated (as most research now is) through the Internet and other digital technologies, and it issued in an intermedial production that engaged its audience in its own kind of research into a question that might productively drive all intercultural encounters: what are we to make of this?—with the emphasis on a historically and culturally positioned but nevertheless inclusive "we" as *makers*. The use of nonhuman technology prosthetically to (re)assemble human others—or in Latour's terms, to reassemble the social—here raises important questions about encounters with otherness more generally. What happens when the borders between subjects and objects are blurred or conflated, and when encounters with the intercultural other are mediated through technology?

A different kind of mediation is at work in chapter 8, which briefly focuses on the contributions of Cahoots Theatre Company (formerly Cahoots Theatre Projects) in mediating among and across the various discourses and initiatives in intercultural theater that have shaped Toronto's intercultural performance ecology since the mid-1980s. Operating largely beneath the public radar, Cahoots has nevertheless sponsored events, taken initiatives, coproduced, and advanced an intercultural performance discourse that, from the very outset, was not based in a ghettoizing identity politics but in genuine efforts to work across real and respected difference.

Unlike part 2 of this volume, part 3 is less concerned with building dramaturgical structures grounded in and developed out of culturally specific forms and practices and more interested in the ways in which borrowed or invented aesthetic and technological forms and discourses have the capacity to mediate performative intercultural exchange in the contemporary world, in collaborations, and in the developing ways in which the discourses of interculturalism and the nature of cross-cultural encounters have evolved since the formative years of identity politics.

SIX | The Modern in Modern Times

> In 1982, the future director of the *Hamlet* that opened this week at Theatre Passe Muraille huddled in a ditch near Iran's border with Pakistan, hiding from a detachment of Revolutionary Guard troops. The young Soheil Parsa . . . had been told by Iran's Islamic-fundamentalist government that he would be conscripted into the army. His pregnant wife had already fled the country, and he was determined to follow her. "It took three days to get to Pakistan, the last eight hours walking by night through the desert," Parsa says. The guides who smuggled him out took most of his money, condemning him to an impoverished start in his country of destination, Canada.
>
> —Ray Conlogue, "Shakespeare with a Persian Twist"

The Islamic revolution in Iran in 1979, from which Soheil Parsa fled three years later (the country remained in "revolutionary crisis mode" until 1983), can be understood in part to have been a response to and retreat from a secular and westernizing modernization of the country that had taken place under the rule of the country's last monarch, the US-backed "shah of Iran" (Mohammed Reza Shah Pahlavi). It was certainly one that resulted, within the newly minted Islamic republic led by the "Supreme Leader," the Ayatollah Khomeini (Grand Ayatollah Ruhollah Khomeini), in the suppression of modernism in the arts, which might usefully be understood as the art world's response to modernity—or what Susan Stanford Friedman calls "different forms of representational rupture . . . in connection with different modernities" (487). As Lebanese Iranian curator and producer Rose Issa wrote in 2001, "Just as Iran's contemporary art scene was taking off, it was stifled by the revolution," and part of that stifling was the voluntary or involuntary exile of many of its artists, including the future artistic director of Toronto's Modern Times Stage Company.

Soheil Parsa had been in his final year of theater school at the University of Tehran in 1979 when he was expelled from university and forbidden to work because he didn't support the revolution. He fled, leaving behind his parents, sisters, and brother, who, as Baha'is, were subject to persecution (Baha'i is a non-Islamic religion). He made his way to Canada via Pakistan, the United Arab Emirates, and India and arrived in Toronto in 1984 speaking almost no English. Not long after his arrival, having taught himself sufficient English and having made a living by delivering newspapers and fast food and driving a school bus—jobs he continued to hold through the first decade of Modern Times' existence—he enrolled in the theater department at York University. Upon his graduation in 1989 he cofounded Modern Times Stage Company with fellow graduates Gregory Danakas, George Mirabelli, and Peter Farbridge. Danakas left the company after one production, Mirabelli after several years. But Parsa has stayed with the company as artistic director from the beginning, together with Farbridge, who was in the first production and remains artistic associate. Only after thirteen years of struggling to fund the company did Parsa and Farbridge begin to receive small salaries as its administrators.[1]

Modern Times' mandate has evolved over the years, but it has been deeply colored by Parsa's experience in Iran and has consistently involved a modernist vision that includes internationalism, inclusive humanism, and formal experimentation. Its mission statement currently reads as follows:

> The company sees in contemporary society a need to identify common values and responds to this by creating theatre work of international focus. In a multilingual and complex world, Modern Times provides disarming and accessible theatre for people in search of new meanings, simple joys and a sense of interdependence.

Artistically and organizationally, Modern Times is committed to

- Being a mutually respectful, culturally inclusive collaboration dedicated to humanist principles;
- Producing provocative, emotional and visceral theatre productions that embrace a global view and transcend narrow ideologies and cultural expectations;
- Searching for new and original forms of creation and expression; and,
- Exploring and taking inspiration from the uniqueness, commonality and differences of the human experience. (Modern Times, "Company Mandate")

As a mission statement this differs little from the predatory intercultural projects of modernist theater artists such as Peter Brook, Jerzy Grotowski, and Eugenio Barba, except, crucially, for its focus on "uniqueness" and "differences" within the human experience, which Modern Times' European models are most often happy to erase in search of a common, undifferentiated humanity. But there is no critique in this mandate of the appropriative practices of universalist humanism or western modernism. Indeed, Soheil Parsa would be delighted to be positioned within the tradition of the great European modernists whose work he admires and from whom he has learned a great deal.

In practice, however, Modern Times consistently probes the intersection of Middle Eastern with western performance forms in a much more evenhanded way than those of Parsa's western models, and its approach might best be described as "new modernist." The company has produced hybrid tradaptations of modernist Iranian plays, Shakespearean tragedies, high modernist European classics, and new intercultural work from some of Canada's least theatrically represented communities, notably Persian/Iranian and, in the case of *The Sheep and the Whale* (discussed in chapter 2), Moroccan Canadian. The company is a key part of the network of "actors" within the intercultural performance ecology of Toronto and a key member of what Yvette Nolan calls its "brown caucus" (Interview). They have coproduced with Cahoots Theatre Company, they have shared an office and personnel with Aluna Theatre, they share creative team and cast members with these and many of the other companies in the network, and they participate through broadly intercultural casting and programming decisions in the larger project of challenging the hegemony of whiteness on the city's stages. And like those of many of the city's intercultural companies, Modern Times' mandate includes consciously offering "culturally-inclusive alternative theatre experiences" (Modern Times, "Home"). On the other hand, Modern Times overwhelmingly defines itself not according to identity politics, as many companies within Toronto's intercultural performance ecology do, or according to any interventionist political model but by a kind of modified or qualified universalism that, at least on the surface, aligns itself with the philosophical and aesthetic projects of western modernism. Indeed, calling what they do "culturally-unspecific theatre," they stage their belief that

> as human beings, we can all simultaneously represent several different or plural identities. We oppose the presumption that people can be uniquely categorized based solely on their religion or culture and seek to demonstrate the multiplicity of the human spirit . . . in our work. (Marsland)

Unlike other members of Toronto's theatrical "brown caucus" who "always cast 'other' in the work" (Nolan, Interview), Modern Times practices something more closely resembling a thematized "color-blind" casting, employing in most of their shows mixed casts of actors from the dominant culture and a wide variety of marginalized cultural and linguistic communities. The company, then, practices what Erika Fischer-Lichte calls the "interweaving" of performance cultures and shares with her a utopian belief in "the transformative power of performance" (Fischer-Lichte, "Interweaving"; Fischer-Lichte, *Transformative*).[2]

Modern Times is perhaps a surprising name for a theater company whose popular reputation, at least in its press coverage, seems to be based on its staged adaptations of ancient Persian fables and whose current mandate focuses on the blending of Middle Eastern and western theatrical forms.[3] But the name is appropriate: central to the company's importance may be its contribution to the rethinking of modernism itself. Indeed, Modern Times can be understood in its politics and artistic practices to be working in its modest way toward the completion of what Jürgen Habermas in 1980 famously (and controversially) called "the unfinished project of modernity"—the extension of the larger humanist project of enlightenment through the creation of a rational and democratic public sphere, one that includes the arts as well as science and morality. According to Habermas, modernity holds "the extravagant expectation that the arts and sciences would not merely promote the control of the forces of nature but also the understanding of self and world, moral progress, justice in social institutions, and even human happiness" (Habermas 45). Habermas is skeptical about the project's potential success, citing "Three Conservatisms"—antimodernism, premodernism, and postmodernism—that work against it (53).

In spite of Parsa's own experience with antimodernism in Iran, and his rejection of postmodern instabilities, Modern Times is more optimistic and, circumventing many of the critiques leveled at Habermas's gender blindness and his eurocentric defense of the enlightenment and its ravages, explicitly extends this extravagant expectation to all of the world's peoples, whatever their genders, sexualities, races, or ethnicities. The company's central project, I suggest, is the relocation and reclamation of modernist aesthetic practices from the appropriative forms of interculturalism practiced in the theater most famously by Peter Brook and Ariane Mnouchkine (and critiqued most famously by Rustom Bharucha [*Theatre*]). At its best Modern Times probes the tensions involved in reappropriative practices "from below" and explores the different kinds of difference that surface when power, in modernist theatrical practice, rests equitably with those modernism has traditionally othered.

In spite of its full participation in the "brown caucus," Modern Times is unique among Toronto's intercultural theater companies in that it is grounded in three intersecting interests: the work of western modernist playwrights and directors that Parsa was exposed to in Iran in the late 1970s, contemporary Persian/Iranian plays and theatrical practices that blend ancient Persian fables and forms with their modernist refashionings, and Sufism, a mystical dimension of Islam that eschews Islamic exceptionalism in favor of an openness to other religious beliefs in a way that resembles the Baha'i faith of Parsa's family. This chapter will explore each of these as mediating factors in the interculturalism of Modern Times, drawing on and contributing to "new modernist" studies' expansive understanding of modernisms as illuminated by Parsa's purposeful blending of East and west (see Mao and Walkowitz).

SOHEIL PARSA, MODERN TIMES, AND WESTERN MODERNISTS

Soheil Parsa studied theater at the University of Tehran at a key moment in Iran's history, when, for better or worse, the country was opening itself to western influences in all spheres of life, including theater. Indeed, the Shiraz Arts Festival, held in the south central Iranian cities of Shiraz and Persepolis between 1967 and 1977, began as a showcase for the royal court under the patronage of the shah's wife, Empress Farah Diba, with one of its purposes being to present contemporary western art and demonstrate the country's openness to intellectual and artistic innovation (Gluck 21; see also "Utopian Stage"). The festival, which frequently focused on the relationships between theater and ritual, attracted to the country a pantheon of western modernist artists, including theater directors Peter Brook, Joseph Chaikin, Jerzy Grotowski, Tadeuz Kantor, and Robert Wilson, whose influence on Iranian directors, according to Iranian American writer Zara Houshmand, was "huge." "That their influence remains powerful after a generation and a revolution," Houshmand argues, "speaks not only to the continuity of this lineage among Iranian theatre artists, but also perhaps to a special cultural fit, a familiarity with the ritual roots of theatre."[4]

As a theater student in Iran at the time, Parsa was not immune to this influence. Indeed, he attended the Shiraz Arts Festival as a teenager in 1971, where he saw Brook's *Orghast* in the ruins of Persepolis, and he viewed films of the festival's series of talk-backs, seminars, conferences, and interviews at theater school from 1975 to 1978 (Parsa, Email). There is no doubt that his working practices as a director today remain very much in line with those articulated by Grotowski in *Towards a Poor Theatre* and by Brook in *The Empty Space*. He describes his work not as imitating ritual but as "creat[ing] a new ritual on the stage" (Modern Times, *Hallaj*), and his process is consistently to simplify, strip away excess detail, and create the kinds of sharp, striking, and self-contained images that are so central to high modernist formalism. Like his models, as he says, he searches for "essences."

Grotowski, Brook, and others have been rightly criticized for practicing an appropriative interculturalism that leaves power within the hands of charismatic western directors while raiding world performance cultures for touches of the exotic, or for so-called primitive energies that might revivify a decadent western tradition. Parsa, however, practices a much more inclusive and reappropriative modernism, as exquisitely crafted as the best of his western models but informed from the inside by the performance forms of the Middle East and filtered through lived experience. Parsa is very much aware, in his deferentially polite way, of the modernist effacement and orientalist exploitation of difference, even as he embraces the austere simplicity of high modernist imagism. And indeed it is the minimalist modernists with which his work is most frequently compared by reviewers. Thus Mira Friedlander compares the "psycho-physical performance style" of *The Eighth Journey of Sinbad* (1992) to that of Grotowski ("Journey"); Jon Kaplan summons Beckett, Genet, and Kafka in describing the world conjured by the 2003 production of *Stories from the Rains of Love and Death* ("Persian Passions"); Kamal Al-Solaylee describes the same show as "a poor man's Kafka; a wannabe Beckett and more-truncated-than-usual Pinter" ("Rains"); and Kaplan finds the central character Gerontion in the 2006 production of Guillermo Verdecchia's *bloom* "ensconced like a figure in a Beckett play" ("Poetry").

Like Brook, Parsa has focused some of his energy on Shakespeare; like Brook (and one of Brook's models, the Polish critic Jan Kott), he considers Shakespeare to be "our contemporary" (Kott); and like Brook, he has staged versions of Shakespeare that are crisp, clear, physical, and stripped of any mannerist fussiness. Also like Brook's, his work is inspired by and infused with Eastern influences. Unlike for Brook, however, those influences are part of Parsa's lived experience (see Kaplan, "Maturing"), and they inform his vision and his belief system as well as his style.

The Modern Times production of *Hamlet* in 1999 is a case in point. As Parsa reported to Ray Conlogue in a preview for the show,

> "It occurred to me that the scene with Yorick's skull was much like the poetry of Omar Khayyam, a similar idea of death, that the body turns to dust and becomes the wall of a house." This led him to reflect on a common Sufi expression for the longing for death, that "the world has become a prison. So when Hamlet says that Denmark is a prison, to me it means that he has already resolved on death. I guess . . . that a Westerner looking at Shakespeare is not so likely to see the Sufi elements." (qtd. in Conlogue)

Mainstream Toronto reviewers may not have seen the Sufi elements in a production whose set consisted of a few bowls and sticks or the specific influence of the Persian *ta'ziyeh-khani* passion play commemorating the martyrdom of the grandson of the prophet,[5] but most commented on the production's "spirituality and mystery" (Al-Solaylee, "Duelling Traditions") or its "stylized Persian aesthetics" (Kaplan and Sumi). Others simply found it "exotic" (Coulbourn, "To Be").

The company's more widely known production of *Macbeth* opened in 1995, was remounted and reconceptualized in 1997, 2003, and 2005, and toured to Montreal and Tehran. This show was more deeply and more directly indebted on a structural and stylistic level to the *ta'ziyeh-khani* in ways that echo the dramaturgical experiments with specific "cultural texts" that I explored in part 2. As such it complicates too simple an understanding of Parsa's indebtedness to a western modernist tradition. According to Zara Houshmand, "Although the religious content of *ta'ziyeh* is anathema to many secular progressive writers [in Iran], the form itself is a treasure-house of minimalist/expressionist theatrical technique," and Parsa's production was described by many as "minimalist in the extreme" (Hustak). There is, then, a complicated lineage to the style of this and other Modern Times shows, as Ray Conlogue suggests when he refers to the company's style of "expressionist acting that [Parsa] first saw with artists like Peter Brooks [*sic*] and Jerzy Grotowski who were invited to Tehran in the late 1970s for an international theatre festival" at which the *ta'ziyeh* was performed.

But the *ta'ziyeh* is not just about minimalist expressionism or even about content that seems entirely appropriate to *Macbeth* (it portrays the historical beginnings of the Shi'ite faith and deals with "martyrdom, doomed battle against impossible odds, and the slaughter of innocents"): "The most critical element of the performance that makes *ta'ziyeh* in its native environment such an emotionally overwhelming experience," Houshmand argues, is the people's "own role as participants at an event not just reenacted but relived in a catharsis of communal mourning." And in many ways it was this emotionally participatory element that the Modern Times *Macbeth* at its most effective replicated—notably in its performances in Tehran, where, as one audience member told the company, "Macbeth . . . is our life" (Logothettis). According to Farbridge, who played an impassioned Macbeth, one performance in Tehran in the middle of a packed crowd "may not have been the best performance we gave, but in terms of our exchange with the audience, I've never felt anything like that in my life" (qtd. in Kaplan, "Maturing"). "I haven't imitated Ta'ziyeh-Khani," Parsa said of the production. "But I've used the form as a springboard to create this piece. I usually try to confront tradition and create something new" (qtd. in Hustak).

What he created was a sparse, austere ritual-in-the-round, with nine barefoot actors playing twenty-eight roles bearing flashlights for swords, wearing scarves and sashes for costumes (with their removal signifying a character's death), along with elasticized headscarves and hand socks and a single prop: a bowl for wine. What set there was, was simple and symbolic, including bedsheets for Birnham wood. Farbridge's Macbeth was, in the words of reviewer Geoff Chapman, "a bewildered victim of alien forces, . . . a blood-soaked Faustian creation who's sold his soul to Satan, at one point joining a coven of revelers as the treacherous hags give him another dose of false pledges about his future." Stavroula Logothettis's Lady Macbeth was described as "a hyperactive sexual machine—a cat on the hot roof of Dunsinane" (Al-Solaylee, "Too Little").

Reviewers, perhaps tipped off by preview articles and a note in the program, were more perceptive about the show's Persian influences than they were to similar underpinnings for *Hamlet*. Although it didn't mention the *ta'ziyeh*, the program explained the show's rationale as a "desire to put a Western classical play into an Eastern theatrical context" and evoked "a world of the invisible, where gods, witches, spirits, and demons live. This world," it explained, "is not part of the day to day culture and experience of Western directors. However, for Soheil Parsa . . . these ideas are the very threads that course through his own creative life, forming part of the framework of his culture" ("Modern Times History"). One critic evoked Brook in citing the "'empty space' purity" of the staging (Al-Solaylee, "Too Little"), but it was clear that this was a show whose modernism was ultimately of a different source and order than that of Brook.

Parsa's theater training in Tehran exposed him not only to the work of western modernist directors but also to playwrights of the European avant-garde such as Genet, Beckett, and Ionesco, whose work influenced him at a fundamental level. When he stages the modernist classics to which his work is so frequently compared, however, Parsa does so with difference as well as deference. Modern Times turned to Genet for its second production (*The Balcony*, 1990), has performed Ionesco twice (*The Chairs*, 2001, and *The Lesson*, 2012), and produced notable productions of *Waiting for Godot* in 2008 and *Blood Wedding* (with Aluna Theatre) in 2015. *The Balcony* was a small-scale show presented for a short run as part of a research-and-development series at Toronto's Theatre Centre, and the scale of the show perhaps dictated a focus on closure and containment that was emphasized by a design consisting of nets that linked, enclosed, and connected audience and stage somewhat in the style of American modernist director Richard Foreman. But Parsa was attracted to the play in large part because its setting (during a revolution) evoked his own experience in revolutionary Iran and because its fusion of illusion and reality was evocative of Persian poetry (see Kaplan, "Italian"). *The Chairs* and *The Lesson* have perhaps been Modern Times' least overtly intercultural work to date and are least directly evocative of non-Western cultural texts. Even here, however, the use of "whiteface" makeup in *The Chairs* worked to racialize whiteness and render it visible, thereby making the futility of the play's action, as an old couple prepares to deliver a discovery (about the meaning of life) to a world that never shows up, legible as a comment on white dominance and destruction. In *The Lesson*, the cross-casting of "audible-minority" actor Costa Tovarinsky as the (female) maid who offers the (white) Professor his Nazi armband also had significantly destabilizing cross-cultural resonances while queering the play's extreme gendering of the relationship between the (male) Professor and his (young, female) student.

But *Waiting for Godot* is perhaps the company's signature treatment of a classic modernist play. The *Godot* was stunningly effective as a brilliantly minimalist staging of this perhaps archetypally modernist play, set on a floating, circular disk whose rake, slanting toward the audience, kept all of the action appropriately and precariously off balance. But the production was also silently subversive, mining and translating through casting the colonialist critique that Beckett hinted at in the relationship between Pozzo and Lucky (tellingly read as English and Irish, respectively, in the long-running Gate Theatre, Dublin, production that is often claimed to be definitive). Parsa cast the formidable and physically dominating Chinese Canadian John Ng in whiteface as the downtrodden Lucky (wearing *jika-tabi*, traditional Japanese work boots), against the much slighter anglo Canadian Stewart Arnott as a domineering, whip-wielding, and racist/fascist Pozzo. The result, in combination with the casting of Peter Batakliev as a Bulgarian Estragon who was in his understated way the equal of Farbridge's Irish, pedantic, but engagingly uncertain Vladimir and of Filipino Canadian Darrel Gamotin as the Boy, was effectively to racialize power relationships, destabilize universalist certainties, and displace western modernist absolutes. The Beckett estate did not allow Parsa to proceed with his planned cross-casting of the role of Lucky, and it prohibited his planned use of sound (which can work to localize a production), but this racialized casting served at least to some extent to circumvent the estate's control (see Perovic). It displaced Beckett from the comfortable realm of universalizing abstraction and perhaps restored his masterpiece to its rightful place as a subtle but powerful, and newly historically situated, critique of imperialism, realizing the localizing potential in production that Alys Moody finds in the script's resistance to historical and geographical specificity.

For me, however, the most telling of Parsa and Modern Times' reconsiderations of western high modernism was the 2006 production of Argentinian Canadian Guillermo Verdecchia's *bloom*, which, like the production of *Godot*, succeeded in circumventing attempts by writers' estates to impose restrictions. *bloom* was originally planned as an adaptation of T. S. Eliot's *The Waste Land*, but because of permission problems with the Eliot estate, the show was finally presented as having been "inspired by" the Modern Times company's studio work with Eliot's modernist epic. And indeed, the play bears only occasional and passing resemblance to the poem that inspired it, at least in terms of its content. There is a range of quotations, citations, and purposeful distortions of *The Waste Land* and other poetry by Eliot, along with many other works, ranging from Buddha's Fire Sermon and Dante's *Inferno* (in Italian), through *Beowulf* and *The Canterbury Tales*, to *Hamlet*, *Lear*, Yeats's "The Second Coming," some Beckett, Richard Dawkins's *Unweaving the Rainbow*, and reports by pilots out of Basra in the 1991 Gulf War. There was even an epigraph in the program and in the published script from the Romanian Jewish German poet Paul Celan's "Psalm," the source of the play's title: "Blessèd art thou. No One. / In thy sight would / we bloom. In thy spite" (qtd. in Verdecchia, *bloom* 96). But the *form* of the show, as a pastiche of citations and fragments from high and popular culture "shored against [our] ruins" (Eliot, "Waste Land" 10), paid tribute to Eliot's method.

The basic situation, the play's postapocalyptic given circumstance, was not drawn from *The Waste Land* itself but was a variation on the situation depicted in its companion poem, "Gerontion": an old man named Gerontion and a boy, in a dry month in "Rat's Alley" (1), reading, talking, singing (or not singing) off-color turns, not playing chess, and waiting for rain while dogs bark, rats scuttle, the jets roar overhead, and a crowd flows over

London Bridge. There is quite a lot of "mixing memory and desire," as Eliot puts it ("Waste Land" 1), mostly Gerontion trying *not* to remember his time as a pilot and his relationship with the long-dead Marie (another trace of Eliot), while the boy is "stirring everything up" (Verdecchia, *bloom* 120), desiring "more." But "more," Gerontion tells him, "is what brought us to this pass" (126).

Most reviewers found in the presence of the Boy "seeds of redemption" (War Child) or "a chance of rebirth" (Kaplan, "Poetry"), and Verdecchia himself, who draws attention in his preface to the published script to the contemporary context of Afghanistan and Iraq, admits, "I'm not sure that the play ends with regeneration, but there's hopefulness that something beautiful may emerge . . . something about the dogged persistence that keeps us struggling on, even if no hope seems possible" (Verdecchia, qtd. in Kaplan, "Old Poem"). It is a distinctly modernist attitude, particularly when the struggling on, and the something beautiful, take the form of such artful, fragile, and inscrutable works of art as *bloom* itself. "I find something both pathetic and beautiful in continuing despite all the evidence that says forget it" (Verdecchia, qtd. in Kaplan "Old Poem"). Ultimately, the show cried out against forgetting. "That's not the story," asserts the Boy. "Is it?" (Verdecchia, *bloom* 142).

bloom is unique, but it is perhaps also representative of much of Modern Times' work in that it is most interesting for its intercultural appropriations of modernism itself, its skirting of the modernist-capitalist alignment over ownership (the Eliot estate), and its representing-with-a-difference the high modernist appetite for the consumption of feminized "other" cultures. Thus the play's unnamed "Boy" is spirited into the world of the aged, vision-impaired, and war-damaged (white, European) Gerontion to bring renewal as "primitive" (and feminized) Eastern art was used by modernists such as Eliot to renew European decadence. Crucially, the role was played (brilliantly) by the cross-cast Indo Canadian actor-dancer-playwright Anita Majumdar, whose play *Fish Eyes* is discussed in chapter 2. Ultimately, *bloom* productively misrepresented Eliot's own work as only one among the fragments that an unsettled "we" shore against our ruins in the savage, postapocalyptic world—the world of today?—in which it was set.

IRANIAN PLAYWRIGHTS AND PRACTICES

Prominent as Shakespeare and the western high modernists are in the repertoire of Modern Times, they do not show up in its seasons as often as do the plays of modern and contemporary Iranian playwrights Gholam-Hussein Sa-edi, Mohammad Rahmanian, Abbas Na'lbandian, and especially Bahram Beyza'ie. The recuperative work of bringing these writers into the western modernist canon is some of the most important that Modern Times performs. But this is modernism that arose, as in much of the Arab world, not simply out of an encounter with Euro-American models (see Carlson); it combines an artistic response to modernity as it manifests itself in Iran with a deep engagement with Persian traditions. Indeed, Zara Houshmand claims a special affinity for modernist forms among certain Iranian playwrights, those (such as Sa-edi, Rahmanian, Na'lbandian, and Beyza'ie) "who weave together [the] three strands of the political, the avant-garde, and the traditional, and who do so with the poetic sensibility that lies at the heart of Iranian cultural expression—not because they are easy, but because they are both challenging and characteristically Iranian."

Iranian Azerbaijani Gholam-Hussein Sa-edi, whose *Oh Fool! Oh Fooled!* Modern Times produced in 1993, was a prolific novelist, short-story writer, screenwriter, playwright, and cultural critic who was arrested and tortured during the shah's regime and exiled during the revolution. In Paris he founded the Association of Iranian Writers in Exile and restarted a quarterly literary magazine that had been banned by the shah, but he eventually succumbed to depression and alcoholism and died in Paris in 1985. *Oh Fool! Oh Fooled!* is a fable about community and the ways in which it responds to perceived external threats. The Modern Times staging was prescient, anticipating by almost a decade the popular anti-Arab, anti-Muslim Islamophobia of many North Americans (and many others) in response to the events of 9/11, 2001, and since.

Playwright Abbas Na'lbandian was deeply influenced by European absurdist theater in his plays of the 1960s and 1970s. His *A Deep, Vast and New Exploration of the Fossils of the Twenty-Fifth Geological Period* was staged by now-exiled Iranian director Arbi Ovanessian at the Shiraz Arts Festival, winning festival and national awards (see Abdi). His was an influential voice in the Arab world, but he was criticized prior to the revolution in Iran for failing to be sufficiently Marxist and was vilified and frequently imprisoned afterward by the Islamic regime. He was eventually driven to suicide in 1989 at the age of forty-two. When Modern Times staged his 1977 play *Stories from the Rains of Love and Death* in 2003, the play's English-language premiere, it had not yet been produced in Iran itself. Parsa, Farbridge, and Brian Quirt used the title for their collected translations and adaptations of Iranian plays, published with Playwrights Canada Press in 2009. The Modern Times production was both violent and sensual, visceral and nightmarish in ways that invoked the playwright's own life and times, but reviewers unfamiliar with Na'lbandian's unique take on specifically Iranian absurdities tended to cite Beckett, Kafka, Pinter, and Genet (Kaplan, "Right"; Kaplan, "Persian Passions"; Al-Solaylee, "Rains"). The comparisons are apt enough, but Na'lbandian's play, consisting of five "folds"—brief scenes that are narratively unconnected and have different "characters" but obliquely cite each other—is less self-contained than are those of Beckett et al, and their anxieties are more grounded: "I just feel like everything is coming apart," says the Father in the third fold. "Little by little it's all becoming—foreign" (Na'lbandian 83).

Among the plays published in the Parsa, Farbridge, and Quirt collection is *Interrogation*, by Iranian director Mohammad Rahmanian. Rahmanian has himself directed a Farsi production of Beyza'ie's *The Battle of Aurash Sade* in Vancouver and Tehran in 2013–14, the play that was the basis for the Modern Times staple *Aurash*, and one that itself combines Persian myth with German playwright Peter Weiss's *Marat/Sade*, famously staged by Peter Brook as part of his Theatre of Cruelty experiment at the Royal Shakespeare Company in 1964. Contributing to the transnational modernism of the 2006 Modern Times production is the fact that *Interrogation* is set in 1964 in postrevolutionary Algeria, where two damaged young Algerian revolutionaries, a boy, Naeem, and a woman, Safiya, are unable to restrain their own violence after the revolution has been won, the boy killing the French woman who loved him, the woman, a victim of torture, detonating a bomb that kills her mother. It is the play's social and historical specificity, its engagement, and its localized particularity in a world where "a hundred more revolutions won't be able to solve these gaps . . . between the French and the Arabs" and where "our history is full of carnage, rapes, and massacres" that constitutes its contribution to a new, transnational modernism (Rahmanian 118, 121). The modernity that this modernism mediates, as Naeem says "*quickly, non-stop*," consists of "colonization, corruption, history, minority, society, land, homeland, occupation, revolution, freedom, conspiracy, terror, traitors, terrorist, machine guns. . . ." "Calm down," his interrogator admonishes him (108).

Sa-edi, Na'lbandian, and Rahmanian, then, have contributed at least as much as Beckett, Ionesco, and Genet to the Modern Times project and aesthetic, but it is Bahram Beyza'ie who has been the company's most frequently produced playwright, dominating the first decade of the company's history and regularly staged since. Indeed, Modern Times' first production after Parsa and Farbridge graduated from York University was *The Conquest* in 1989, an adaptation of Beyza'ie's screenplay *Salandar*, and they have gone on to do four more: *The Four Cases*, 1991; *The Eighth Journey of Sinbad*, 1992; *The Death of the King*, 1994 and 2016; and *Aurash*, first staged in 1998 and remounted frequently since. Beyza'ie, best known as a member of a leading Iranian literary family and a prominent filmmaker of the Iranian new wave, has written over fifty plays in which he draws directly on the work of Pirandello, Beckett, and Ionesco but forges his own uniquely Iranian oeuvre. The plays translated, adapted, and produced by Modern Times are also and primarily versions of Persian fables and their modernism is deeply grounded in Persian culture. In the late 1950s and early 1960s Beyza'ie did extensive research on ancient and pre-Islamic Persian literature and culture, he subsequently studied traditional Iranian theater, arts, and painting, and he has had a dominant influence in the development of a non-western identity for modern Iranian theater and film.

Modern Times' *The Conquest* (1989) was the work of a young director, but one already blending Eastern and western asceticism to tell the story on a sand-covered stage of a silent Sufi mystic tormented by soldiers wielding weapons. *The Four Cases*, two years later and after Parsa's first foray into Genet, featured what was to become the director's trademark physicality in the staging of another Persian fable transformed by Beyza'ie and drawing on the playwright's own interest in puppetry, together with dance and clown. It told the charged political allegory of four humans who build a monstrous scarecrow to protect themselves but who in the end lose their freedom to their own creation. Parsa continued to experiment with Persian puppet theater in a modernist context the following year in the world premiere of Beyza'ie's 1960s play *The Eighth Journey of Sinbad*, but the show was perhaps more notable for the development of his physical theater aesthetic. Where movement in *The Four Cases* had been frenetic, Parsa, working in a coproduction with Toronto Island–based Phyzikal Theatre, was moving toward the kind of minimalism that is the hallmark of his mature style. "I'm emphasizing a kind of minimalist movement as a way of refining our technique," he told Jon Kaplan in 1992 (Kaplan, "Irani Playwright"). In *Sinbad* Beyza'ie linked together and revisited the story of Sinbad from *The Arabian Nights* with the twelfth-century Persian Sufi poet Farid ud-Din Attar's *The Conference of the Birds*, which, it will come as no surprise to learn, had also been adapted by Peter Brook and taken on tour throughout Africa in 1972. In Beyza'ie's version Sinbad's seven journeys are in search of enlightenment, not wealth, as are the journeys through seven valleys in *The Conference of the Birds*. Parsa drew on the conflated traditions of the *ta'ziyeh* and the poor theater to stage the conflated fables in the round on a central dais and used minimal costumes and no set pieces, trusting the actors' bodies and voices to create the play's worlds and characters.

Parsa's directorial style and imprint were firmly in place by the time he directed Modern Times' fourth play by Beyza'ie in 1994, *The Death of Yazdgird,* translated by Parsa and Farbridge as *The Death of the King,* which immediately preceded the company's celebrated and much remounted productions of *Macbeth* and *Aurash.*[6]

The play is technically set in 642 CE and concerns the death of Yazdgird III at the time of the Muslim invasion that effectively ended the Persian Empire. But it's no history play. Beyza'ie turns the story into a bleak modernist metatheatrical fantasia about a family who may or may not have killed the man who may or may not have been the king. Much is made of the fact that, when push comes to shove (and it does), no one can tell the difference between a destitute miller and a king. But it doesn't really matter anyway, because the wolf—in the form of the first of centuries of invaders and occupiers—is already at the gate. As the Magu (priest) prophesizes at the play's outset, "When the millennium ends, the Age of the Lamb will be over, the Time of the Wolf will begin and Daevas [demons] will dance on the corpses of the angels" (Beyza'ie, *Death* 30). For Parsa and Modern Times, the show represents the company's fully developed minimalist style, which I think of as Iranian Canadian theatrical modernism. This involves a blend of striking visual imagery produced largely through light and movement and supported by evocative soundscapes most often inspired by Middle Eastern musical styles, used to tell ancient fables with contemporary applications in response to a complex and specifically Iranian Canadian modernity. The modernism of this work is inherent in the ancient Persian forms in which Beyza'ie's work is steeped. And this new, engaged modernism is what provides the hyphen—the mediation between cultures—in Modern Times' Persian-Iranian-Canadian work.

Beyza'ie's *Aurash,* first staged in 1998 as translated and adapted by Parsa with dramaturge Brian Quirt and edited by Peter Farbridge, is the style's best exemplar, and it is not incidental that the company has produced this show not only in Toronto but in various of the world's most troubled contact zones.[7] The program for the 2010 Toronto remount calls *Aurash* "a very special part of our company's history, present and future. In this piece, we see the heart of Modern Times' aesthetic—it is a true collaboration between Persian myth and storytelling and our local artists' influence and interpretation" (Modern Times, Program, *Aurash*). The production was nominated for and won several Dora Mavor Moore awards (for outstanding lighting design, sound design, direction, and adaptation/

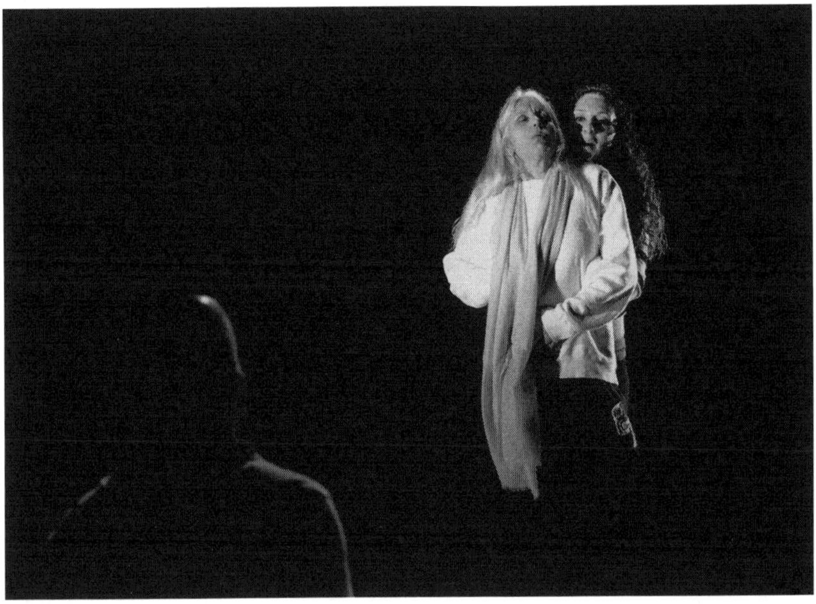

Fig. 7. Ron Kennell, Jani Lauzon, and Bahareh Yaraghi in rehearsal for the Modern Times production of Bahram Beyza'ie's *The Death of the King*, 2016. Photo by Ric Knowles.

translation), and it garnered high praise from reviewers: "Everything about this production works" (Citron, "Poetic"). It has become, indeed, the company's signature piece, carving out a new modernist vision that is at once sparse, austere, and rooted in Persian tradition.

The myth on which the play is based is itself a simple one, the story of a lowly shepherd turned stableman for the defeated Persian army who is forced to determine his country's borders and his people's fate by firing an arrow from the top of Mount Elborz. The arrow never lands, Aurash disappears, and the fate of his people, with classic modernist ambiguity (see Empson), remains unclear. Reviewers of the production heard "strong statements on a raft of issues, from the horrors of war and the greed of leaders, to the plight of ordinary soldiers who are pawns in a vicious chess match between armies, to a plea for universal peace and a borderless world" and found contemporary resonances with Canadian soldiers in Afghanistan (Citron, "Poetic"). But the actors pointed to its commentary on "the ambiguity of victory and enslavement, heroism, leadership and sacrifice" (qtd. in Kaplan, "Aurash").

The play, originally written by Beyza'ie for a solo actor, is performed by four actors in the Modern Times stagings, indicated in the script only by "A," "B," "C," and "D," together narrating and performing an epic folktale and playing a cast of thousands using the simplest of devices. The roles assigned to the actors have varied with each remount, including the varied assignation of narrators and characters by letter, sometimes making thematic associations (as when, in the published text, the same actor, "C," plays and thereby compares the idealist champion archer, Kashvad, and the realist traitor, Hoomann), sometimes working across gender roles (as in the original staging, when Joan Heney played the Persian commander, or in the 2010 remount in Toronto, when the Métis Algonquin actor Michelle Latimer played Aurash). In every case the piece has employed Modern Times' characteristically expressive physicality, as in the opening, when, in "a rapid montage of scenes of war—the cast enacts tableaux of murder and mayhem, each vignette more violent than the next. A woman is savagely raped. A soldier is graphically eviscerated," a bloody battle is enacted, "impaled bodies lay strewn across the battlefield and captured soldiers are marched off to prison" (Citron, "*Aurash*"; Wagner). As reviewer Vit Wagner says, "That Parsa and company convey the horror and magnitude of the event so succinctly is no small feat—considering that it's done with a cast of four." But this physicality is combined with scenes of dialogue and with a kind of choric narration, with all cast members doubling as narrators, producing simple, clear, poetic, and yet curiously theatrical moments:

D Drums again.
B Trumpets again.
A A falcon soars through the sky like a javelin.
B And the people cry out, the people of this land with their loudest cry, say:
D "Yes, Aurash, go, go, to the enemy and tell them you will fire the arrow,
B And wherever your arrow lands will be our land,
C Wherever your arrow lands!"
D And Aurash goes toward the enemy and cries:
A "I will fire the arrow. And wherever my arrow lands will be our land."

(Beyza'ie, *Aurash* 14)

Among the "characters" embodied in turn by the actors, in addition to kings, commanders, corporals, and soldiers, are the ghost of Aurash's father (who advises him, "Your heart must release the arrow, not your arm"

[19]) and the mountain itself (which warns him off). At one point three actors play Aurash simultaneously, as "Aurash stands in front of Aurash" (17), physicalizing his internal debate and staging an archetypally modernist self-alienation; at another that debate and that alienation are voiced in a powerful wrenching between first and third person in a monologue:

> A Who is Aurash?—who was unknown at dawn, and now at sunset has the eyes of the world upon him. He was a warrior whose most dangerous weapon was his shepherd's crook. Who is Aurash?—an ignorant farmer who won't even curse a man who steals from him. Who is Aurash?—a curved back that has been loaded and loaded but never complained. I am Aurash, a man once devout and pious. I was taught only to love: I turned my back on spite. But now there are scorpions in my head; now a man, a wicked man called Aurash has stained me with disgrace. He is Aurash, standing on the other side of the earth, on the peak of a mountain, like a mirror, facing me, and his heart is my arrow's aim. He is a man so wretched, so disgraced, that he was condemned before he was tried. I am Aurash, the one who at sunrise was ignorant, and now, at sunset, knows something about the world. And he, Aurash, screams: "I wish I didn't know."
>
> B Aurash is frightened by his own cry. In front of a silent endless sky, he trembles.
>
> (21–22)

The actors' work was supported, again in characteristic Modern Times fashion, by clear and simple staging—described by reviewer Paula Citron as "economical yet majestic" ("Poetic")—and powerful, evocative, and perfectly coordinated sound (by Richard Feren) and lighting (by Philip Cygan in 1998 and Andrea Lundy in 2010)—which feature as independent forces or even "characters" in reviews of almost all of the company's shows (see Citron, "Poetic"). And like the acting, none of this was naturalistic, the lighting, for example, employing primary colors, strobe effects, and even putting the flickering of onstage glow tape to use as stars (see Hicton). In its original staging at the backspace at Toronto's Theatre Passe Muraille, Parsa reversed the perspective, placing the audience in what is usually the tiny stage space and locating the action among the steeply raked bleachers. In later incarnations of the show the stark set, designed by Parsa and Setarweh Delzendeh, consisted primarily of a round, sand-colored floor mat and a platform box. Differently colored flags were used for the different armies, and the costumes, also designed by Delzendeh, consisted of plain pants and tunics with two-color convertible sleeves on the forearms, which, switched from red to yellow, alternately indicated their roles as enemies or as Persians. In all of this, the key was minimalist simplicity. As actors Ron Kennell and Todd Hammond reported to Jon Kaplan, "'Soheil works with nonliteral, abstract images and continues to strip them down as a production develops. . . .' 'We're looking for the essence of an idea or an action rather than its representation. . . .' 'What we hope to present is a narrative of essence rather than of story. The result is poetic, multifaceted and richer than any literal stage presentation.' . . . Parsa's catchphrase in rehearsals is 'simplify.' He constantly pares down elements of a production, everything from props to movement, to their essence" (Kaplan, "*Aurash*").

SUFISM

If the search for an essential simplicity defines the style of Parsa and Modern Times, that search derives not only from western modernist and ancient Persian sources but also from an abiding fascination on the parts of both Parsa and Farbridge with a transcendent and transnational brand of religious Sufism, originally a mystical dimension of Islam that shares some elements with Parsa's family's Baha'i faith as well as with Buddhist, Taoist, Hindu, Jewish (Kabbalah), and Christian mystic traditions from all parts of the world. In Modern Times' understanding, as represented through the "study guide" to their 2009 production of Parsa and Farbridge's *Hallaj*, the central goal of this mysticism is "to attain unity, truth, and a purer, more fundamental state of existence" (Modern Times, *Hallaj* 7). Their interest is in a Sufism "that can be flexibly interpreted" beyond the strictly Islamic tradition (10). Crucially, the company is interested in the artistic form of Sufi practices and rituals, including the practice of Dhikr, "a devotional act of repetition that influences the music, dance, and rhythm patterns of Sufi arts" (10) as it influences those of Modern Times. For Modern Times, those arts include not only the company's characteristic rhythmic use of movement but its reliance on Sufi poetry, which Parsa and Farbridge are deeply steeped in, notably the poems of Rumi (Maulana Jalaladdin Balkhi, 1207–73) and his meditations on Tawhid, the doctrine of oneness or unity that transcends geographical and cultural borders. In many of the company's productions, from *Waiting for Godot* to *The Eighth Journey of Sinbad* and the remount of *The Death of the*

King, this unity is consciously represented by stagecraft that involves or invokes circles (see Friedlander, "Updating").

Sufism has been part of Modern Times from the outset. As I have indicated, the company's first production, Beyza'ie's *The Conquest* in 1989, took as its focus a silent Sufi mystic (played by Farbridge) tormented by two soldiers who tried to force him to speak, while three years later Beyza'ie's *The Eight Journey of Sinbad* was based in part on Farid ud-Din Attar's thirteenth-century Sufi poem *The Conference of the Birds*, an allegory about a Sufi master leading his students to enlightenment. The Modern Times production was tailored to focus on this archetypal search for truth (as opposed to riches) through veils and layers of lies and illusion. Even their 1999 production of *Hamlet*, as noted above, was initially inspired by Parsa's insight that Hamlet's meditation on Yorick's skull resonated with Sufi expressions of longing for death (Conlogue). But the company's most overt and extensive engagement with Sufism to date, and one of its most highly regarded productions, was Farbridge and Parsa's own new play, *Hallaj*, first produced at the Richmond Hill Centre for the Arts in September 2009 and later revised and remounted at Buddies in Bad Times in November–December 2011.

The play, loosely based on the life and martyrdom of the ninth- to tenth-century Sufi mystic Mansur Al-Hallaj (played by Farbridge), is set in Hallaj's prison cell in Baghdad on the eve of his torture and execution. Hallaj was a legendary and widely loved Sufi poet, teacher, and philosopher who ran afoul of the authorities because of his antiauthoritarian teachings, his promotion of charity and spirituality over formal religious practices and of compassion over judgment or violence, and his encouragement of Muslims to forego the haaj (or "hajj"), the pilgrimage to Mecca that is required of all able-bodied Muslims at least once in their lifetime, in order to put the money they thereby save to better uses:

> Let's extinguish the fire of hell and set heaven ablaze so we may turn once more to the message of God's love—charity. *Cheers of the crowd.* Every year many of us save hundreds upon hundreds of dirhams to spend on our pilgrimages to Mecca. I too have made the haaj. When I arrived, I saw an empty house of stone. I came to see the Master of the House. What have I to do with the house? *Reactions of shock from the crowd.* Look! *He produces a stone.* Do you feel compelled to make the pilgrimage? Then find a stone, place it on the ground, walk around it seven times and spend the money you have saved on clothes for the poor, on liberating a slave, on feeding an old and hungry man! (Farbridge and Parsa 12)

"Religion," he argues, understandably offending the religious authorities, "is the form, the shell, not the inner reality. I refuse to stop at the shell and regard it as absolute. Religion serves as the first training ground for a devotee, but like a raft it must be discarded after crossing the river" (24).

The action of the play, punctuated by flashbacks, focuses on efforts by the authorities and Hallaj's friends and family to convince him to recant his heretical views on "man's unity with God" (1), which challenge the caliph. Throughout, he communes with Christ in his cell and studies "the philosophers, atheists, magicians, Christians, Jews, neo-Hellenists, Zoroastrians, Manicheans, Hindus and Buddhists" on his travels (2), en route to his dangerously democratic discovery and revelation that God is in himself, and by implication in everyone ("The blade that touches me, touches God! I am The Truth!" [39]). Hallaj and his wife, Jamil, finally welcome their deaths, which are presented less as the cathartic purging of the heroic individual represented in western tragedy than as the annihilation of the self in an ultimate, ecstatic union with one another, with God, and with the universe.

The production was notable in rehearsal, as are all Modern Times productions, for its relentless search for "truth" and "essences" not unlike that of the show's subject. Here as elsewhere Parsa pares away at script and presentation to achieve simplicity of form and expression of which Hallaj himself might be proud. His democratic rehearsal hall, welcoming creative input from all, seems a far cry from the guru-like intensity of the western modernist masters or the authoritarianism of the play's caliph and the system he represents. *Hallaj* was notable, too, for its engagement with earth, with bodies, and with movement, asserting not only the grounded and embodied (versus textual) nature of theater studies' engagement with modernism that Penny Farfan has recently affirmed (xiii) but also a contemporary performative engagement with the Sufi arts, and the ritual practice of *Dhikr* in particular. The show characteristically included choric movement in its representation of the classroom of Hallaj's Sufi master, Junayd; of the meeting and marriage of Hallaj to Junayd's daughter, Jamil; of riots and revolution; of Hallaj's travels; and of his torture and death. But it also included representations of a Punjabi dance that Hallaj tries to teach Jamil and, crucially, of Hallaj's trance-like, repetitive devotional movements that re-create those of *Dhikr* ceremonies incorporating music, dance, meditation, and trance (movements that reviewers characteristically called "ecstatic fits," which in their own orientalizing vision they nevertheless found to be "mesmerizing" [Al-Solaylee, "Only"]). *Hallaj*'s incorporation of Sufi art practices into its new, modernist vision, however, doesn't replicate the western modernist raiding and decontextualizing of the cultural forms of the primitive "other"; rather, it engages in thematic, philosophical, and theological as well as formal ways with ongoing, living cultural arts and practices as they are embedded in the lives and belief systems that produced and continue to engage them. And it does so in a way that fossilizes neither the source materials nor the company's own work. As Parsa said recently of the company's 2014 dance-theater piece, *Forgiveness* (discussed in the conclusion), and in contradistinction to the typically hermetically sealed works of European high modernism as they tightly contain their anxieties with the passage of time, "It's not finished. None of our work is ever finished" (Parsa, Personal communication).

CONCLUSION

Theater, in its messy materiality, vulgar theatricality, and formal impurity, has had a vexed relationship with the theorists, historians, border police, and manifesto writers of modernism (see Ackerman and Puchner), and until recently it has been largely ignored even within the expansive global project of what has come to be called new modernist studies (see Farfan).[8] Intercultural theater has had an even more vexed relationship with the modernist project, a relationship that came to a head in the intercultural theater wars of the 1980s and 1990s (see Knowles, *Theatre & Interculturalism*). The interculturalism of Modern Times Stage Company, however, is less troubled by this narrowly western modernism than it is mediated through transnational modernist forms, specifically through a modernist theater practice that responds to a newly complex and globally diasporic modernity and that pays attention, as Penny Farfan argues, "to modernism's local, material, corporeal, lexical, and interactive dimensions in performance" (xiii). It is a theatrical modernism, that is, that tries to respond to modernity in all its faces and facets, wherever and whenever it occurs. The modern in Modern Times responds directly to what Alys Moody, in an essay on *Waiting for Godot* in post-Katrina New Orleans, considers to be the localizing potential made available by the very ahistoricism of the modernist classic. When applied to the intersecting diasporas that constitute the city of Toronto, as it is in the work of Modern Times, this potential is realized as "a cross-border dialogue, a transnational process rather than a transnational identity" (Moody 541), one that engages the western modernist, ancient and contemporary Persian/Iranian, and local intracultural Torontonian in vital conversation aimed at advancing, if not completing, modernity's fabled and utopian "unfinished project."

SEVEN | # The Intermedial Intercultural and the Limits of Empathy[1]

Aluna Theatre's Nohayquiensepa (with Jessica Riley)

The space between cultures at Modern Times is mediated by new modernist formalism. At the Latin Aluna Theatre, which shares an office with Modern Times, formalist mediations are very differently effected through the interdisciplinary and, specifically, the intermedial, and in this case they mediate cultural forms both intraculturally within Toronto and transnationally across the Americas. The mediation effected by intermediality at Aluna, however, is not so much about the technological as posthuman "other," at least not in the cyborgian senses articulated by N. Katherine Hayles or Donna Haraway, as it is about the posthuman*ist*, postdramatic, postempathetic use of technology in the performative *reassemblage* of the other—the other "we" don't know—*as* human.[2]

Apart from the well-known work of individual artists such as Argentinean Canadian Guillermo Verdecchia and Chilean Canadians Carmen Aguirre and Rosa Laborde, Latin theatre came late to Toronto, with the founding by Colombian Canadian Béatriz Pizano and German Canadian Trevor Schwellnus of Aluna Theatre in 2001 and by Marilo Nuñez of Alameda Theatre Company in 2006 until its closing in 2014. Alameda's mandate was the development, presentation, and support of new work by Canadian Latinx playwrights and theater artists. Aluna, on whose signature production, *Nohayquiensepa*, this chapter focuses, is explicitly international, interdisciplinary, and intercultural; its practice has engaged the intersection of Latinx Canadian and intermedial work.

We attended *Nohayquiensepa (No One Knows): A Requiem for the Forcibly Displaced* as part of Aluna's first biennial Panamerican Routes/RUTAS panamericanas[3] Festival, which took over Toronto's Theatre Passe Muraille for three weeks in May 2012.[4] The crowd in the lobby and spilling out onto Ryerson Avenue was charged with energy. English and Spanish mixed in lively conversations about the festival's workshops, classes, and showcases and about the two shows most had already seen: *Urban Odyssey*, an interdisciplinary dance–puppet theater piece by Federico Restrepo and Loco7 of Bogotá and New York; and *Parting Memories*, a performance piece by the luminous Violeta Luna of Mexico City and San Francisco. Yet to come on the main stage was *Blue Box* by Carmen Aguirre, of Valdivia (Chile) and Vancouver.

Nohayquiensepa was in good company. All of these shows had been invited by Aluna's founders, Béatriz Pizano and Trevor Schwellnus, with the explicit purpose of "going beyond divisions and making connections" to achieve a festival that was "Interdisciplinary. From Across the Americas" (Aluna, Program, Panamerican). Their own interdisciplinary video-dance theater performance was listed as having arrived by way of a Pan-American route that passed through Medellín, Montevideo, Mexico City, Caracas, Bogotá, Edmonton, Ottawa, and Toronto, all cities directly involved in its development. In addition to complex prerecorded and (mostly) live video projection, live drawing on screen, original sound and music, and striking choreography, the show used spoken text in both English and Spanish. In doing so, *Nohayquiensepa* made significant interventions into the fraught and often appropriative practice of intercultural performance through the mediation of the intermedial and the interdisciplinary. The show created environments for artists and audiences in which differences could come together on equal terms and new, self-reflexive and nonappropriative ways of seeing and relating to difference could be proposed and explored. But the progress toward understanding was not easy.

When the audience entered the main space at Theatre Passe Muraille on that evening in May 2012, they saw a large screen downstage on which a "live" hand was drawing shapes, squares, crosses, words, and phrases that at first seemed random. When the house lights dimmed to black, the screen went blue and the shapes of two female dancers in outstretched skirts appeared in silhouette behind the screen—moving through water, perhaps?—but soon emerged to the front and engaged in ritual movements based on the Colombian *cumbia* (a dance form tracing back to Yoruban traditions in West Africa),[5] making offerings in the direction of the audience and lighting candles at the sides of the forestage that would remain lit throughout the show. This ritualistic sequence was followed by the projection of an animated map of the Magdalena River region of coastal Colombia, fragments of a corporate report from a Canadian mining company, and the again shadowy, silhouetted figure of a man who seemed to be presenting it. This show was full of shadows. This in turn was followed by projected

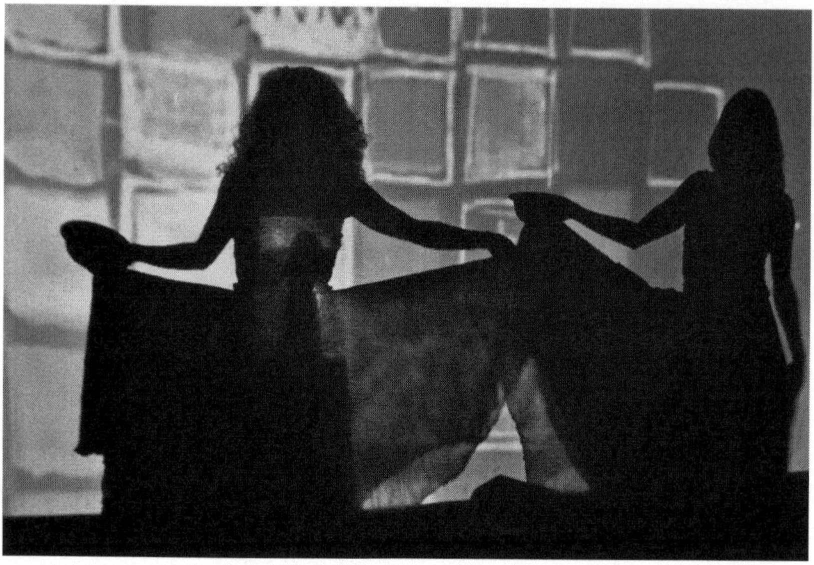

Fig. 8. Victoria Mata and Lilia Leon dance in silhouette behind the blue screen at the opening of Aluna Theatre's *Nohayquiensepa,* while Lorena Torres Loaiza draws live on screen. Photo by Katherine Fleitas.

charts, with the occasional intervention of the live on-screen hand highlighting phrases such as "missing persons," and "AFRO COMMUNITY FACES EVICTION BY ANGLO GOLD ASHANTI IN COLOMBIA." The sequence dissolved into a "soup," as the creators put it (Riley and Knowles),[6] of seemingly naked bodies on the stage floor, their images shot from above and projected onto the again-blue screen, while their limbs also reached up to form disconnected on-screen silhouettes. This complex image was accompanied by reverberating, watery music that was oddly serene. We were fifteen minutes into the show before a word was spoken, and even when words were introduced they were fragmentary, and they characteristically moved freely between the show's dominant spoken languages.

What were we to *make* of this? To answer this question, we need as in previous chapters to consider briefly the company's history and process before moving to a closer analysis of the creation of *Nohayquiensepa* and its reception within the context of the Panamerican Routes/RUTAS panamericanas Festival.[7]

Aluna Theatre was founded in 2001 by Pizano as artistic director and Schwellnus as artistic producer out of a felt need to create roles for Latino, and particularly Latina, actors—chiefly Pizano herself—and to develop a process—one that they would ultimately describe as "design dramaturgy"—to accommodate Schwellnus's ambitions and interests as a scenographer. The company's mandate, however, has evolved over the years. Its cultural specificity as Latin American has given way to a more interculturally Pan-American vision that foregrounds Indigeneity, while at the same time Aluna's work has become increasingly intermedial and interdisciplinary. In exploring the relationships between the intercultural and intermedial in the work of Aluna, specifically in their signature piece, *Nohayquiensepa*, we are particularly interested in the ways in which the show used the intermedial and interdisciplinary to mediate across cultural and national difference by producing an affective longing that is different from and more productive than the kind of "crude empathy" that Jill Bennett finds critiqued by Brecht: "feeling for another based on the assimilation of the other's experience to the self" (Bennett 10).[8] Indeed, *Nohayquiensepa* may serve as an example of a different kind of work—and a different kind of empathy—not unlike the kinds that Bennett says "refuse to yield to sympathetic identification" but allow the viewer to "*feel into* another": "it stages a perceptual experience that threatens to take us outside of ourselves" (34, emphasis in original)—to unsettle us.[9]

According to its published mandate, "Aluna Theatre is a not-for-profit charitable company that creates, develops, produces and presents artistically innovative and culturally diverse performance work with a focus on Latin Canadian and women artists" (Aluna, "Artistic Mission").[10] The company's focus on the (implicitly multicultural) Canadian experience, on international outreach, on collaboration, on language, and on hybridities of various kinds is a result of its evolution, its experiences working with theater artists in Colombia and elsewhere since 2008, and its increasing politicization in the realms of human rights and social justice.[11] It is also the result of an increasing awareness of the problematics of the term *Latin America*, particularly as it relates to the Indigenous peoples of the Americas. Returning from working in the Amazon region in Brazil in 2012, Pizano describes an encounter with a man who told her, "We're not Latin American. We're Indigenous." This acute awareness of Indigeneity across the Americas is reflected in company's name ("Aluna is a Kogi[12] word that refers to an inner world of spirit and memory through which the world around and outside of us is kept in balance" ["Aluna Up + Coming"]); in an Aluna dance/theater production, *Ixok'*, by Edgar Flores and Carmen Samayoa, which concerns Indigenous women and the struggle of the Mayans in the face of the 1978–84 genocide in Guatemala; and in the coproduction of the Panamerican Routes/RUTAS panamericanas Festival since 2014 with Native Earth Performing

Arts. It is also reflected in an increasingly engaged interest in what Pizano calls "this [multicultural] experiment that is Canada."

The integration of the intermedial and intercultural has been incipient, however, in all of Aluna's work and is reflected not only in Pizano's interests but in those of Schwellnus, who holds a fellowship with the Chalmers Foundation to explore the integration of artistic disciplines and intercultural practices. Indeed, they describe the company's earliest work, *Meeting Place,* created by Schwellnus and directed by Pizano at Toronto's Summerworks Festival in 2003, as "a post-dramatic montage." Pizano's trilogy of plays about women and war, *For Sale* (Theatre Centre, fall 2003), *Madre* (Theatre Passe Muraille Backspace, 2008), and *La Comunión* (Buddies in Bad Times, 2010), have increasingly been developed scenographically in the studio, incorporating live video into the process, not simply the production, so that the actors could work with the projections actively. Their powerful and decidedly postdramatic 2014 devised piece, *what I learned from a decade of fear*—the decade and more since the events of 9/11—incorporated live camera work; the onstage use of an overhead projector and laptop to control sound, light, and projections; surveillance and interrogation footage; and techniques to explore a post-terror surveillance society. "We didn't want wallpaper," Schwellnus says of *Nohayquiensepa,* indicating an impulse to move beyond video and other intermedial dimensions as purely aesthetic effects toward their incorporation as inherent, integral dramaturgical elements informing how and what the performance evolves to communicate. At the same time, *La Comunión,* the third play in Pizano's trilogy, introduced the mixing of languages that has also become important to the company's work and did so through a characteristic emphasis on the intrinsic communicative potential of design elements. Rather than the traditional use of surtitles, Aluna's strategy, since *La Comunión,* has been to incorporate such textual translations into the "literary architecture" of the design as an essential move toward the hemispheric perspective cultivated by a multilingualism that might be understood as the linguistic side of the interdisciplinary and intercultural. As Schwellnus puts it, "Visual poetry is a way to transcend language"—including, we suggest, the exclusions and silos of monolingualism.

A major turning point in the company's process came in 2008 when its members worked in Bogotá with a diverse team of ten Canadian and fourteen Colombian artists on *the defenestration project,* a cross-cultural collective creation in collaboration with Bogotá's Corporación Colombiana de Teatro, Toronto's Theatre Revolve (theater for young women), and Toronto's Tridha Arts Association (for the creation of international coproductions, especially between Canada and Latin America). The director of the project was Patricia Ariza, the award-winning artistic director of La Corporación.[13] The process, first developed in the 1960s by Teatro La Candelaria to help find a unique Colombian voice (and a kind of Jungian collective unconscious for Colombia, according to Pizano and Schwellnus), was adapted by Aluna for the creation of *Nohayquiensepa*. The process involves a tripartite focus on the ensemble, the space of creation, and the audience. It consists of unmotivated improvisation (improvisers are not told what to improvise about) in front of members of the ensemble who stand in for future audiences, noninterpretative reflection (observers simply describe what they see as "a chain of actions"), and reflective analysis.

Nohayquiensepa is a result of Aluna's adaptation of this process to its own cultural and creative contexts. This involved finding ways to work with—and against—artists coming out of conventional North American conceptions of theater, modifying the year-long Colombian process to suit Canadian theater-making timetables, and introducing some of the characteristics of Aluna's style and working methods into the process of collective devising. For example, for Schwellnus, who directed and designed *Nohayquiensepa* as "lead artist," "video projection works best when the performer works with it from the beginning, making it part of her space."

Consequently, he says, "my twist on [La Corporación's] formula is to make the room in which we work part of the improvisation, by proposing (and adapting) environments in real time. The improvs, based on some source material and ideas, are analyzed, and then we do another round. Everyone in the room creates, but the director definitely assembles and tweaks the work as the process matures and the improvs slowly transform into a series of related sequences" (Trilling).

Thus the emphases on ensemble, space, and audience learned from La Corporación were adapted through Aluna's characteristic "design dramaturgy." Aluna constitutes its Toronto studio as a "meeting place," to invoke at once the title of its first production and the supposed Huron-Wendat name for the city in which it is located. As I've noted in the introduction, *Toronto* is popularly believed to derive from the Huron-Wendat word for "meeting place"[14] and to invoke the city's history, even before contact, as a place in which different cultures and (First) Nations came together—a point of intercultural mingling that also evokes a Pan-American history predating the borders of nation-states and such concepts as "Canada" and "Latin America." The studio, then, serves consciously as the locus for the intersection of the (multi)cultural, transnational, and (multi)medial, an intersection that provides the Aluna process with much of its generative

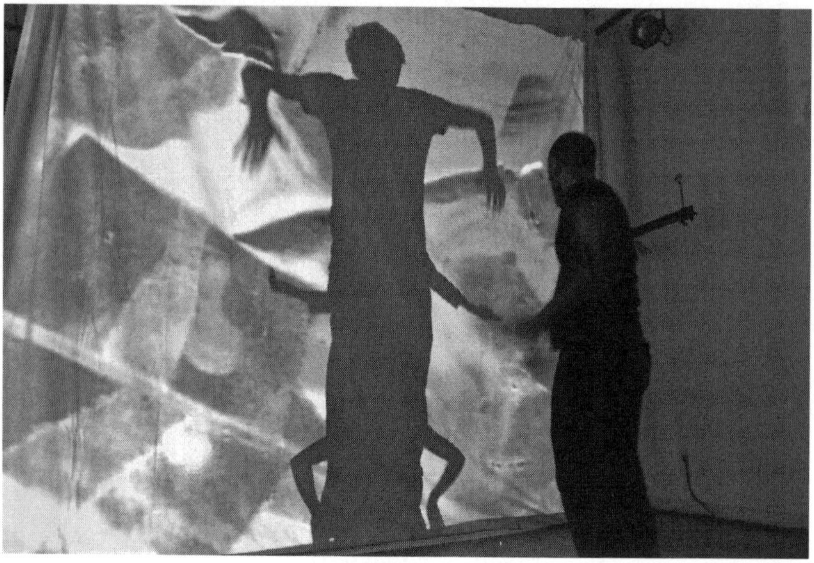

Fig. 9. Live video was incorporated into the process of creation for *Nohayquiensepa*, not simply the production. In this rehearsal photo Carlos Gonzáles-Vio (as Claudio) works on the show's "running" sequence while facing the on-screen image so that he can work with the shadow image as the choreography evolves. Photo by Trevor Scwhellnus.

force. The emphasis on audience in the creation process, moreover, extends beyond improvisation exercises that involve participants responding to the work as spectators. At later stages, in its multiple Pan-American iterations, *Nohayquiensepa* continued to evolve in response to spectatorial feedback, most notably in the company's critical discovery, on performing an early version of the piece in Bogotá to an invited "first audience" of the families of people being killed in Colombia, that the play was—in at least one major way—about Canadian mining practices. Thus the ensemble creation of the show, in its particular spaces of creation, is integrally related to the eventual involvement and engagement of the spectator.

The ensemble, too, was essential to the role played by interdisciplinarity in the development of *Nohayquiensepa*. Reflecting on this, Pizano and Schwellnus speak of the "freedom" from traditional North American—for them, specifically Torontonian—dramaturgies that intermediality and interdisciplinarity, as well as collaborative development practices, have allowed them. Pizano and Schwellnus talk about the excitement of working with choreographer Olga Barrios and other dancers, citing the dancers' freedom from post-Stanislavskian assumptions about motivation that can sometimes constrain actors. Modeling a different approach to development, "the dancers just launch" into the process, as Schwellnus puts it, giving the rest of the ensemble "something right off the bat to react to" and helping members unused to the "risky [Colombian-influenced creation] process" to overcome their conventional inhibitions. As Pizano puts it, "We had to shut up as actors. Because they [the dancers] don't ask—they start going, and going, and going, and they start finding." Resisting impulses toward conventional western acting and dramaturgy, performers from both disciplines engaged in cross-cultural, cross-genre "jamming with composer Thomas Ryder Payne in the rehearsal hall." Likewise, intermedial "jamming," with live drawing by Colombian Canadian Lorena Torres Loaiza, with cameras, projections, abstract shadows, and Mylar, and with codirector Heather Bratten as observer-describer, produced a process that resisted traceable, causational, appropriative narratives. "We didn't want to re-enact anything," says Schwellnus, describing a process not of "explaining but explor[ing]," a process that avoided approaches to acting that require the performer to absorb rather than present the "character" she is playing. "Throughout the creation process we always tried to reflect from our own perspective. We were not trying to embody somebody else unless a very particular moment demanded it." What Schwellnus is describing echoes in theatrical terms Dominick LaCapra's "empathic unsettlement," a kind of critical, self-reflexive empathy, "a virtual, not vicarious experience . . . in which emotional response comes with respect for the other and the realization that the experience of the other is not one's own" (40). "Empathic unsettlement," according to LaCapra, "poses a barrier to closure in discourse" (41).

The process cut across cultural backgrounds and influences as well as across creative disciplines, with company members from throughout the Americas and Europe. Different parts of the show were inspired by the *cumbia* dance form, by Indigenous songs, and by pre-Columbian art. The influence of western dramaturgy entered the mix during the stages of reflection and analysis. Schwellnus and the company assembled the pieces out of the creative, "interwoven" dramaturgical material to constitute, through alternative ways of working, what is essentially an alternative performance form that is, in Hans-Thies Lehmann's terms, postdramatic: it is not based on (re-en)acting, in the traditional sense of creating "characters," but on the prompting and reacting that characterize Aluna's creation process and the reception of its work by audiences.

Nohayquiensepa, which is based on stories from the Magdalena River in

Colombia and the devastating effects of Canadian mining operations there, is loosely focused on the largely subconscious final moments of a hunted man and the local people who react to his death. It has been variously described over the several manifestations in the course of its development as a cri de coeur for victims of violence, a requiem, and "an investigation on what it means to be on the fringes of violence—to confront its effects not in our personal lives, but where public meets private":

> It is about the death of strangers, and what people do to cope with the realities of violence when we have our own seemingly disconnected lives to live. What kind of answers could we propose in the face of human rights violations against people we don't know? Nothing truly honest (no hay quien sepa—there is no one who knows)—and yet we feel the pull of that need to try to answer the why and how of resolving someone else's pain. (Aluna, Program, *Nohayquiensepa*)

It is also about using the techniques of collective and collaborative creation across disciplinary, artistic, and cultural difference to find "new ways of creating hybrid performances" (Aluna, Program *Nohayquiensepa*).

The show uses the intermedial to mediate key issues in intercultural performance on several fronts, all of which are related to the initial and overarching issue of empathy and its limits across difference as raised by the project's inciting impulse to explore our "capacity for empathy"[15] through the question "how do we deal with the death of a stranger?" Debates about empathy have been renewed in theater and performance studies in the past decade in part because of cognitive studies discourses around the discovery by Vittorio Gallese in 1996 of "mirror neurons" in macaque monkeys (see Gallese et al.; Gallese). Theater, performance, and dance studies scholars such as Bruce McConachie, Rhonda Blair, and Susan Leigh Foster have been quick to explore the implications of these theories for theater and performance. Foster's work, *Choreographing Empathy: Kinesthesia in Performance*, is particularly pertinent to our discussion here because of her attention to social and cultural determinants that frame empathetic responses. Perhaps less well known to the field is the work of trauma scholars such as Sarah Ahmed, Jill Bennett, and Dominick LaCapra, who are useful in addressing our own concern with empathy's tendency to "eat" its other, appropriating and ultimately negating the other's experience by making it one's own. LaCapra warns against "unchecked identification, vicarious experience, and surrogate victimhood" (40), while Sarah Ahmed characterizes empathy as "a 'wish feeling,' in which subjects 'feel' something other than what another feels in the very moment of imagining they could feel what another feels" (*Cultural Politics* 30). "Even when we feel we have the same feeling," she argues, "we don't necessarily have the same relationship to the feeling" (10). Bryoni Trezise parses Ahmed's argument as "intimating that at the heart of empathy there exists an important, but often overlooked, discordance between an intention to enact it and the actuality of performing it." "Perhaps," she suggests, "empathy might always already be diverting itself from its own central cause" (216). Finally, both Ahmed and Susan Leigh Foster relate empathy to the cultural production of "the stranger" in ways that illuminate *Nohayquiensepa*'s central question concerning how we relate to the death of a stranger, both historically and in the contemporary context of globalization, multiculturalism, and technological intervention. Ahmed argues that "emotions may involve 'being moved' for some precisely by fixing others as 'having' certain characteristics. The circulation of objects of emotion involves the transformation of others into objects of feeling" and thereby "objectifies"—makes objects of them (*Cultural Politics* 11). In her earlier book, *Strange Encounters*, Ahmed speaks of this reifying and objectifying "fixing" of others as an act of (creative? rhetorical?) figuration that "*invents the figure of the stranger with a life of its own insofar as it cuts 'the stranger' off from the histories of its determination*" (5, emphasis in original): "It is the very gesture of getting closer to 'strangers' that allows the [reifying] figure to take shape" (4). And as Foster points out, empathy has as part of its history and genealogy a definitional field that involves recognition and therefore the very constitution of the (unrecognizable) other as other, in the service of justifying the colonial project (see S. Foster 142–47).

Jill Bennett nevertheless holds out hope for LaCapra's "empathic unsettlement," finding in the contemporary visual and performance art world's response to trauma "the possibility—for both artist and viewer—of 'being spectator of one's own feelings'" (23)[16] in a way that allows for the kind of self-reflexive, nonappropriative empathy that was addressed in chapter 2 and that we are exploring here in the creation and reception ("for both artist and viewer") of *Nohayquiensepa*. Indeed, we suggest that *Nohayquiensepa*, in foregrounding the limits to proximity between strangers (onstage and in its performer-spectator dynamic), works against the impulse to elide the distance that Ahmed sees as part of the reification of the stranger through what she calls "stranger fetishism" (*Strange Encounters* 5).

Initially for the Aluna company, the question "how do we deal with the death of a stranger?" was prompted by the story of Colombians in Puerto

Berrio who were dealing with the deaths of other Colombians, strangers from upriver rendered all the more strange and unknowable by the fragmentation of their remains. Retrieving these unidentifiable body parts from the Magdalena, the people there adopted the remains, giving names to the strangers and creating a mausoleum in which to bury them. Entering into this project, Schwellnus and Pizano themselves became part of the question, extending it into the realms of the intercultural and intermedial by the nature of their involvement and working process. The story first came to the attention of Pizano and Schwellnus mediated and mediatized; that is, it came by way of a televised news story and it led to Internet research. Thus artists in Canada, now, were "dealing with the deaths of strangers"—and with how strangers deal with the deaths of strangers—across media and culture, and their next step was to use intermediality and interdisciplinarity to work through this extended strangeness and directly explore our "capacity for empathy." This exploration intriguingly brought together the suturing made possible by the technologically "posthuman," by traditionally "kinaesthetic" kinds of connections that Susan Leigh Foster explores in the history of dance, and by the "phenomenological aural experience" that Marcus Cheng Chye Tan finds in what he calls "acoustic interculturalism" (36).[17] These suturings were combined with a degree of detachment that was produced through a frustrated need to perform semiological decoding—to comprehend—that was highlighted throughout the production in ways that we explore below. The pure affective power of Barrios's choreography, Schwellnus's videography, and Ryder Payne's soundscape can, in fact, be understood to produce the longing for meaning and understanding that the performance itself productively frustrates. Ultimately, then, the problem of dealing with the deaths of strangers extends one step further, to *Nohayquiensepa*'s audiences, who can be understood directly to engage the initial impulse of the project, to test, mediate, and experience the power and limits of empathy in ways that reflect the paths traced by the artists' own intercultural and intermedial process of discovery as they worked through an evolving sense of the politically, psychologically, and affectively charged initial question.

The production might be understood to produce what Bennett calls "affective responses [that] can be thought provoking as well as emotive [and] can produce a form of empathy that is more complex and considered than a purely emotional or sentimental reaction" (24). She draws on Gilles Deleuze's notion of the encountered sign that, "far from foreclosing on thought, . . . agitates, compelling and fuelling inquiry rather than simply placating the subject" (36), becoming "the means by which thought proceeds and ultimately moves toward deeper truth" (37). And that truth, arrived at "when one allows the violence of an affective experience to truly inform thinking," can, for Bennett, "inform understandings both about the nature of relationships to others and about the *political* nature of violence and pain" (56, emphasis added). For as Ahmed argues,

> The call of such pain, as a pain that cannot be shared through empathy, is a call not just for an attentive hearing, but for a different kind of inhabitance. It is a call for action, and a demand for collective politics, as a politics based not on the possibility that we might be reconciled, but on learning to live with the impossibility of reconciliation, or learning that we live with and beside each other, and yet we are not as one. (*Cultural Politics* 390)

The "strength of the Arts," Schwellnus writes, is "the sensitivity to hear the softer voices that don't cut through the daily noise of our overmediated lives" ("Why"). Given that Schwellnus's own art is intermedial theatrical design, this assertion expresses the paradox of media as both the barrier to and the agent of intercultural exchange that operates in the development and reception of *Nohayquiensepa*. Intermedial effects that are integral to the creation and presentation of the work frequently express, simultaneously, both the impulse toward and the self-reflexive limitations of empathy. This paradox is closely related to the intermedial paradox discussed by Bruce Barton in his essay "Paradox as Process: Intermedial Anxiety and the Betrayals of Intimacy." Barton productively discusses the ways in which intermediality, by heightening the anxiety and vulnerability of both performers and spectators, can simultaneously heighten the possibilities of intimacy. He talks about the tensions between "vicarious identification" and "an intimacy informed by investments in lucidity, consistency, and comprehension," and he usefully (for our purposes) cites "Yvonne Spielman's assertion that the primary mode of intermedia performance is 'self-reflection'" (581). We are attempting here to extend his insights on intimacy into the different but related realm of empathy. In *Nohayquiensepa*, however, the issue is less about the anxiety that intermediality might produce in spectators than about the capacity for intermediality to mediate between the production of direct kinesthetic or phenomenological response, as suggested above in the work of Barrios and Ryder Payne, and the self-reflection produced by fragmentation and the frustrated longing for semiological "lucidity, consistency, and comprehension" as well as for direct, *un*mediated human connection. The large screen, for example, which dominates the setting (particularly in the first half of the show, when it is located far downstage in the position of a proscenium curtain), at one level represents the tantalizing possibility of easy access to another's experience implicit in our regular engagements with televised news or with naturalistic dramas or films. The screen in *Nohayquiensepa*, however, intrudes on the space in ways that also serve to remind us that this perception of access is illusory, that there is inscrutable life behind, before, and at the peripheries of its projected representations, which in *Nohayquiensepa* the audience literally *sees through*. And throughout the production the screen is used at once to produce and complicate our empathetic relationship to the action. Like the show in which it features, the screen is full of shadows.

When Pizano as actor finally, at first timidly, speaks, over fifteen minutes into *Nohayquiensepa*, she offers a narrative, and with it the tantalizing possibility of some access to meaning, a definitive elaboration on the series of images, on screen and onstage, that have been presented thus far. Speaking in front of a screen onto which is projected a disembodied hand, Pizano (or the "character" she presents) names and begins to narrate (imagine into being) the life of the Magdalena victim she has adopted. As she describes his life with increasing confidence, the disembodied hand on screen gains a body: a live camera pans up the arm until the torso and head of "Claudio" (Uruguayan Canadian actor Carlos González-Vio) come into view behind her.

What is at issue here is the limits of Pizano's access to the unknowable victim: he both is and isn't reachable through Pizano's creative attempt to know him—in Ahmed's terms, to "figure" him—and this self-reflexive articulation of the limits of empathy—and the possibilities of creativity—in communication between strangers is made explicit by the operations of the intercultural and intermedial in this scene. They communicate, she in English, he in Spanish, from stage to screen, seeming to reenact conversations drawn from his life. They speak lines in unison. He comments on—even contradicts—the details of her narrative. For spectators such as us, fluent in only one of the two languages, there are limits to understanding the nature of this interaction. Indeed, there are other, nonlinguistic limits as well, which taken together serve to disrupt the spectator's certainty about what she is seeing: if Pizano, or the character she is presenting, has conjured this "Claudio" imaginatively and technologically from an unknown fragment or body part, if she has given him life through imagining his life story, then who is this man that we see on screen? Is he the embodiment of her fabrication, a fragment turned into a man? Is he the man, the victim, who became Pizano's fragment? Or is he a kind of techno-cyborg, a posthuman figure

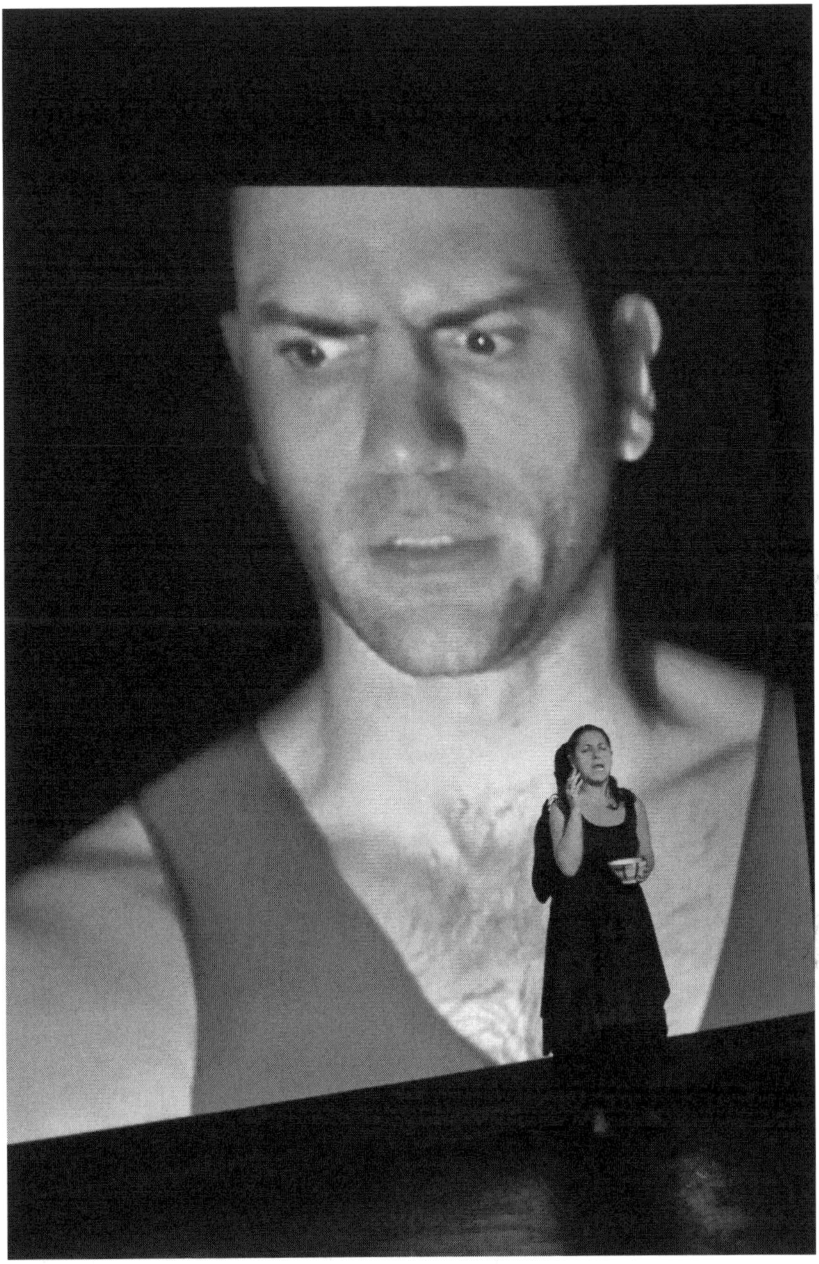

Fig. 10. The live camera pans up from the fragmented image of a hand to reveal the torso, then head of Carlos González-Vio (Claudio) as Béatriz Pizano names and describes the imagined character's life with increasing confidence. Photo by Katherine Fleitas.

reconstituted on screen through full-body prostheses and technological wishful thinking?

At one level, Pizano virtually breathes (on-screen) life into the body fragment that she has discovered in a synecdoche of the way in which the technology provided by the intermedial show itself prosthetically reassembles the bodies of the unknown victims in Puerto Berrio. At the same time, however, we are made self-reflexive by the seemingly provisional ontological status of the "characters," including the "hunted man" that the show is purportedly about. As we "*see [ourselves] feeling*," in Bennett's phrase (47, emphasis in original)—as we "catch [ourselves] in the act" (123)—we are made aware of the limits of empathy across difference through the mediating and mediatized disruption of an impulse toward intercultural engagement that is potentially appropriative and distorting. We experience a type of empathy that "comes into play when . . . we inhabit the space—the difference—between ourselves and others" (Bennett 123), and our certainties about shared understanding, in this instance, are experientially unsettled. As LaCapra argues, such unsettlement "places in jeopardy harmonizing or spiritually uplifting accounts of extreme events from which we attempt to derive reassurance or a benefit (for example unearned confidence about the ability of the human spirit to endure any adversity with dignity and nobility)" (41–42). This unsettlement, this detached wish for empathy, we suggest, is a common function and effect of digital and social media encounters with "the other" that include online petitions and fundraising appeals that create safe spaces for neoempathetic responses to safely distant "others."

And then Pizano exits and "Claudio" comes to life. González-Vio enters the auditorium through the audience-center aisle, climbing onto the stage and beginning violently to interact with his silhouettes/doubles on the screen. To the ragged, unsettling sound of machinery, he runs, literally shadowed by a multifigured, multilimbed image behind him, seeming to run from the screen toward the (embrace of?) the audience, but trapped in motion, making no progress. The surprise of first seeing an embodied rather than on-screen Claudio is not, however, accompanied by a greater sense of empathetic identification. Perhaps because of our familiarity with filmic naturalism, the on-screen figure seemed somehow more engaging, more "real," than this nevertheless desperate figure enmeshed in his own shadows in an increasingly claustrophobic mise-en-scène. Claustrophobic, that is, until, in an extraordinary moment, the screen that has kept the stage so foreshortened to this point lifts in what Pizano and Schwellnus call "the opening-up moment" and the stage is taken over by dancers as the screen, with seemingly independent, nonhuman agency, adjusts and settles itself farther upstage.

Thus the freedom from conventional dramaturgical constraints that Pizano and Schwellnus cite as the product of their interdisciplinary and intermedial, collaborative development processes also operates in the possibilities for reception that emerge in performance. As indicated in our description of the play's first "dramatic" moments, through Pizano's narration and animation of the life of "Claudio," *Nohayquiensepa* invokes and disrupts assumptions that commonly inform conventional theatrical reception, at least in Canada. Audience members seeking to know "what does it mean?" both get their answer and don't. Indeed, as Pizano aptly notes, spectators asking "what does it mean?" register not only the disruption of their inherited assumptions but also, significantly, their engagement: "That [is] the thing they are so interested in." This fixation conveys the theatrical power of the unexplained, replacing "what does it mean?" with "what are we to make of this?"; like the artists and their original subjects, replacing the need for comprehension (and therefore control) with the impulse to imagine or create.[18] Drawn in by the disruption of convention and denied the conventional routes to meaning associated with control and comprehension (with any pretension to complete or discrete, definitive or unquestioned understanding), the spectator becomes aware of the possibility of an alternative, nonappropriative communication model—a model, even, for a different form of empathy—one that includes the reflexive recognition of its own limits and incompleteness.

The most ostensibly "dramatic" scene in the piece occurs at the midpoint of its hour-long duration and might serve as a further example. Here the more traditional "character" of a journalist is introduced (though one with neither backstory nor through line). The audience's expectation of a conventional "scene" is initially evoked with the sound of a ringtone and an opening line spoken realistically into a cell phone—"Hello, yeah, I'll be right there." There is even a revealing expository detail: "I woke up this morning in a hotel. . . . I thought I'd learn some Spanish before I got here, but you know how that goes. Best intentions . . ." However, the staging of the scene and the incorporation of projections disrupt these expectations of realism, as they do expectations of human-to-human cross-cultural understanding. The reporter's interview subjects are bodies writhing on the floor, projected on screen in a wash of blue light that evokes the Magdalena and its victims of violence, and his extending microphone becomes a fishing line, dredging the river for its secrets. Most of these secrets are delivered in Spanish, which the journalist struggles to translate and relays to us in fragments: "something about a door . . . flowers, water, and salt," "something about a mountain . . . ," "something about no water in the tank." Eventually one of the women "climbs" him, literally enmeshing him in a struggle that he initially ignores. When he finally drops his microphone to the floor, another woman crawls to it, crying out in Spanish and eventually crying *tout court,* as the journalist moves his body, apparently experiencing pain akin to that which is registered in the woman's voice. His writhing seems to respond to something that is not there; the unseen assailant who prompts the woman's cries seems also to prompt the journalist's contortions. Or do the cries themselves bring on the journalist's pain? Is his pain analogous to hers, brought on by the same assailant, or is it an echo, a personal expression at a remove, an onstage depiction of Ahmed's "wish feeling" empathetic experience that creates distinct, subject-specific emotion in the place of any direct appropriation of feeling or experience? This uncertainty is amplified by our own empathetic impulses, prompted simultaneously by the aural encounter with the woman's suffering and the onstage image of the writhing man. As in Ahmed's definition of empathy, we are powerfully affected by this feeling, prompted to "imagin[e] we [can] feel what another feels," but the very fragmentation of this feeling, the onstage illustration of the dislocation of empathetic "wish feeling," fractures and makes plain the limits to this impulse toward a unifying—and universal—experience of suffering. Meanwhile, the upstage screen shows images of the squares that we had seen in the preshow, which we come to understand to be the individual graves of a large mausoleum, and as the journalist points to or touches these cells, the projected hand of the live drawer blacks them out while the previously writhing and whispering bodies on the stage floor assume fetal positions, deadly still, and are projected onto the screen from overhead cameras. The scene dissolves into a video of walking feet that fill the screen as a voice-over sings lines from Emilíana Torrini's haunting "Beggar's Prayer," highlighting the refrain, "Mama said eventually this hurting will end."[19]

The sequence seems to cry out for an empathetic response, as we see the journalist move from his initial casual composure to kinesthetically embodying and enacting a version of his subject's struggles, as we ourselves witness and experience viscerally something that resembles at a distance the wrenching pain of the depicted victims, and as we finally hear the moving lyrics of the song. But neither the journalist nor the dancers are figures who invite identification, and finally the video that accompanies the song, featuring the apparently indifferent feet of passers-by, serves as a distancing, and puzzling, distraction from conventional pity or fear. The audience in Canada understands that something terrible has happened and through other clues in the production knows that this ecological and human disaster is an outcome of the practices of Canadian mining companies and the policies of Canadian governments. But we are not allowed to own the grief that we see depicted, to feel the pleasures of purgative identification, or to let ourselves emotionally off the hook for what we are coming to understand. Perhaps what we experience is less the vicarious and dubious pleasure of empathetic involvement and more the longing to respond actively and adequately to something that we experience through the mediation of technology and cannot fully access or comprehend.

The audience's experience of this central sequence, moreover, once again replicates that of the theater company, as the journalist's questions and research into the ultimately unknowable may be seen to represent those of the company itself, while the audience's piecing it all together—"something about body parts and a river," perhaps, "something about ecological disaster," "something about mining"—replicates both.[20] Here and throughout the show the show's audiences, like its creators, are "working within environments," reacting to prompts rather than witnessing reenactments that are always and inevitably inadequate. In these ways the show models and prompts an affective, differently empathetic way of connecting across difference that is at once powerful, provocative, deeply moving, and openly mediated.

Against the backdrop of the apparently indifferent passing feet, the transition from this sequence to the next occurs through the limited and ultimately unsettling onstage depiction of the spectator's impulse to reach out across difference and offer assistance. Pizano crosses the stage and reaches out to aid a dancer, lifting her from the ground, but this ostensibly simple act of assistance is implicitly complicated by the operations of costumes and props. Pizano, dressed in what registers as the first recognizable "costume" in the performance, wears a corporate ensemble, glasses and a jacket. Is this, then, to be understood as an empty gesture by a corporate flunky? Far from a fulfillment of our fantasy for an easy connection across difference, Pizano's costume reminds us of the contentious issue of "corporate social responsibility" (CSR) that is to be the subject of a public debate as part of the festival, immediately following *Nohayquiensepa* on one of the days we were in attendance. Though the dancer accepts Pizano's assistance in rising from the stage floor, she notably rejects Pizano's proffered microphone, refusing to be "given" a voice.

Moments later, this refusal is repeated by the audience. Extending the microphone in our direction, Pizano invites spectators—specifically the

Torontonian audience of which we were a part—to fill the gap left by the dancer's refusal, to say what needs to be said in response to the suffering we've witnessed. Finding the audience silent, however, the corporate figure herself attempts to speak, but she too finds herself lost, stuck at the expression of self, literally as (grammatical) subject, uttering "I . . . ," and struggling to move beyond it. At the same time, the screen functions intermedially to extend the implications of this limited "I." As the show has evolved, the hand of the live drawer has come to feel like an extension of the audience, and here, as it visibly transcribes and then falters in its self-expression, "I . . . ," spectators are once again invited to reflect on the limits of empathetic engagement. Across languages, too, we see this expressed, as González-Vio comes forward to utter, and falter at, his own "Yo . . . ," duly recorded by the hand on screen. The hand that writes, finally, completes in Spanish the sentence that neither Pizano nor González-Vio was able to finish giving voice to, and in so doing expresses the limits to knowledge across difference, to certainty in the face of violence, to the capacity for words to atone for the devastating practices of Canadian mining companies in Colombia, adding on screen "no se" ("[I] . . . don't know"). As the show's title tells us, no one does.

Not knowing, the limits to knowledge and therefore to empathy, is then illustrated experientially by what the creators call the "eulogy scene." The performers line up, initially one behind the other and later in a row across the base of the screen, and deliver eulogies in overlapping languages and voices. Arising directly out of one of the improvisation exercises used to create the piece, in which the performers were asked to offer eulogies to strangers, the scene is staged in order to recapture what emerged in the development process as an "exercise in listening." The scene remains unscripted, so the actors, improvising every night, are forced not only to create but to listen to one another in performance. "The listening is key," Schwellnus says, "giving your thing, but also letting someone else talk. It was like creating a choir." Experiencing these multiple, bilingual, and overlapping speeches from the position of a spectator, however, the effect of this listening exercise is to disrupt any expectation that what we hear, in the theater, defines and delineates our ability to make meaning, that what we receive as spectators is what we need to know. Here, instead, the experience highlights the limits to our knowledge, to our ability to make meaning. We can't hear everything, no matter how hard we try; we are necessarily limited in our access to the experiences of others. Thus we experience the impulse to understand, straining as we do to distinguish particular voices, to make whole the fragments of speech we are able to discern while simultaneously confronting experientially the limits to that understanding.

Moreover, those fragments that we do piece together serve to make plain the very real limits to meaningful cross-cultural communication surrounding the mining practices of Canadian companies in Colombia. The English fragments discernible in this eulogy scene range from bureaucratic ("I would have preferred more time to prepare something more suitable on this terrible day. I want you to know that the company is . . . regretful;" "[It is] inappropriate for me at this time to comment as the investigation is going on; however we believe in the community. We believe in the project") to ridiculous (a "closet vegetarian" impulsively confesses, "When there is a chicken I eat chicken"), and they compete against Spanish voices for provisional dominance, as the microphone passes from hand to hand in midsentence, even midphrase. At one point, one of the figures is asked about life in Canada. "It's a good life," she responds, to which the questioner replies, "Señora, we also want a good life."

Here, as in many other scenes in *Nohayquiensepa,* the onstage action is accompanied by the on-screen hands of Lorena Torres Loaiza, engaged in live drawing in dialogic, intermedial response to the action (the hands rarely prompt or precipitate what happens onstage). Loaiza's live drawing, in an instance of process-as-performance, re-creates the responsive, collaborative, intermedial dynamics of the collective creation of *Nohayquiensepa.* The artist's hands, in the development process and in the live performance, help to create the space in which the performers, and later the audience, come together. Perhaps most importantly, however, the projected hands also have the potential to literalize reception, at certain points in the show functioning as live, responsive prosthetics for the audience, within which the artist herself is physically situated (the technical requirements of the show necessitate her positioning in the tech booth) and out of which the hands are literally projected. In the eulogy scene, as elsewhere, Loaiza's projected, prosthetic hand serves as a potential conduit for spectators' own responses both to that which is represented and to the experiential discoveries fostered by the performance. As the eulogists speak, the artist's hand makes marks over their bodies in groups of five slashes on a projected transparency, keeping a kind of tally that, digitally multiplying to cover the entire surface of the constantly shifting transparency, comes to resemble the bars of a kind of prison for the eulogists.[21]

Perhaps enacting a sort of justice on the part of the audience, this tally keeping simultaneously reads as futile, experienced as it is alongside the

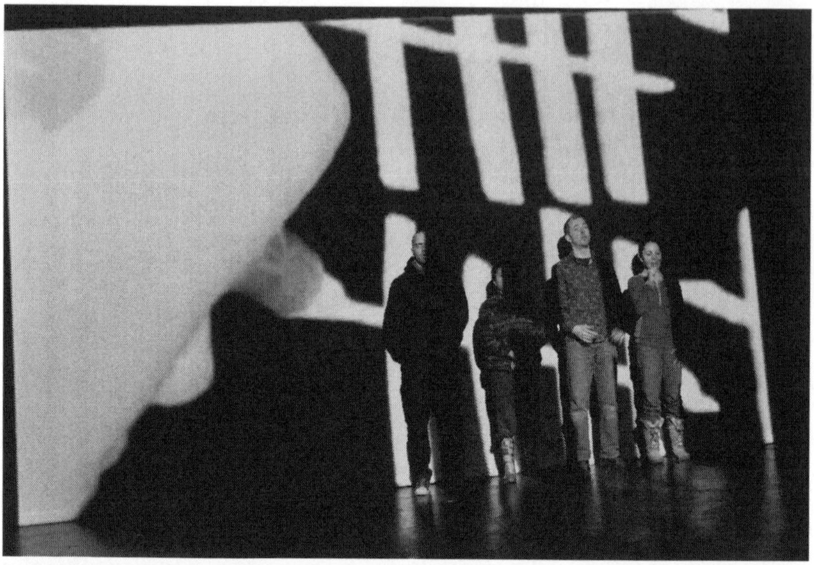

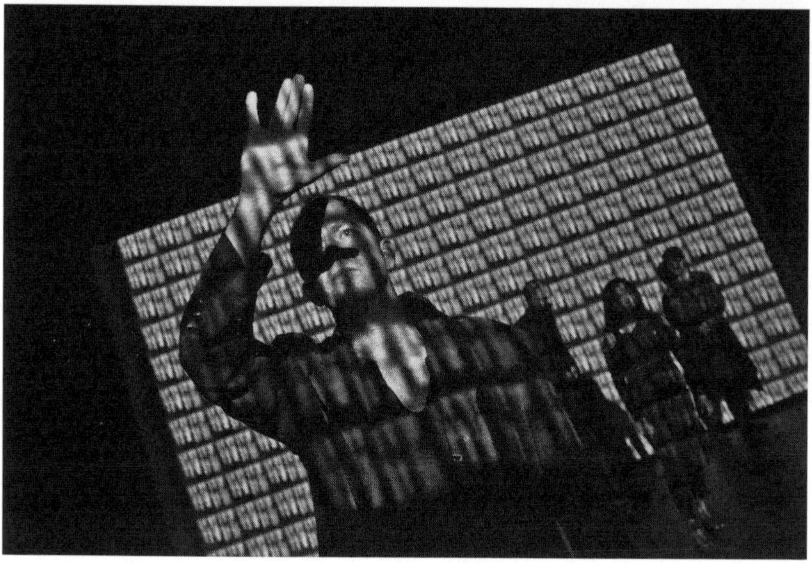

Figs. 11 and 12. The hand of artist Lorena Torres Loaiza, projected live, keeps a count as Carlos Gonzáles-Vio, Mayahuel Tecozautla, Christopher Stanton, and Béatriz Pizano deliver their overlapping eulogies to strangers in Spanish and English. The tally escalates "digitally" as they speak. Photo by Katherine Fleitas.

impossible aural track keeping of the listening exercise itself: we simply can't hear everything that's said.

The hands often do things in response to the action that we want to do. But the impulse toward identification (those hands are "my" hands, with all the attendant intercultural implications concerning the appropriations effected by traditional empathetic cross-cultural response), as with other, similar impulses, is evoked only to be disrupted. The intermediality of the hands' projection on screen, for example, prosthetics for the artist's limbs as they are for the audience's impulses, serves as a constant reminder that those hands are manifestly not "mine," serving as another instance of the tension between the prosthetic potential of the intermedial and its limits. A culminating instance of the productive affect of this dynamic comes in the final moments of the show. The hands—fully established, by now, as both "my hands" and not—engage in their penultimate task: the piecing together of fragments of a torn-up letter that has spilled out of an envelope addressed to the "Minister of Foreign Affairs and International Trade Canada." As the hands assemble the fragments (echoing the earlier on-screen piecing together of the body of "Claudio"), the audience may recognize words and phrases that had seemed random in the live drawing during the preshow. Fully assembled, the letter reads,

> Let me be clear, saying these things to you today puts my life in danger. Already, four Embeca leaders have been killed by paramilitary forces for challenging the negative impact of the Urra mega project. . . . Anyone who dares to speak out about Urra is accused of being involved with the guerillas and with that pretext, both our communities and leadership have been deemed a military target.

It is signed "Kimy Pernia Domico."

For those in the know, the letter has documentary force. The words are taken from a deposition made by Kimy Pernía Domicó,[22] a leader of the embattled Embera Katío Indigenous People, to a Canadian parliamentary commission in 1999. Domicó had come to Canada to draw attention to the hunger, disease, and rainforest habitat destruction on the Upper Sinú River in northern Colombia brought about by a hydroelectric megaproject funded in part by Canada's Export Development Corporation. On June 2, 2001, he was abducted by three gunmen believed to belong to army-backed paramilitary groups and has not been seen since. In January 2007 paramilitary leader Salvatore Mancuso confessed to participating in Domicó's murder.

Literalizing as it does the repeatedly evoked and limited impulses to

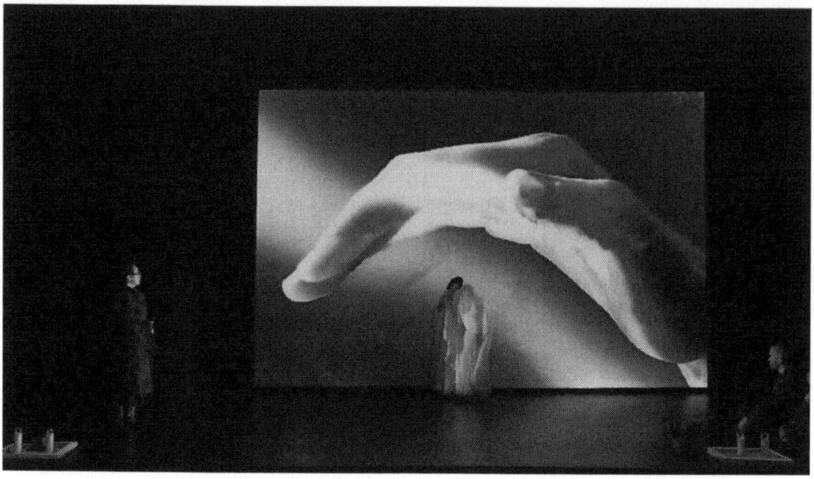

Fig. 13. Lorena Torres Loaiza's projected hand functions as an audience prosthetic to shelter *cumbia*-inspired dancers Victoria Mata and Lilia Leon as Béatriz Pizano and Carlos González-Vio watch. Screen capture from video by Trevor Schwellnus.

make meaningful wholes out of fragmentary parts, which also recalls the larger project's impetus, this on-screen assembly of the letter is the culmination of our identificatory impulse toward the hand as audience and artist prosthetic throughout the production. In this moment, our longing to make sense of what we have been presented with, even to assign or assume responsibility, is to some extent fulfilled. A whole and comprehensible document emerges, and it demands our attention. The question of what to do with this letter—posed by the fact that it is directed to a minister of the Canadian government—is raised by way of our evolving sense of the on-screen hands as audience prosthetic.

This culminating moment of identification and complicity precedes the hands' final intervention. While the letter is assembled and as the show draws to a close, the two *cumbia* dancers, with the same outstretched white skirts that they wore at the opening, reappear, by now identified with the peoples of the Magdalena region, after which the artist's hand, protective now, arches on the screen above them, seeming to fulfill the audience's urge to offer shelter.

The sheltering of the dancers expresses our longing through a gesture that is not appropriative but that symbolizes and provokes social engagement and responsibility. A numbered list of names appears on the screen, the disappeared, to which is added, as number 667, "Kimy Pernia Domico, Disappeared, June 2001." And as the rest of the cast and the audience watch, the women . . . dance.

This dance—a celebration, a wake?—and the shelter of a prosthetic hand that represents at once an audience's need and its inability to protect, both longing and incapacity for empathetic identification, juxtaposed so closely with the letter and the long and growing list of the disappeared, are productively unsettling rather than purgative, posthumanist rather than posthuman, enabling and provoking rather than forestalling or replacing thought and action. We feel ourselves feeling. In the words of Susan Leigh Foster in another context, the dancers "foreground the partiality and incompleteness of empathy even as they invite viewers to dance along with them" (218).

EIGHT | Cahoots

> Cahoots
> 1. go cahoots, to share equally; become partners:
> They went cahoots in the establishment of the store.
> Also, go in cahoot with, go in cahoots.
>
> 2. in cahoot/cahoots,
>
> in partnership; in league.
> in conspiracy: in cahoots with the enemy.
> —*Dictionary.com*[1]

The first theater company in Toronto with an explicitly intercultural mandate was Cahoots Theatre Projects (now Cahoots Theatre Company). Cahoots has played a central role in the developing discourses and practices of intracultural performance in the city. In 1990, early in the company's life, it sponsored a galvanizing conference of minority playwrights, Write About Now, and its artistic directors have consistently been leaders in the developing discourses around multiculturalism, interculturalism, and diversity in the theatrical life of the city. Meanwhile the history of the company is a kind of microcosm of the way in which difference in new play development has evolved in the city over the past three decades.

Cahoots was founded in 1986 by Beverly Yhap, a Chinese Trinidadian Canadian whose mixed race had *always* led her to question traditional 1980s versions of identity politics that underscored the mandates of many of the culturally specific, feminist, and queer theaters that had emerged in Toronto in the late 1970s and 1980s. The company was initially formed to bring the late Jesse Glenn Boyden's play *Skull Riders*, first produced in Vancouver, to Toronto's Winchester Street Theatre. A dark, expressionist western set in Montana in 1902, by a white male playwright and featuring a cast of five white men, *Skull Riders* is not typical of what Cahoots, then touted as a company whose goal was to produce works "that stretch the boundaries of form and expression" (Cahoots Theatre Projects), would proceed to produce.[2] The company did stage a notable production of *The Phoenix Cabaret* in 1988, a tradaptation by Henry Beissel and Jia-Lin Peng of two Chinese one-act plays by Xie Min, banned in China, about the Cultural Revolution and its aftermath. But it didn't fully assume its leadership role in Toronto's and Canada's intercultural performance ecology until it got involved with Write About Now, billed as "The First Canadian Conference of Visible Minority Playwrights," in June 1990.

The conference featured keynote addresses by pioneers Tomson Highway (Cree), Maria Campbell (Métis), and Rick Shiomi (Japanese Canadian); sessions, mostly practical, on responsibility, resources, self-determination, and nurturing ; a resolution to adopt "people of colour" (rather than "visible minorities") as a working term; and a cabaret evening of performances and readings. The conference was held, symbolically, at the Toronto city hall's council chambers; the readings were at Factory Theatre's Studio Café. The conference was ahead of its time in grounding itself in Indigeneity, particularly in Maria Campbell's keynote and Anishinaabe Lenore Keeshig Tobias's address to white allies to be prepared to "step back and be forgotten" and to "defer to the voices of the people you're working for" (Write About Now, "Discussion"). Significantly, the company's first production following the conference was of Delaware Nation playwright Daniel David Moses's dark comedy *Big Buck City*.

In retrospect, however, Write About Now was perhaps most notable for Beverley Yhap's own contribution, following up on her 1988 article in *Canadian Theatre Review* that had presciently pointed to a shift that had taken place among artists of color since the days of Black Theatre Canada and Theatre Fountainhead (see appendix 1 and chapter 5): these new artists, she argued, were "committed to making concerns known and understood *on their own terms*. . . , uncompromisingly, challenging the host community to move beyond recognition to self-criticism" (Yhap 25). At Write About Now she presented a "shopping list" for different constituencies that is still relevant:

- for the public (including arts councils): she asked that artists of color be recognized as "exactly that" rather than be adopted as white, therefore imposing white standards, "because traditions are not shared across the board, and they involve historical inequities." She asked that members of the public and of funding bodies "educate themselves about diverse cultures so that work can be appraised in a knowledgeable climate";

- for communities: she asked that they learn to recognize artistic creativity as distinct from advocacy or promotion, integrating arts activity into the fabric of the community;
- for artists: she asked that they take responsibility to define themselves in relation to their communities, to be informed and to inform others about the cultural underpinnings of their work;
- finally, she argued, for the conference attendees: "we all in this room have a general responsibility as members of Canadian society to monitor the workings of this society, its institutions, how they're funded, where the funding comes from and how it's allocated, who pays and who profits." (Write About Now, "Responsibility")

In a CBC Radio Noon interview promoting the conference, responding to Grenadian Canadian Richardo Keens-Douglas's "I mean white's a colour too, right?" and speaking out of her own position as Chinese Trinidadian Canadian, Yhap lamented "the notion that culture is one monolith."

In the wake of this conference Yhap and Cahoots emerged as leaders in the discourses surrounding intercultural performance in Toronto, and each subsequent artistic director of the company has extended that leadership role. Indeed, Yhap herself, along with her successor at Cahoots, Korean Canadian Jean Yoon (with Linda Hill), were among a group of artists of color, mainly women such as Brenda Kamino, Dawn Obokata, Sandi Ross, Sally Han, and others, who worked tirelessly in the 1990s as lobbyists, board members, spokespeople, and activists to change policy at arts councils and professional organizations in order to improve access, profile, working conditions, and funding for minoritized artists. Yoon, coartistic director of Cahoots from 1992 to 1994, has been particularly vociferous in her address, both externally to organizations such as Canadian Actors Equity and the Ontario Arts Council and within the community, where she has consistently urged her fellow Asian Canadian artists to work in solidarity, keeping in mind "the bigger picture" ("Chinese") and to provide and demand adequate compensation for their work: "I'm an artist. Pay me" ("Reflections" 85). She has also made significant contributions to the historical record in talks she has given, panels she has participated in, and articles she has contributed to *Canadian Theatre Review* ("Chinese") and *The Canadian Encyclopedia* (Berger and Yoon).

Taken together, the leaders of Cahoots have tackled topics such as culture, multiculturalism, cultural diversity, equity, solidarity, funding, casting, representation, racism, and culturally specific performance forms, and they have done so with considerable sophistication and grace. The company's mandate has shifted over the years, but it has been consistently "dedicated to the creation, development and production of new works that investigate the complexities of Canada's cultural diversity" and has in recent years made explicit the intention to "examine the intersections of these cultures" (Cahoots Theatre Company, "Mandate"). This mandate has, of course, been the site of debate, particularly around terms such as *culture* and *diversity*. Perhaps Argentinian Canadian Guillermo Verdecchia, artistic director from 1998 to 2003, citing both Beverly Yhap and Jean Yoon, set the tone in arguing for an understanding of culture as "a process, not a finished thing. Culture is a living system: open, dynamic, and responsive" ("Seven Things" 107). Invoking Gloria Anzaldúa's "borderlands" theory (as he had done in his award-winning 1993 play *Fronteras Americanas: American Borders*), he committed the company to a focus on "the fluidity of culture[s] . . . , their points of intersection, of overlap, of fusion. We should," he argued, "focus on the shifting border zones."

> It seemed to me that Cahoots could address not only race, ethnicity, and nation of origin, but also gender and sexuality, self-identification, language, class, religion, ability, hybridity, and all the really interesting inventions, concoctions, proposals, and definitions that human beings come up with as we negotiate our existential condition. ("Seven Things" 107)

Unlike multiculturalism, then, which Verdecchia defined as "the official policy of promoting polyethnicity" (108), cultural diversity could address the diversity *internal* to cultures, broadly understood, and he crucially included in his understanding of diversity a vision and acknowledgement of "visibly diverse audiences" (108).

Verdecchia's essay was first published in 2003. By 2008 his successor as artistic director, Chinoy (Chinese Filipino) Canadian Jovanni Sy, was lamenting the language of cultural diversity, which, he felt, had "outlived its usefulness." Given what he felt was the obvious diversity of Canada, "doesn't it make more sense for us to describe Cahoots simply as 'a company that produces new Canadian plays,'" he asked (Cahoots Theatre Company, Red Hut, 11 April 2008). Intriguingly, Beverly Yhap responded to his blog post with her own assertion that "diversity isn't a choice" for Canadians of color *or* "of pallor": it just is. Once again pointing to her own mixed heritage, she pleaded, "When we talk about diversity, let's please really yes talk about diversity" (Cahoots Theatre Company, Red Hut, 11 April 2008).

Sy responded with a striking example of what he was trying to address:

> In February 2007, Cahoots (with Modern Times and Theatre Passe Muraille) produced Bobby Theodore's translation of Ahmed Ghazali's *The Sheep and the Whale*, an epic drama mounted with seventeen performers. In keeping with the play's themes, our cast's ethnic origins spanned all parts of the globe. I found it quite thrilling to see them fanned out taking their curtain call at the end of each performance. Obviously I wasn't alone. Three separate reviews pointed out how exceptional it was to see a show that looked like modern-day Canada.
>
> At the same time *The Sheep and the Whale* was running, Tarragon mounted their outstanding production of [Lebanese Québécois] Wajdi Mouawad's *Scorched* (translated by Linda Gaboriau). Much of the play's action takes place in an unnamed Middle Eastern country engulfed in civil war. To the best of my knowledge, the cast of ten had no actors of Middle Eastern descent.

Indeed, the cast, not unexceptionally for the relatively conservative Tarragon Theatre (whose directors presumably felt they were doing a Québécois and therefore white European play), was all somatically white. Sy continued,

> While we were being praised for reflecting Canada's pluralism, I never read a single word pointing out that *Scorched* . . . represented a bold experiment in cross-cultural casting. In other words, a predominantly "white" cast portraying Arabs was so "normal" that it didn't even merit comment. . . .
>
> As lovely as it was to be publicly praised for the United Colours of Benetton feel of *The Sheep and the Whale*, I would gladly trade places so that our show's multiculturalism went unnoticed while *Scorched* got praise for its edgy and daring use of non-traditional casting. (Cahoots Theatre Company, Red Hut, 15 April 2008)

Casting, of course, has been much discussed, though the discourse has moved on from early and problematic topics such as "color-blind casting" (problematic because it purports to erase somatic difference that has unavoidable semiotic value) and "best actor for the job" regardless of race or ethnicity to nuanced considerations of "nontraditional casting," the representation of difference through maintaining culturally specific worldviews and the intercultural constitution of the entire creative team. But this "moving on" has been uneven within and across communities, highly divisive, and controversial, as when, in 2015, Algonquin playwright Yvette Nolan's award-winning postapocalyptic play *The Unplugging* was co-produced by Factory Theatre and Native Earth Performing Arts with a widely diverse creative team. (As Factory artistic director Nina Lee Aquino, former artistic director of Cahoots, said, "we are allies" ["Open letter"]). After an intensive but unsuccessful search, the team, including Aquino, Nolan, and Ryan Cunningham, the Métis Cree artistic director of Native Earth, cast white actors in the play's central Indigenous roles,[3] a decision that was seen as problematic and deeply offensive by many in the Indigenous community.

In addition to debates around identity politics, culture, diversity, and casting, Cahoots has actively engaged in discussions of the personal and public responsibilities of artists, audiences, and reviewers, including the responsibilities of artists to the communities they represent, the responsibility of reviewers to acknowledge their position, and the responsibility of reviewers and audiences to be open to other forms and acknowledge different contextual factors (see Offord). Indeed, current artistic director and award-winning Chinese Canadian playwright, librettist, actor, and director Marjorie Chan's response to reviews of Cahoots's production of what was possibly the first Afghan Canadian play, Kawa Ada's epic postdramatic family drama *The Wanderers* in 2014, was a model of sensible and restrained commentary in the face of extraordinary critical obtuseness, reductiveness, and arrogance:

> Asking a culturally specific story to be told through a specific lens is asking for that culture to be placed in a box of your own understanding. Why do we even have our own specific expectations of the artistic voice of a cultural minority? Expectations of form, lead to expectations of content, lead to expectations of voice, lead to the loss of the unique cultural perspective of the artist. Does all culturally-diverse work have to live in the same established aesthetic?
>
> Cahoots' mandate is one of inclusion and pluralistic values. We believe that all stories are important and deserve to be shared. We entrust and empower our artists to share the specifics of their perspective and as such, an artist needs to have the ability to be able to tell the story in the form that they want to tell it. Kawa Ada should be considered on his own terms. His experience is unique and indeed, so is his aesthetic. He writes episodically, mimicking the se-

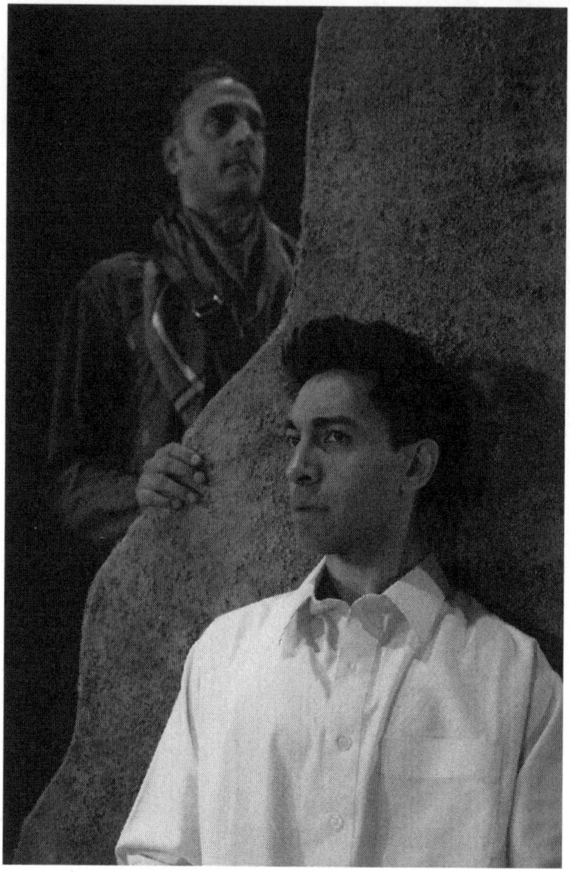

Fig. 14. Omar Alex Khan and Kawa Ada in the Cahoots Theatre Company production of Ada's *The Wanderers*. Photo by Dahlia Katz Photography.

> lected memories of PTSD survivors. He writes elliptically, as befits an indirect style of Afghan storytelling. He writes poetically, because he is an artist.

"If we are not able to discuss or understand plays from different cultural perspectives without being diminishing," she asks, "how can we even begin to live and understand one another?" ("Closing Thoughts").

Chan articulates her priorities for the company as threefold:

1. Mentorship/community engagement: "For us to truly serve marginalized groups," she argues, "Cahoots must be able to address everyone at every level of access." She therefore prioritizes, first, refugees and newcomers, followed by emerging artists, and fi-

nally, play development, with production placed at the center of the mission.

2. Diversity of practice: "It is very challenging," she says, "to develop works that don't have their basis in text, as it takes more time and certainly more resources." She talks about building "diversity of audience through diversity of practices. . . . I am unconvinced that aesthetics are the same around the globe, so by that reasoning a culturally diverse company must embrace different forms, instead of continuously holding up the mainstream or the dominant idea of theatre."
3. Partnerships: "I strongly believe that as a smaller organization Cahoots can benefit strongly with partnerships with others. The more that we are able to collaborate, the more work that we are able to do, and the more artists that we can serve." (Email)

But Cahoots has not only consistently provided leadership around the published discourses of diversity within the city's intercultural performance ecology, it has also been a central node in the intercultural meshworks through its practice. It initially pioneered a movement away from identity politics toward a model of "Coming Together," as its first in a series of Lift Off! play development festivals was called. Later Cahoots worked with a broadening definition of "culture" beyond the usual multicultural mix, and beyond multiculturalism, toward a practice and understanding of "diversity" that *encouraged,* rather than simply managed, tolerated, or even celebrated, difference.

As we saw in chapter 1, Mayte Gómez has critiqued the first Lift Off!, organized by coartistic directors Jean Yoon and Lynda Hill in 1993, for reinforcing discourses of universalism, for failing to instantiate dramaturgical models that are structurally heterogeneous, and for failing to occupy its own cultural and physical space. But in the same essay she also celebrates the fact of the festival's having created "strategic alliances" across difference (38). Indeed, she argues,

> The festival's workshops and public readings were a triumph for activists in cultural policy. In Lift Off! as a collective event dozens of artists from several cultures assumed without apology the roles of protagonists as creators and organizers. As a group they owned the means of production which made their work possible. They gained access to public funding, chose to work on specific scripts which were of interest to them, were able to have their work developed by

> actors from the same cultural groups, had a public reading in which they were (and very importantly too, were perceived as being) the sole protagonists, and had an opportunity to voice the issues and struggles they believed are important in Canada. . . . In this way, artists of diverse cultures reclaimed their voices as full protagonists in the theatre community and in society at large. (38)

Ever since that first Lift Off! Festival, in which six plays were developed cross-culturally by playwrights in the Indigenous, Asian, South Asian, and arguably African Canadian communities (*Belle*, about two slaves and a suffragette during Reconstruction in the late-1860s United States, was controversially written by white playwright Florence Gibson), Cahoots has been a central node for everyone in the "brown caucus." From 1993 to 2006 (Lift Off! 2006 took place in Hong Kong as part of Festival Canada), and again since its revival by Marjorie Chan in 2014, Lift Off! has continued to develop new plays from diverse communities. Play development has continued in other forms as well, including a playwright-in-residence program that has hosted such diverse artists as Tara Beagan, Jo SiMalaya Alcampo, Thomas Morgan Jones, Jani Lauzon, Leah-Simone Bowen, and Suvendrina Lena. Cahoots has also run a "playwright's hothouse" unit involving four to six writers from diverse backgrounds. In both the hothouse and the residency programs, moreover, it has recently expanded its mandate to actively explore queer, disability, and Deaf cultures. Under Nina Lee Aquino the mandate was expanded beyond race, nation of origin, and ethnicity to encompass gender, sexuality, ability, language, and class, as originally proposed by Verdecchia in 2003 ("Seven Things," 107). Following this, and in addition to the support that has been given to numerous queer artists of color (particularly women), Aquino included white queer playwright extraordinaire Sky Gilbert (founding artistic director of Buddies in Bad Times, North America's largest queer theater) as a member of the playwright's hothouse in her first year as artistic director. In 2011 she appointed white playwright-director Thomas Morgan Jones to the position of playwright in residence and developed his text-and-movement piece, *Sam in Three*, about his diagnosis with multiple sclerosis. The show has so far received a workshop production at Buddies in Bad Times' Rhubarb! Festival. Receiving a full production in 2016 under Marjorie Chan was the extraordinary play *Ultrasound*, by Adam Pottle, who may be the first professional playwright in Canada who identifies as Deaf. The play, involving a Deaf and hearing-impaired couple facing the prospect of having a hearing baby, incorporates American Sign Language (ASL) and surtitles as an intrinsic part of its design and dramaturgy. Alongside the production the company under Chan held a four-week series of Crossing Gibraltar workshops for emerging Deaf artists of color and have created DATT, a multimedia guide ("The Deaf Artist & Theatre Toolkit") to help theater companies engage with Deaf and hearing impaired artists and audiences and address the currently dominant ablist theatrical culture that prevails in Toronto and Canada (See Cahoots Theatre Company, "DATT").

That *Ultrasound* was performed as Cahoots's mainstage production for the season was key, because the public face of the company and its broadest reach are through its mainstage productions and coproductions. These have consistently broken new ground over the years, particularly in seeking out and supporting under-represented groups such as queer artists of color and in presenting professional productions from communities previously unrepresented in Toronto theater (such as the city's Moroccan, Afghani, Korean, and South Asian communities). As former artistic director Jovanni Sy says, "Whoever is granted the least license to speak in our society is the voice we most need to hear. This principle is essential in a world where voices of dissent are quashed in the name of 'homeland security.' As Canadians, it is our special responsibility to speak the truth. To be the voice of the outsider" (qtd. in Nothof).

Conclusion

Place [is] a heavily trafficked intersection.
—Dwight Conquergood, "Performance Studies: Interventions and Radical Research"

Much of this book has focused on individual theater companies that participate in various interconnected ways in the intercultural performance ecology of the city, but it has dealt only implicitly, through recurring names, intersecting activities, and visibly multiple subject positions, with the networks and interactions that constitute that ecology. Few theater workers from nondominant communities limit their work to a single theater company or cultural community; most work across a broad range of companies and activities in varying degrees of solidarity, practicing a new, rhizomatic interculturalism from below that is the subject of this conclusion. Here I will pull together some of the strands that run through the book in an analysis of the intercultural performance ecology of Toronto as heterotopic space, a site of alternate ordering in which both practitioners and audiences come together in an interculturalism that is multiple, fluid, and dynamic, modeling an emerging rhizomatic practice for other increasingly multicultural cities around the globe.

While many chapters of this book have treated theater companies, cultural communities, and even specific shows as case studies as though they were operating in isolation from one another, in fact these companies increasingly function interdependently, there are more frequent coproductions among them every year, more of them are identifying as intercultural rather than as culturally specific, and most companies in the intercultural meshwork now list on their websites and blogs recommended current shows by other likeminded companies. Thus b current, once defined by its focus on the African Caribbean Canadian community, mainly women, now supports and coproduces work by other companies, promotes itself as supporting artists "from all the diasporas" (Factory Theatre, Program), and in 2014–15 collaborated with Aluna (Latino/a), Sulong (Filipino), Buddies in

Bad Times (queer), and Factory Theatres. Factory Theatre itself, long self-defined as "the home of the Canadian playwright," under the artistic directorship of Nina Lee Aquino now includes in its profile and mandate "diverse theatrical voices," "culturally diverse artists," and, significantly, "our diverse audience" (Factory Theatre, "About Us").

Individual artists over the course of a few years might work with an entire spectrum of companies and with other artists of a stunning diversity of cultural backgrounds and affiliations. The artistic director of one company will write plays that are staged by another company and perform in work with still others. Actors come together in a wide range of combinations, working with one another on their shows and discussing and learning from other shows that they have each seen or worked on. The increasingly diverse audiences of most shows include artists who are at work on others and directors who are looking to cast others still. Companies share information on the broadly intercultural pool of actors, directors, designers, technicians, and producers who move freely across the intercultural performance ecology of the city. All of this activity perhaps provides a window into the fecundity of cross-fertilization that can occur when artists who play multiple roles as creators, playwrights, artistic directors, actors, and others in one another's work come together as culturally situated "actors" (or actants)—this is no universalist "melting pot"—in a performance ecology that is fluid, provisional, and productively uneven, one in which, as I said in the introduction, citing Kershaw, anything that occurs within the ecosystem effects everything else within that system. All of these artists and actors are deeply engaged in the exploration of how their own (often complex) cultural positioning inflects their own work and their work in collaboration with others, and how those collaborations, in a kind of recursive loop, redound upon their own creative practice. In almost every show in which they participate each engages consciously in negotiation across real and acknowledged difference in what in chapter 1, citing Ella Shohat and Robert Stam, I called "mutual and reciprocal relativization" (359), and what Indigenous scholars and artists might call honoring relationships.

In the introduction I framed Toronto's intercultural performance ecology using the language of rhizomes, radicants, networks, and "meshworks." In this conclusion I want more explicitly to invoke Ingold's "meshworks" by looking at some of the "uneven and fluctuating distribution of agency" (92) in which some actants have temporarily and provisionally acquired different degrees and kinds of agency over the past few decades and where certain hubs and nodal points, often small companies with explicitly intercultural mandates, have from time to time exerted an influence on the entire performance ecology of the city in a kind of "butterfly effect" that has often been disproportionately large.

One relatively recent development among some of the leading intercultural companies has been the increasing cultivation of international, hemispheric, and transnational networks and connections beyond the city and country, either through the organization of festivals and their ancillary events, through an idiosyncratic brand of touring, or through work with specific, targeted companies or communities. Thus Aluna Theatre, in addition to its own shows such as *Nohayquiensepa,* the subject of chapter 7, organizes a biennial Panamerican Routes/RUTAS panamericanas Festival that not only brings companies from throughout the Americas to perform, give workshops and master classes, and attend conference sessions in the city but also, through its programs, maps the companies' travels and connections across the continents, tracing genealogies of their work hemispherically. MT Space Theatre holds a similar biennial event in nearby Kitchener, the IMPACT Festival, featuring culturally diverse work from Canada and around the world—in 2015 Morocco, Iran, Australia, Halifax, Toronto, Edmonton, Vancouver, and Whitehorse as well as local intracultural work were represented—with a special emphasis on interdisciplinary, intercultural, and physical theater productions. Both companies mix the local with the international, neither privileges familiar work from or created for the international touring circuit, and both increasingly ground their events in Indigenous perspectives, organizers, and performances.

Other companies, as we have seen with Native Earth's Honouring Theatre project, have organized touring *with* other Indigenous theater companies, in this case from Australia and Aotearoa New Zealand, eschewing national dominant-culture diplomatic brokerage. And Cahoots Theatre Company, the subject of chapter 8, has recently revived its Crossing Gibraltar community initiative program, first mounted in 2007 in conjunction with its coproduction (with Modern Times) of Ahmed Ghazali's refugee-crisis drama *The Sheep and the Whale*. This "adaptive" program's internationalism is locally grounded, focused as it is on refugees and recent immigrants to Toronto. Forming partnerships with organizations such as the Canadian Centre for Victims of Torture (2008), Access Alliance Multicultural Health and Community Services (2008, 2009, 2014), and Native Earth Performing Arts (2009), it has variously focused on Rohinga and Tanzanian youth (2008), on Karen and Burmese youth from the Mae Lah Oon refugee camp in northern Thailand (2008), on dance (2009), on a writing workshop for adult women (2014), on the Deaf and hearing-impaired community (2016), and on youth from specific troubled Toronto neighborhoods.

Among the most adventurous companies in terms of its transnational operations has been Modern Times Stage Company, whose work is the subject of chapter 6. Modern Times has engaged in a range of international collaborations, including its "Dialogues Project," staging *Aurash* with local artists, actors, youth, and war veterans in some of the world's most fraught contact zones, including Havana (1999),Tehran (2002), Mostar (2009), Bogotá (2010), and Sarajevo (2010). In 2009 *HamletZar*, an experimental collaboration with the Danish company Goosun Art-ilery, explored Shakespeare's *Hamlet* in the context of the ancient Zar ritual from southern Iran. Its 2014 collaboration, *Forgiveness: A Theatrical Poem*, was with Don*Gnu, Bora Bora, and Laboratoriet, all from Aarhus, Denmark, as well as Dreamwalker Dance Company from Toronto. *Forgiveness* was a significant departure for Modern Times. While the company's work has always been physical, *Forgiveness* moved into the realm of dance theater, with a cast made up of familiar Modern Times actors Peter Farbridge and Stavroula Logothettis, together with Danish dancers Elkær Nielsen and Kristoffer Louis Andrupgård Pedersen from Don*Gnu and Chinese Canadian Andrea Nann of Dreamwalker, described by one reviewer of the show as "surely one of the most expressive and accomplished interpretive dancers in North America" (Garebian).[1] The result was an evocative mixed-media meditation on the theme of forgiveness, housed in a sheer white set by designer Lindsay Ann Black, with dangling microphones, a cassette recorder, and five chairs, abetted by a color-filled and geometrical lighting plot by Michelle Ramsey and a powerful soundscape by Thomas Ryder Payne "incorporating breathing, faint singing, night sounds and other elements, [that] works on the subconscious to suggest an unsettling world" (Kaplan, "Beyond"). The show was transnational and intercultural not only in its personnel but in its content. It was inspired by a story from the war in Bosnia and Herzegovina, in which a man forgives his father's killer, but it ranges in its subject matter from petty resentments and failures to forgive on the mundane, interpersonal level to specific atrocities, crimes against humanity, and vacuous apologies delivered by the United States, Canada, Iran, Croatia, Cambodia, South Africa, and Serbia. In one sequence a dying war criminal asking for water changes culture and ethnicity as his successive doctors and caregivers treat or turn against him.

But the heart of Toronto's intercultural performance ecology is *intra*cultural, functioning across cultures *within* the nation rather than transnationally, and there are many significant hubs and nodal points in the intracultural meshwork that constitutes the ecosystem. These have variously included, in addition to Cahoots, as discussed in chapter 8: the feminist

Nightwood Theatre during its post-1989 mandate to focus on women of color; Young People's Theatre (from 2001 to 2011 Lorraine Kimsa Theatre for Young People), which has long been notable for its attention to the cultural mix in the schools that it serves and for hiring artists who reflect that mix; Buddies in Bad Times, which in the past decade has understood its queer mandate to accommodate all kinds of difference and which has included considerable coproduction with companies such as Native Earth, Modern Times, and Aluna in its season planning; and currently Factory Theatre under Nina Lee Aquino.

The site I'd like to highlight in conclusion, however, is the Aki Studio. If, as I've suggested, Cahoots is a key nodal point in the *discursive* meshwork that constitutes intercultural performance in Toronto, its participation as one of the resident companies at the Aki Studio, along with fu-GEN Theatre and Kaha:Wi (Indigenous) Dance Theatre, represents a material, physical point of "coming together" for many of the city's communities of difference, theatrical and otherwise. The studio has been administered since its opening in 2012 by the Indigenous Native Earth Performing Arts. It is housed in the Daniels Spectrum, built as a "community cultural hub" (Daniels Spectrum), part of the redevelopment and renewal of the huge and long-troubled Regent Park social housing project in the city's old east end. Run by the controversial not-for-profit urban development organization Artscape, the accessible, eco-friendly Daniels Spectrum houses performance, exhibition, and meeting spaces and hosts arts and community organizations such as Native Earth, COBA (Collective of Black Artists), and the Centre for Social Innovation, as well as individuals from the neighborhood who want to simply read, do homework, play the colorfully painted community piano in the lobby, or just "hang out" (Daniels Spectrum). It is also home, on its northwest corner, to the Paintbox Bistro, a fashionable Mediterranean restaurant that takes seriously its participation in the redevelopment of the neighborhood, offering jobs and on-the-job training to marginalized people on social assistance and generally serving people in, while attracting people to, the once widely shunned neighborhood (see Pataki). Aki Studio, Native Earth, and the resident companies belong here.

Ever since the earliest days of culturally specific and intercultural theater, when Vera Cudjoe and Jeff Henry were building the city's first African Canadian theater companies, a key and central problem has been the control of space, as white artistic directors curated seasons in which work by individuals and companies from othered cultures might or might not be scheduled according to priorities that those individuals and companies might not share. Even programming at rental spaces is out of the control of companies, which are forced to be nomadic. Native Earth has struggled mightily since 2012 with the responsibilities of administering the Aki Studio space and programming it in such a way as to make it at once financially viable and accessible to the "brown caucus" to which it feels responsibility—and even here, many small, struggling, culturally specific companies often can't afford the rent that Native Earth is forced to charge. Nevertheless, Native Earth itself, the resident companies, and others *have* made good use of the attractive, accessible, well-equipped, and flexible 120-seat black-box theater, including companies with mainstream aspirations, such as the African Canadian Obsidian Theatre, which opened its popular and critically acclaimed show *The Mountaintop* there in 2014, holding the opening night reception in the Paintbox Bistro.

As this book has argued, the intercultural performance ecology of Toronto has been generative since at least the mid-1980s, and in spite of the historical and ongoing fact of real material differences in access, funding, and resources that have worked to prevent the emerging and newly vital practices of intercultural theater that I have been describing from taking their full and proper places on the mainstages of Toronto and other world cities, progress has been and is being made. At Aki Studio, and now at Factory Theatre, formerly marginalized and colonized peoples have access to the means of production and are in full control of their own representation. That Aki Studio is under the administration of the First Peoples of this meeting place is key, as is the primacy of Indigenous relationships to land and place as marginalized groups begin to assert new relationships to the places, spaces, and processes of production. *Aki*, it is worth noting, is the Anishinaabemowing word that encompasses earth, land, and place. In the introduction I outlined the principles of Indigenous research methodologies as articulated by Indigenous scholars, including relationality, responsibility, respect, and reciprocity, that extended to "all my relations," human and nonhuman. Aki Studio and Native Earth are run according to similar principles. As Native Earth states on its website, "In service of our mandate and mission, the company strives to operate according to 7 traditional principles which inform decisions in all undertakings. It is our belief that these tenets not only honour Indigenous values, but are universal to all cultures in various manifestations . . . : Courage, Generosity, Tolerance, Strength of Character, Patience, Humility, Wisdom" ("About Us").

Appendix 1

The Intercultural Performance Ecology of Toronto

What follows is an incomplete summary and description of the companies that have been the primary focus of my research. It is not an attempt to map Toronto's entire theater scene, commercial and not-for-profit. Many theaters across the city include work that crosses cultures, sometimes cast "other," and share personnel with the companies on which I focus. For broader considerations of theater in Toronto that might contextualize this study, I encourage readers to consult Michael McKinnie's *City Stages* and Laura Levin's edited collection *Theatre and Performance in Toronto*. I am conscious that the organization of the descriptions I undertake below risks reifying identity categories in ways that distort the degree to which the companies and communities share personnel and resources and problematize such categories through various kinds of solidarity and cooperation as well as through fluid and multiple community memberships. A listing such as this also risks distorting or minimizing the degree to which the work of many of these companies is interdisciplinary, intermedial, or defiant of categorization: I have included companies, for example, that focus mainly on movement-based theater but not those whose primary focus is dance, in spite of the fact that this distinction is far from clear-cut; I have included companies whose work is devised, site-specific, or performance-based but not those branded simply *as* performance or performance art. Mostly I have focused on communities of color and have included companies with which I have worked or have some relationship or specific interest and that are active players in the intercultural performance ecology of the city.

Indigenous Theater

There are four active companies in Toronto dedicated to producing theater by and about the first peoples of what is now Canada. Two of these are well established and two relatively new, in addition to which the members of Turtle Gals Performance Ensemble, which folded in 2008, remain independently active and influential and carry on the work initiated by the company.[1] Turtle Gals was founded in 1999 by Jani Lauzon (Métis), Monique Mojica (Guna and Rappahannock), Michelle St. John (Wampanoag), and Sandra Laronde (Teme-Augana-Aninshinaabe), who left the company before its first production. Turtle Gals was a creation company dedicated to the exploration of the members' own stories and concerns, as representative of those of Aboriginal and mixed-race women hemispherically throughout the Americas. Turtle Gals created and performed their own devised work exclusively and were dedicated to formal hybridity and the integration of traditional and contemporary performance forms: "As artists we envision a continuum of past, present, and future expressed as stories using our bodies and voices. We draw on traditional forms of story telling, oratory, song and dance integrating them with current technology and popular culture to develop nonlinear multi-disciplinary theatre forms. We will use our work to contribute to a paradigm shift in the consciousness of colonial culture as an empowerment model for Aboriginal youth and as a healing tool for individuals and communities" (Turtle Gals, Information). Turtle Gals was a direct descendent of New York's Spiderwoman Theater, and its hemispheric, hybrid, and contemporary work with the development of new forms of Indigenous theater has continued in the work of the founders, most directly in that of Monique Mojica and her collaborators as discussed in chapter 4.

The fourth founding member of Turtle Gals, Sandra Laronde, left the company almost immediately after its founding and served a brief stint (with Alejandro Ronceria and Daniel David Moses) as part of an Artistic Directorate of Native Earth Performing Arts in 1998–2000 before moving on to found Red Sky Performance in 2000, where she remains artistic director. Red Sky is an internationally touring dance-theater company that concerns itself with the contemporary celebration of transnational Aboriginal identities, bringing together Indigenous artists from Canada, Mexico, Australia, the Torres Straight Islands, Mongolia, and elsewhere. In drawing on traditional Indigenous forms "to articulate a contemporary dance process while creating new movement vocabularies" (Todd 24), Laronde skirts dangerously close to the familiar high modernist practice of renewing western "high culture" by incorporating, absorbing, and commodifying Indigenous forms and staging them, sometimes virtually unaltered, for the gaze of mainstream audiences in proscenium venues. Similarly, her courting of new audiences through celebratory Aboriginal dance risks exoticism and collusion with problematic official multiculturalisms even as it risks deflecting national and international attention away from Canada's mistreatment of its Native population (see Knowles, "Red Sky" 131–37). But Laronde presses on, refusing to allow herself to be discouraged by what she sees as the debilitating type of negativity left over from colonialism. Typically, she moves forward, creating work for and increasing the profile of Aboriginal performers in Canada and abroad, insistently rewriting dominant media representations of Native peoples by eschewing racist stereotypes and replacing them with representations of astonishing beauty and skill, and exploiting tactically, in Michel de Certeau's sense (*Practice* 34–39), the pieties of Canada's "official multiculturalism" in order to advance the cause globally of Aboriginal people in the arts.

Signal Theatre was founded in 2011 by Plains Cree actor, director, dancer, and choreographer Michael Greyeyes, who has also worked as a dancer, choreographer, and advisor for Red Sky and as a director for both the Chocolate Woman Collective and Native Earth. Signal explores both physical and text-based theater and moves through the disciplines of dance, opera, music, design, and the spoken word to create work that, according to its mandate, "reflects and privileges indigenous knowledges, as well as international creation methodologies that situate physical rigour and exploration as the centre of the work." "Our vision is to enrich the Canadian landscape through public performance/interventions and to broaden the social and political awareness of our audiences both at home and internationally" (Signal). Already fully integrated with the dance and theater ecology of Toronto, Signal has collaborated with the Chocolate Woman Collective on the development of *Side Show Freaks and Circus Injuns*, discussed in chapter 4. Its first and signature dance/theater production, *from thine eyes* (2011), with text by Yvette Nolan, was a collaboration with Native Earth Performing Arts and its second major production, *A Soldier's Tale*, with text by Native Earth/ARTICLE 11's Tara Beagan, had its premiere at the Fleck Dance Theatre in Toronto in 2014.

Native Earth Performing Arts is Canada's oldest and longest-standing Indigenous theater company, founded in 1982 by Denis Lacroix and Bunny Sicard to develop and present Aboriginal theater, dance, and performance. Since then it has been central to the development of Native and other intercultural theater in Toronto, and that position has been solidified by its acquisition in 2012 of the Aki Studio Theatre in the Daniels Spectrum in the culturally diverse Regent Park area as its performing venue, which it runs as the host of three resident companies: Cahoots (intercultural) Theatre Company, fu-GEN Asian Canadian Theatre Company, and Kaha:Wi (Indigenous) Dance Theatre. Native Earth came into prominence during the 1986–92 artistic directorship of Tomson Highway (Cree) through the attention attracted by the productions and tours of his plays *The Rez Sisters* (1986) and *Dry Lips Oughta Move to Kapuskasing* (1989). Highway secured government funding, hired full-time staff, and inaugurated the company's mandate, which remains "to provide a base for professional Native performers, writers, technicians, and other artists; to encourage the use of theatre as a form of communication within the Native community, including the use of Native language; to communicate to audiences experiences that are unique to Native peoples in contemporary society; and to contribute to the further development of theatre in Canada" (Native Earth, "About Us"). Under the artistic directorship of Yvette Nolan (Algonquin, 2003–11) and Tara Beagan (Ntlaka'pamux, 2011–14) emphasis was given to development, apprenticeships, and internships and to dance and multidisciplinary work rather than simply theater, and the company's artistic vision is now described as one that "is both inclusive and reflective of the artistic directions of members of the Aboriginal community who participate in the arts" (Native Earth, "About Us"). Under Nolan and Beagan the company officially espoused a model that adheres to "7 values": courage, generosity, tolerance, strength of character, patience, humility, and wisdom (Native Earth, "About Us").

Métis actor Ryan Cunningham succeeded Beagan as artistic director of Native Earth in 2014 but has shown no signs of radically changing the company's focus or direction. A combination of national mandate, strategic solidarity across difference, and attention to the specific voices of the original creators of almost exclusively new work issues at Native Earth in an extraordinarily varied repertoire. The work presented is cognizant of longstanding Aboriginal performance structures and traditions but is also conscious of a political commitment to intervention in the contemporary lives of Native peoples. This range of cultures and contents is matched by the range of cultural forms that the company's productions mine. If Native Earth has no single, identifiable house style, it characteristically serves Canada, from Toronto, as "gathering place," where the country's various and diverse First Nations meet theatrically and constitute themselves as a strong diasporic community.

Tara Beagan left Native Earth in 2014 to found a new company, ARTICLE 11, with Mushkegowuk Cree designer Andy Moro. This new company is named after article 11 of the UN's 2007 Declaration of Rights of Indigenous Peoples, which states, "Indigenous peoples have the right to practise and revitalize their cultural traditions and customs. This includes the right to maintain, protect and develop the past, present and future manifestations of their cultures, such as archaeological and historical sites, artifacts, designs, ceremonies, technologies and visual and performing arts and literature" (United Nations). The company espouses a holistic and collaborative working philosophy, with an evolving mandate to serve "Indigenous, mixed blood, feminist, non-discriminatory and mindfully accountable peoples" in ways that prioritize the Indigenous perspective and Indigenous artists but "also inherently include the non Indigenous population" (Beagan and Moro). The company has become known for its variable-content collaborative installation *DECLARATION*, staged variously at Fort York (2013), the Royal Ontario Museum (2015), and the National Arts Centre (2015); for *The Ministry of Grace*, a 2014 experimental piece in a tent at Fort York; and for *Reckoning*, a 2016 triptych in movement, video, and text inspired by the Canadian Truth and Reconciliation Commission inquiry into the residential school system and staged at the Theatre Centre.

Asian Canadian Theater

Asia is a troubled and necessarily intercultural term that has real meaning only in diaspora. *Asian Canadian* is even more troubled and more intercultural, in that it involves not only the yoking together of people from very different and often conflicting "home" cultures but also the forging of new intercultural subjectivities within the Canadian nation-state. And in Canada, *Asian* tends to mean *East Asian*. In spite of important work by individual South Asian Canadian playwrights such as Dilara Ally (*Mango Chutney*, 1996), Sheila James (*A Canadian Monsoon*, 1993; and *All Whispers/No Words*, 1995), Sunil Kuruvilla (*Rice Boy*, 2003), Anita Majumdar (*Fish Eyes*, 2004, discussed in chapter 2; *The Misfit*, 2008; *Same Same but Different*, 2014; and *The Fish Eyes Trilogy*, 2015), Anusree Roy (*Pyaasa*, 2007; *Letters to My Grandma*, 2009; *Roshni*, 2010; *Brothel #9*, 2011; and *Sultans of the Street*, 2014), and Ravi Jain (*A Brimful of Asha*, 2012), there has been no long-standing theater company devoted to work from the Indian subcontinent in Toronto since the folding in 2012 of Rasik Arts, which was founded in 1997 by white artistic director Sally Jones and dedicated primarily to the presentation of plays and artists from India.

The (East) Asian Canadian theater scene remains, however, as it was for Jean Yoon in 2002, "fluid, vibrant, and inclusive" ("Chinese" 5). It began with two forerunners, the Chinese United Dramatic Society, established in 1933 and lasting into the early 1990s (Yoon, "Chinese" 6, 10); and the Canasian Artists Group, founded in 1981, flourishing for a few years before floundering, and then briefly revived in the early 1990s as Canasian Theatre (Yoon, "Chinese" 6, 8). And there have been a number of Asian Canadian theater companies active in Toronto since, many of them run by women but most relatively short-lived. These include Yoon's Loud Mouth Asian Babes, founded in 1995 and "dedicated to the development and production of new Canadian works by, for, and about Loud Mouth Asian women who may or may not be Babes, Loud Mouth Asian Babes who may or may not be women, and Loud Mouth Babes we really dig. Irrepressible, aggressively irreverent. Theatre for the Dis/Oriented and Culturally Confused" (qtd. in E. Lee 71). Loud Mouth Asian Babes was founded and run by Korean Canadian actor and playwright Jean Yoon as "Seoul Babe/Artistic Director" until 2007, producing Yoon's own work, including *Sliding for Home* and *Borders* (1995), *The Yoko Ono Project* (2000), and its one-person version *Yes Yoko Solo* (2002). A second company, k'Now Theatre, was founded by Chinese Canadian Keira Loughren to produce her play *Little Dragon* in 2002–3 and has since successfully produced Norman Yeung's *Pu-Erh* (2010) under Loughren's direction. The most recent of these companies is Filipina Canadian Catherine Hernandez's interdisciplinary Sulong Theatre, whose mandate is to produce theater that is by and about women of color. Founded in 2010, the company has staged the collective creation *Future Folk* (2010, about Filipina caregivers in Canada), Hernandez's *Eating with Lola* (2010, about the playwright's attempts through food and memory to connect with her deceased maternal grandmother), and Hernandez's *Kilt Pins* (2011, about sexuality in a Catholic high school), along with the fundraising performance projects *Queer Family Quilt* (2012) and *Operation Lifeboat* (2012), in the latter of which Hernandez submerged herself to the chin for twenty-four hours in sympathy with flood victims in the Philippines, generating active online responses worldwide.

But perhaps the most significant Asian Canadian companies currently operating are Carlos Bolusan Theatre (the subject of chapter 3) and fu-GEN Theatre. While Carlos Bulosan emerged from and is dedicated to a specific cultural community, fu-GEN emerged from an explicit and expressed need to find a stable home for new Asian Canadian work, broadly defined. fu-GEN was founded in 2002 by Leon Aureus, Nina Lee Aquino, Richard Lee, and David Yee to develop and produce Asian Canadian plays, serve Asian Canadian theater artists, and, as the current mandate says, "build a stronger, truly multicultural Canadian community by breaking down stereotypes through education and development of a strong cultural artistic base" (fu-GEN). Nina Lee Aquino served as its first artistic director until 2012, when David Yee was appointed, first as interim artistic director, then as the company's second artistic director, which he remains.

fu-GEN has developed and mounted a string of major new Asian Canadian plays since its first major production of Leon Aureus's award-winning *Banana Boys* in 2004, adapted from Terry Woo's novel. These have included Catherine Hernandez's *Singkil* (2007), David Yee's award-winning *paper SERIES* (2007) and *lady in the red dress* (2009), Byron Abalos's *Brown Balls* (2011), and Adrienne Wong, David Yee, and Donald Woo's *sex tape project* (2012). In addition, the company has developed and nourished innumerable new writers and plays through its annual playwright's "Kitchen" and its Potluck Festival (including major work produced elsewhere, such as Ins Choy's *Kim's Convenience*, Jovanni Sy's *A Taste of Empire*, and Norman Yeung's *Pu-Erh*). Finally, fu-GEN has consolidated a national Asian Canadian theater community through its GENesis: Asian Canadian Theatre Festival in 2010, which issued in a published volume, *Asian Canadian Theatre*, as a companion to Aquino's two-volume *Love and RelASIANships*, the first ever national anthology of Asian Canadian plays (Aquino and Knowles; Aquino, *Love*).

Africanadian Theatre

Although Black theater in Canada has a history dating back to at least 1849 (see Breon, "Black"; Breon, "Growth"; Saddlemyer 14; Sears, Introduction iv), the first professional Black theaters were an outgrowth of a wave of immigration from the West Indies that began in the 1960s. In Toronto this took the form of Black Theatre Canada (BTC), founded in 1973 by a Trinidadian immigrant woman, Vera Cudjoe, and Theatre Fountainhead, founded the following year by Trinidadian Jeff Henry, who moved to Toronto to work at York University after having been a founder of Black Theatre Workshop in Montreal in 1971, an outgrowth of the Trinidad and Tobago student association at McGill University (see Henry; Bayne).

Theatre Fountainhead, though it was Caribbean in sensibility, was nevertheless pan-African in practice. Its first production was Nigerian Wole Soyinka's *The Swamp Dwellers*; subsequent work included plays by the likes of Athol Fugard, Barrie Keefe, and Samuel Beckett, and significant effort was invested in providing professional-level (western) training for Black theater artists and mounting school tours to "areas where there was a preponderance of Caribbean youth" (Henry 32). BTC was more unapologetically Caribbean from the outset, and although it staged such work as *A Raisin in the Sun*, Lorraine Hansberry's iconic African American play, in 1978, under Vera Cudjoe it was more consistently dedicated to the early development of a Caribbean Canadian performance aesthetic. This took the form of staging work by Caribbean writers such as Trevor Rhone, Roderick Walcott, Daniel Caudieron, and Mustapha Matura and bringing to Canada major Caribbean performers such as Paul Keens Douglas and, crucially, Louise Bennett, all of which introduced and exposed the community to Afro-Caribbean performance forms that had a powerful influence on new work developed by the company and by many others in subsequent years. BTC also made direct contributions to the cultivation of an Afro-Caribbean diasporic dramaturgy by developing such things as playwright Amah Harris's school-touring *Anansi Tales* beginning in 1977, structured by the stories and rhythms of African folktales (Gingell, "jumping" 11n12), and by producing the award-winning "Caribbean" *Midsummer Night's Dream*, directed by Azra Francis in 1983. BTC folded in 1988 and Theatre Fountainhead two years later, but between them (and indeed together, for a short time, as Black Theatre Alliance),[2] they had helped to develop a generation of Black, largely Caribbean theater artists who would lead the way in subsequent years. Their alumni included BTC's Amah Harris, whose company Theatre in the Rough focused much of its efforts on training Black youth through its hugely influential Fresh Arts program. In the 1990s the mantle was briefly passed to director Colin Taylor's Theatre WUM, which mounted six major productions between 1991 and 1994, though Taylor's play choice did not focus solely on African Canadian work.

Toronto is now home to four major continuing Black theater companies in addition to d'bi.young anitafrika's watah theatre institute, discussed in chapter 5. The AfriCan Theatre Ensemble, founded in 1998 by Modupe Oloagun, who remains its artistic director, is dedicated to "making African Theatre accessible to Canadians through performance, education, research, and professional development of classics and new creations originating from or inspired by Africa." The company explicitly articulates among its goals the creation of "cultural exchange between Africa and Canada" and the forging of "human relationships across cultures, creeds, ethnicities, ideologies, genders, and social classes" (AfriCan). It has staged major African plays, including Ola Rotimi's *The Gods Are Not to Blame* (1999) and *Our Husband Has Gone Mad Again* (2000), Zakes Mda's *And the Girls in Their Sunday Dresses* (2001), Ama Ata Aidoo's *Anowa* (2003), Wole Soyinka's *Death and the King's Horseman* (2004), Tawfiq al-Hakim's *The Fate of a Cockroach* (2005), Femi Osofisan's *Esu and the Vagabond Minstrels* (2006) and *The Engagement* (2011), Gcina Mhlophe's *Have You Seen Zandile* (2008), and Biya Bandele's *Brixton Stories* (2012). In the early years much of this work was tinged with a kind of compensatory nostalgia for the homeland, but the company's productions have become increasingly sophisticated, and its range has also expanded to include new Canadian adaptations such as

Efua Sutherland's *The Marriage of Anansewa,* adapted by Bayo Akinfemi and Modupe Oloagun for production in 2009, and the Junction Avenue Theatre Company's *Sophiatown,* adapted by Oloagun and produced in 2010. It also expanded to producing new work, including American playwright Jeff Stetson's *The Meeting* (2013) and the new African Canadian plays *The Full Nelson,* by Donald Carr (2005); *Coma,* by Jude Idada (2013); and Oloagun's own *Lost* (also 2013).

The most prominent of the current African Canadian Companies—indeed, it claims to be "Canada's leading culturally diverse theatre company" (Obsidian)—is Obsidian Theatre, which was founded to considerable publicity in 2000 by a consortium of thirteen African Canadian theater artists, including Bajan (Barbadian) Canadian Alison Sealy Smith, its founding artistic director; Guyanese Canadian Djanet Sears, the matriarch of African Canadian Theatre and founder in 1997 of the galvanizing Afri-Canadian Playwrights Festival;[3] and Jamaican Canadian actor and director Philip Akin, its current artistic director and a Black Theatre Canada alumnus. Obsidian's mandate is diasporic, "dedicated to the exploration, development, and production of the Black voice" (Obsidian) through productions of work from the African diaspora, new play development programs, training programs, and partnerships. Its goal is unabashedly to crash the mainstream, and to this end it has cooperated with such "mainstream" theaters as the Stratford and Shaw Festivals, Mirvish Productions, and Canadian Stage.

Obsidian has staged prominent productions of such Canadian plays as Djanet Sears's *Adventures of a Black Girl in Search of God* (2002, its first production), George Boyd's *Consecrated Ground* (2004), Joseph Jomo Pierre's *Pusha Man* and *Born Ready* (2005) and *Hip Hop: Who Stole the Show?* (2006), Colleen Wagner's *The Monument* (2006), Austin Clarke's novel *The Polished Hoe* (adapted for the stage by Alison Sealy-Smith and Colin Taylor, 2007), Marcia Johnson's *Late* (2008), Beth Graham's *The Gravitational Pull of Bernice Trimble* (2013), Meghan Swaby's *Venus's Daughter* (2015), and Lisa Codrington's *Cast Iron* (2005, with Nightwood Theatre) and *Up the Garden Path* (2016). And early on it staged a powerful production of Jamaican playwright Trevor Rhone's *Two Can Play* in 2005 and an adaptation of Aboriginal Australian playwright Wesley Enoch's *Black Medea* in 2008. But in addition to its new Canadian work, the company's main focus, especially in recent years, has been on the African American canon, including August Wilson's *The Piano Lesson* early on (2003) and later Lynn Nottage's *Intimate Apparel* (2008, revived in 2010) and *Ruined* (2011), Dael Orlandersmith's *Yellow Man* (2009, with Nightwood Theatre), Suzan-Lori Parks's *Topdog/Un-*

derdog (2011–12, in association with the Shaw Festival), and Lynn Ahrens and Stephen Flaherty's musical, *Once on This Island* (2014). It also produced, somewhat anomalously, canonical non-Black American playwright Tony Kushner's *Caroline, or Change* in 2012. Its 2014–15 season featured Katori Hall's *The Mountaintop* (in association with the Shaw Festival) and the musical *The Wild Party,* by Michael John LaChiusa and George C. Wolf.

The other two major African Canadian companies operating in Toronto, b current and Theatre Archipelago, are discussed in more detail in chapter 5. b current was founded in 1991 by ahdri zhina mandiela to nurture exploration, engage community, and develop talent that reflects the aesthetics, language, and speech of the Black diaspora. Since then it has been involved in the development of innumerable plays and of two generations of African Canadian interdisciplinary theater and performance artists and has produced, often in collaboration with other companies, over a dozen mainstage plays, ranging from mandiela's own *dark diaspora . . . in* dub! in 1991 to Nicole Brooks's *Obeah Opera* in 2012. That the latter was a coproduction with Theatre Archipelago is not surprising: b current has frequently collaborated with Archipelago since Rhoma Spencer founded the company in 2005 with a production that grew directly out of b current's 2004 rock.paper.sistah's development festival. Theatre Archipelago is dedicated to serving "as a catalyst for propagating Caribbean theatre in the diaspora" and staging plays "by Canadian and Caribbean playwrights at home and abroad" (Theatre Archipelago).

Latinx Canadian Theater

Apart from the well-known work of individual artists—Argentinean Canadian Guillermo Verdecchia (many plays, including *The Noam Chomsky Lectures,* with Daniel Brooks, 1990; the award-winning *Fronteras Americanas/ American Boarders,* 1993; *Ali & Ali and the Axis of Evil,* with Camyar Chai and Marcus Youssef, 2004; and *bloom,* 2006) and Chilean Canadians Carmen Aguirre (over twenty plays, including, in Toronto, *Chile Con Carne,* 1999; the award-winning *Refugee Hotel,* 2009; and *Blue Box,* 2012) and Rosa Laborde (seven plays, including *Dish,* 2007; *Léo,* 2008; and *Hush,* 2010)—Latino theater came late to Toronto with the founding, by Colombian Canadian Béatriz Pizano and her partner Trevor Schwellnus, of Aluna Theatre in 2001. Aluna, whose signature production, *Nohayquiensepa,* is the focus of chapter 7, is explicitly international, interdisciplinary, and intercultural, addressing within its plays and their audiences "people [who] are complex individuals who exist beyond the restrictions of cultural labels" (Aluna, "Artistic Mission"). It has staged productions of the collective creation *For Sale* (2003, about Columbian women dealing with armed insurgency), Pizano's *Madre* (2008, about guilt, memory, and mothers), *La Comunión* (2010, about the life of a child soldier), and Pizano, Schwellnus, and Lyon Smith's *what I learned from a decade of fear* (2014, "A Karmic Accounting/Interrogation Ritual to atone for a decade of repression, war, and paranoia"). The company has also cooperated internationally with La Corporación Colombiana de Teatro and others on a collective creation, *Defenestration* (2008), with the Red Snow Collective on Chinese Canadian Diana Tso's *Red Snow* (2012, about the rape of Nanjing) and on other ongoing projects, including biennially since 2012 the extraordinary Panamerican Routes/RUTAS panamericanas Festival, complete with performances, workshops, and a conference, since 2014 in collaboration with Native Earth Performing Arts.

A second Latin Canadian company joined Aluna in 2006, when Alameda Theatre was founded by Chilean Canadian Marilo Nuñez as "an avenue for Latin voices" (Alameda) with the primary mandate of developing, staging, and supporting new work by Canadian Latin American playwrights and theater artists. In subsequent years, in addition to an aggressive development program that included a playwright in residence and an annual De Colores Festival presentation of four new plays each year, the company mounted full productions of Nuñez's own *Three Fingered Jack & The Legend of Joaquin Murietta* (2006), Carmen Aguirre's award-winning *The Refugee Hotel* (2009) and *Chile Con Carne* (2013), and Amaranta Leyva's *The Intruder* (2011). Unfortunately Nuñez closed the company in 2014 for personal reasons.

Intercultural Companies

In addition to the companies with culturally specific mandates of varying degrees of cultural specificity, from Carolos Bulosan's "Filipino Canadian" to the more expansive "Caribbean Canadian" of Theatre Archipelago to the baggy and inclusive "Asian" or "Native" or "African" Canadian, there are a number of companies in Toronto whose mandates, in different ways, are more broadly and explicitly cross- or intercultural. These include the broadly diverse, approaching-the-mainstream Young People's Theatre, which has been staging culturally specific and intercultural work and engaging in "color blind" hiring since the 1990s. Also prominent has been the feminist Nightwood Theatre, particularly in the period between 1989 and 2008 when it produced or coproduced a series of major works by Aboriginal, African Canadian, and Asian Canadian women such as Monique Mojica (*Princess Pocahontas and the Blue Spots*, 1990), ahdri zhina mandiela (*dark diaspora . . . in* dub!, 1991), Diana Braithwaite (*The Wonder Quartet*, 1992), Lillian Allen (*Love and Other Strange Things*, 1993), M. NourbeSe Philips (*Coups and Calypsos*, 1993), Diane Roberts (*The Coloured Girls Project*, 1995), Dilara Alley (*Mango Chutney*, 1996), Djanet Sears (*Harlem Duet*, 1997, and *Adventures of a Black Girl in Search of God*, 2002), Marjorie Chan (*China Doll*, 2004, and *A Nanking Winter*, 2008), and Lisa Codrington (*Cast Iron*, 2005). In this period Nightwood also staged *Smudge* (2000), by vision-challenged playwright Alex Bulmer, extending its understanding of cultural diversity—which has always included diverse genders and sexualities—to disability cultures. Since the mid-2000s Nightwood has focused less on Canadian work and less on cultural difference in its shift toward a more international and mainstream profile. Other, smaller companies include, notably, Why Not Theatre, founded in 2007 by South Asian Canadian artistic director Ravi Jain and dedicated to "inventive, experimental, cross-cultural collaborations" (Why Not Theatre). In addition to organizing workshops with prominent international artists and hosting international productions, Why Not has produced Dean Gilmour, Michele Smith, Ravi Jain, and Adam Paolozza's *Spent* (2010), Jain's own *A Brimful of Asha* (2012), and Nicholas Billan's award-winning *Iceland* (2012), each of which has toured nationally and/or internationally.

But currently the most significant companies explicitly dedicated to cross- or intercultural work in the city are Modern Times Stage Company, the subject of chapter 6, and Cahoots Theatre Company, which is discussed in chapter 8.

Appendix 2

List of Artists

The following is a partial list of Toronto theater artists discussed in *Performing the Intercultural City*, together with some of the companies, plays, and shows they have been associated with as writers, actors, directors, or designers. It does not include all artists whose names have been mentioned (the index does that), but in addition to those whose work has been discussed at length it includes artists who are only briefly mentioned but whom I judge to have had a major impact on the intercultural performance ecology of the city. The list is intended for readers who may not have any familiarity with the artists named in the book, particularly those in part 1, and who want to keep track of their key work, identifications, and affiliations.

Ada, Kawa (Afghan Canadian)
- Buddies in Bad Times
- Cahoots Theatre Company
- Factory Theatre
- Soulpepper Theatre
- *Bombay Black*
- *The Canny Afghani*
- *carried away on the crest of a wave*
- *The Death of Mrs. Ghandi and the Beginning of New Physics (a political fantasy)*
- *Iceland*
- *paper SERIES*
- *Sister Mary's a Dyke?!*
- *The Wanderers*

Aguirre, Carmen (Chilean Canadian)
- Alameda Theatre Company
- Aluna Theatre

Nightswimming Theatre
Blue Box
Chile Con Carne
Refugee Hotel

Akin, Philip (Jamaican Canadian)
Black Theatre Canada
Obsidian Theatre
Shaw Festival
Black Medea
The Mountaintop

Ancheta, Karen (Filipina Canadian)
Carlos Bulosan Theatre
fu-GEN Theatre Company
In the Shadow of Elephants
Singkil

anthony, trey (Jamaican Canadian)
trey anthony studios
da kink in my hair
How Black Mothers Say I Love You

Aquino, Nina Lee (Filipina Canadian)
Cahoots Theatre Company
Carlos Bulosan Theatre
Factory Theatre
fu-GEN Theatre Company
Native Earth Performing Arts
Young People's Theatre
Acquiesce
Banana Boys
Miss Orient(ed)
People Power
Scarberia
Singkil
Sister Mary's a Dyke?!
Sultans of the Street
The Unplugging
The Wanderers

Aureus, Leon (Filipino Canadian)
Carlos Bulosan Theatre
fu-GEN Theatre Company
Banana Boys
In the Shadow of Elephants
People Power

Beagan, Tara (Ntlaka'pamux)
ARTICLE 11
Native Earth Performing Arts
Signal Theatre
DECLARATION
Free as Injuns
Ministry of Grace
Miss Julie: Sheh'mah
Reckoning
A Soldier's Tale

Bou-Matar, Majdi (Lebanese Canadian)
MT Space Theatre
Theatre Passe Muraille
Body 13
The Last Fifteen Seconds
Seasons of Immigration to the West

Brooks, Nicole (Afro-Caribbean Canadian)
b current
Theatre Archipelago
Obeah Opera

Candido, Romeo (Filipino Canadian)
Carlos Bulosan Theatre
Factory Theatre
fu-GEN Theatre Company
Romance of Magno Rubio
Singkil
The Unplugging

Chan, Marjorie (Chinese Canadian)
Cahoots Theatre Company

Common Boots Theatre
Tapestry Opera
China Doll
The Enchanted Loom
The Madness of the Square
A Nanking Winter
Paper SERIES
Sanctuary Song
Tails from the City
Ultrasound

Chau, Jackie (Chinese Canadian)
Factory Theatre
fu-GEN Theatre Company
Native Earth Performing Arts
The Fish Eyes Trilogy
Pu-Erh
Singkil

Choy, Ins (Korean Canadian)
fu-GEN Theatre Company
Soulpepper Theatre
Banana Boys
Kim's Convenience

Cortez, Rose (Filipina Canadian)
Carlos Bulosan Theatre
fu-GEN Theatre Company
In the Shadow of Elephants
People Power
Singkil

Cudjoe, Vera (Trinidadian Canadian)
Black Theatre Canada

Cunningham, Ryan (Métis Cree)
Native Earth Performing Arts

Del Rio, Bobby (Chinese Canadian)
Professionally Ethnic

Farbridge, Peter (Irish Canadian)
Modern Times Stage Company
Hallaj
Hamlet
Macbeth
Waiting for Godot

Favel, Floyd (Plains Cree)
Chocolate Woman Collective
Chocolate Woman Dreams the Milky Way

Ford-Smith, Honor (Jamaican Canadian)
Sistren Theatre (Jamaica)
Theatre Archipelago
Fallen Angel and the Devil Concubine

Garcia, Nicco Lorenzo (Filipino Canadian)
Carlos Bulosan Theatre
In the Shadow of Elephants
People Power

González-Vio, Carlos (Uruguayan Canadian)
Aluna Theatre
Modern Times Stage Company
Death of the King
Hallaj
Nohayquiensepa (No One Knows): A Requiem for the Forcibly Displaced

Greyeyes, Michael
ARTICLE 11
The Chocolate Woman Collective
Native Earth Performing Arts
Red Sky Performance
Signal Theatre
Almighty Voice and His Wife
from thine eyes
Sideshow Freaks and Circus Injuns
A Soldier's Tale

Harris, Amah (Dominican Canadian)
Black Theatre Canada
Theatre in the Rough
Anansi Tales

Henry, Jeff (Trinidadian Canadian)
Theatre Fountainhead

Hernandez, Catherine (Filipina Canadian)
Buddies in Bad Times
Carlos Bulosan Theatre
Factory Theatre
fu-GEN Theatre Company
Nightswimming Theatre
Sulong Theatre
Theatre Passe Muraille
Eating with Lola
Future Folk
In the Shadow of Elephants
Kilt Pins
Singkil

Highway, Tomson (Cree)
Native Earth Performing Arts
Dry Lips Oughta Move to Kapuskasing
Ernestine Sushwap Gets Her Trout
The (Post)Mistress
The Rez Sisters
Rose

Jain, Ravi (Indo Canadian)
Factory Theatre
Why Not Theatre
A Brimful of Asha
Iceland

Jean-Pierre, Edwige (Congolese and Haitian Canadian)
b current
Buddies in Bad Times
Factory Theatre

Obsidian Theatre
Theatre Archipelago
The Big Mess
Even Darkness is Made of Light
Our Lady of Spills

Kantule, Oswaldo De León (Guna)
Chocolate Woman Collective
Chocolate Woman Dreams the Milky Way

Koo, Camellia (Chinese Canadian)
Cahoots Theatre Company
Factory Theatre
fu-GEN Theatre Company
Obsidian Theatre
Shaw Festival
Banana Boys
benu
blood.claat
carried away on the crest of a wave
paper SERIES
Singkil
The Unplugging
word!sound!powah!

Laborde, Rosa (Chilean Canadian)
Aluna Theatre
Buddies in Bad Times
Factory Theatre
fu-GEN Theatre
Dish
Hush
Léo
Paper SERIES

Laronde, Sandra (Teme-Augana-Aninshinaabe)
Native Earth Performing Arts
Red Sky Performance
Turtle Gals Performance Ensemble
Caribou Song

Mistatim
Raven Stole the Sun
Tono

Lauzon, Jani (Métis)
Cahoots Theatre Company
Modern Times Stage Company
National Arts Centre
Native Earth Performing Arts
Paper Canoe Productions
Turtle Gals Performance Ensemble
Death of a Chief
The Death of the King
I Call Myself Princess
The Only Good Indian
Prophecy Fog
The Scrubbing Project
A Side of Dreams
The Triple Truth

Loaiza, Lorena Torres (Colombian Canadian)
Aluna Theatre
Nohayquiensepa (No One Knows): A Requiem for the Forcibly Displaced

Loring, Kevin (Nlaka'pamux)
Where the Blood Mixes

Loughren, Keira (Chinese Canadian)
k'Now Theatre
Nightwood Theatre
China Doll
Little Dragon
Pu-Erh
The Yoko Ono Project

Majumdar, Anita (Indo Canadian)
Modern Times Stage Company
Bloom
Bombay Black

Fish Eyes
Rice Boy
Same Same but Different

mandiela, ahdri zhina (Jamaican Canadian)
b current
Black Theatre Canada
Obsidian Theatre
Theatre Archipelago
dark diaspora . . . in dub!
I Marcus Garvey
Obeah Opera
who knew grannie?

Mangosing, Christine
Carlos Bulosan Theatre
In the Shadow of Elephants
People Power

Mengesha, Weyni (Ethiopian Canadian)
Carlos Bulosan Theatre
Soulpepper Theatre
Stratford Festival
Why Not Theatre
blood.claat
da kink in my hair
Kim's Convenience
People Power
The Small Room at the Top of the Stairs

Mojica, Monique (Guna and Rappahannock)
Chocolate Woman Collective
Native Earth Performing Arts
Turtle Gals Performance Ensemble
Chocolate Woman Dreams the Milky Way
Princess Pocahontas and the Blue Spots
The Rez Sisters
The Scrubbing Project
Sideshow Freaks and Circus Injuns

Moro, Andy (Mushkegowuk Cree)
ARTICLE 11
Chocolate Woman Collective
Native Earth Performing Arts
Red Sky Performance
Signal Theatre
Chocolate Woman Dreams the Milky Way
DECLARATION
Free as Injuns
Ministry of Grace
Reckoning

Moses, Daniel David (Delaware)
Cahoots Theatre Company
Native Earth Performing Arts
Almighty Voice and His Wife
Big Buck City
Brébeuf's Ghost
Coyote City
The Indian Medicine Shows

Ng, John (Chinese Canadian)
ARTICLE 11
fu-GEN Theatre Company
K'Now Theatre
Modern Times Stage Company
Native Earth Performing Arts
Red Snow Collective
Acquiesce
Ching Chong Chinaman
Free as Injuns
Hallaj
Pu-Erh
Reckoning
Waiting for Godot

Nolan, Yvette (Algonquin)
Factory Theatre
Native Earth Performing Arts
Turtle Gals Performance Ensemble

Annie Mae's Movement
The Birds
Death of a Chief
Job's Wife
The Only Good Indian
Tombs of the Vanishing Indian
The Triple Truth
The Unnatural and Accidental Women
The Unplugging
Video

Nuñez, Marilo (Chilean Canadian)
Alameda Theatre
Aluna Theatre
Modern Times Stage Company
Chile Con Carne
Hallaj
Refugee Hotel
Three Fingered Jack & The Legend of Joaquin Murietta

Ocampo, Martha (Filipina Canadian)
Carlos Bulosan Theatre

Oloagun, Modupe
AfriCan Theatre Ensemble

Parsa, Soheil (Iranian Canadian)
Aluna Theatre
Cahoots Theatre Company
Modern Times Stage Company
Aurash
The Balcony
Blood Wedding
Bloom
The Chairs
The Conquest
The Death of the King
The Eighth Journey of Sinbad
Forgiveness
The Four Cases

Hallaj
Hamlet
Interrogation
The Lesson
Macbeth
Oh Fool! Oh Fooled!
The Sheep and the Whale
Stories from the Rains of Love and Death
Waiting for Godot

Peña, Flerida (Filipina)
Buddies in Bad Times
Cahoots Theatre Company
Carlos Bulosan Theatre
fu-GEN Theatre Company
Sister Mary's a Dyke!?

Pierre, Joseph Jomo (Trinidadian Canadian)
Factory Theatre
Obsidian Theatre
Theatre Passe Muraille
3D Atomic Entertainment
Born Ready
Pusha-Man
Shakespeare's Nigga
Twisted

Pizano, Béatriz (Colombian Canadian)
Aluna Theatre
Modern Times Stage Company
Panamerican Routes/RUTAS panamericanas Festival
Red Snow Collective
Blood Wedding
La Comunión
For Sale
Madre
Meeting Place
Nohayquiensepa (No One Knows): A Requiem for the Forcibly Displaced

Red Snow
what I learned from a decade of fear

Preuss, Clare (Swiss Canadian)
Alameda Theatre Company
b current
Cahoots Theatre Company
Carlos Bulosan Theatre
Factory Theatre
fu-GEN Theatre Company
Native Earth Performing Arts
Nightwood Theatre
People Power
Singkil
The Unplugging

Punzalan, Alexander (Filipino)
Carlos Bulosan Theatre
Factory Theatre
fu-GEN Theatre Company
In the Shadow of Elephants
The Unplugging

Roy, Anusree (Indo Canadian)
Factory Theatre
Stratford Festival
Theatre Passe Muraille
Brothel #9
Letter to My Grandmother
Pyaasa
Roshni
Sultans of the Street

Schwellnus, Trevor (German Canadian)
Aluna Theatre
Buddies in Bad Times
Modern Times Stage Company
La Comunión
The Death of the King
For Sale

Hallaj
Madre
Meeting Place
Nohayquiensepa (No One Knows): A Requiem for the Forcibly Displaced
Red Snow
Shakespeare's Nigga
The Sheep and the Whale
Waiting for Godot
what I learned from a decade of fear

Sears, Djanet (Guyanese Jamaican Canadian)
AfriCanadian Playwrights Festival
Nightwood Theatre
Obsidian Theatre
The Stratford Festival
Adventures of a Black Girl in Search of God
Afrika Solo
Harlem Duet

Smith, Alison Sealy (Barbadian Canadian)
Nightwood Theatre
Obsidian Theatre
Stratford Festival
Theatre Fountainhead
Young People's Theatre
Adventures of a Black Girl in Search of God
Coups and Calypsos
Good Night Desdemona (Good Morning Juliet)
Harlem Duet
The Piano Lesson
The Polished Hoe

Spencer, Rhoma (Trinidadian Canadian)
AfriCan Theatre Ensemble
b current
Theatre Archipelago
Fallen Angel and the Devil Concubine
I Marcus Garvey

Just Jazz
Obeah Opera

St. John, Michelle (Wampanoag)
Native Earth Performing Arts
Turtle Gals Performance Ensemble
Annie Mae's Movement
The Only Good Indian
The Scrubbing Project
Tombs of the Vanishing Indian
The Triple Truth

Sy, Jovanni (Chinoy [Chinese Filipino] Canadian)
Cahoots Theatre Company
The Sheep and the Whale
A Taste of Empire

Taylor, Drew Hayden (Ojibway)
Native Earth Performing Arts
Red Sky Performance
AlterNative
The Berlin Blues
The Bootlegger Blues
Dead White Writer on the Floor
Girl Who Loved Her Horses
Only Drunks and Children Tell the Truth
Raven Stole the Sun
Someday

Tso, Diana (Chinese Canadian)
Aluna Theatre
Jumblies Theatre
Red Snow Collective
Young People's Theatre
Comfort
Red Snow

Verdecchia, Guillermo (Argentinian Canadian)
Cahoots Theatre Company
Carlos Bulosan Theatre

Modern Times Stage Company
Soulpepper
Ali & Ali & the Axis of Evil
A Taste of Empire
bloom
Fronteras Americanas/American Borders
Miss Orient(ed)
The Noam Chomsky Lectures

Villasin, Fely (Filipina Canadian)
Carlos Bulosan Theatre
Miss Orient(ed)

Villasin, Nadine (Filipina Canadian)
Carlos Bulosan Theatre
fu-GEN Theatre Company
In the Shadow of Elephants
Miss Orient(ed)
People Power
Singkil

Yee, David (Chinese Scottish Canadian)
Buddies in Bad Times
Cahoots Theatre Company
Factory Theatre
fu-GEN Theatre Company
Tarragon Theatre
Acquiesce
carried away on the crest of a wave
lady in the red dress
paper SERIES
the sex tapes project
Singkil

Yhap, Beverley (Chinese Trinidadian Canadian)
Cahoots Theatre Projects
The Phoenix Cabaret
Skull Riders

Yoon, Jean (Korean Canadian)
Cahoots Theatre Projects
Factory Theatre
Loud Mouth Asian Babes
Young People's Theatre
Borders
Kim's Convenience
Sliding for Home
Yes Yoko Solo
The Yoko Ono Project

young anitafrika, d'bi. (Jamaican Canadian)
AfriCan Theatre Ensemble
Tarragon Theatre
Theatre in the Rough
watah theatre institute
androgyne
da kink in my hair
the sankofa trilogy (*blood.claat, benu,* and *word!sound!powah!*)
yagayah: two.womyn.blackgriots

Notes

INTRODUCTION

1. *A Taste of Empire* was written and performed by Jovanni Sy, directed by Guillermo Verdecchia, and produced by Cahoots Theatre Company at the demonstration kitchen at Toronto's St. Lawrence Market, 29 June–24 July 2010. I worked on it as dramaturge and preview director.

2. For an expanded history of the developments traced in this paragraph see Knowles, *Theatre & Interculturalism*. In trying to explode the binaries articulated here and avoid the ways in which the discourses of intercultural theater have tended to reify participating cultures as stable and clearly distinguishable from one another I am working in the spirit of Erika Fischer-Lichte's critique of the term *intercultural theatre* ("Introduction"; "Interweaving"). I have not, however, adopted her term *interweaving performance cultures* because of its silence, even in the German *Verflechtungen*, about who is doing the weaving. I also share Rustom Bharucha's unease about the efficacy of the new term in displacing, rather than doing away with, the pitfalls of the discourses of "intercultural theatre" (Bharucha, "Hauntings") and the practices of what Daphne Lei has recently called "HIT" ("hegemonic intercultural theatre") (571).

3. Chapter 7, written in collaboration with Jessica Riley, shifts to yet another, collaborative voice.

4. Marcus also says that "multi-sited ethnographies inevitably are the product of knowledge bases of varying intensities and qualities. To do ethnographic research . . . on the social grounds that produce a particular discourse of policy [as in my chapter 1] requires different practices and opportunities than does fieldwork among the situated communities such policy effects [as in subsequent chapters]. To bring these sites into the same frame of study and to posit their relationships on the basis of firsthand ethnographic research in both is the important contribution of this kind of ethnography, regardless of the variability of the quality and accessibility of the research at different sites" (84).

5. Although Foucault may not be in this instance, I am understanding *textual* here in its broadest sense to include performance texts and cultural texts, defined by Yuri Lotman as "any carrier of integral ('textual') meaning including ceremonies, works of art, as well as 'genres' such as 'prayer', 'law', 'novel', etc." (6)—and I would argue, written, spoken, and performed languages. See also chapter 3, note 64.

6. I am indebted to Joanne Tompkins for drawing my attention to Hetherington's work.

7. Hetherington's point is similar to one made by Deleuze and Guattari: "There are knots of aborescence in rhizomes, and rhizomatic offshoots in roots" (20).

8. Thanks to Māori theatre artist David Geary, now working in Canada, for confirming this translation of *mana*. Smith later, and in a different context, usefully translates it as "our standing in our own eyes" (173).

9. Bourriaud, unlike other critics of multiculturalism cited in chapter 1, does not cite official policies such as those of Australia or Canada, nor does he analyze local practices or applications of what he calls "a vague ideology of sorts" (*The Radicant* 164).

10. Bourriaud isn't always very attentive to specifics—a problem overarching western theory often has—as when he reads the Canadian philosopher Charles Taylor and his writings about multiculturalism's "politics of recognition" as referencing a US context (*The Radicant* 164). See chapter 1, note 19.

11. The Anishinaabe (there are variant spellings) refers to the peoples often referred to in Canada as Ojibwe (or Ojibway), and in the US as Chippewa.

12. The derivation is from Henry Scadding and John Dent's 1884 book *Toronto: Past and Present*, is disputed, and is probably inaccurate (see Natural Resources Canada; Merritt), but it has legs, and it is certainly the case that the area that is now Toronto served as a precontact site of cultural and economic exchange and was later a trading post (see Sanderson and Howard-Bobiwash).

PART ONE

1. For consideration of some of these conditions as they apply to Toronto theater, see Knowles, *Reading*; Knowles, "Reading Material"; Levin; McKinnie; and Wallace.

CHAPTER ONE

1. By "the multicultural script" I mean the composite discourse of documents that have emerged since the 1971 federal White Paper instituted multiculturalism as a policy, including the 1988 Act, the 1996 review, and the Annual Reports that have accumulated since.

2. I am using *archive* and *repertoire* as they have been influentially explicated by Diana Taylor.

3. Information about the history of multiculturalism here is derived primarily from Esses and Gardner and from Abu-Laban and Gabriel 105–28, but see also Berdichewsky; Bibby; Breton; Gwyn; and Reitz and Breton. Bannerji convincingly disputes the dominant view that the 1971 policy came about in response to "demand from below," arguing that it was in fact "an ideological elaboration from above . . . which rearranged questions of social justice, of unemployment and racism, into issues of cultural diversity and focused on symbols of religion, on so-called tradition. Thus immigrants were ethnicized, culturalized and mapped into traditional/ethic communities" (44–45).

4. See Bannerji 30. The editors of a special issue of the *Canadian Journal on*

Urban Research on "Our Diverse Cities" provide statistics on immigration as of 2006—almost half a million immigrants in the past quarter century, 43 percent to Toronto, where almost 50 percent of the population is now foreign born. They also indicate a significant increase in immigrants from Asia, Latin America, and Africa (Carter et al. 1).

5. I am quoting clauses 3(1)a and 3(1)j of the Act from Multiculturalism and Citizenship Canada's *The Canadian Multiculturalism Act: A Guide for Canadians*, which functions as a kind of annotated "critical edition."

6. Bourriaud's critique of multiculturalism is a generalized one not deriving from any particular policy, so it isn't surprising that he finds it to be "a vague ideology of sorts" (*The Radicant* 165). His critique of Taylor is one I agree with, but his concomitant assertions that "one would have to be rather naïve to believe in a contemporary work of art that would be the natural expression of the culture from which its author comes" is slippery and seems a rhetoric ("contemporary" vs. "natural expression") that begs the larger question. It allows him, for example, to argue for the "double dialogue" of interculturalism: "one that the artist maintains with his or her tradition and a second dialogue between the artist's tradition and the corpus of aesthetic values inherited from modern art" (165–66). Where the latter "corpus of values" comes from is not made clear by Bourriaud, but it is found in those artists who *he says* "are important today" (166), rendering his claim somewhat self-fulfilling. The argument that "the artist reflects less his or her culture than the mode of production of the economic (and thus political) sphere in which he or she moves" (165), coupled with the argument that we are all working within a globalized economy, strikes me as a dangerous surrender. See also introduction, note 10.

7. See also Bannerji, especially 151–74.

8. Gunew discusses "the somatic technology constituted by the learning of [standard] English" (63) as "a kind of virus inhabiting the body" (61).

9. Founding Cahoots Theatre Projects artistic director Beverly Yhap wrote in 1988, "There will always be a place for folklore and heritage activities. However, for the serious theatre professional, dedicated to the development of his/her craft, willing to test the material before the glare of a larger public, there must be funding at the professional level. Multiculturalism, with its lower funding base, cannot be the automatic dumping ground for work that has ethnic content. This promulgates a double standard, and reinforces the notion that professional theatre is what white people do" (30).

10. In Toronto this came primarily from the Canada Council, the Ontario Arts Council, and the Toronto Arts Council.

11. In June 2013, for example, the Harper government announced that it would use $12 million of existing funding to promote "Canadian History," leading up to the 150th anniversary of confederation in 2017 (see De Sousa). In practice this meant *diverting* existing funds to promote a particular conservative vision of settler Canada, as is evident from the government's concomitant $25 million spent to change the name and mandate of the Canadian Museum of Civilization to "The Canadian Museum of History." The museum had until this time featured First Nations histories and those of the country's diverse immigrant populations, and the change has been widely seen as conservative re-

trenchment and a rewriting of Canadian history to suit its ideological agenda (see Geddes).

12. I use *white* here and throughout this book not as an essentializing category of race but as indicating normalized access to power, privilege, and funding.

13. These phrases have recurred in political speeches since the 1990s. They are quoted here from a foundational 1994 speech by Sheila Finestone (Liberal Secretary of State Multiculturalism and Status of Women) in which they appear in rapid succession (qtd. in Abu-Laban and Gabriel 116).

14. An exception to this trend is the accession of two artists of color—Nina Lee Aquino (Filipina) and Nigel Shawn Williams (Afro-Jamaican Canadian)—to the artistic directorship of one of the city's most prominent midrange venues, Factory Theatre, "the home of the Canadian playwright." That this happened in the wake of a huge public outcry over the firing in 2012 of founding and former artistic director Ken Gass—a controversy in which for some the elephant in the room was the fact that a large percentage of Gass's support came from dominant-culture artists—is a significant complication. In the fall of 2014 Williams stepped down to assume the role of associate artistic director, a position from which he resigned in spring 2016; Aquino is now sole AD.

15. Aaron was played in the premiere by the playwright.

16. For scholarly analyses of the creation, production, and reception of *The Death of a Chief*, see Simmonds; and Knowles, "*The Death*."

17. Yvette Nolan has pointed out the ways in which Toronto's "Indian diaspora" represents a closing in rather than a dispersion, as Native peoples covering wide swaths of land were forced into unnaturally choked off and lifeless urban locations—like Toronto (interview).

18. Nolan is clear that she is not essentializing race. She includes among the "brown caucus" companies such as Mammalian Diving Reflex that are somatically "white" but determinedly "other."

19. For productive analyses of the evolution of the establishment and evolution of theater spaces in postindustrial downtown Toronto, see McKinnie.

20. According to the 2011 census, Brampton's population was 38.4 percent South Asian, 32.9 percent white, and 13.5 percent Black.

CHAPTER TWO

1. Landsberg's concept of prosthetic memory is compelling, but her work is worrisomely indifferent about the distinction between the memory of actual events that did not happen to the remembering subject and the inculcation of manufactured cultural memories through the use of powerful mass media.

2. *The Fish Eyes Trilogy* includes *Fish Eyes*, *Boys with Cars*, and *Let Me Borrow That Top*. Its full production as a trilogy was at Vancouver's PUSH Festival in January 2015.

3. Confusingly, West Bengal is in eastern India, bordering on Bangladesh, which is also Bengali.

4. I am quoting from the unpublished script used for the 2005 production at Toronto's Theatre Passe Muraille. The text varies somewhat when performed

in different cities. Its (so far) final form is recorded in the 2016 Playwrights Canada Press publication of the trilogy.

5. In the play itself, Norma twice tells Mimi, "You've been dancing the Singkil your entire life" (Hernandez, *Singkil* 25, 82), the second time giving her the dated photograph.

6. These quotations are taken from rehearsals in which I participated. I worked on the show with Nina Lee Aquino as an associate dramaturg; preproduction dramaturgy was by the Algonquin Yvette Nolan, another example of intercultural crossings within Toronto's performance ecology.

7. These transformations were more a function of Aquino's production than of Hernandez's script, which calls for a much more traditional version of the Singkil at the end (see Hernandez, *Singkil* 100)—another example of the negotiation of subjectivities in diaspora.

8. The play mounts a searing critique of economic globalization as productive of the kinds of human displacement that it represents, the details of which are beyond the scope of this chapter. The production itself, however, represents a grassroots transcultural collaboration that speaks back to corporate globalization.

9. The gendered fact of Hassan's occupying the central subjectivity while Hélène plays a largely symbolic role is disturbing and leads almost inevitably to a rape that may be emblematic but is nevertheless played out on the body of a woman—though in production it happened offstage. The relative bleakness of this production as opposed to *Fish Eyes, Singkil, Body 13*, or *The Scrubbing Project* is related to its being gendered male and taking place in an overwhelmingly masculine shipboard setting.

10. Although Bou-Matar remains with the company and continues to direct its shows, the artistic directorship was taken over in July 2016 by Gujarati (West India) Canadian Pam Patel.

11. My account of the show and its creation derives from my having participated in its creation as dramaturge. I am listed in the unpublished script as one of the co-creators.

12. The play is mostly in English but also includes significant and lengthy passages in Twi (a dialect of Akan spoken mainly in Ghana), Gujarati (spoken in Gujarat, West India), and Arabic (in this instance as spoken in Lebanon and Syria).

13. Monique Mojica left the ensemble in the summer of 2006 and was replaced by Falen Johnson and Cheri Maracle before the company folded in 2008.

14. The complexities of *The Scrubbing Project*, of the vast body of scholarship on Holocaust memory, and of the burgeoning field of mixed-race studies make a thorough exploration of this stunning moment beyond the scope of this chapter, which focuses on intercultural memory.

PART TWO

1. For an analysis of such contemporary Canadian dramaturgical forms and structures, see Knowles, *The Theatre of Form*.

2. The concept of diaspora is a problematic one for Indigenous peoples precisely because they have not followed the pattern of global dispersion that defines "diaspora" for other communities; rather, they are diasporic on the land over which they had once traveled freely. As Nolan says,

> Many of us didn't necessarily belong to a certain place. We belonged to big swaths of ground that we traveled on. And as contact happened, as settlers arrived, we were forced into smaller and smaller spaces. So ironically, our diaspora moves in the opposite direction—it is *to* the urban centers because of the terrible spaces that we were put in. The diaspora for us is from traditional huge lands to tiny little urban spaces that are completely, as in this place [Toronto's Distillery District], *dead* land, covered up with concrete, dead water at the base of the city. Toxic. Smoggy. No animals. So it's interesting that our diaspora is a closing in, rather than a spreading out. (Interview)

3. I have selected here only those Caribbean countries that are significantly represented in the Toronto theatrical community. There are, of course, dozens of others.

CHAPTER THREE

1. After its production, *Carding,* in 1984, the running of the workshop devolved onto Martha Ocampo and Fely Villasin in the de facto roles of producer and artistic director, respectively. The workshop's early activities extended beyond theatrical production to include such things as the publication of a pamphlet by Ocampo and Villasin entitled *Mag-usap Tayo . . . Let's Talk: A Guide to Educating on Violence against Women in the Filipino-Canadian Community* (Ocampo and Villasin). According to Fely Villasin, "Our use of theatre was to raise awareness about the issues: torture, imprisonment. . . . We were raising the profile of the political movement [against Marcos]" (qtd. in Grant 17). According to Nina Lee Aquino, "Carlos Bulosan exists because of the need for the community to express itself. It acts like a bridge between home there and home here. . . . It's an outlet for the community to gather, celebrate, or mourn the history and celebrate the future" (qtd. in Knowles, "Between" 77).

Named after the blacklisted 1930s Filipino American farm laborer and labor activist, poet, and novelist Carlos Sampayan Bulosan (*America Is in the Heart*), the workshop regularly staged shows in Toronto between 1984 and 1997. Many of the shows were advertised and staged in both English and "Pilipino" (as it is called on the show's posters) and dealt with such things as immigration (*Carding,* 1984, 1986; *No Boundaries,* 1995), the plight of Filipino domestic workers in Canada (*If My Mother Could See Me Now/Inay Kung Alam Mo Lang,* 1989, 1990), the evolution of Filipino society (*Ten Fingers/Sampung Mga Daliri,* 1991), the writings of Carlos Bulosan (*Carlos Bulosan: A Trilogy,* 1992), violence against women in the Filipino community (*Home Sweet Home,* 1993–94), generational differences within that community (*Noong Kapanahunan Ko . . . Not on My Time,*

1994), the revolution against Spanish rule in the Philippines (*Walang Sugat/Undefeated*, by Severino Reyes, 1996, 1998), and the Katipunan revolutionaries (*Images of 1896*, by the Philippines Educational Theatre Association [PETA], 1997).

2. Since it turned professional the company has received Toronto Arts Council and Ontario Arts Council Operating funding, Canada Council for the Arts Equity Capacity Building funding, and Project funding. It has also received support from Canadian Heritage for the Tales from the Flipside festival and has received capacity-building money from Ontario's Trillium Foundation. Nadine Villasin, the company's second artistic director, credits the Canada Council's Equity funding that began in 2003 with jump-starting the company's growth as a professional theater company under her direction. After almost two decades of project-to-project funding, CBT grew to an annual operating budget of over $100,000 in less than two years. By 2011 it had risen to approximately $200,000. Since then the company has struggled and its funding has declined (see chapter 3, note 3). I am grateful to Martha Ocampo for information on the Carlos Bulosan Cultural Workshop, to Nadine Villasin for details about the structure and funding of the Carlos Bolusan Theatre and its transition to professional status, and to current artistic producer Leon Aureus for updates on the company.

3. The lengthy process of development of the CBT collective's *In the Shadow of Elephants* was suspended when the company was caught in the position of neither having funding to proceed nor being eligible for further funding until it had done a public presentation of the show. During this time Nadine Villasin resigned as artistic director in 2010 and was replaced by Renna Reddie in the role of "artistic producer." Reddie engaged in important development work but was unable to mount mainstage productions until the funding situation at the company was clarified. Reddie resigned in July 2012 and was replaced by Leon Aureus, who has retained the title of artistic producer. The staging of *Elephants* in June 2013 provided the company with a new starting point, but it had lost its operating funding from the Toronto and Ontario Arts Councils and continues to struggle to regroup. It has resumed operations and has staged readings at the annual Kultura Festival, and its Playwriting Unit has continued operations. As of summer 2016 it is running a series of "Tagsibol" (time of rebirth) workshops for young Filipino artists and has initiated another collective creation, *Anak*, under Aureus and actor-director Karen Ancheta.

4. Nina Lee Aquino's engagement with the story didn't end with *People Power*, to which she wrote and performed in what might be considered a "prequel." Her play *Every Letter Counts* explored her own relationship as a child to Ninoy Aquino in the time leading up to his return to the Philippines from exile, which resulted in his immediate assassination on the runway as he disembarked the plane. *Every Letter Counts* was produced at Factory Theatre in January–February 2013.

5. The show was revived in a revised form in September–October 2010, when it opened Teesri Duniya Theatre in Montreal's thirtieth anniversary season to enthusiastic reviews. For the remount, Rose Cortez, who had left the collective, was replaced by Aura Carcueva.

6. Mangosing is dangerously close here to making claims to an "authentic

Filipino identity" that is grounded in appropriated Indigenous practices, as American, Canadian, Australian, and New Zealand national identities have been. The difference here, I think, is that in the case of Carlos Bulosan's work a fundamentally mixed-race population is rediscovering long-suppressed (and living) parts of its own subjectivity.

7. The "Family Compact" (so called by their opponents) refers to the small clique of men who held a firm grip on power in Upper Canada (later Ontario) between 1810 and 1840.

8. Sir Francis Bond Head was the Lieutenant Governor of Upper Canada in 1837, and according to the script of the play the rebel leader William Lyon Mackenzie "could rarely resist punning on his name" (Salutin and Theatre Passe Muraille 24). Like the People Power Revolution, the 1837 revolution in Upper Canada—called in Canadian dominant-culture history texts a "rebellion"—was also a more-or-less spontaneous people's revolt against injustice and nepotism.

9. I don't wish to take credit away from the powerful and inventive staging of director Nina Lee Aquino, working with movement designer Clare Preuss and the company; rather, I want to point to the improvisatory creation process through which these scenes were first imagined.

10. The revised version of the play in Montreal in 2010, which eliminated some awkward audience contact and one character and worked on the details of language use, received no such comments.

11. See, however, Caroline Mangosing's letter to the editor in response to Robert Cushman's scathing review, in which she also corrects several pertinent misrepresentations: "Mr. Cushman . . . writes: 'It rarely sounds like people talking.' I find this offensive and racist. When I watched the play I saw myself represented in an authentic way. This play was not produced for the very limited and narrow view of a white theatre critic who can so flippantly reduce the work to 'bad theatre' and not have any idea what this kind of production brings to the Filipino-Canadian community and the broader, more open-minded community of Toronto who want to learn a little bit more of the history of a people who make up 3% of the GTA's [Greater Toronto Area's] population" (Mangosing).

12. Even Holthe's novel tends to be pro-American, and the web presence of information on the Philippines in World War II overwhelmingly smacks of US propaganda and prominently—inevitably—features General Douglas McArthur's famous "return." Even the archive on the earlier Philippine-American War, though it increasingly includes a Filipino perspective, tends to focus on the United States and to frame the struggle as a political one within the United States. Elinor Fuchs and Joyce Antler's documentary play *Year One of Empire,* entirely sympathetic to the Filipinos, is nevertheless exclusively made up of quotations from American politicians, diplomats, and soldiers.

13. I worked on the show as dramaturge throughout the development process, including attending these workshops. What follows draws upon this work.

14. As indicated in note 5 to the introduction, Lotman uses *cultural text* to refer to "any carrier of integral ('textual') meaning including ceremonies, works

of art, as well as 'genres' such as 'prayer', 'law', 'novel', etc" (6). As Balme notes, "A key criterion for a cultural text is that it is only fully comprehensible within the culture that uses it" (4), and as he also notes, "such a text outside of its context may not even be recognized as a . . . carrier of meaning at all" (4). In truly syncretic theater, however, "cultural texts retain their integrity as bearers of precisely defined cultural meaning" (5).

15. The creation of *In the Shadow of Elephants* was interrupted by circumstances that almost destroyed the company, mostly driven by arts councils' demands that a "product"—a production—be presented before the company would be eligible for further funding. See chapter 3, note 3.

CHAPTER FOUR

1. Dule, in the Guna language (Dule Gaya), means simply "people," or "the people," implicitly the Guna people. Thus dule wagwa is a girl person and Dule Gaya the language of the people.

2. This quotation is from Mojica's introduction to an unpublished draft transcription of the words of the play. This transcription was never understood by Mojica or the Chocolate Woman Collective to be the show's "script," which as will become clear exists in its current form as nine scrolls of newsprint with pictographic annotations. Nevertheless, quotations from the play in this chapter are necessarily from this production transcription.

3. *Chichi* is fermented sugarcane juice used for ritual purposes; a *chichi* ceremony is held for the coming of age of young girls.

4. Although not an enrolled citizen of the Chickasaw nation, Allen traces Chickasaw ancestry through his maternal line (C. Allen, *Trans-Indigenous* 250n11).

5. Although the neoclassical style dominates US federal buildings on and around Capitol Hill and the National Mall, there are many distinctive architectural styles on view in the US capital, including the distinctively different National Museum of the American Indian, designed by Douglas Cardinal, a Blackfoot architect from what is now Canada, which sits uncomfortably as a "national" museum among others on the mall but carves out its curvilinear difference amidst 4.25 acres of landscape re-creating various ecosystems in the Americas.

6. The "nesting" phenomenon and other geometrical and astronomical alignments are confirmed by the aircraft-based remote sensing technology LiDAR (light detection and ranging). See Romain and Burks, "LiDAR Analysis," and Romain and Burks, "LiDAR Assessment," cited in C. Allen, "Serpentine" 830–31n10.

7. Quotations from *Side Show Freaks and Circus Injuns* are from fragments of work in progress from various workshops over several years.

8. The process is long and arduous—it takes years and many workshops to bring a show to completion, as it took years to build many of the mounds—and the team interrogates each step closely to ensure that we remain true to the dramaturgical principles that we have distilled from the mounds and earth-

works that are our models and do not slip into the taken-for-granteds of dominant theatrical practice in the west. Envisioning and early writing for the show began as early as 2005 with writing Mojica did as "outtakes" from *The Only Good Indian*, a show developed with Turtle Gals Performance Ensemble. Research began in earnest in 2011 as a result of an International Development Grant from the Ontario Arts Council and a Research/Creation Grant from the Social Sciences and Humanities Research Council of Canada. The first full creation workshop took place in June 2012; the first public presentation of *Side Show Freaks and Circus Injuns* of any kind was a workshop at the Canadian Federation for Advanced Research's Belonging Differently meetings in Banff, Alberta, in August 2012. There have been subsequent small-scale meetings and workshops involving parts of the team since, and a workshop that included the design team in December 2013 issued in a public presentation. The mound-building process continued in a five-week creation workshop in Toronto in the summer of 2014 that focused on visual imagery and design (it has been a principle of the process that the design will evolve in a parallel progression with the dramaturgy) and a ten-day workshop in Chickasaw territory, Sulphur, Oklahoma, in December of that year in which a full draft of the first section of the show was completed. There have been small-scale, focused workshops and presentations since, including one in March 2016 in which Tara Beagan served as dramaturge, as the collective investigates further funding opportunities.

CHAPTER FIVE

1. For a sense of the debate about the relative importance to African Canadian culture of taking a culturally nationalist (George Elliot Clarke) or a diasporic stance (Rinaldo Walcott), see Clarke, *Odysseys Home*; Walcott, "Rhetorics of Blackness"; and Walcott, *Black Like Who?*. In these works Clarke and Walcott are primarily discussing literature and, in Walcott's case, popular culture, but both have also published on African Canadian theater making similar arguments (see, for example, Clarke, "Afro-Gynocentric Darwinism"; Clarke, "Must All Blackness"; and Walcott, "Dramatic").

2. The other Black Toronto theater that emerged as a direct result of this wave of immigration was Theatre Fountainhead, founded in 1974 by Trinidadian Jeff Henry, who moved to Toronto to work at York University after having been a founder of Black Theatre Workshop in Montreal in 1971, an outgrowth of the Trinidad and Tobago student association at McGill University (see Henry; Bayne). Though it was Caribbean in sensibility, Theatre Fountainhead was pan-African in practice. Its first production was Nigerian Wole Soyinka's *The Swamp Dwellers*. Subsequent work included plays by the likes of Athol Fugard, Barrie Keefe, and Samuel Beckett, and significant effort was invested in providing professional level (western) training for Black theater artists and mounting school tours to "areas where there was a preponderance of Caribbean youth" (Henry 32). Theatre Fountainhead ended operations in 1990, but like BTC it made a significant impact and fostered a host of Black theater artists,

many of them Caribbean and many of them women, who would carry on the work in subsequent years.

3. Interestingly, when Jamaican-born ahdri zhina mandiela directed *A Midsummer Night's Dream* in Toronto's High Park almost twenty-five years later in 2007, the *Toronto Star* review opened with "There's a joyful Caribbean atmosphere to this year's Dream in High Park" (Crew).

4. In addition to b current and Theatre Archipelago, these include: the AfriCan Theatre Ensemble, founded in 1998 by Modupe Oloagun and dedicated to making African theater accessible to Canadians through performance, education, research, and professional development of classics and new work originating from or inspired by Africa; and Obsidian Theatre, founded in 2000 by a consortium of African Canadian artists, including its founding artistic director, Alison Sealy Smith; Djanet Sears; and a BTC alumnus the Jamaican-born actor-director Philip Akin, its current artistic director. Obsidian's mandate is diasporic and its goal is to crash the mainstream. Although its most recent successes have been with African American plays (notably by Lynn Nottage, Suzan-Lori Parks, Dael Orlandersmith, and Katori Hall), it too has staged work by Afro-Caribbean playwrights and developed new work by African Canadian playwrights of Caribbean descent. See appendix 1 for more detail.

5. Spencer had worked in the theater in Trinidad and Tobago before coming to Canada to do an MFA in theater at York University. Upon graduating she spent two years working with the AfriCan Theatre Ensemble, grounding herself in the aesthetics of African theater before (re)turning her attention to the Caribbean and founding Theatre Archipelago. As the resident company of the Papermill Theatre at the Todmorden Mills Museum and Arts Centre on Pottery Road, Theatre Archipelago was Toronto's first Black theater company with its own performance space.

6. An exception to the male dominance of theater in the Caribbean is the well-known Sistren Theatre Collective in Jamaica, whose mission is to actively transform the status of women in society. But Sistren is unique, and it functions as a grassroots, community-based collective rather than a place of employment for theater professionals.

7. Also see Knopf for an account of Canadian dub poets' critiques of Canadian multicultural policy.

8. Although the Theatre Archipelago production credited the play to the Groundwork Collective, the published version is more specific, naming as authors Patricia Cumper, Honor Ford-Smith, Carol Lawes, Hertencer Lindsay, and Eugene Williams. Jamaican Canadian Honor Ford-Smith, a founder of Sistren in Kingston, Jamaica, explains the various roles played in the collective creation in her introduction to the play (236–40).

9. *Obeah Opera* has been remounted and restaged several times since its premiere, most recently in August 2015 at the Young Centre for the Performing Arts, where it was coproduced by Nightwood Theatre and Culchaworks and directed by Kim Weild.

10. mandiela had anticipated herself in 1985, developing and workshopping a script by Mariam Fikrete, when she "created a stage ritual (used as scene

transitions) which was carved & stylized from the language & music of Jamaicans" (qtd. in A. Lee 83). She returned to this type of transition in 2003 with *Honouring the Word* (see mandiela, Smith, and Sears).

11. Canadian dub pioneer Lillian Allen contends that "without reggae, dub poetry could never have existed. And without two remarkable figures of the twentieth century, Louise Bennett . . . and Bob Marley . . . , there would be no dub poetry" (12). Allen also points to the influence of Bennett on Marley, to whom he looked "for inspiration and . . . as a reference point" (14). For the influence of Louise Bennett on Canadian women dub poets, see Gingell, "Coming Home."

12. Rastafarianism, or "rasta," is a Christian religious movement that emerged in Jamaica in the 1930s and worships the Ethiopian emperor Haile Selassie (1892–1975), whose original title was "Ras Tafari" and who resisted Italian invaders of Ethiopia. Selassie is understood to be a manifestation of the creator, Jehovah (or "Jah"). The movement rejects "Babylon" (corrupt western values) and the politics of the nation-state and locates "Zion" (Ethiopia, or Africa) as the birthplace of humanity. Interpreting the bible as a narrative of Black exile and return, it attempts to reclaim traditional African values, including peace, love, and respect for human beings and nature. Its Afro-centrism aligns it with Garveyism. Interestingly, Weyni Mengesha, director of the Toronto premiere of Jamaican Canadian trey anthony's wildly successful play *da kink in my hair,* is the great-great-granddaughter of Haile Selassie (see Mohammed).

13. Spoken word poetry is a latecomer in relation to dub, emerging in the late 1980s and early 1990s out of rap and hip-hop culture intercut with the legacy of performances of the beat poets in the United States in the 1950s and 1960s. Rap is a musical (as opposed to poetic) genre, the origins of which are also Jamaican (by way of reggae and turntabling), and both rap and dub have roots in the tradition of the West African griots (storytellers, poets, and praise singers). Arguably, however, rap has been co-opted by the American and multinational music industry, while dub has been more successful at resisting assimilation and appropriation. d'bi.young anitafrika argues in an interview that "dub has retained . . . so much of its integrity," while "hip hop has become one of the most strategic American neo-colonial tools" (Flynn and Marrast 52).

14. Empowerment, hope, and even celebration are central to dub and help to differentiate it from other postcolonial forms that focus more narrowly on resistance, and from other forms of performance poetry (see L. Allen 12, 20). This spirit carries forward into the theater forms developed by ahdri zhina mandiela and d'bi.young anitafrika that I discuss below, which are nothing if not celebratory.

15. Susan Gingell, in a note to her 2006 interview in which mandiela includes shange among her influences, says that mandiela calls *dark diaspora . . .* "a choreopoem" (Gingell, "jumping" 5), and Loretta Collins also asserts that mandiela was "certainly influenced by Shange's choreopoem" (52). mandiela also talks about the influence of *for coloured girls,* along with Jamaican American playwright and director Vinette Carroll's *Your Arm's Too Short to Box with God* (A. Lee 8).

16. Collins is using Yusef Komunyakaa's phrase "vertical velocity" "to de-

scribe the speed and pulsating orality" of American spoken word poetry (Collins 46; Komunyakaa 3). Collins's article is the best analysis to date of *dark diaspora . . . in* dub!, but its focus is on the techniques mandiela uses to inject the energy of performance onto the printed page rather than on the play as a theater piece.

17. Lorde called her 1982 autobiography, *Zami*, a "biomythography," and the term has been picked up with variations by many, including mandiela's friend and collaborator Djanet Sears, who has referred to her play *Afrika Solo* as an "auto-biomythography" (Sears, Afterword 95), and mandiela's protégée, d'bi.young anitafrika, who has often referred to her own work as "biomyth theatre," or "biomyth monodrama" (Email).

18. For accounts of the development of *dark diaspora . . .* see mandiela, "evolution" x–xii; and A. Lee 83. The first production as listed in the Sister Vision publication is the workshop production at the Toronto Fringe in 1991, but the play received a subsequent full production in 1992 at the Beaverhall Studio Gallery. The play has recently been revived and revised in a new performance at Aluna Theatre's Panamerican Routes/RUTAS panamericanas Festival in Toronto in fall 2016. mandiela reprised the role of poet maestra—this time named "the Praisesinger"—in the production of *Honouring the Word: a test of commitment* that she co-compiled with Alison Sealy Smith and Djanet Sears for the celebratory opening of the 2003 AfriCanadian Playwrights Festival, consisting of excerpts from sixteen plays by African Canadian playwrights (see mandiela, Smith and Sears).

19. "I feel stranded without collaboration," mandiela told Susan Gingell in 2006 ("jumping" 13).

20. The "ring shout" was a form of religious expression practiced by African slaves in Trinidad, Jamaica, and elsewhere, involving moving in a circle, clapping, stomping, and crying out. Like the ring shout, the more familiar "call and response" has its origins in Africa, and particularly in African music and African forms of religious and political participation.

21. The production was mounted by Obsidian at the Factory Theatre mainspace in association with Factory Theatre.

22. The phrase *signifying on* of course invokes African American street poetry ("signifyin'") and involves quoting from, repeating, doubling, and extending the resonances of (usually vernacular) words and cultural forms. See Gates.

23. She doesn't reproduce the original lyrics of the familiar gospel song and only invokes the key, familiar phrase, "comin' for to carry me home," but she rings significant changes on the lyrics:

> swing low, sweet low
> sweet chariot/sing low
> sweet/sweet low (mandiela, *who knew grannie* 84)

24. Nyabinghi consist of three membrane drums (bass or thunder, funde, and repeater) of three different pitches that are played in 4/4 time as part of rasta "groundation" (ceremony). Its roots are in Africa, and its rhythms are the bases of reggae.

25. mandiela is expansive in her woman-centeredness but reluctantly agreed in an interview by the author with mandiela, Alison Sealy Smith, and Rhoma Spencer that her work is, indeed, woman-centered (Knowles, "Having").

26. young anitafrika articulates these principles differently in different places. See "Theatre Is Territory: anitafrika," where rhythm in this list is replaced with "musicality"; and, from her interview with Flynn and Marrast,

> I am a staunch dub poet. Which means that I respect the rules of dub poetry, which tell me to write in rhyme and tell me that the work has to be political, which tells me that the work has to have a serious analysis, which tells me that the work has to be able to hold people's attention when it is performed. (46)

For accounts of young anitafrika's background, influences, and politics, see her "wombanifesto" and "Dub Poetics and Personal Politics."

27. young anitafrika founded her anitAFRIKA! dub theater studio in Toronto as a school, "an institution that espouses the kinds of values I was taught," launching it on August 19, 2008, with a five-day artist development conference called "storyteller.groundings.fest." The studio also held antioppression workshops, creative living courses, mentorships, lectures, and classes, all grounded in the principles that became the **sorplusi** method (see young anitafrika, "Dub Poetics"), and offered to "young people who are discriminated against due to their race, class, gender, sexual orientation, ability, and more" (young anitafrika, "wombanifesto"). A key element, however, was the artist residency program, housing five to ten artists per year at no cost to the residents. In 2010 she moved the studio with her to Cape Town and renamed it the pan afrikan performing arts institute, and in 2013, after her return to Toronto, she established the watah theatre institute and watah school in the upscale Distillery District, which continues to operate under similar principles.

28. Quotations in this essay are from the earlier scripts and do not reflect revisions made for the Tarragon production or for the publication of the trilogy.

29. The "Maroons" (mountaineers) were slaves who escaped to the mountains in seventeenth- and eighteenth-century Jamaica. The First Maroon War, in 1729, was the result of the Jamaican government's campaign attempting to wipe out the Maroons, to whom slaves continued to flee. The Maroons fought back and in 1739 successfully negotiated with the British for their freedom and the ownership of their land in exchange for support against foreign invasion and an agreement to capture and return future runaway slaves. Subsequent disputes over adherence to the treaty led to the Second Maroon War in 1795, at the end of which, and in defiance of a negotiated peace agreement, three hundred Maroons were transported to what is now the Canadian province of Nova Scotia.

30. blood.claat is nation language meaning "bloodied cloth." It is now used as a profoundly misogynist curse word in Jamaica (as when the thuggish policeman in *word!sound!powah!* threatens benu, "all of yuh getting the blood.claat firing squad. Yuh hear mi?" [11]). But originally, of course, it simply referred to the cloth worn during menstruation.

31. As this book goes to press, young anitafrika is about to premiere *Bleeders*, the third show in her second trilogy, *Orisha*, at Toronto's Summerworks Festival in August 2016. Parts 1 and 2, *Esu Crossing the Middle Passage* and the award-winning *She MamiWata & the Pussy Witch Hunt*, opened respectively at the Storefront Theatre in April 2016 and the Backspace at Theatre Passe Muraille in May 2016.

CHAPTER SIX

1. This chapter, like most writing about Modern Times, focuses on Soheil Parsa, but it is important to acknowledge Farbridge as a strong influence, not only as an actor, cotranslator, and coauthor of much of the company's work but as a strong presence as artistic associate, one who shares Parsa's minimalist aesthetic and his interest in Sufism. Some of the information on the company's early days and current vision derive from its 2012 "Planning Profile," prepared with consultant Jane Marsland (see Marsland).

2. Fischer-Lichte eschews the use of *intercultural theatre* because of its associations with what Daphne Lei has recently called "hegemonic intercultural theatre" (571) and because she feels that the term implies the stultification of cultures. I prefer to retain the word *intercultural* and its cognates because of its focus on "the contested, unsettling, and often unequal spaces *between* cultures," where negotiation, flow, and exchange can happen (Knowles, *Theatre & Interculturalism* 4).

3. The company's name is in fact an acknowledgement of the influence of Charlie Chaplin on Parsa, who attributes his decision "to take art seriously" to a viewing at age seventeen of Chaplin's film *Modern Times* (Furey). Some of the material from this chapter is based on an early interview with Soheil Parsa in Toronto's Distillery District, 6 March 2007, followed by a conversation at Table 17 restaurant on Toronto's Queen Street East on 20 February 2014; on a number of other conversations and emails; and on my participation in the development workshops and rehearsals for *Hallaj* in 2008, 2009, and 2011; for the revival of *The Death of the King* in a new translation in 2016; and currently on the forthcoming devised piece *Thirst*.

4. The influence would seem, moreover, to have been reciprocal. According to both Houshmand and Gluck, the Persian passion play *ta'ziyeh-khani* performed at the Shiraz Festival in 1971 "fascinated Brook and Grotowski" (Houshmand) and "influenced avant-garde Western theatrical directors Peter Brook, Jerzy Grotowski, and Joseph Chaiken" (Gluck 22). As I argue below, the *ta'ziyeh* has also been formative for Parsa.

5. A partial exception to this is Yemen-born Kamal Al-Solaylee of Toronto's *Globe and Mail*, who was exiled to Beirut and Cairo before moving to London and then Canada and who noted in his review "the influence of the Persian tradition of the Passion Play" ("Duelling Traditions"). Al-Solaylee's period as theater reviewer for the *Globe and Mail* was curious. A gay critic of West Asian and Middle Eastern background, Al-Solaylee was nevertheless notoriously hard on plays by queer, culturally specific, or intercultural playwrights and

companies and adopted the detached, universalist critical positioning required of *Globe and Mail* reviewers.

6. Beyza'ie's play was written in 1980 and revised by the playwright in 2003. The Modern Times production was based on a translation of the 1980 version; the published translation from which I am quoting is an updated translation of the version performed by the company "with some of Beyza'ie's revisions" (Parsa, Farbridge, and Quirt). Parsa and Farbridge did a new translation when the company restaged the play in 2016.

7. In addition to the original Toronto production in 1998 and its remount there in 2010, the show has been staged, mainly with local casts and in different languages, in Havana in 1999 at the Centro Cultural Bertolt Brecht; in Tehran in 2002 at the Fadjr International Theatre Festival; in Mostar (Bosnia and Herzegovina) in 2009; in Bogotá in 2010 at the Festival Iberoamericano, Casa del Teatro Nacional; and in Sarajevo, also in 2010, at the International Teatarfest. The concept of "contact zones" as places where cultures meet, class, and negotiate is Mary Louise Pratt's.

8. The recent exception is Penny Farfan's 2013 special issue of *Theatre Journal* on "Modernism," consciously set in quotation marks.

CHAPTER SEVEN

1. The phrase "the limits of empathy," though not new, reentered popular discourse through a September 2011 article with that title in the *New York Times* by David Brooks. "The problem comes," Brooks writes, "when we try to turn feeling into action."

2. It is notable that late twentieth- and early twenty-first-century theatrical practices of the posthuman and postdramatic have tended to be by dominant-culture artists, in spite of theorizations that are race and gender driven, such as Haraway's explicit feminism. At the moment when hitherto othered cultures have staked the claim to humanity and to dramatic self-representation, the human and dramatic in theater have, along with representation, become passé. Aluna Theatre's use of intermediality would seem to work contrary to this trend.

3. Aluna uses the spelling *Panamerican* to reflect the Spanish *panamericana*. We have retained their usage when referring to the festival but elsewhere have used the more standard *Pan-American*.

4. Some of the festival's workshops also took place at Buddies in Bad Times, Nightwood/Tapestry Studios in the Distillery District, and Aluna's own studio space.

5. For a version of the *cumbia* closest to what was used in the production, see Xiomara.

6. All subsequent quotations from Pizano and Schwellnus are from Riley and Knowles unless otherwise indicated.

7. Our analysis is based on two performances of the play that we attended at this festival and a video of a festival performance provided to us by Trevor

Schwellnus. All quotations from the performance are from that video. But we have also consulted a video of the earlier, 26 March 2011, performance in Toronto (see Schwellnus, "*Nohayquiensepa*"), and Ric Knowles attended earlier workshop presentations of the show there.

8. Brecht never uses the word *assimilation,* and the passage in "The Short Organum" that Bennett cites is talking about an actor's empathetic identification with her or his character, which he calls "the crudest form of empathy": "What should I be like if this or that were to happen to me?" (Brecht 195). But Bennett's phrase accurately represents the force of Brecht's argument.

9. Bennett's work may be understood to be an extension of the work on cultural memory done by scholars such as Marianne Hirsch, Marita Sturken, and others, as discussed in chapter 2. It is striking, given *Nohayquiensepa*'s focus on Colombia as seen from Canada, that Bennett twice invokes "the plight of Colombians" when discussing the need "to understand their situation insofar as this entails an acknowledgement of an alterity, irreducible to our own experience," and "the failure of the First World to think outside of itself—to understand its differences from other places" (19, 21). One of Bennett's case studies, moreover, is the work of Colombian visual artist Delores Salcedo (50–54, 60–69), whose work is often discussed under the rubric of memory studies.

10. More specifically,

> The artistic mission of Aluna Theatre is to embrace the myriad of voices, cultures, and stories of our population, which are transforming the landscape of Canadian theatre. In our plays, works in translation, and international co-creations, people are complex individuals who exist beyond the restrictions of cultural labels. We encourage new hybrids of theatre evolved from a rich collaboration of experiences, performance traditions and media by engaging both emerging and established theatre professionals. Our work reaches out to diverse audiences in Canada and abroad. We build liaisons that promote art as a way to empower, and a way to share with each other and the world the idea of living in harmony. (Aluna, "Artistic Mission")

11. The company history provided on its website now includes, in addition to an emphasis on its goals of redressing the mis- and under-representation of diversity and on its efforts "to form a new and distinct theatrical language of presentation," an indication that "for over a decade, Aluna Theatre has been attempting to shift the scales of imbalance by bringing social justice, equality, and human rights to the forefront of all productions."

12. The Kogi are Indigenous to Colombia, the unconquered descendants of the Tairona civilization, living primarily in the higher regions of the Sierra Nevada (see Meija).

13. The program for Aluna's 2012 Panamerican Routes/RUTAS panamericanas Festival, where both *Nohayquiensepa* and *Ixok'* were performed and where Ariza offered a workshop on collective creation, describes her as "one of the most important women in Latin American Theatre": "She is Artistic Director of

La Corporación Colombiana de Teatro, a beacon of hope and awareness in engaged theatre in a context of civil war. In 2007 she was given the Prince Claus Award (Denmark) for her efforts in counteracting injustice, restoring social memory, for her energetic commitment to the reduction of conflict and for her outstanding work over the decades to empower the disadvantaged, enabling them to transform their lives through cultural activities" (Aluna, Program, Panamerican; for more information on Ariza and the company, see Corporación Colombiana de Teatro. See also Cawley for information on Teatro La Candelaria, the country's first independent experimental theater, with which La Corporación is associated).

14. The etymological claim is disputed (as I've also noted in the introduction, note 12), but it has the force of popular tradition behind it, and the historical role of Toronto as actual meeting place is not in question.

15. This description of the inciting impulse behind *Nohayquiensepa* was offered by Schwellnus during the Panamerican Routes/RUTAS panamericanas Festival conference session "Theatre and the Law II: The New Gold Rush and Corporate Responsibility" on Friday, 25 May 2012.

16. Bennett is quoting from Swiss psychologist Édouard Claparède's 1911 work "La question de la 'mémoire' affective," where he argues that "it is impossible to feel emotion as past. . . . One cannot be a spectator of one's own feelings" (qtd. in Bennett 22). Trezise sees in Bennett's position a conflict, not only with Claparède but also with Ahmed, for whom "empathy only ever operates in the future, as a wish, as deceptively multiple or even *dissimulating*" (Trezise 216, emphasis in original).

17. "Sound/music," Tan argues, can "create new culture-scapes" (43).

18. Jill Bennett also proposes a shift away from "what does it mean?" as the question to ask an artwork, but rather than "what are we to make of this?" she proposes "'how does it work?—how does it put insides and outsides into contact in order to establish a basis for empathy" (45).

19. For the complete lyrics of the song, see Torrini.

20. As scholars and theater historians we experienced a further replication of this process in piecing together fragments and traces of a show that, as we have worked on it, exists only in our memories and reconstructions and in archival videos of its different iterations. In piecing together our account of the show's first "dramatic" scene, discussed earlier in the chapter, we built a complex argument concerning a particular unsettling split-screen effect, only later realizing that the documents we were working with were rehearsal videos made for the purposes of introducing a new actor into the cast. The split-screen effect we had so carefully analyzed had never existed in any performance before an audience.

21. The pun here, in which slashes—numbered in groups of five and made by the fingers ("digits") of the live artist's hands—are digitally multiplied through technology, is entirely intentional.

22. The accents seem inadvertently to have been dropped from Domicó's name. For more information on Domicó, see, among many online sources, Council of Canadians. For information on the Embera Katío's struggle, see, also among many online sources, World Rainforest Movement.

CHAPTER EIGHT

1. Cahoots Theatre Company, in announcing its name change from Cahoots Theatre Projects, says that "the word cahoots comes from the word for a small cabin, either the French cahute or the Dutch kajuit. Thus, to be in cahoots with someone means, literally, to live with someone in a confined space, implying both close collaboration and constructive tension. The name Cahoots Theatre Projects was coined in the spirit of flexibility, and was indicative of a time when there was not enough culturally diverse work on stage to merit more than project-to-project operations" (Cahoots Theatre Company, *2013/2014 Annual Report*).

2. Cahoots is not alone in this. Buddies in Bad Times, North America's largest queer theater, and Nightwood, Canada's longest-standing feminist theater, were both founded with experimental formalist mandates that, like that of Cahoots, changed after one or two initial productions.

3. The two female leads were played by Spanish Canadian actor Allegra Fulton and Diana Belshaw, a white-identified actor who was just beginning to explore her Māori heritage. The supporting male role was played by Turkish Canadian actor Umed Amin.

CONCLUSION

1. Nann grounded the show's opening sequence, following a taped vocal collage, with a stunningly affective dance. The full sequence was described by Keith Garebian as follows: "Nann . . . touches the long, dangling microphone cord, then the recorder, next the chair, her finger tracing meticulously an unbroken line right onto the floor and then to her own chair, suggesting by this movement that gesture can invite narrative through imaginative speculation. She then sits, legs splayed wide apart, and pulls a hood over her face. The cool tension of this sequence yields to a hot tension when she performs what can only be described as a silent corporeal opera of stifled feeling, articulated by tension in her neck and the tonic and twitch muscles that inhibit or impel larger movement. Her 'opera' is supplemented by the violent tension of hyperkinetic male and female bodies in spastic movement in a rapid and dangerous choreography of bodies banging about and chairs being overturned or flung in an almost orgiastic ecstasy to mid-Eastern music. . . . The acoustic texture is thickened by low-keyed chanting and a soundtrack catalogue of some things that people hate. Respite comes briefly but amusingly and self-consciously when Farbridge, momentarily winded by the intense choreography, pauses to enjoy watching the audience watch him breathe."

APPENDIX 1

1. The Chocolate Woman Collective, discussed in chapter 4, is dedicated primarily to the work of former Turtle Gal Monique Mojica, and Paper Canoe

Projects is dedicated to producing the work of former Turtle Gal Jani Lauzon. The third founding member of Turtle Gals, Michelle St. John, now works primarily in film production.

2. Jeff Henry (33) explains that Black Theatre Alliance was largely an administrative fiction devised by himself and Vera Cudjoe to fend off an attempt by the Canada Council for the Arts to fold the companies together.

3. Sears is also author of the highly acclaimed *Harlem Duet* and *Adventures of a Black Girl in Search of God* and editor of the first national anthology of African Canadian plays, the two-volume *Testifyin': Contemporary African Canadian Drama*.

Works Cited

Abdi, Mohammed. "Theatre, a Response to a Need: An Interview with Arbi Ovanessian." *Gozaar: A Forum on Human Rights and Democracy in Iran*. 23 December 2008. Web. 11 February 2014.

Abu-Laban, Yasmeen, and Christina Gabriel. *Selling Diversity: Immigration, Multiculturalism, Employment Equity, and Globalization*. Peterborough, ON: Broadview, 2002. Print.

Ackerman, Alan L., and Martin Puchner, eds. *Against Theatre: Creative Destructions on the Modernist Stage*. Basingstoke, UK: Palgrave Macmillan, 2006.

"AfriCan Theatre Ensemble." Web. 22 January 2014.

Ahmed, Sarah. *The Cultural Politics of Emotion*. London: Routledge, 2004. Print.

Ahmed, Sarah. *Strange Encounters: Embodied Others in Post-coloniality*. London: Routledge, 2000. Print.

Alameda. "Alameda: An Avenue for Latin Voices: About Us." Web. 11 November 2013.

Alland, Sandra. "Word & Stage: rock.paper.sistahs." *Xtra* (Toronto) 39 (March 2006). Web. 12 July 2011.

Allen, Chadwick. "Serpentine Figures, Sinuous Relations: Thematic Geography in Allison Hedge Coke's *Blood Run*." *American Literature* 82.4 (2010): 807–35. Print.

Allen, Chadwick. *Trans-Indigenous: Methodologies for Global Native Literary Studies*. Minneapolis: U of Minnesota P, 2012. Print.

Allen, Lillian. Introduction. *Women Do This Every Day*. Toronto: Canadian Scholars Press, 1993. 11–21. Print.

Al-Solaylee, Kamal. "Duelling Traditions Fuel Fresh Adaptation." *Eye Weekly* 13 (May1999): 21. Print.

Al-Solaylee, Kamal. "Only a Perfect Martyr Mars the Beautiful Tale of Hallaj." *Globe and Mail* 23 November 2011. Web. 10 April 2014.

Al-Solaylee, Kamal. "Rains Pours on Mystery of Life." *Globe and Mail* 11 November 2003: R4. Print.

Al-Solaylee, Kamal. "Too Little Text in the Brew." *Globe and Mail* 11 March 2005. Web. 14 May 2007.

Aluna Theatre. "Artistic Mission." Web. 1 September 2011.

Aluna Theatre. "History." Web. 1 September 2011.

Aluna Theatre. *Nohayquiensepa (No One Knows): A Requiem for the Forcibly Displaced*. Prod. Aluna Theatre. Panamerican Routes/RUTAS Panamericanas Festival, Theatre Passe Muraille, Toronto. 22–27 May 2012. Performance.

Aluna Theatre. Program. *Nohayquiensepa (No One Knows): A Requiem for the Forcibly Displaced*. Toronto. August 2009. Print.

Aluna Theatre. Program. Panamerican Routes/RUTAS Panamericanas. 15–27 May 2012. Print.

Aluna Theatre. "*what I learned from a decade of fear.*" Web. 11 January 2015.

"Aluna Up + Coming." Web. 1 September 2012.

Appleford, Rob, ed. *Aboriginal Drama and Theatre.* Toronto: Playwrights Canada, 1990. Print.

Appleford, Rob. "'No, the Centre Should Be Invisible': Radical Revisioning of Chekhov in Floyd Favel Starr's *House of Sonya.*" *Modern Drama* 45.2 (2003): 246–58. Print.

Aquino, Nina Lee, ed. *Love and RelASIANships: A Collection of Contemporary Asian Canadian Drama.* 2 vols. Toronto: Playwrights Canada, 2009.

Aquino, Nina Lee. Interview with the author. Distillery District, Toronto. 22 October 2006.

Aquino, Nina Lee. "Open letter to Michelle St. John & Co." 13 May 2015. Unpublished ms.

Aquino, Nina, and Ric Knowles, eds. *Asian Canadian Theatre.* Toronto: Playwrights Canada, 2011.

Aquino, Nina, and Nadine Villasin. *Miss Orient(ed). Canadian Theatre Review* 125 (2006): 83–99. Print.

Archibald, Jo-Ann. *Indigenous Storywork: Educating the Heart, Mind, Body and Spirit.* Vancouver: U of British Columbia P, 2008. Print.

Balme, Christopher. *Decolonizing the Stage: Theatrical Syncretism and Post-colonial Drama.* Oxford: Oxford UP, 1999. Print.

Bannerji, Himani. *The Dark Side of the Nation: Essays on Multiculturalism, Nationalism, and Gender.* Toronto: Canadian Scholars, 2000. Print.

Barton, Bruce. "Paradox as Process: Intermedial Anxiety and the Betrayals of Intimacy." *Theatre Journal* 61.4 (2009): 575–601. Print.

Bayne, Clarence S. "The Origins of Black Theatre in Montreal." *Canadian Theatre Review* 118 (2004): 34–40. Print.

Beagan, Tara. "Free as Injuns." 1 September 2012. Unpublished playscript.

Beagan, Tara. *Miss Julie: Sheh'mah. New Canadian Realisms: Eight Plays.* Ed. Roberta Barker and Kim Solga. Toronto: Playwrights Canada, 2012. 244–328. Print.

Beagan, Tara, and Andy Moro. "ARTICLE 11: *The Ministry of Grace.*" 2013. Grant application. (Emailed to Ric Knowles, 7 November 2013.)

Bennett, Jill. *Empathic Vision: Affect, Trauma, and Contemporary Art.* Stanford: Stanford UP, 2005. Print.

Berdichewsky, Bernardo. *Racism, Ethnicity and Multiculturalism.* Vancouver: Future, 1994. Print.

Berger, Jeniva, and Jean Yoon. "Theatre, Multicultural." *The Canadian Encyclopedia.* 2011. Web. 28 July 2015.

Beyza'ie, Bahram. *Aurash.* Trans. and adapted Soheil Parsa with Brian Quirt. Ed. Peter Farbridge. Parsa, Farbridge, and Quirt, *Stories* 1–24. Print.

Beyza'ie, Bahram. *The Death of the King.* Parsa, Farbridge, and Quirt, *Stories* 25–62. Print.

Bharucha, Rustom. "Hauntings of the Intercultural: Enigmas and Lessons on the Borders of Failure." *The Politics of Interweaving Performance Cultures: Be-*

yond Postcolonialism. Ed. Erika Fischer-Lichte, Torsten Jost, and Saskya Iris Jain. New York: Routledge, 2014. 179–200. Print.

Bharucha, Rustom. *Theatre and the World: Performance and the Politics of Culture*. London: Routledge, 1993. Print.

Bibby, Reginald W. *Mosaic Madness: The Poverty and Potential of Life in Canada*. Toronto: Stoddart, 1990. Print.

Bimm, Jordan. "A Taste of Chocolate." *NOW* 2–9 July 2011. Web. 28 July 2015.

Bissoondath, Neil. *Selling Illusions: The Cult of Multiculturalism in Canada*. Toronto: Penguin, 1994. Print.

Blair, Rhonda. *The Actor, Image, and Action: Acting and Cognitive Neuroscience*. New York: Routledge, 2008. Print.

Bogard, Travis. *Contour in Time*. 1972. Rev. ed. New York: Oxford UP, 1988. Web. 17 January 2015.

Boru, Brian. From *That's Show Business* 3 (14 August 1974): 4, 7. *Canadian Drama and the Critics*. Rev. ed. Ed. L. W. Conolly. Vancouver: Talonbooks, 1995. 157–59. Print.

Bourriaud, Nicolas. *The Radicant*. Trans. James Gussen and Lili Porten. New York: Lukas and Sternberg, 2009. Print.

Bourriaud, Nicolas. *Relational Aesthetics*. Trans. Simon Pleasance and Fronza Wood with the participation of Mathieu Copeland. Dijon, France: Les Presses du Réel, 2002. Print.

Bradshaw, James. "Capturing the Rhythm of the Heart." *Globe and Mail* 22 March 2010: R2. Print.

Brecht, Bertolt. *Brecht on Theatre: The Development of an Aesthetic*. Ed. and trans. John Willett. London: Methuen, 1964. Print.

Breon, Robin. "Black Theatre Canada: A Short History." *Canadian Theatre Review* 118 (2004): 25–28. Print.

Breon, Robin. "The Growth and Development of Black Theatre in Canada: A Starting Point." *Theatre History in Canada* 9.2 (1988): 216–28. Print.

Breton, Raymond. "Multiculturalism and Canadian Nation Building." *The Politics of Gender, Ethnicity and Language in Canada*. Ed. Alan Cairns and Cynthia Williams. Toronto: U of Toronto P, 1986. 27–66. Print.

Brook, Peter. *The Empty Space*. London: Macgibbon and Kee, 1968. Print.

Brooks, David. "The Limits of Empathy." *New York Times* 29 September 2011. Web. 18 November 2013.

Butler, Judith. "Performative Acts and Gender Constitution: An Essay on Phenomenology and Feminist Theory." *Performing Feminisms*. Ed. Sue-Ellen Case. Baltimore: Johns Hopkins UP, 1990. 270–82. Print.

"Cahoots." *Dictionary.com*. Web. 25 July 2015.

Cahoots Theatre Company. *2013/2014 Annual Report*. Web. 28 July 2015.

Cahoots Theatre Company. "DATT." Web. 10 December 2016.

Cahoots Theatre Company. "Mandate." Web. 15 July 2013.

Cahoots Theatre Company. "Red Hut: A Meeting Place to Discuss Art, Culture, and Diversity." Blog. 22 July 2015.

Cahoots Theatre Projects. Program. *Skull Riders*. By Jesse Glenn Bodyan. Winchester Street Theatre, Toronto. June 8, 1986. Print.

Cajete, Gregory. *Native Science: Natural Laws of Interdependence*. Santa Fe, NM: Clear Light, 2000. Print.

Canada Council. Web. 11 January 2015.

Carlos Bulosan Theatre. "Mandate." Web. 8 March 2010.

Carlson, Marvin. "Negotiating Theatrical Modernism in the Arab World." *Theatre Journal* 65.4 (2013): 523–35. Print.

Carter, Jill. "*Chocolate Woman* Visions an Organic Dramaturgy: Blocking-Notation for the Indigenous Soul." *Indigenous Women in Canada: The Voices of First Nations, Inuit, and Métis Women*. Spec. issue of *Canadian Women's Studies* 26.3–4 (2008): 169–76. Print.

Carter, Jill. "Writing, Righting, 'Riting'—*The Scrubbing Project: Re*-members a New 'Nation' and Reconfigures Ancient Ties." *alt.theatre: cultural diversity and the stage* 4.4 (2006): 13–17. Print.

Carter, Tom, Marc Vachon, John Biles, Erin Tolley, and Jim Zamprelli. Introduction. *Our Diverse Cities: Challenges and Opportunities*. Spec. issue of *Canadian Journal of Urban Research* 15.2 Supplement (2006). i–viii. Print.

Cawley, Margeurite. "Colombia's 1st Independent Theatre Continues to Influence, Create, Innovate." *Colombia Reports* 15 June 2011. Web. 1 September 2012.

CBC Radio Noon. Interview with Beverly Yhap, Monique Mojica, and Richardo Keens-Douglas.14 June 1990. Radio.

Chambers, Ross. "Ophaned Memories, Foster Writing, Phantom Pain: The *Fragments* Affair." Miller and Tougaw 92–111. Print.

Chan, Marjorie. "Closing Thoughts." *Cahoots Insider*. 22 March 2014. Web. 13 July 2015.

Chan, Marjorie. Email to the author. 6 June 2015.

Chapman, Geoff. "Age-Old Serial Killer Tale Told with Faustian Twist." *Toronto Star* 22 October 1995. Web. 14 May 2007.

Chaudhuri, Una. "The Future of the Hyphen: Interculturalism, Textuality, and the Difference Within." *Interculturalism and Performance: Writings from PAJ*. Ed. Bonnie Marranca and Gautam Dasgupta. New York: PAJ, 1991. 192–207. Print.

Citron, Paula. "*Aurash*: A Mythic and Gripping Archer's Tale." *Globe and Mail* 18 May 2012. Web. 6 January 2015.

Citron, Paula. "Poetic Text and Physical Theatre Bring a Mythic Tale Alive." *Globe and Mail* 18 May 2010. Web. 10 September 2012.

Citron, Paula. "When Marriage Goes Very, Very Bad." Rev. of *Twilight Café*, by Tony Hall, prod. Theatre Archipelago, dir. Rhoma Spencer, perf. Raven Dauda and David Collins. The Theatre Centre, Toronto. *Globe and Mail* 19 May 2007: R8. Print.

Clarke, George Elliott. "Afro-Gynocentric Darwinism in the Drama of George Elroy Boyd." *Canadian Theatre Review* 118 (2004): 77–84. Print.

Clarke, George Elliott. "Must All Blackness Be American? Locating Canada in Borden's *Tightrope Time* or Nationalizing Gilroy's *The Black Atlantic*." *African-Canadian Theatre*. Ed. Maureen Moynagh. Toronto: Playwrights Canada, 2005. 11–28. Print.

Clarke, George Elliott. *Odysseys Home: Mapping African-Canadian Literature*. Toronto: U of Toronto P, 2002. Print.

Collins, Loretta. "Snow on the Canefields/(the De-icing of a Canadian City): Jamaican-Canadian Identity and Kinetic Language in ahdri zhina mandiela's *dark diaspora . . . in dub: a dub theatre piece.*" *Sargasso: A Journal of Caribbean Language, Literature, and Culture* (2001): 39–63. Print.

Conlogue, Ray. "Shakespeare with a Persian Twist." *Globe and Mail* 14 May 1999: C9. Print.

Connerton, Paul. *How Societies Remember*. Cambridge: Cambridge UP, 1989. Print.

Conquergood, Dwight. "Performance Studies: Interventions and Radical Research." *TDR: The Drama Review* 46.2 (2002): 145–56. Print.

Cooper, Afua. "Redemption Dub: ahdri zhina mandiela and the Dark Diaspora." *Testifyin': Contemporary African Canadian Drama*. Ed. Djanet Sears. Toronto: Playwrights Canada, 2000. 1:441–45. Print.

Cooper, Afua. "Utterances and Incantations: Women, Poetry, and Dub in the Black Diaspora." *Utterances and Incantations: Women, Poetry and Dub*. Ed. Afua Cooper. Toronto: Sister Vision, 1999. 1–10. Print.

Cooper, Carolyn. *Noises in the Blood: Orality, Gender, and the "Vulgar" Body of Jamaican Popular Culture*. Durham, NC: Duke UP, 1995. Print.

Corporación Colombiana de Teatro. Web. 1 September 2012.

Coulbourn, John. "Theatre Review: *Body 13*." *Toronto Sun* 21 January 2013. Web. 25 February 2013.

Coulbourn, John. "To Be or Not to Be an Exotic Hamlet." *Toronto Sun* 15 May 1999: 34. Print.

Council of Canadians. "Update: Remembering Water Justice Activist Kimy Pernia Domico." 27 September 2012. Web. 28 July 2015.

Crew, Robert. "Theatre in the Park Worth Seeing." *Toronto Star* 4 July 2007. Web. 18 November 2013.

Cushman, Robert. "On This Front, It's Not So Popular: Carlos Bulosan Theatre's People Power Depicts the Marcos Years in the Philippines." *National Post* 19 April 2008: TO 22. Web. 7 May 2008.

Daniels Spectrum. "About." Web. 22 July 2015.

Davis, Andrea. "Sex and the Nation: Performing Black Female Sexuality in Canadian Theatre." *African-Canadian Theatre*. Ed. Maureen Moynagh. Toronto: Playwrights Canada, 2005. 107–22. Print.

de Certeau, Michel. *The Practice of Everyday Life*. Trans. Stephen Rendall. Berkeley: U of California P, 1988. Print.

de Certeau, Michel. *The Writing of History*. Trans. Tom Conley. New York: Columbia UP, 1988. Print.

Deleuze, Gilles, and Félix Guattari. *A Thousand Plateaus: Capitalism and Schizophrenia*. Trans. Brian Massumi. Minneapolis: U of Minnesota P, 1987. Print.

Deloria, Philip. *Playing Indian*. New Haven, CT: Yale UP, 1998. Print.

Del Rio, Bobby. *Professionally Ethnic. Canadian Theatre Review* 139 (2009): 69–78. Print.

Denzin, Norman K., Yvonna S. Lincoln, and Linda Tuhiwai Smith, eds. *Handbook of Critical and Indigenous Methodologies*. Los Angeles: Sage, 2008. Print.

Derrida, Jacques. *Of Grammatology*. 1967. Trans. Gayatri Chakravorty Spivak. Baltimore: Johns Hopkins UP, 1975. Print.

De Sousa, Mike. "Harper Government to Focus $12 Million in Funding on Promoting Canadian History." *Canada.com.* 11 June 2013. Web. 13 November 2013.

Dlodo, Awakhiwe. "*Miss Orient(ed)* Explores Cultural Identity." *Concordian* 9 March 2005. Web. 17 April 2008.

Donald, Minty. "Entided, Enwatered, Enwinded: Human/More-Than-Human Agencies in Site-Specific Performance." *Performing Objects and Theatrical Things*. Ed. Marlis Schweitzer and Joanne Zerdy. Basingstoke, UK: Palgrave Macmillan, 2014. 118–31. Print.

"Dub Poet Opens Own Theatre Space." *Xtra* 20 August 2008. Web. 18 November 2013.

Dupuis, Chris. "Rhoma Spencer Tackles Marcus Garvey and Discovers Something about Journeys along the Way." *Xtra* 9 March 2011.Web. 10 March 2011.

Earth Works: Virtual Explorations of the Ancient Ohio Valley. Cincinnati: U of Cincinnati, CERAC Centre for the Electronic Reconstruction of Historical and Archaeological Sites, 2007. CD-ROM.

Eliot, T. S. "Gerontion." 1–2. The Poetry Foundation. Web. 17 October 2013.

Eliot, T. S. "The Waste Land." 1–10. The Poetry Foundation. Web. 17 October 2013.

Empson, William. *Seven Types of Ambiguity*. London: Chatto and Windus, 1930.

Esses, Victoria M., and R. C. Gardner. "Multiculturalism in Canada: Context and Current Status." *Canadian Journal of Behavioural Science* 28.3 (1996): 145–60. Print.

Factory Theatre. "About Us." Web. 23 July 2015.

Factory Theatre. Program. *Twisted*. By Charlotte Corbeil-Coleman and Joseph Jomo Pierre. Factory Theatre, Chicago. February 2015. Print.

Farbridge, Peter, and Soheil Parsa. "Hallaj." 18 November 2012. Unpublished playscript.

Farfan, Penny. "Editorial Comment: 'Modernism.'" *Theatre Journal* 65.4 (2013): x–xiii. Print.

Favel, Floyd. "Poetry, Remnants and Ruins: Aboriginal Theatre in Canada." *Canadian Theatre Review* 139 (2009): 31–35. Print.

Favel, Floyd. "The Shadowed Path." Unpublished ms.

Favel, Floyd. "The Theatre of Orphans/Native Languages on Stage." Appleford, *Aboriginal Drama* 32–36. Print.

Favel, Floyd. "Waskawewin." *Topia* 24.1 (2005): 113–15. Print.

Favel Starr, Floyd. "The Artificial Tree: Native Performance Culture Research." Appleford, *Aboriginal Drama* 69–73. Print.

Fischer-Lichte, Erika. "Interweaving Cultures in Performance: Different States of Being In-Between." *New Theatre Quarterly* 25.4 (2009): 391–401. Print.

Fischer-Lichte, Erika. "Introduction: Interweaving Performance Cultures—Rethinking 'Intercultural Theatre': Towards an Experience and Theory of Performance beyond Postcolonialism." *The Politics of Interweaving Performance Cultures: Beyond Postcolonialism*. Ed. Erika Fischer-Lichte, Torsten Jost, and Saskya Iris Jain. New York: Routledge, 2014. 1–21. Print.

Fischer-Lichte, Erika. *The Transformative Power of Performance: A New Aesthetics*. Trans. Saskya Iris Jain. New York: Routledge, 2008. Print.

Flynn, Karen, and Evelyn Marrast. "Dubbin' Revolution: An Interview with d'bi young." *Obsidian III* 5.2 (2004–5): 35–58. Web. 12 July 2011.

Ford-Smith, Honor. "Playing Contrapuntally: An Introduction to *Fallen Angel and the Devil Concubine*." *3 Jamaican Plays: A Postcolonial Anthology (1977–1987)*. Ed. Honor Ford-Smith. Kingston, Jamaica: Paul Issa, 2011. 233–40. Print.

Foster, Cecil. *Where Race Does Not Matter*. Toronto: Penguin, 2005. Print.

Foster, Susan Leigh. *Choreographing Empathy: Kinesthesia in Performance*. New York: Routledge, 2011. Print.

Foucault, Michel. "Of Other Spaces." *Diacritics* 16.1 (1986): 22–27. Print.

Foucault, Michel. Preface. *The Order of Things: An Archaeology of the Human Sciences*. New York: Vintage Books, 1973. xv–xxiv. Print.

Francisco, Luzviminda. "The First Vietnam: The U.S.-Philippine War of 1899." *Bulletin of Concerned Asian Scholars* 5 (1973): 2–16. Print.

Friedlander, Mira. "Journey of Sinbad Exhausts Audience." *Toronto Star* 7 May 1992: C8. Print.

Friedlander, Mira. "Updating of Sinbad Fable Merges Persian, Canadian Dramatic Styles." *Toronto Star* 30 April 1992: F6. Print.

Friedman, Susan Stanford. "Planetarity: Musing Modernist Studies." *Modernism/Modernity* 17.3 (2010): 471–99. Print.

Fuchs, Elinor, and Joyce Antler. *Year One of the Empire: A Play of American Politics, War, and Protext. Taken from the Historical Record*. Boston: Houghton Mifflin, 1973. Print.

fu-GEN Asian Canadian Theatre Company. "Mandate." Web. 10 December 2016.

Furey, Anthony. "All the World's a Stage." *Canadianimmigrant.ca*. 5 February 2009. Web. 24 January 2009.

Gallese, Vittorio. "Empathy, Embodied Simulation and the Brain: Commentary on Aragno and Zepf/Hartmann." *Journal of the American Psychoanalytic Association* 56 (2009): 769–81. Print.

Gallese, Vittorio, Luciano Fadiga, Leonardo Fogassi, and Giacomo Rizzolatti. "Action Recognition in the Premotor Cortex." *Brain* 119 (1996): 593–609. Print.

Garebian, Keith. Rev. of *Forgiveness*, by Peter Farbridge, Soheil Parsa and Barbara Simonsen. Modern Times, BoraBora, Laboratiet, Don*Gnu, and Dreamwalker. Black Box Theatre, Toronto. *Stage and Page* n.d. Web. 25 March 2014.

Gates, Henry Louis, Jr. *The Signifying Monkey: A Theory of Afro-American Literary Criticism*. New York: Oxford UP, 1988. Print.

Geddes, John. "How Stephen Harper Is Rewriting History." *Maclean's* 29 July 2013. Web. 2 November 2013.

Ghazali, Ahmed. "The Sheep and the Whale." Trans. Bobby Theodore. 10 December 2006. Unpublished production script.

Gingell, Susan. "Coming Home through Sound: See-Hear Aesthetics in the Poetry of Louise Bennett and Canadian Dub Poets." *Journal of West Indian Literature* 17.2 (2009): 32–48. Print.

Gingell, Susan. "jumping in heart first: an interview with ahdri zhina mandiela." *Postcolonial Text* 2.4 (2006): 1–15. Print.

Gluck, Robert. "The Shiraz Arts Festival: Western Avant-Garde Arts in 1970s Iran." *Leonardo* 40.1 (2007): 20–28. Print.

Gómez, Mayte. "'Coming Together' in Lift Off '93: Intercultural Theatre in Toronto and Canadian Multiculturalism." *Essays in Theatre/Études Théâtrales* 13.1 (1994): 45–60. Print.

Grant, Cynthia. "The Carlos Bulosan Cultural Workshop: A Discussion with Fely Villasin." *Canadian Theatre Review* 117 (2004): 17–19. Print.

Grotowski, Jerzy. *Towards a Poor Theatre*. New York: Simon and Schuster, 1968. Print.

Guattari, Félix. "The Three Ecologies." Trans. Chris Turner. *New Frontiers* 8 (1989): 131–47. Print.

Gunew, Sneja. *Haunted Nations: The Colonial Dimensions of Multiculturalisms*. London: Routledge, 2004. Print.

Gwyn, Richard. *Nationalism without Walls: The Unbearable Lightness of Being Canadian*. Toronto: McClelland and Stewart, 1995. Print.

Habermas, Jürgen. "Modernity: An Unfinished Project." Trans. Nicholas Walker. *Habermas and the Unfinished Project of Modernity*. Ed. Maurizio Passerin D'Entrèves and Seyla Benhabib. Cambridge: Polity Press, 1996. 38–55. Print.

Hague, Mel. "Dramaturge's Notes." *Shakespeare's Nigga*. By Joseph Jomo Pierre. Toronto: Playwrights Canada, 2013. [iii]. Print.

Halbwachs, Maurice. *On Collective Memory*. Ed. and trans. Lewis A. Cosner. Chicago: U of Chicago P, 1992. Print.

Haraway, Donna. *Modest-Witness@Second Millennium.FemaleMan-Meets OncoMouse: Feminism and Technoscience*. New York: Routledge, 1997. Print.

Haraway, Donna. *Simians, Cyborgs, and Women: The Reinvention of Nature*. New York: Routledge, 1991. Print.

Harkness, James. Translator's Introduction. *This Is Not a Pipe*. By Michel Foucault. Trans. and ed. James Harkness. Berkeley: U of California P, 1983. 1–12. Print.

Hayles, N. Katherine. *How We Became Posthuman: Virtual Bodies in Cybernetics, Literature, and Informatics*. Chicago: U of Chicago P, 1999. Print.

Hayles, N. Katherine. "Interrogating the Posthuman Body." *Contemporary Literature* 38.4 (1997): 755–62. Print.

Hayles, N. Katherine. "Refiguring the Posthuman." *Comparative Literature Studies* 41.3 (2004): 311–16. Print.

Henry, Jeff. "Black Theatre in Montreal and Toronto in the Sixties and Seventies: The Struggle for Recognition." *Canadian Theatre Review* 118 (2004): 29–33. Print.

Hernandez, Catherine. Interview with the author. Factory Theatre, Toronto. 29 January 2007.

Hernandez, Catherine. *Singkil*. Toronto: Playwrights Canada, 2009. Print.

Hetherington, Kevin. *The Badlands of Modernity: Heterotopia and Social Ordering*. London: Routledge, 1997. Print.

Hicton, Douglas. "Iranian Epic Sets Audience Aquiver." *Eye* 28 May 1998: 23. Print.

Hirsch, Marianne. *Family Frames: Photography, Narrative, and Postmemory*. Cambridge, MA: Harvard UP, 1997. Print.

Hirsch, Marianne. "Marked by Memory: Feminist Reflections on Trauma and Transmission." Miller and Tougaw 71–91. Print.

Holledge, Julie, and Joanne Tompkins. *Women's Intercultural Performance*. London: Routledge, 2000. Print.

Holthe, Tess Uriza. *When the Elephants Dance*. New York: Random House, 2002. Print.

Houshmand, Zara. "Iran in Theater." *Literary Border-Crossings In Iran*. Spec. issue of *Words without Borders* (July/August 2003). Web. 23 March 2014.

Howe, LeAnne. "Embodied Tribalography: Mound Building, Ball Games, and Native Endurance in the Southeast." *Studies in American Indian Literatures* 26.2 (2014): 75–93. Print.

Howe, LeAnne, and Monique Mojica. "Side Show Freaks and Circus Injuns." June 2012. Unpublished script fragments.

Hustak, Alan. "The Ever-Versatile Macbeth: Toronto Company Melds Traditions for New Take." *Gazette* (Montreal) 27 January 1997: B5. Print.

Huyssen, Andreas. *Present Pasts: Urban Palimpsests and the Politics of Memory*. Stanford, CA: Stanford UP, 2003. Print.

"Indigenous Peoples in the Philippines." International Work Group for Indigenous Affairs. Web. 13 November 2013.

Ingold, Tim. *Being Alive: Essays on Movement, Knowledge, and Description*. London: Routledge, 2011. Print.

Issa, Rose. "Post Revolution, Art's Revelation." *Times Higher Education*. 13 April 2001. Web. 4 February 2014.

Kamboureli, Smaro. Introduction. *Making a Difference: Canadian Multicultural Literature*. Ed. Smaro Kamboureli. Toronto: Oxford UP, 1996. 1–16. Print.

Kamboureli, Smaro. *Scandalous Bodies: Diasporic Literature in English Canada*. Toronto: Oxford UP, 2000. Print.

Kaplan, Jon. "*Aurash* Actors Thrive on Roundtable Riff." *NOW* 14–20 May 1988: 95. Print.

Kaplan, Jon. "Beyond Hurt." Rev. of *Forgiveness*, by Peter Farbridge, Soheil Parsa and Barbara Simonsen. Modern Times, BoraBora, Laboratiet, Don*Gnu, and Dreamwalker. Black Box Theatre, Toronto. *NOW* 27 February–6 March 2014. Web. 14 August 2014.

Kaplan, Jon. "Irani Playwright Gives Sinbad a Second Look." *NOW* 30 April–6 May 1992: 47. Print.

Kaplan, Jon. "Italian Theatre Piece Has Universal Appeal." *NOW* 12–18 April 1990: 37, 40. Print.

Kaplan, Jon. "Maturing Macbeth: A Decade after Playing Doomed Hero in Persian-Edged Production, Actor Understands Disillusionment." *NOW* 3–9 March 2005. Web. 25 July 2007.

Kaplan, Jon. "Old Poem, New Bloom: Guillermo Verdecchia Takes Inspiration from T.S. Eliot's *The Waste Land*." *NOW* 23 February–1 March 2006. 72. Print.

Kaplan, Jon. "Parkdale Passions." *NOW* 18 May 2006. Web. 16 January 2015.

Kaplan, Jon. "Persian Passions: Adaptation of Iranian Script Looks at Love, Death and Forbidden Desires." *NOW* 30 October–5 November 2003. Web. 24 January 2009.

Kaplan, Jon. "Poetry Not Wasted: Modern Times' Take on *The Waste Land* Conjures Up Strong Imagery." *NOW* 9–15 March 2006. Web. 25 July 2007.

Kaplan, Jon. "Right as Rains." *NOW* 13–19 November 2003. Web. 26 July 2007.

Kaplan, Jon. "Vocal Villasin: Nadine Villasin, Artistic Director of Carlos Bulosan Theatre." *NOW* 17–24 April 2008. Web.14 April 2010.

Kaplan, Jon, and Glenn Sumi. "Persian Pulse Beats in Modern Hamlet." *NOW* 20–26 May 1999: 75. Print.

Kershaw, Baz. "Oh for Unruly Audiences! Or, Patterns of Participation in Twentieth-Century Theatre." *Modern Drama* 42.2 (1998): 133–54. Print.

Kershaw, Baz. *Theatre Ecology: Environments and Performance Events*. Cambridge: Cambridge UP, 2007. Print.

Kershaw, Baz. "The Theatrical Bisophere and Ecologies of Performance." *New Theatre Quarterly* 16.2 (2000): 122–30. Print.

Keung, Nicholas. "Filipino Centre Unites Generations." *Toronto Star* 28 November 2005: B4. Print.

Kilborn, Joslyn. "Body on Body on *Body 13* Playing at Toronto's Theatre Passe Muraille." *Mooney on Theatre* 18 January 2013. Web. 29 July 2015.

Knopf, Kerstin. "'Oh Canada': Reflections of Multiculturalism in the Poetry of Canadian Women Dub Artists." *Revue Lisa/Lisa e-journal* 3.2 (2005). Web. 23 March 2011.

Knowles, Ric. "'Between Home There and Home Here': An Interview with Nina Lee Aquino." *Canadian Theatre Review* 125 (2006): 75–82. Print.

Knowles, Ric. "*The Death of a Chief*: Watching for Adaptation; or, How I Learned to Stop Worrying and Love the Bard." *Shakespeare Bulletin* 25.3 (2007): 53–65. Print.

Knowles, Ric. Dramaturgical notes. *When the Elephants Dance*. 25 October 2009. Unpublished notes.

Knowles, Ric. "'Having a Whole Lot of Show Going On': Diasporic Caribbean Theatre in Toronto: A Conversation with ahdri zhina mandiela, Alison Sealy Smith, and Rhoma Spencer." *Theatre Research in Canada,* forthcoming. Print.

Knowles, Ric. "Native Performance Culture, Monique Mojica, and the *Chocolate Woman* Workshops." *Crosstalk: Canadian and Global Imaginaries in Dialogue*. Ed. Diana Brydon and Marta Dvorak. Waterloo, ON: Wilfrid Laurier UP, 2012. 73–93. Print.

Knowles, Ric. "Reading Material: Transfers, Remounts, and the Production of Meaning in Contemporary Toronto Drama and Theatre." *Essays on Canadian Writing* 51–52 (1993–94): 258–95. Print.

Knowles, Ric. *Reading the Material Theatre*. Cambridge: Cambridge UP, 2004. Print.

Knowles, Ric. "Red Sky, Native Earth: Performing Toronto's 'Indian Diaspora.'" *Essays in Theatre/Études Théâtrales* 21.1 (2002): 119–40. Print.

Knowles, Ric. *Theatre & Interculturalism*. Basingstoke: Palgrave Macmillan, 2010. Print.

Knowles, Ric. *The Theatre of Form and the Production of Meaning: Contemporary Canadian Dramaturgies*. Toronto: ECW Press, 1999. Print.

Komunyakaa, Yusef. Foreword. *Listen Up! Spoken Word Poetry*. Ed. Zöe Anglesey. New York: One World/Ballantine, 1999. 1–3. Print.

Kott, Jan. *Shakespeare, Our Contemporary*. Garden City, NY: Anchor Books, 1966. Print.

Kovach, Margaret. *Indigenous Methodologies: Characteristics, Conversations, and Contexts*. Toronto: U of Toronto P, 2009. Print.

Kukathas, Chandran. *The Liberal Archipelago: A Theory of Diversity and Freedom*. Oxford: Oxford UP, 2003. Print.

LaCapra, Dominick. *Writing History, Writing Trauma*. Baltimore: Johns Hopkins UP, 2001. Print.

Landsberg, Alison. *Prosthetic Memory: The Transformation of American Remembrance in the Age of Mass Culture*. New York: Columbia UP, 2004. Print.

Latour, Bruno. *Reassembling the Social: An Introduction to Actor-Network Theory*. Oxford: Oxford UP, 2005. Print.

Law, John. "Actor Network Theory and Material Semiotics." Version of 25 April 2007. 18 May 2007. Web. 13 October 2013.

Lee, Angela. "ahdri zhina mandiela: encountering signposts." *Canadian Theatre Review* 83 (1995): 5–8. Print.

Lee, Esther Kim. "'Patient Zero': Jean Yoon and Korean Canadian Theatre." Aquino and Knowles 62–78. Print.

Lehmann, Hans-Thies. *Postdramatic Theatre*. Trans. Karen Jürs-Munby. London: Routledge, 2006. Print.

Lei, Daphne. "Interruption, Intervention, Interculturalism: Robert Wilson's HIT Productions in Taiwan." *Theatre Journal* 63.4 (2011): 571–86. Print.

Levin, Laura, ed. *Theatre and Performance in Toronto*. Toronto: Playwrights Canada, 2011. Print.

Li, Peter. "A World Apart: The Multicultural World of Visible Minorities and the Art World of Canada." *Canadian Review of Sociology and Anthropology* 31.4 (1994): 365–91. Print.

Lo, Jacqueline, and Helen Gilbert. "Toward a Topography of Cross-Cultural Theatre Praxis." *TDR: The Drama Review* 46.3 (2002): 31–53. Print.

Logothettis, Stavroula. "Backstage in Tehran: Canadian Actress Stavroula Logothettis Visits Another Part of George W. Bush's 'Axis of Evil.'" *Maclean's* 3 March 2003. Web. 14 May 2007.

Lorde, Audre. *Zami: A New Spelling of My Name*. 1982. Freedom, CA: Crossing Press, 1994. Print.

Lotman, Yuri. "Theses on the Semiotic Study of Cultures (as Applied to Slavic Texts)." *Structure of Texts and Semiotics of Culture*. Ed. Jan van der Eng and Mojmir Grygar. The Hague: Mouton, 1974. 1–28. Print.

Luhning, Holly. "Accountability, Integrity, and *benu*: An Interview with d'bi young." *alt.theatre: cultural diversity and the stage* 8.1 (2010): 10–17. Print.

Lyons, Scott. *X Marks: Native Signatures of Assent*. Minneapolis: U of Minnesota P, 2010. Print.

Majumdar, Anita. "Fish Eyes." 2006. Unpublished playscript.

Majumdar, Anita. *The Fish Eyes Trilogy*. Toronto: Playwrights Canada, 2016. Print.

Majumdar, Anita. Interview with the author. Epicure Café, Toronto. 7 March 2007.

mandiela, ahdri zhina. "about this dub." Mandiela, *dark* vii–ix. Print.

mandiela, ahdri zhina. "an africanadian theatre aesthetic trek . . ." *Canadian Theatre Review* 118 (2004): 69–70. Print.

mandiela, ahdri zhina. *dark diaspora . . . in* dub!: *a dub theatre piece*. Toronto: Sister Vision, 1991. Print.

mandiela, ahdri zhina. "evolution of this dub." Mandiela, *dark* x–xiii. Print.

mandiela, ahdri zhina. notes from the playwright/director. Program. *who knew grannie*. Prod. Obsidian Theatre Company. Factory Theatre, Toronto. March 2010. Print.

mandiela, ahdri zhina. *Speshul Rekwes*. Toronto: Sister Vision, 1985. Print.

mandiela, ahdri zhina. "who knew grannie: a dub aria." Working draft. February 2010. Unpublished playscript.

mandiela, ahdri zhina. *who knew grannie: a dub aria*. Toronto: Playwrights Canada, 2012.

mandiela, ahdri zhina, Alison Sealy Smith, and Djanet Sears. *Honouring the Word: a test of commitment*. *Canadian Theatre Review* 118 (2004): 6–24. Print.

mandiela, ahdri zhina, and Rachel Van Fossen. "Mirroring Duality: A Dialogue about *yagayah*." *Testifyin': Contemporary African Canadian Drama*. Ed. Djanet Sears. Toronto: Playwrights Canada, 2003. 2:351–55. Print.

Mangosing, Caroline. "Filipino Play Is Authentic." *National Post* 23 April 2008: A19. Web. 7 May 2008.

Mao, Douglas, and Rebecca L. Walkowitz. "The New Modernist Studies." *PMLA* 123.3 (2008): 737–48. Print.

Marcus, George E. *Ethnography through Thick and Thin*. Princeton, NJ: Princeton UP, 1998. Print.

Marsland, Jane. "Modern Times Planning Profile." 2012. Unpublished MS.

McClintock, Anne, Aamir Mufti, and Ella Shohat, ed. *Dangerous Liaisons: Gender, Nation, and Postcolonial Perspectives*. Minneapolis: U of Minnesota P, 1997. Print.

McConachie, Bruce. *Engaging Audiences: A Cognitive Approach to Spectating in the Theatre*. New York: Palgrave Macmillan, 2008. Print.

McKinnie, Michael. *City Stages and Urban Space in a Global City*. Toronto: U of Toronto P, 2007. Print.

Meija, Louis. "KOGI: Lost Tribe of Pre-Colombian America." Web.1 September 2012.

Merringer, Ian. "Photo Gallery: Carnival's Cutting Figures." *Globe and Mail* 29 July 2011. Web. 18 November 2013.

Merritt, Shaun. "Toronto: Meeting Place or Fish Corral?" *Nuit Blanche* 8 February 2007. Web. 30 September 2012.

Miller, Nancy K., and Jason Tougaw, ed. *Extremities: Trauma, Testimony, and Community*. Urbana: U of Illinois P, 2002. Print.

"Modern Times History & Philosophy." Program. *Macbeth*. Prod. Modern Times Stage Company in association with Buddies in Bad Times Theatre. Dir. Soheil Parsa. 17 October–5 November 1995. Print.

Modern Times Stage Company. "Home." Web. 14 February 2013.

Modern Times Stage Company. "Company Mandate." Web. 24 January 2009.

Modern Times Stage Company. *Hallaj: The Study Guide*. September 2009. Print.

Modern Times Stage Company. Program. *Aurash*. By Bahram Beyza'ie. Trans.

and Adapted Soheil Parsa and Brian Quirt. Prod. Modern Times Stage Company. Dir. Soheil Parsa. 14–29 May 2010. Print.

Modern Times Stage Company. Program. *bloom*. By Guillermo Verdecchia. Dir. Soheil Parsa. 24 February–19 March 2006. Print.

Mohammed, Nassir. "Weyni Mengesha." *Ethioscope* 8 August 2013. Web. 30 June 2016.

Mojica, Monique. "Artist Statement." Draft application to the Ontario Arts Council Creators Reserve Play Development Fund. 13 January 2013. Typescript.

Mojica, Monique. "Chocolate Woman Dreams the Milky Way." *Indigenous Women in Canada: The Voices of First Nations, Inuit, and Métis Women*. Spec. issue of *Canadian Women's Studies* 26.3–4 (2008): 160–68. Print.

Mojica, Monique. *Chocolate Woman Dreams the Milky Way*. Production draft. 22 May 2011. Unpublished typescript.

Mojica, Monique. Email to the author. 30 May 2013.

Mojica, Monique. "An Excerpt from 'Scoring the Body through Indigenous Aesthetic Principles: Indigenous Dramatic Arts in Theory, Process and Practice.'" *Canadian Theatre Review* 146 (2011): 61–62. Print.

Mojica, Monique. "In Plain Sight: Inscripted Earth and Invisible Realities." *New Canadian Realisms*. Ed. Roberta Barker and Kim Solga. Toronto: Playwrights Canada, 2012. 218–42. Print.

Mojica, Monique. "Outside/Inside." Monologue improvised at the creation workshop for *Side Show Freaks and Circus Injuns*. Cahoots Theatre Company studio, Toronto. June 2012. Unpublished typescript.

Moody, Alys. "*Waiting for Godot in New Orleans*: Modernist Autonomy and Transnational Performance in Paul Chan's Beckett." *Theatre Journal* 64.4 (2013): 537–57. Print.

Moss, Laura, ed. *Is Canada Postcolonial? Unsettling Canadian Literature*. Waterloo, ON: Wilfrid Laurier UP, 2003. Print.

MT Space. *Body 13*. Prod. MT Space Theatre at Theatre Passe Muraille, Toronto. January 2013. Performance.

Multiculturalism and Citizenship Canada. *The Canadian Multiculturalism Act: A Guide for Canadians*. Ottawa: Minister of Supply and Services Canada, 1991. Print.

Na'lbandian, Abas. *Stories from the Rains of Love and Death*. Trans. Soheil Parsa with Peter Farbridge. Parsa, Farbridge, and Quirt, *Stories* 63–96. Print.

Native Earth Performing Arts. "About Us." Web. 20 November 2013.

Native Earth Performing Arts. Program. *Honouring Theatre*. Canadian Tour, Fall 2006. Print.

Natural Resources Canada. "The Real Story of How Toronto Got Its Name." Web. 21 October 2013.

Nightwood Theatre. "Mission and Mandate." Web. 8 November 2013.

Nolan, Yvette. "Death of a Chief: An Interview with Yvette Nolan." Interview with Sorouja Moll. Native Earth Performing Arts Office, Distillery District, Toronto. 12 March 2006. *Canadian Adaptations of Shakespeare Project*. Web. 7 July 2006.

Nolan, Yvette. Interview with the author. Native Earth Performing Arts Office, Distillery District, Toronto. 29 June 2006.

Nothof, Anne. "Cahoots Theatre Projects." *Canadian Theatre Encyclopedia*. 25 January 2014. Web. 25 July 2015.
Obsidian Theatre. Web. 22 January 2014.
Ocampo, Martha. Interview with the author. Toronto. 30 March 2010.
Ocampo, Martha, and Fely Villasin. *Mag-Usap Tayo . . . Let's Talk: A Guide to Educating on Violence against Women in the Filipino-Canadian Community*. Toronto: Carlos Bulosan Cultural Workshop, 1993. Print.
Offord, Alexander. "Responsibility in Theatre." Panel, Toronto Fringe, 8 July 2014. *YouTube*. Web. 24 July 2015.
O'Neill, Eugene. *Desire under the Elms: A Play in Three Parts*. Rev. 2nd ed. New York: Boni and Liveright, 1925. Project Gutenberg Australia, 2004. Web. 15 January 2015.
Ortiz, Simon. "That's the Place Indians Talk About." *Wicazo Sa Review* 1.1 (1985): 45–49. Print.
Ouzounian, Richard. "Giving the People Their Due: Performers Share Own Memories of the 1986 Filipino Revolution." *Toronto Star* 10 April 2008. Web. 15 April 2008.
Parsa, Soheil. Email to the author. 30 March 2014.
Parsa, Soheil. Interview with the author. Balzac's, Distillery District, Toronto. 6 March 2007.
Parsa, Soheil. Personal communication. Table 17, Queen Street East, Toronto. 20 February 2014.
Parsa, Soheil, with Peter Farbridge and Brian Quirt, eds. *Stories from the Rains of Love and Death: Four Plays from Iran*. Trans. Soheil Parsa with Peter Farbridge and Brian Quirt. Toronto: Playwrights Canada, 2007. Print.
Parsa, Soheil, Peter Farbridge, and Brian Quirt. Translators' Note. Parsa, Farbridge, and Quirt, *Stories* vii. Print.
Pataki, Amy. "Paintbox Bistro: Review." *thestar.com*. 25 January 2013. Web. 22 July 2015.
Patias, Lilias. "Obeah Opera Shakes, Rattles and Rolls, Then Brings Down the (Master's) House." 3 March 2012. Web.18 November 2013.
Pavis, Patrice. *Theatre at the Crossroads of Culture*. Trans. Loren Kruger. London: Routledge, 1992.
Perovic, Lydia. "Vladimir and Estragon Return to Toronto." *Toronto Arts Council Newsletter* Spring 2008: [2].
Philip, Marlene NourbeSe. "Signifying Nothing: Why the Media Have Fawned Over Bissoondath's *Selling Illusions*." *Border/Lines* 36 (1995): 4–11. Print.
Pierre, Joseph Jomo. *Shakespeare's Nigga*. Toronto: Playwrights Canada, 2013. Print.
Pratt, Mary Louise. "Arts of the Contact Zone." *Profession* 91 (1991): 33–40. Print.
Process Panel—ahdri zhina mandiela, Ed Roy, and Paul Thompson. The Canadian Festival of Ideas and Creation, 10 May 2006. Web. 22 April 2011.
Qadeer, Mohammed, and Sandeep Kumar. "Ethnic Enclaves and Social Cohesion." *Our Diverse Cities: Challenges and Opportunities*. Spec. issue, *Canadian Journal of Urban Research* 15.2 supplement (2006): 1–17. Print.
Rahmanian, Mohammed. *Interrogation*. Trans. Soheil Parsa. Parsa, Farbridge, and Quirt, *Stories* 97–127. Print.
Reilly, F. Kent, III. "People of Earth, People of Sky: Visualizing the Sacred in

Native American Art of the Mississippian Period." *Hero, Hawk, and Open Hand: American Indian Art of the Ancient Midwest and South.* Ed. Robert V. Sharp. Chicago and New Haven, CT: Art Institute of Chicago in association with Yale UP, 2004. 125–37. Print.

Reitz, J. G., and Raymond Breton. *The Illusion of Difference: Realities of Ethnicity in Canada and the United States.* Toronto: C. D. Howe Institute, 1994. Print.

Riley, Jessica, and Ric Knowles. Interview with Béatriz Pizano and Trevor Schwellnus. 29 August 2012.

Roach, Joseph. *Cities of the Dead: Circum-Atlantic Performance.* New York: Columbia UP, 1996. Print.

Romain, William F. *Mysteries of the Hopewell: Astronomers, Geometers, and Magicians of the Eastern Woodlands.* Akron, OH: U of Akron P, 2000. Print.

Romain, William F., and Jarrod Burks. "LiDAR Analysis of Prehistoric Earthworks in Ross County, Ohio." *Current Research in Ohio Archeology 2008.* Web. 3 March 2008.

Romain, William F., and Jarrod Burks. "LiDAR Assessment of the Newark Earthworks." *Current Research in Ohio Archeology 2008.* Web. 3 February 2008.

Saddlemyer, Ann, ed. *Early Stages: Theatre in Ontario 1800–1914.* Toronto: U of Toronto P, 1990. Print.

Salutin, Rick, and Theatre Passe Muraille. *1837: The Farmers' Revolt: A Play.* Toronto: James Lorimer, 1976. Print.

Sanderson, Frances, and Heather Howard-Bobiwash, ed. *The Meeting Place: Aboriginal Life in Toronto.* Toronto: Native Canadian Centre of Toronto, 1997. Print.

Sassen, Saskia. *The Global City: New York, London, Tokyo.* 2nd ed. Princeton, NJ: Princeton UP, 2001. Print.

Scadding, Henry, and John Charles Dent. *Toronto: Past and Present: Historical and Descriptive. A Memorial Volume for the Semi-centennial of 1884.* Toronto: Hunter, Rose, 1884. Print.

Schwellnus, Trevor. "*Nohayquiensepa (No One Knows)*, Toronto March 26 2011." Vimeo. Web. 28 September 2012.

Schwellnus, Trevor. "Why a Festival of Theatre for Human Rights?" 20 May 2012. Web. 11 September 2012.

Sears, Djanet. Afterword. *Afrika Solo.* Toronto: Sister Vision, 1990. 95–101. Print.

Sears, Djanet. *Harlem Duet.* Winnipeg: Scirocco, 1997. Print.

Sears, Djanet. Introduction. *Testifyin': Contemporary African Canadian Drama.* Ed. Djanet Sears. Toronto: Playwrights Canada, 2000. 1:i–xiii. Print.

Severi, Carlo. "Kuna Picture-Writing: A Study in Iconography and Memory. *The Art of Being Kuna: Layers of Meaning among the Kuna of Panama.* Ed. M. L. Salvador. Los Angeles: UCLA Fowler Museum of Cultural History, 1997. 245–72. Print.

Shohat, Ella, and Robert Stam. *Unthinking Eurocentrism: Multiculturalism and the Media.* London: Routledge, 1994. Print.

Signal Theatre. "Signal." Web. 20 November 2013.

Simmonds, Jason Woodman. "Native Earth Performing Arts's *The Death of a Chief*: Unearthing Shakespeare's *Julius Caesar*." *Performing Indigeneity.* Ed. Yvette Nolan and Ric Knowles. Toronto: Playwrights Canada, 2016. 167–96. Print.

Simon, Roger, with Mario Di Paolantonio and Mark Clamen. "Remembrance as Praxis and the Ethics of the Interhuman." *The Touch of the Past: Remembrance, Learning, and Ethics*. By Roger Simon. New York: Palgrave Macmillan, 2005. 132–55. Print.

Simpson, Leanne. *Dancing on Our Turtle's Back: Stories of Nishnaabeg Re-creation, Resurgence and a New Emergence*. Winnipeg: Arbeiter Ring, 2011. Print.

Slemon, Stephen. "Resistance Theory for the Second World." *Postcolonial Studies Reader*. Ed. Bill Ashcroft, Gareth Griffiths, and Helen Tiffin. London: Routledge, 1995. 104–110. Print.

Slotkin, Lynn. "Review: *Body 13*." *Slotkin Letter*. 21 January 2013. Web. 14 July 2015.

Smith, Kristen. "The Filipino Community in Canada at a Glance." *Canada.com*. 12 November 2013. Web. 13 November 2013.

Smith, Linda Tuhiwai. *Decolonizing Methodologies: Research and Indigenous Peoples*. London: Zed Books, 1999. Print.

Solga, Kim. "One Dead White Guy at a Time: *Miss Julie: Sheh'mah*." *New Canadian Realisms: Eight Plays*. Ed. Roberta Barker and Kim Solga. Toronto: Playwrights Canada, 2012. 239–43. Print.

Spencer, Rhoma. Interview with Andy Barry. "Metro Morning." CBC Radio Toronto. 23 May 2006. Radio.

Sturken, Marita. "Narratives of Recovery: Repressed Memory as Cultural Memory." *Acts of Memory: Cultural Recall in the Present*. Ed. Mieke Bal, Jonathan Crewe, and Leo Spitzer. Hanover, NH: UP of New England, 1999. 231–48. Print.

Syerah. "Summerworks Theatre Festival: Fish Eyes." *Mybindi.com*. 2000. Web. 5 April 2007.

Tan, Marcus Cheng Chye. *Acoustic Interculturalism: Listening to Performance*. Basingstoke, UK: Palgrave Macmillan, 2012. Print.

A Taste of Empire. By Jovanni Sy, dir. Guillermo Verdecchia, prod. Cahoots Theatre Company. Market Kitchen, St. Lawrence Market, Toronto. 29 June–24 July 2010. Performance.

Taylor, Diana. *The Archive and the Repertoire: Performing Cultural Memory in the Americas*. Durham, NC: Duke UP, 2003. Print.

Taylor, Drew Hayden. "A Comedic History of Aboriginal Proportions." *Performing Indigeneity*. Ed. Yvette Nolan and Ric Knowles. Toronto: Playwrights Canada, 2016. 158–66. Print.

Taylor, Drew Hayden. *Me Funny*. Vancouver: Douglas and McIntyre, 2006. Print.

Theatre Archipelago. "About Us." Web. 17 April 2011.

"Theatre Is Territory: 10 Questions: d'bi young anitafrika." *praxistheatre.com*. Web. 28 April 2011.

"Theatre Is Territory: 10 Questions : Christine Mangosing." *praxistheatre.com*. Web. 21 April 2008.

Todd, Rebecca. "Enlivening the Land: Red Sky's Integrative Approach." *dance current* (March 2003): 22–25. Print.

Torrini, Emilíana. "Beggar's Prayer Lyrics." *Metro Lyrics*. N.d. Web. 15 February 2013.

Treutler, Lise. "Who Is the Fairest Filipina of Them All? Teesri Duniya Theatre Explores the Canadian Minority Identity." *McGill Tribune* 24 March 2003. Web. 17 April 2008.

Trezise, Bryoni. "Spectatorship That Hurts: Socìetas Rafaello Sanzio as Meta-affective Theatre of Memory." *Theatre Research International* 37.3 (2012): 205–20. Print.

Trilling, Geneviève. "Interview Series: *Nohayquiensepa.*" Interview with Trevor Schwellnus, 18 July 2009. Summerworks Theatre Festival. Web. 2 September 2010.

Turtle Gals Performance Ensemble. Information sheet. Turtle Gals Performance Ensemble office, Toronto. Files.

Turtle Gals Performance Ensemble. Promotional flyer. *The Scrubbing Project.* Co-produced Turtle Gals Perfrmance Ensemble, Native Earth Performing Arts, and Factory Theatre at Factory Theatre, Toronto. 2002. Print.

Turtle Gals Performance Ensemble. *The Scrubbing Project. Staging Coyote's Dream: An Anthology of First Nations Drama in English.* Ed. Monique Mojica and Ric Knowles. Toronto: Playwrights Canada, 2009. 2:323–66. Print.

Ty, Eleanor. "Affect, Family, and the Past in Two Plays by Catherine Hernandez." Aquino and Knowles 212–22. Print.

United Nations. "United Nations Declaration on the Rights of Indigenous Peoples." 13 September 2007. Web. 20 November 2013.

"A Utopian Stage: Festival of Arts Shiraz-Persepolis. " Whitechapel Gallery, London, UK. 21 April–4 October 2015. Exhibition.

Varty, Alexander. 'd'bi young Addresses Legacy of Colonialism." *Straight.com.* 28 May 2008. Web. 18 November 2013.

Verdecchia, Guillermo. *bloom. Another Country/bloom.* Vancouver: Talonbooks, 2007. 93–144. Print.

Verdecchia, Guillermo. "Seven Things about Cahoots Theatre Projects." *"Ethnic," Multicultural, and Intercultural Theatre.* Ed. Ric Knowles and Ingrid Mündel. Toronto: Playwrights Canada, 2009. 106–14. Print.

Villasin, Nadine. Interview with the author. Theatre Passe Muraille, Toronto. 22 March 2010.

Vizenor, Gerald. *Fugitive Poses: Native American Indian Scenes of Absence and Presence.* Lincoln: U of Nebraska P, 1998. Print.

Wagner, Vit. "A Simple Story of Complexity." *Toronto Star* 17 May 1998: B6. Print.

Walcott, Rinaldo. *Black Like Who?: Writing Black Canada.* Toronto: Insomniac, 2003. Print.

Walcott, Rinaldo. "Dramatic Instabilities: Diasporic Aesthetics as a Question for and about Nation." *Canadian Theatre Review* 118 (2004): 99–106. Print.

Walcott, Rinaldo. "Rhetorics of Blackness, Rhetorics of Belonging: The Politics of Representation in Black Canadian Expressive Culture." *Canadian Review of American Studies* 29.2 (1999): 1–24. Print.

Wallace, Robert. *Producing Marginality: Theatre and Criticism in Canada.* Saskatoon, SK: Fifth House, 1990. Print.

War Child. "Bloom Update." *War Child News.* Web. 25 July 2007.

Wasserman, Shoshanna. "21st Century Mound Builders." Document downloads / past press releases. American Indian Cultural Center and Museum. 5 August 2008. Web. 21 March 2012.

Weber-Pillwax, Cora. "What Is Indigenous Research?" *Canadian Journal of Native Education* 25.2 (2001): 166–74. Print.

Weimann, Robert. *Author's Pen and Actor's Voice: Playing and Writing in Shakespeare's Theatre*. Ed. Helen Higbee and William West. Cambridge: Cambridge UP, 2000. Print.

Westfall, William. From *Canadian Historical Review* 59 (1978): 71–75. *Canadian Drama and the Critics*. Rev. ed. Ed. L. W. Conolly. Vancouver: Talonbooks, 1995. 161–63. Print.

Why Not Theatre. "About." Web. 30 July 2015.

Wilson, Shawn. *Research Is Ceremony: Indigenous Research Methods*. Halifax, NS: Fernwood, 2008. Print.

World Rainforest Movement. "Colombia: The Embera Katio's Struggle for Life." 27 September 2012. Web. 13 November 2013.

Worthen, W. B. *Shakespeare and the Force of Modern Performance*. Cambridge: Cambridge UP, 2003. Print.

Write about Now First Canadian Conference of Visible Minority Playwrights. "Discussion and Resolutions." Toronto, 24 June 1990. Panel.

Write about Now First Canadian Conference of Visible Minority Playwrights. "Responsibility." Toronto, 23 June 1990. Panel.

Xiomara. "Colombian Cumbia Dance Performance with Xiomara." *YouTube*. 27 September 2012. Web.

Yhap, Beverly. "On Their Own Terms." *Canadian Theatre Review* 56 (1988): 25–30. Print.

Yoon, Jean. "Chinese Theatre in Canada: The Bigger Picture." *Canadian Theatre Review* 110 (2002): 5–11. Print.

Yoon, Jean. Keynote address. The Shipping of Souls Conference. Theatre Passe Muraille, Toronto. 26 February 2007. Presentation.

Yoon, Jean. "Reflections on the 'Roots' Panel and 'The Generational Divide.'" Aquino and Knowles 79–85. Print.

young, debbie, and naila belvett. *yagayah: two.womyn.black.griots*. *Testifyin': Contemporary African Canadian Drama*. Ed. Djanet Sears. Toronto: Playwrights Canada, 2003. 2:349–90. Print.

young anitafrika, d'bi. *benu: a biomyth monodrama: the sankofa trilogy part II*. 2010. Script.

young anitafrika, d'bi. *blood.claat/sangre*. Spanish trans. queen nzinga maxwell edwards. Toronto: Playwrights Canada, 2005. Print.

young anitafrika, d'bi. "Dub Poetics and Personal Politics." *Notes from Canada's Young Activists: A Generation Stands Up for Change*. Comp. and ed. Severn Cullis-Suzuki, Kris Frederickson, Ahmed Kayssi, and Cynthia Mackenzie, with Daniel Aldana Cohen. Vancouver: Greystone, 2007. 137–48. Print.

young anitafrika, d'bi. Email to the author. 12 April 2011.

young anitafrika, d'bi. "wombanifesto." *dbiyoung.net*. 30 April 2011. Web. 13 November 2013.

young anitafrika, d'bi. *word!sound!powah!: a biomyth monodrama: the sankofa trilogy part III*. 4th draft. 2010. Unpublished playscript.

Index

Note: bolded page numbers reflect the most substantial writing about an entry.